WARRIORS

Darkness Over Freelandia

Kent Larson

Warriors: Darkness over Freelandia

Copyright 2013 by Kent Larson
Cover design by Michael Malone
Interior illustrations by Rebecca Ross

Library of Congress Control Number: 2013951981
ISBN Number: 978-1-939456-09-0

First Printing November 2013
Printed in the USA

Cover images purchased and used by permission of istockphoto.com and Malone
Photography

Published by Search for the Truth Publications
3275 Monroe Rd.
Midland, MI 48642
www.searchforthetruth.net

A Note to Parents

This is the last installment of the Freelandia Trilogy. In Book 1, we were introduced to a young blind orphan girl named Maria who has an extraordinary singing ability. Extraordinary really does not describe it adequately. Supernatural would be better, for it is a gifting from God, a spiritual gifting the likes of which the world has never experienced. The first book takes place entirely within thecountry of Freelandia, a land highly secluded geographically but rich in resources and more importantly, rich in spiritual awareness of the one true God. As such they have been blessed immensely with prosperity and peace for hundreds of years. Biblical New Testament spiritual gifts are widely exercised and even expected (see I Corinthians chapters 12-14 in particular, though in the story Discerners really have a combination of several of the listed Gifts of the Spirit).

In the first book Maria's astounding gift is experienced by many, and she is befriended by several of the most important people in the country. At the Academy of Music, life would seem rather idyllic …except for the ominous impending threat of war with the Dominion, a demon-empowered country bent on world conquest.

We also met Ethan, the son of the Chancellor, who also has a most unusual supernatural gifting, which is used to thwart an assassination attempt on his father. Book 1 ends with Grand Master Gaeten, Ethan's exceptionally skilled but blind mentor, heading into Dominion territory to spy out their plans against Freelandia.

Book 2 follows Gaeten and his assistant Nimblefoot as they learn about the imminent invasion the Dominion has planned against Freelandia. We are also introduced to the School of Engineers, where God is pouring out ideas for new inventions to be used in the upcoming war. Meanwhile, Maria finds that her gifting extends well beyond singing to also encompass playing musical instruments. Ethan is seduced, kidnapped and taken aboard a disguised Dominion ship which escapes even as the Freelandian navy is attacked by a much larger Dominion armada. The naval clash has both physical and spiritual ramifications, and Maria and the Academy of Music learn that their worship of God has significant impact against the evil forces arrayed against Freelandia. This realization precipitates a major reorganization within the Academy, and God brings about spiritual awakening and revival first at the Keep and then to the entire country ... and even to the chained Ethan.

This then is the setting for Book 3. Ethan is being taken to the Dominion, which plans on extracting the great amount of knowledge he has of Freelandian defenses and on using him as a hostage or worse against his homeland and his parents, the Chancellor and Chancelloress of Freelandia. Maria is preparing the entire Academy of Music to become worship warriors. The engineers are creating weapons and defenses the likes of which are totally unknown in their world. The Dominion is preparing for an all-out war that pits not only their navy and army against Freelandia, but also demonic spiritual forces as well.

You are invited to join in on what is prayerfully more than a simple adventure. Unlike Freelandia, our world is full of books depicting worldly adventures that sadly not only fail to mention or give credit to God, but which even seem to revel in ignoring the Creator. They assign the supernatural to demons, but not to angels, experiences to luck or chance and not to our Savior, and success to human ability instead of to God's grace. If you begin to wonder if God could really be like He is depicted in the story, then I have accomplished some good. If you catch a spark of what living with Holy Spirit's power might be like, if it makes you give glory to our wonderful loving God in any way, then all of the efforts to write it and get it into your hands were well worthwhile. May this story be known for any blessings it brings.

Kent Larson
Awestruck worshiper of the Most High God
2013

Acknowledgements

riting a story that grows into a three volume trilogy is no small undertaking. I wish to thank my family for their patience both in releasing my time to write/edit and for their patience as I worked to create each subsequent installment ... just think what reading this story would be like if you had to wait days for each new chapter! In particular my wife Sue deserves a lot of credit for all of the proof-reading, edit helps and the many other contributions. I also want to thank the fellowship group from my local church who weekly encouraged me to "keep going".

As the books took shape, one person in particular had the vision to see them published. A special thanks to Bruce Malone and *Search for the Truth Ministries*. Without a brother coming alongside to lead me through the publication process – I'm not sure these books would ever have become a reality. Thanks also to his wife Robin for the many encouraging words, the expert help of their daughter-in-law Beth for content editing and ideas for streamlining the storyline, and to Rebecca Ross for bringing the story alive with her beautifully detailed illustrations.

Finally, I would like to express thanks and appreciation for the encouragement of too many others to name – fellow believers who took the time to read and comment on the early versions of this story. May God reward your efforts as these books bless many lives.

Dedication

This book has been written to bring the glory of Jesus. To God be the glory for the things He has done! Praise to Emmanuel (the God-who-is-with-us), which can also be understood to mean "God-in-us". What a concept for every Christian, "God-in-me"!

About the Author

*The author and his family: wife Sue, sons Ben and Matt,
daughters Sarah and Rachel (son Jonathan is not pictured)*

Kent Larson's occupation may not be what you would expect for a writer of Christian fiction with a theme centered on the praise and worship of God. He is a material scientist at a leading chemical company. But he sees no conflict between these, as science proclaims the wonder of our Creator at every level for those who would simply acknowledge Him. The author and his family live in the middle of lower Michigan on nearly five acres - surrounded by a forest filled with animals - at the edge of where the Michigan population tapers off into a rural and rustic setting. On quiet evenings he and his family can step out onto their back porch, gaze at the starry host above, and feel even closer to the God who created it all.

Chapter 1

Reflections

aster Warden James dwarfed his desk and looked like he had been sitting far too long. He was a man of action who had many administration duties. He carried them out very thoroughly, but deskwork ill-suited his broad shoulders. He looked up from his desk as his naval commander entered the room and spoke first. "So what is your status report?"

"Well sir, our ships damaged in the battle with the Dominion fleet are being repaired far faster than I had even hoped, and as part of that all are getting the latest weaponry that the engineers have dreamed up. I was quite unsure about those new fangled launchers, fireball bombs and floating barrel mines, but they surely worked well against even the biggest frigates we came up against. And if we can get a few of those Thunderclap of God devices I think we even might stand up to those humongous Dreadnaughts we've been hearing about."

"I presume you are upgrading the full complement of weaponry for every ship?"

"Indeed we are, though it seems like something new is coming from the School of Engineering every other day. It is difficult to keep up with the training on all the new things they are delivering."

"Try to keep up! How long do you think you need before every naval ship has been outfitted and ready to sail?"

"Oh, I'd say two to three weeks. And the shipbuilders are in a tear making new sloops too. I personally think they are bragging, but I was told they believe they can deliver one new ship every week. That sounds preposterous to me, but then again, those engineers have swarmed all over the ship building yards and every dockyard is humming along real efficient-like, and they seem to have a small army of volunteer workmen."

"Yes, I toured it yesterday to see for myself. It's incredible. The Master Shipbuilder even told me he thought they could further ramp up production to increase their output yet this month, and retrofits are taking less than a fourth of the time they used to since the engineers have standardized mounting brackets and tools. It is unbelievable how much faster changes and upgrades go with quality interchangeable standardized parts! Have you heard any word from our outer patrol vessels … any chance one of them might catch those Dominion spies who kidnapped the Chancellor's son Ethan?"

"Not likely, not likely at all. Besides, it looks like a merchant ship from any distance, especially if they hide their catapults under heavy cloth. I am sorry to say that it appears they got clean away."

"Well then, it is up to God to stop them. At least our friends the Alterians should only be a day or so behind them."

The Alterian ship was speedy, but so was the Dominion merchant ship. Both passed the straggling Freelandian vessels returning to port, and they could readily see battle damage. The Alterian captain knew he was nearly a day behind and did not know for sure where the other ship was going, but he suspected they would be destined for one of only a few high-security Dominion naval ports thought to be staging grounds for the coming invasion fleet, and Kardern was the closest.

A few days out of Freelandia they began to pass surviving Dominion war ships limping along with significant damage, each group with several intact escorts. The Alterians steered clear of those, but with only minor course adjustments so as to avoid any suspicion. A few days out of Kardern they passed one of the big frigates, which appeared to also have taken damage. It was moving slowly and had several other ships in close proximity, but they remained too far away to identify each. Once past, they steered directly toward the docks of Kardern.

Ethan noticed they were slowing. He groaned, wondering if the next step of his ordeal was about to begin. He heard muted shouts and the sound of the launch boat he had noticed in the stern being bumped along the hull as it was lowered. The spy ringleader Murdrock could be heard giving out harsh commands, and Ethan was pretty certain that individual was boarding the launch. Shortly there was the noise of oars in water moving away. A few minutes later light steps could be heard slowly descending the stairs into the hold where Ethan lay bound. In a moment Taleena sauntered into his field of view. This was not the sweet teenage-looking girl who had seduced, drugged and led him into a trap. Even in the dim light Ethan could see that she looked much older now, and dressed like a wayward woman that he would have never been tempted by.

"Hello there, dear Ethan." Taleena moved close and caressed his check with a hand. Ethan flinched away as strongly as his bindings would allow. "Oh, still angry at me? I suppose you would be. I played quite the

temptress, didn't I? Don't worry, today is not when you will be delivered to the Overlord. No, Murdrock wanted to obtain official naval escort for the remaining few days of our journey, and to hear first hand of how badly we defeated the Freelandian fleet. He was rather surprised not to find the ships out in blockade formation and to see so many damaged Dominion vessels heading south. Now what do you suppose that means? I guess we will find out soon enough. Regardless, while the 'cat's away the mice will play'. I only have a few minutes before the guard will wake up." She glanced over her shoulder at a small creaking noise and then turned back with a sneering smile. "He got so very tired right after I was nice enough to give him a drink of hot mead. Imagine that!

Now, dear Ethan, I have something to give to you. With you here there is little real need of me – the Overlord can wring every ounce of Freelandian defense information right out of your sweet little head. I can't let that happen. No, it must be obvious that I am the main asset. But don't worry; you will still be needed, at least as a figurehead. At least your body will be needed alive and well. But your memory … well now, that may just be in competition with the future I am planning." Taleena moved even closer and removed something from a bag she was carrying. "You will not feel much unpleasantness … and besides, you won't recall it anyway!"

Ethan smelled something foul being brought up close to his face and he fruitlessly struggled to move away. The gagging smell began to overwhelm him and in desperation he held his breath as long as he could. Taleena patiently waited. In less than a minute Ethan could no longer restrain himself and gasped for breath. As he did so, his lungs filled with the acrid fumes from the cloth Taleena was holding over his face. As he gagged and coughed she laughed unpleasantly and roughly shoved a small ball of foul paste up each of his nostrils.

"There now, that out to do it. In a few minutes the smell will clear and no one will be the wiser … and most especially you."

The sun was high in the afternoon sky at the lake where Maria had started her morning. Most of the people who had come out to the revival had returned, though some lingered on and new people from surrounding towns kept straggling in. Minister Polonos and several other ministers remained, and God's presence seemed to have sunk in to permeate the surroundings.

Chancellor Duncan was back at his same office with his same duties and activities, yet everything seemed new and fresh and more REAL somehow. Decisions seemed to flow far easier and he went about his day humming the main melody Maria had been playing … or at least a tiny part of it that he could remember that had somehow seemed to be an indistinguishable part of the surrounding creation. He still did not know how that could be … but it just was.

There were many decisions to make. The whole country was gearing up in defensive preparations, and that required a tremendous amount of organizing, planning and coordinating. So much time could be lost if the preparations were done incorrectly, or wastefully. Yet today it seemed like everything was just falling into place. Preparations were all going at re-markable speed, and Duncan felt confident that if they had several months more they could put up a truly formidable defense of their homeland.

Yet he knew that their hope did not lie with their activities or achieve-ments … it lay squarely on their God. And that was what he had to cling to when he thought about Ethan. His son was in the hands of the Dominion, but even more so he was in the hands of God. Somehow, this was going to turn out for God's glory and purpose. Yet that did not mean Ethan would come out unscathed. Duncan had to prepare for the worst.

It was of only slight comfort when the former Dominion Dark Magician Turlock had within hours of the kidnapping come and told them Ethan would have been drugged and certainly was taken bound aboard the ship that had escaped. He explained that Ethan would be held securely but safely by the Dominion master spy Murdrock and would be transported to one of the main port cities of the Dominion. From there, Turlock had not wanted to speculate … but it stood to reason that since Ethan had intimate knowledge of many Freelandian defenses, he would be forced to divulge much of what he knew.

Turlock had tried to console Duncan, saying that most interrogations used a variety of drugs to make the subject more talkative without the need to utilize more … violent … methods. Duncan had shuddered, and they had ended the meeting with earnest prayer.

Turlock and James lingered for some time in earnest discussion. Fi-nally James nodded and Turlock strode out of the room with new-found purpose.

Vocal Master Veniti normally sat in any chair with straight-back posture that made him seem especially formal. Yet today Vitario thought he looked, well, somewhat relaxed as he sat in the Grand Master's office chair. As Vitario gestured, Master Veniti began. "I admit I was highly skeptical about the supposed spiritual overtones that you and Maria claimed were part of her musical repertoire."

"What changed your mind?"

"I … I think that young lady was getting to me, with all her talk of worship being the true purpose of music and song. It seemed to resonate in some hollow part of me, a part long ago walled off to the point I rarely remembered it. Hearing her descriptions of her 'special place' with God re-awakened a kind of spiritual hunger. God began to work on me. Then I felt the pull … I've heard some calling it 'the call' yesterday to go out to the lake … to the revival. It was so strange. Some deep part of me felt like it was being tugged on, felt the need to go along with the others. And when I arrived, Maria was still playing and others had joined in. I think I saw you there with your viola?"

Vitario leaned forward, his eyes bright. "Yes, I felt it too, and strongly. It was a little like how we played the other day in the amphitheater, but different too. This was a mixture of joy and peace and unity and wonder all joined together with the most beautiful sunrise over the perfect lake." Vitario sighed. "Somehow we seemed joined and intertwined with creation worshiping the Creator."

Veniti nodded vigorously. "Yes that, and even more. It was like a part of me had been asleep, but was awakened there to a world with greater vibrancy and color and, well, awe. There is so much beauty I find that I was taking for granted, walking right by without even noticing! Somehow God's presence was … was THERE, manifestly present and all creation reflected it." Veniti uncharacteristically leaned over Vitario's desk and looked at the head of the Music Academy, his face beaming. "And the music! Oh, Vitario … I have never, ever experienced anything so wonderful, so fulfilling, so inspiring! And as good as all of you were who were playing, it was obvious you were accompanying Maria … I think all of creation there in those surroundings was accompanying Maria!"

Vitario sat back, misty eyed. "Or was she accompanying the song of joy and thanksgiving creation has been and is singing all along, that we normally just ignore or cannot hear?"

That rocked Master Veniti. He sat back so rapidly his chair actually skidded backward a few inches. "Really? Do you suppose …?" A tear was forming in his eyes. Normally he would have figured this was getting out of hand, out of his carefully crafted facade of control. Now … now he figured being out of his own control may well be a sign he was letting his God be in control.

"Well, regardless of what I can or cannot explain – I believe your and her story now."

Vitario smiled warmly, but then a quizzical look came over his features. "But even before that, at our staff meeting, you stood up quite boldly in her defense."

"Yes, I did, didn't I?" Veniti chuckled. "I think I knocked the socks off several in the room with that! Those others who were so opposed to her … I could not sit any longer. They did not know her, did not know her gifting. I admit I had only acknowledged a tiny part of it myself. She has such talent, Vitario! Her voice is so capable. She could do even so much more, with some refining."

"That is one of the reasons I asked you to personally work with her. She has a great gift from God, but it is still housed in a very little girl – a rather weak and fragile vessel. She is very willing, very sincere … but also … well … ignorant of so much of what we teach."

"But what of the inadequacies she voiced so strongly? What sorts of things are lacking?"

Vitario narrowed his eyes and looked upward in thought. "I think we need to expose Maria to a wider variety of music types. However, since she seems to feel that God has a specific use for her … and the entire Academy for that matter… in the war against the Dominion, I think we should start with music that may perhaps be more suited along those lines, such as marches. I am thinking of asking Senior Apprentice Ariel to directly guide her studies – and I am thinking of bringing Ariel before our Master review board sometime very soon … I think she is ready and I now have several vacancies to fill. What about you – do you have any changes in Maria's training planned?"

Master Veniti pondered that a moment and then looked more serious. "I'm not sure, though we do have several more 'militaristic' songs I could introduce her to. I am concerned though with her stamina – she is indeed a wisp of a girl. She has made admirable progress in her breathing and lung capacity, and she is much stronger in her lower octave range than when she started. While I prefer singers to work without accompaniment to start, marches have such a strong beat that I may need to borrow a few apprentices on snare and bass drums, and maybe a trumpet player or two. I think we should get started soon though – we really do not know how much time we may have."

"You are surely right there, Veniti. And I think the whole Academy needs a similar program of study – an abrupt change. If nothing else we need to change our focus – I now realize that the real purpose of singing and music is to glorify God. We have always strongly pushed apprentices to achieve perfection, that such excellence was the main goal of all we stood for, all we did. But now ..." Vitario leaned forward again, his voice more animated and forceful. "Now I want to create excellent worshipers, musicians that express God's majesty and glory, that are themselves powerful worshipers and that are capable of bringing their audiences along with them in expression of that worship. I think we need a quite serious shake-up in our Academy."

"Yes, and none too soon. And it must start with us Masters, and flow downward."

"Indeed. Yet it first began with our newest, least experienced apprentice ... Maria!"

Robby held Arianna's hand as they walked back to the Engineer's facilities. They too had found themselves drawn to the lake and had also experienced the spiritual awakening to an even deeper relationship to the living God. In turn, they were drawn even closer to each other.

"Ye know, me love, a few days back ye mentioned somethin' to me in the cabin o' the ship that fishyed ye outa the water."

"Oh, did I? I must have forgotten. After all, I had quite a pounding when my basket hit the water. It may have knocked me silly for awhile. I suppose I could have said just about anything then …"

Robby's eyes had gone quite wide and the color drained from his face as he turned to look at her deadpan face. The twinkle in her eyes however gave her away. "Ach, lass, donna be doin such messing 'round with me head like that! Tis enough to give a strong man a heart attack like poor old Brentwood."

Arianna stopped walking and put her head down over Robby's chest. "Seems to me, Chief Engineer, that your heart is beating just fine, other than a tad fast right now!"

Robert pulled her face up to meet his. "I canna wait no longer! I was so mightily 'fraid when you went all a'tumbling down from the sky, like me angel herself just a'had her wings clipped off all a sudden. I wondered to meself why I was waiting. No sir, no longer! I asked ye then but you twernt ready to answer."

"Bobby, whatever are you babbling on about?" Arianna's eyes were beaming up into his even as she smirked.

He grinned down at her. "Arianna, will the smartest and prettiest engineer in all the world take the likes of me to be her husband?"

She impishly grinned back. "Well, when I find her I will ask …"

Robert's eyes flashed dangerously.

"But in the meantime, I guess I will have to fill in for her." Arianna took a short step back and eyed Robby up and down critically. "Chief Engineer, I most certainly find your specifications to be in order and your construction appears to be rather sound … maybe a wee bit soft in the noggin, but I figure I can get that squared away and ship-shape with some hard work. I think I will accept your offer, once it is officially and properly presented!"

Bobby looked rather flustered, but Arianna's smile and eyes could not be withstood for more than a moment. He dropped to one knee and lifted her hand in his. "Arianna, will ye be me bride?"

She smiled sweetly down. "Yes sir, Robert, I would be most delighted to!"

The hillsides along the pathway reverberated for what seemed like several minutes with a deafening "Y E E H A A W!"

Ethan was semi-delirious. His forehead was beaded with sweat and he could not concentrate on any given thought for more than a few seconds. Memories kept flooding his mind. He fought against the confusion and noise, but whatever it was that Taleena had forced upon him was more powerful and soon he succumbed. He did not hear the scow return and be lifted to the deck, or the ship he was on lift anchor and return to their journey. Ethan's drug fogged mind was lost in a fantasy world, reliving memories.

A fresh blanket of snow had fallen in the high mountain town of Bartleton. With his mother and father meeting with the town council to discuss mining production and trade issues, the eight year old Ethan was left outside to play with the many other children whose parents were similarly occupied. The townspeople had moved the snow from the area in front of the main town buildings into the small park nearby, creating several quite large 'mountains' of snow that were the delight of the children.

Ethan clambered up the steep sides of one of the large snow piles. Some of the older children were at the peak, and a particularly large boy was triumphantly proclaiming himself 'king of the hill'. That signaled to all the males in the vicinity that he was the target to be immediately deposed from his throne. Not wanting to be left out of the fun, the much smaller Ethan scrambled to the top, barely dodging the flying bodies of others who reached the pinnacle before him and found their abilities wanting. Within a moment of reaching the objective, strong arms gave him a mighty shove and he joined the downward avalanche of bodies. The new snow was soft and cushioning, and the backwards momentum carried the tumbling Ethan to the very bottom of the hill. Grinning ear to ear, he picked himself up and charged back up the hill. He found himself climbing near a handful of other similarly sized youngsters, who all began converging on the 'king'. However, as they neared the top once more, it became apparent that the latest ruler had gathered a small consort of subjects around him to assist in holding the vaunted height. They all paused in concern – their much smaller size made a headlong rush obviously useless.

The young boys glanced at each other and wordlessly reached a pact. One charged forward as the others closely followed. That first boy made to launch himself at the nearest antagonist, who was just tossing back down the hill another challenger. At the last moment the younger boy dived to wrap his arms around the ankles of the defender. Another of the newly formed team charged upward and became rapidly tangled in the arms of the taller boy. Meanwhile, yet another team member added his own body to the pile-up and this gave enough momentum to topple the defender from his post. The younger boys disengaged instantly even as the older boy began to fall, and so did not have very far to recover their altitude advantage. Other former 'kings' nearby had also been similarly deposed of their lofty thrones and for a brief minute the new reigning members rejoiced. Then the usurping battles began again.

Ethan's group stood triumphant on one of the lesser peaks. However, the recently dethroned combatant was not about to be trumped by a group of lesser mortals. He solicited the assistance of a cohort of roughly the same age and size and they charged for the top.

This was pure boy fun. As the first challenger made to climb the last few sloped steps to attempt to regain his position, Ethan leapt forward and up, directly into the outstretched arms and head. The momentum toppled the older boy backwards and both he and Ethan tumbled down the slope in a tangle of gangly arms and legs. Several others of the smaller boys saw the outcome and copied it with the other clambering combatants to achieve the same effect, leaving a smaller number of their young group retaining the prized geography.

The battle raged on for quite some time, but eventually the steep climbing took its toll on short tired legs and Ethan, along with his new-found friends-at-arms conceded the hill to others and looked for less leg-demanding pursuits. The snow that was currently falling was of the wet, heavy kind that was nearly perfect for making snowmen – which was being eagerly worked on by a number of the young girls from the town – and also for the more manly activity of making snowballs. Toward this end his cohort cast about for which war to join and soon found themselves somewhat sheltered behind a low drift across a no-man's-land from another group of youngsters whose makeup was of similar numbers though perhaps a year or two older in age.

Snowballs flew in volleys across the short span between the groups. Ethan and two others began to feverishly create a cache of especially well packed and rounded snowballs, and crouched with an armload each. A nod to their compatriots produced a heavier supporting cover volley and the three intrepid warriors swarmed up and over their makeshift protection and charged the other group's bunker behind their own low drift of snow. They made it about half way across before their opponents noticed the impromptu invasion force and let loose suppressing snowball fire.

Life seemed so good. Ethan began throwing his armload cache as quickly as he could, though few actually hit their mark. He was not very practiced at the snowball throwing art form. But as he staggered forward, tossing icy bombs as he went, he began to notice faint bluish streaks in the air in front of him that seemed to trace out the trajectory of his projectiles. That was odd. A reddish line appeared in his vision that seemed to intersect directly with his … WHAM! A particularly well thrown snow ball crashed into his chest, knocking him backwards a step. Other red lines appeared, though most were rather faint and trailed away off to one side or another, or even over his head. A bright red line sprouted into the air and seemed to come directly into his eyes. He winced and ducked, and felt the breeze from a snowball that passed through the empty air where his head had just been located.

As the first volley ended with defenders restocking their weapons, Ethan picked one of his two remaining snowballs and prepared to launch it at the nearest boy, who was frantically scooping and packing additional snow into a projectile. Ethan saw a blue arc in the air reaching from his upraised arm and ending at his opponents unprotected head. Curiously, he tried to throw the snowball to follow that blue line and was fairly successful, scoring a direct hit on his target. Of course, that drew attention to his situation – standing out in plain sight and within easy range, and with only a single snowball now in his hands. The 'enemy' singled him out and the next volley was aimed exclusively in his direction.

Ethan barely noticed, as his concentration was on those odd blue and red lines. What were they? Where did they come from? Even as those thoughts formed, a host of red arcs appeared. Some were fainter than others like before, but several were bright, angry red and terminated at some point on his body. Without warning, time stopped.

Well, it did not really stop, but that was what it seemed like to Ethan. Sounds died away and the light took on an off-cast coloration. The red arcs remained, but now the snowballs following the trajectories painted in his sight lazily edged forward. Then Ethan saw a blue ribbon which started with his body and seemed to kink and bend in a complicated pattern that caused it to avoid every red line completely. This was strange stuff indeed! Enthralled, Ethan began to move, contorting his body along the prescribed blue path. He could only move very slowly, though it seemed faster than the movement of the snowballs toward him. The blue path moved with him, in his time frame, and the snowballs began to pass above, before and beside him. None connected. A moment later normal time resumed and Ethan found himself still standing, clutching his lone snowball, unscathed.

He looked about in wonder. How had that happened? A movement caught his eye as one of Ethan's opponents, highly frustrated that his enemy in plain sight had not so much as been wounded by the last volley, stood and charged forward, a snowball in each hand, to deliver his own vengeance. Even as this antagonist pulled back his arm to throw from only ten feet away, time again slowed to a near standstill. Ethan automatically began to move in the clearly marked blue pathway, easily avoiding the first perfectly aimed throw – perfectly aimed at the spot where Ethan had been. The thrower was fast, and the second ball went airborne, aimed at the new location his prey had somehow moved to.

The second snowball, precisely aimed, also completely missed its intended target and the larger boy looked on with astonishment. How had that little runt moved so fast! How could he have possibly missed? Reality of his own unprotected situation sunk in and the boy made a very speedy turn and ran back to his position of relative safety behind the low snow bank. Just as he dived over the drift a snowball, precisely following a blue line invisible to everyone else, solidly scored with the back of his head.

The eight year old and current day Ethan both smiled as the scene faded amongst swirls of other memories.

Chapter 2

A Blackness Over Kardern

The Alterian ship edged into a berth in the commercial docks at Kardern and a gangplank was lowered. Even before stern faced Dominion inspectors could begin to board, a dark hooded sinister-looking figure made its way off the ship. The chief inspector hastily backed off the plank and gave wide berth. The dock area was a bustle of people going this way and that, yet a clear pathway almost magically formed around the lone, shuffling figure as he disembarked.

Turlock looked both directions, finding no one looking back at him. No one present would dare challenge him. The Alterians had suggested he begin looking for a wizened blind man with a young street urchin in the various taverns near the dockyards, especially near the military docks. He knew Kardern's layout from previous visits, and he headed in prescribed direction, always alert for the potential presence of other Dominion magicians.

No one noticed him shudder inside his robes. He never wanted to be associated with Magicians again, and his skin prickled even wearing the costume. That was how Turlock thought of it. It was a costume and he was now an actor. He figured he could bluster his way around most lower level Magicians readily enough, but also knew that in the spiritual realm he now stood out as considerably different. Scowling, he shuffled along.

Several Alterians, meanwhile, began to fan out, observing and noting everything. They too headed toward the military wharves, where they had noticed several damaged warships as they had sailed into the harbor.

Kardern was a buzzing beehive of activity. When the fleet left, Gaeten thought things would quiet down, but instead more people had been arriving. It appeared to the Master Watcher that the city was turning into a staging area, getting ready for the expected invasion. But a darker, more ominous undercurrent was welling up too.

Gaeten heard the murmurings that someone was coming, someone important, but no one was really talking about it in any detail, at least not in public. It had the whole town nervous. Nimby mentioned seeing many more magicians wandering about in their black cowled robes, all seeming on most serious business. Several times they had had to take alternative routes about the town to avoid any close encounters with the sinister figures, and the one time that they had come near Gaeten had felt dread and heaviness, as though the sun was dimming and all that was good and joyful in the world was draining away. That spiritual darkness and oppression surrounding the magician had lifted once they had passed. Whoever was coming, many preparations seemed to be required. More soldiers were also arriving, and being put up in make-shift housing off to one side of the city.

Then today several ships had straggled into the dock, battered and listing. Nimby had described their condition, and the dockyard workers they questioned said the sailors spoke of a terrible battle where many Dominion ships had been lost and the mighty naval fleet had been sent running to lick their wounds. Rumors began to circulate of some new and terrible magic the sailors had encountered near the coast of Freelandia. The sailors spoke of fire breathing demons that had swooped down on their ships, spitting flame and burning metal balls, and of ocean monsters who rose from the depths to bite holes right through hulls with explosive force. They were jittery and afraid of what terrible demons and gods seemed to be found in those far northern waters that had destroyed dozens of ships. Gaeten wondered just what the engineers had cooked up – whatever it was, it must have been rather effective, and the highly superstitious sailors were attributing all sorts of magical causes and effects to it.

Gaeten chuckled. With each passing person the tales were growing larger and more outlandish … sun-bright flashes of light in the sky high above ships, followed by a booming thunderclap and burning metal rain. A few stories were even going around of metallic balls that shot right through sparing and upper decks to be found buried in the hull planks. Ha! No catapult was capable of delivering that kind of damage! Gaeten thought it more likely some Dominion catapult crew had somehow had a load of grapeshot that had failed to launch and instead was shot down into their own hold. Regardless, the exaggerations were having a significant impact. Whereas before the bravado of the Dominion sailors was galling, and Gaeten had been getting more and more concerned that perhaps there really was something to their presupposed superiority, now a form of morbid dread was overtaking the town concerning the fearsome magic unleashed against their fleet.

So, while he was cautious about what was happening here in Kardern, he was also optimistic. The Dominion had apparently suffered a significant naval defeat and a fear of Freelandia – and of the God who protected them – was spreading. That could only work to the advantage of Freelandia. Now he needed to find out more about who was coming to Kardern, and why that might be significant – and as always, when the Dominion was planning on their invasion.

Nimby brought over their evening meal at the roadhouse tavern they had chosen this day, which was situated near the barracks reserved for newly arrived Dominion soldiers. "I don't like it here, 'grandfather.'"

Gaeten was sitting at a table, seemingly mindlessly passing a coin between his fingers while actually listening intently to various conversations. "Why is that?"

"There are many Southern fighters ... can't you smell that sickly sweet odor they all have? And they seem to look right through me. I don't expect very good pickings here – and you may do well not to try any fancy tricks either – these people look like they would just as soon stick you with those huge swords and axes they carry as talk to you."

"Bring me to an empty spot near them – I presume they are mainly sitting together?"

"Yes, all the Southerns are sitting in one area ... it looks like even the other Dominion soldiers are not going very near them."

"Good. I hear that they are especially superstitious. Let's see about that."

Nimby looked at him rather dubiously, but nonetheless led him over to a table rather near the strange Southerns. Gaeten affected a slight list, as though his drinking was starting to affect him, and absently swatted at the many flies that were commonplace at these taverns. He heard some nearby soldiers – not from the southern tables – in low conversation. Gaeten caught a few words that seemed to be questioning the ships with obvious battle damage at the docks.

With a decided drunken lisp he spoke out. "I hear …" again he absently swatted at the pestering flies "…that the sailors at the docks are saying 'demon fire' shot down from the heavens on them. I heard another say that the gods were spitting steel balls at them."

The soldiers across from Gaeten had wide eyes, and looked nervously around to see what the other patrons' reactions would be to such brash statements. When no one appeared to be paying any attention, one of them worked up some bravery to answer. "Hogwash, old man. No such things as demons and gods. Naw … they musta just run into some new fangled super-sized northern enemy ships that had 'specially big catapults, that's all. Our Dreadnaughts will be like mountains to their hillocks. No such thing as 'demon fire'! You're just full of old wives-tales, old geezer."

Gaeten turned toward the several tables full of Southerns, who were speaking in some unintelligible guttural language of their own. They were all hulking, brutish looking men who glared out of slitted eyes at everyone else in the tavern. "Oh … no such things as demons or demon fire, eh? I bet our southern friends would disagree with you." He waited a few moments, but only heard somewhat more agitated guttural noises at those tables. "I heard clear as day several sailors say that they had several high ranking Dark Magicians present who commanded demon fog to accompany them northward. But the enemy ships could see right through it, and snuck up on 'em, then called on some fearsome northern demons to start hurling fire and steel down on them. And some are talking about sea devil monsters that rose from the deep to feed on Dominion ships. That northern magic must'a been mighty powerful, more powerful than our Dominion magicians could handle as their demon fog just evaporated away." Gaeten punctuated his sentences with further fly swats.

A maid walked by to light candles, and Gaeten carefully listened to her actions to better judge the distances between the various tables, and then ordered a tankard of particularly strong drink.

The regular soldiers must have been emboldened after Gaeten's first remark, since now several laughed coarsely. "You are an old blind fool to believe those fairy tales! Those sailors are just making up fanciful stories to cover up what really happened – they probably ran into some unexpected fog and ended up ramming each other! Leave the demons and gods to the scary fairy tales we tell our children to make them behave!"

A chair scraped backwards noisily, but the speaker was on a roll and did not hear it. "Oh … watch out, old man … demon fire's gonna spit out from your candle and get you! You never know when one of them de … de …" his words ended in a gurgle as a particularly large Southern warrior whom Gaeten had heard moving up behind the other soldiers lifted the speaker up out of his chair with a humongous hand around the hapless man's neck. In a moment the soldier's feet were dangling in the air and he was gasping for what little air he could still get around the clamping grasp.

An impossibly deep growly voice sounded. "You not mock what you not understand. You not underestimate spirits and principalities of enemy. That is quick way to meet them … in afterlife." The big man dropped the soldier without any warning, and the smaller man collapsed down onto the floor laboring to breathe. His companions began to rise to defend the honor of their comrade, and immediately two tables full of the southerns rose as well. Other soldiers all across the tavern were watching intently and several had also risen and were fingering their weapons.

The man on the floor stumbled to his feet, drawing in ragged breaths. He drew his dagger and charged at the man who had held him, stabbing viscously upward. The Southern man hardly moved, and certainly did not even try to step aside. Instead he took a partial step forward and with surprising speed grabbed the knife wielding hand in mid swing in his own massive paw. The attacker was stopped dead in his tracks, unable to move his hand at all. His face turned red, and even as he tried to twist away the much larger warrior lifted upwards. Again the soldier found himself dangling completely off the floor. He sputtered and was gearing himself to try a kick when he felt something very sharp poking his chest. He looked down at a huge dagger whose point was already through his shirt.

"You learn to respect what you not know, little man. Pray you never run into a demon, face-to-face. Where we from, they are common. You also learn to respect your elders, like yonder blind man. Now be thankful tonight I rather drink ale than your blood!" He lowered the soldier slowly, proving his immense strength. With a final squeeze that evoked a gasp of pain from the astonished solider he released the imprisoned hand and in a show of contempt and superiority he slowly turned his back on them and walked back to his table.

The soldiers did not really know what to do. They looked at each other with bewildered expressions. Then a soldier across the room who was from a different barrack began to laugh uproariously, and in a moment was joined with most of the other tavern patrons. Humiliated, the soldiers near Gaeten paid their tab and stomped out.

Gaeten, however, was not likewise finished. Without turning toward the Southerns he continued. "Perhaps our northern enemy is indeed protected by demons, at least in their homeland. But our ships met them out at sea, supposedly a goodly day's journey from their borders. Surely the gods of Freelandia cannot have power that extends so far from their homeland."

The Southern speaker addressed him. "You speak as one with knowledge of spirits. In our homeland are those who see more in spiritual world than our own. Some say being blind to world gives better vision to other realms."

Gaeten needed to be very, very careful now. "Yes, leader-warrior. The spiritual world is very, very real to me … as I know it is to you. Our enemies may have enlisted forces greater than we have anticipated; perhaps some air and sea gods we do not know. We will have to entice our own protective spirits to be with us even closer when we attack. We will need even stronger magic to overcome the northerners."

"Hmph. We be ready, ancient one. We be protected by our strongest spells and enchantments, and our own demons will fight for us. I not afraid of Freelandian spirits, but I keep eyes open and pray to our gods. Maybe I give extra sacrifices to unknown sky and sea gods."

"That may be wise, valiant one. Yet I wonder … if the northern sky spirits can be so strong even many miles out to sea, could they possibly … possibly even be here, spying on us now?"

That got some attention. The other Southerns began to grumble in the odd guttural tones uneasily. "Do you know something, you-who-sees-the-spirits? Have you seen something?"

"Those others … you were good to stop them. Mocking the spirits is always dangerous. It calls attention from them and … they come to investigate."

The voices became more agitated now, and Gaeten could hear many at the Southern tables shift about with unease. The warrior spoke in a hushed voice even as he nervously glanced about. "What … do … you … see and hear?"

Gaeten smiled inwardly, but his outward expression was deadly serious. Still with his back to them he continued. "The air spirits are angry tonight. They feel they may need to demonstrate their power and might to the unbelievers yet here. I … I hear a whisper …" Gaeten's hands shot upward as if to ward off blows, flinging them backwards over his head. "I heard them say men would drop like flies!"

Even as the words left his mouth, several of the flies he had caught and lightly crushed rained down on the nearest Southern table. As they hit, two of those at that table leapt backwards in fear, clutching at amulets hanging from rough leather strings around their necks.

Gaeten took a swig of his strong drink and swished it around his mouth. What he planned next was unpleasant, but should be rather entertaining. At least the alcohol should be highly antiseptic. "Ohhhhh," Gaeten gurgled out as he clamped a hand over his mouth. He staggered to his feet and turned, stumbling over to a nearby table of intently watching and listening Southerns. He slammed his forehead down on the table and then craned his neck back upward, his face at their level. He opened his mouth widely and the few still living flies he had transferred there from his other hand buzzed out in bewildered drunken aerial circles.

That put them over the top. Color drained from their faces and eyes bugged out at the sight of the strangely buzzing flies zig-zagging in loopy circles before them and at one that was moving in staggered steps up Gaeten's cheek. The big men began to shout in horrified tones in their native tongue. As the flies flew further toward them they broke rank and in panic dashed away from the table, and that began a stampede of all the Southerns out of the tavern.

Gaeten cleared his throat and noisily spit. He reached around the table before him to find a tankard and took a quick gulp, only to roll that about his mouth a moment and then splutter it out in a cough. Ugh, he thought. That tasted even worse than the fly he thought he had swallowed. The Southerns indeed were a very superstitious lot, and that could be used against them if done carefully. He would have to consider how to build on the rumors further. The Freelandian demons were going to become extraordinarily fearsome … as everyone would soon know.

Turlock was given very wide berth by all passersby, and even tavern bouncers stayed well away from him too. He had surveyed half a dozen taverns in as many blocks, and yet had not noticed anyone meeting the description the Alterians had given. The town seemed to have nearly as many taverns as soldiers. The search was going to take longer than Turlock had expected. He hoped the Alterians were more successful in finding the merchant ship that might have brought Ethan here … if Kardern was even the destination port. Turlock prayed for Ethan's safety and deliverance, and that he could find this blind Gaeten fellow soon. Whose plan had it been to send an old blind man out as a spy anyway?

As other merchant ships began arriving at ports both within and outside of the Dominion, encrypted dispatches of all sorts were carried by runners from the ships. One by one those letters began to be delivered to Watchers leased out from Freelandia as the world's most elite and respected body-guards and military consultants. The messages were all simple and short. Aunt Lydia's one and only nephew had gone on vacation unexpectedly to ports unknown. If anyone happened to see or hear from him, or from his blind uncle Garth, they were asked to kindly assist in any way possible. Aunt Lydia and her entire extended family would be extremely grateful.

Chapter 3

Arrivals

aster Oldive pushed back from his desk and stretched. He grinned at the ceiling when his hands did not touch the side walls. He had his own office now, a proper one quite unlike the cramped space he had only a short time ago.

"Don't get too comfortable, Master Oldive – we have a war to prepare for!" James grinned broadly to convey his words were only a good-natured jest.

"Oh, hello Master Warden! Do you always sneak up on people, or am I honored with special attention today?" Oldive grinned back.

"Watchers can be as silent as a shadow when they are on a mission."

"And what might that mission be today, Master Warden?"

James chuckled. "Please, call me James. I was looking for Robby, is he hiding somewhere around here?"

"And you can call me Oldsy, most people around here do. Robby said he had to visit the Master Shipwright on some urgent matter – likely to settle some squabble between the engineers working there and the ship builders. They get along pretty well, but sometimes those old salts can't get past their traditional ways of doing things."

James shrugged wryly. "And sometimes you engineers don't accept the fact that in battle what can go wrong often does, and the more complicated a contraption or procedure is, the more likely it will break or not be used correctly. I'll take reliability over clever innovation anytime fighting breaks out. Though I will give it to you, those Thunderclaps of God certainly seemed to work out above my expectations."

Oldive's grin grew. "Yes, those were impressive, weren't they! Is there anything I can help with Mas …, I mean, James?"

James took on a more serious expression and pulled up an empty chair to sit. "Yes, I think so. Robby said you were his second-in-command. I wanted to get an update for a meeting I have with Chancellor Duncan later today. Perhaps hearing it from you would add another dimension of perspective … unless you think Robby would prefer I hear it only from him?"

"No, I am sure it is perfectly fine for me to give you an update. Since I am not positive what he has filled you in with I apologize ahead of time if I am repeating anything you have already heard."

James nodded in affirmation, and so Oldive continued. "We have quite a cadre of apprentice engineers split into several teams working on sillarium spring weapons of all sorts. The many volunteers flooding in from the city and countryside have been put to active work. The mines have tripled their outputs, and the smelters were producing metal as fast as it can be fashioned into the various parts needed for weapon assembly. Additional capacity for production is being added daily, and efficiency seems to increase by the hour. The largest springers are heading to the coastal defenses, along with engineers to implement a strenuous training schedule to get the gunners up to speed with them as quickly as possible."

James nodded. "Yes, Robby has mentioned that. It sounds like it is all progressing quite well."

"Yes, but it is both exhilarating and frustrating." Oldive scowled and shook his head. "We see the new technology implemented but it also has some rather exasperating aspects. The speed of new inventions and advancements is occurring at a rapid pace. Nearly every day some apprentice or another is coming up with an improvement, and designs are evolving so fast that after a few weeks the latest models are considerably superior to prior builds. Yet so many launchers are needed that as soon as we build and test them, they are deployed out to the coasts. And your Watchers have insisted that the channel defense get their catapults replaced as soon as possible. So, ironically, the most important positions for the coastal defenses of Freelandia are getting the models that are now the least advanced … though still superior to the old original catapults. The closer you get to the Keep itself, the newer the model of spring-a-pult becomes."

James lifted one eyebrow quizzically. Oldive chuckled as he continued, "At least that is the name some of the apprentices have given the larger versions! I just pray there will be enough time to update the earliest versions before the Dominion comes. And it is not just the coastal defenses. A similar situation exists on our ships. The first priority was to outfit existing ships, but at least they could be deployed wherever desired versus the fixed position coastal defenses. But the latest and greatest ships are getting the latest and greatest weaponry. Some of those ship mounted launchers are particularly cleverly outfitted, making those that the Dominion ships have already encountered seem antiquated."

James shrugged. "That is always the case with an army and navy. We try to both standardize and yet bring along updated equipment. I've heard about most of the ship mounted versions of your launchers, but I've heard you have also been improving on the smaller hand-mobile models?"

"You have heard right, James." Oldive leaned forward and became more animated as he began to talk about one of his 'pet' projects. "The swivel mounted units that you have seen before have been much improved, but we are still ironing out details for the man-portable units that can be rapidly deployed. Crews are being trained on using the smallest tubes, which should be quite effective at very close range against even lightly armored enemies. However, Minister Polonis has made it quite clear that the hellhounds would need something larger, and the pachyderms that some of the Southerns will likely ride into battle required something much more substantial, yet ideally such a device would still need to be moved about by at most two or three Freelandian soldiers."

At the mention of the huge beasts known to accompany some of the Dominion war campaigns James frowned deeply. "I admit we do not have strong back-up options to stop those. We really need you to deliver a workable solution. On another topic, what is going on with the integration of the launchers with Engineer Arianna's bombs?"

Oldsy smiled. "Robby finally promoted Arianna to Master – I have been suggesting it for weeks! It will take some time to get used to calling her by that title. Of course, if the Dominion holds off long enough there might be another new title for her ... Mrs. Macgregor!"

James smiled. "I wondered how long that last item was going to take! Watching those two together makes you think they have been together for years. But can you update me on what is happening with those pressure bombs?"

Oldive turned more serious again. "Arianna is turning out improvements in her pressure canisters at a right smart pace and we have been interchanging apprentices to each other's teams to ensure the newest launchers will deliver the newest gas bombs most effectively. She has delegated most of the work to other engineers so that she can concentrate on the lighter-than-air floating bags – they call them 'bubbles' now. They have potential to deliver quite large bombs out over the bay to greater distances than even our best launchers, and they might be able to better time the release of the devastation. I must admit I considered the reports of what happened to the merchant ship nearly unbelievable … until Arianna duplicated it for all to witness … minus of course the nearly fatal ride she took after triggering off the first one."

Oldive leaned back and grinned. "And Robby has most adamantly demanded that she stay firmly grounded! In fact, the Chief Engineer is not too keen on any of the manned bubbles. He asked for work to concentrate on smaller versions that could be launched from shore with timed fuses. While one very large bubble could deliver a huge payload, multiple smaller ones could more easily be moved about on the coast to catch the most favorable breeze and deliver many smaller "Thunderclaps of God" to blanket a given target area. Production of the floating sea mines is also going at a frantic pace, and swamp gas and mud are being scoured for all over the countryside."

Oldive leaned forward now and frowned very seriously. "The big question of course is how long do we have? If the Dominion was scared off from their first naval defeat, perhaps we might have more time for even better preparations."

James nodded. "We are all praying for that, Master Old …, I mean, Oldsy. And we will all still work feverishly in the meantime."

Ethan did not feel the ship reach the dockyard. He felt rough hands untying his hands and feet, but in his delirious state it seemed like flies alighting on him, and he absently waved them away. He was half dragged along out of the hold with his hands tied behind his back. Murdrock looked on disgustedly. His prize possession apparently had come down with some sickness, and that would surely lessen his immediate value … and he dare not die. That could be disastrous.

Murdrock assigned a burly sailor to carry the boy off the ship to eliminate the chance of any accidents, and he followed closely to meet the waiting contingent of fancifully dressed honor guards that had cleared a wide area along the dockside around the ship. Several hooded Dark Magicians stood by, along with an emissary from the city Mayor to ensure smooth transactions of whatever was needed. A light sheet had been thrown over the limp form of the captive to disguise his identity from watching eyes, and as soon as he, Murdrock and Taleena had disembarked the guards tightly surrounded them several layers deep.

Murdrock looked on warily. He had expected more fanfare, though he acknowledged that secrecy may be a better tactic for now. The honor guard surprised him. He had expected a squad or two of Dominion soldiers, maybe even from an elite unit. But as he examined the trappings of the guards he realized they must belong to … an Overlord! Murdrock nearly stumbled when that thought flashed through his mind. Here? An Overlord? He pushed his chest out all the more. High honor indeed … and perhaps his best chance yet of getting the notice – and advancements – he felt he so surely deserved.

Taleena had taken note of the insignia too, and was already plotting how to discredit both Murdrock and poor little Ethan while emphasizing her own merit and detailed knowledge of Freelandian defenses. She had several of her best wardrobe selections and the best of the jewelry that had not been discovered in a satchel, along with her special bag of potions. If possible she wanted to give one final dose to Ethan, one that would make his delirium irreversible and lethal. She figured it would not be too terribly difficult to worm her way for one last visit to the boy, wherever it was they were going to hold him. Things seemed to be going oh so very smoothly according to her plan.

The retinue moved out of the dockyard and traversed through the streets of Kardern to the old castle/fort that had been built here over a hundred years before and that now served as the region's main governmental and military outpost. Though the need for such a massive structure was no longer evident, it had been kept and expanded for its current uses, and it remained a very imposing structure with quite secure ... and very private ... prison cells.

Even for a bustling Dominion port city flush with soldiers, the procession was unusual enough to be noted by quite a few onlookers and sailors. It would just add to the considerable rumors already spreading throughout the city that someone of great importance was coming, or possibly could already have arrived. And more than a few soldiers recognized the advance honor guard insignia as belonging to none other than an Overlord. While a few marveled and wondered about what great importance that might bring to their town, the few soldiers and sailors who had ever been around an Overlord before just shuddered and shut their mouths. The coming of an Overlord always brought trouble. Already the number of Dark Magicians wandering about seemed to have swelled significantly, and more seemed to prowl the streets every day.

When the party reached the castle, an administrator greeted them and led Murdrock, Taleena, and the others to VIP quarters that were reserved for them. Murdrock noted that the special guards seemed rather commonplace throughout the castle, and in particular noted that several seemed to be stationed in the hallway outside the guest rooms. He scowled. He did not like at all the inference that might be drawn from that. But before he would even consider checking out his quarters in detail he demanded to see and thoroughly inspect where his prisoner would be kept. A highly secure dungeon cell had been prepared, but Murdrock would have none of it – given the obvious serious sickness, Murdrock demanded that Ethan be placed in a VIP room just down the hallway from himself and Taleena. This caused quite a fuss, but when Murdrock threatened that any worsening of the prisoner's sickness due to inadequate facilities would be immediately reported to the highest officials, a room was rapidly prepared in the VIP hall and two guards were put into Ethan's room itself, as though the lad could somehow escape out of the bed to which he was chained. Senior Healers were called immediately, and Murdrock assured all that he himself would be present and would have to agree to anything administered ... it was HIS prisoner, make no mistake about it.

For her part, Taleena enjoyed the obvious discomfort and stress that Murdrock seemed to be under. She had her own plans for the kidnapped prisoner, once the Overlord came to understand her own considerable importance. She was just a tad bit concerned about the Healers, however. Taleena had very carefully concocted her mix of poisons so that it would closely mimic several rather common southern maladies, and a couple of the ingredients were from plants known only in the region where she had grown up. Yet it was always possible they could come up with some form of antidote to counter the relatively low dosage she had administered – and that had to be prevented at all costs. She wanted Ethan alive for awhile longer, certainly until he could be brought before the Overlord and shown to be uselessly incoherent and unlikely to recover. That would surely cement her own most VIP status. And then ... then she would see that Murdrock received his oh-so-just reward for the way he had treated her! Why, without her they would not have gotten Ethan at all, and she would not have a head full of the Freelandian defense details that Ethan had showed and explained to her.

Thinking of that, Taleena once again went about repeating the phrases she had memorized to aid in recalling those details. The phrases themselves meant nothing, indeed they were somewhat gibberish, but each word was associated with a detail she had seen or heard. Taleena smiled at her own creativity. Even if she was drugged into divulging information against her will, it was unlikely much more than these phrases would easily be extracted – she purposely and frequently repeated them and drilled them into her memory.

No one was going to take away her prize, her destiny. Now she began to prepare one last dose that would put Ethan's weakened condition over the terminal edge. He could not be allowed to recover. His death would seal her own fate. She figured she would get one and only one chance to administer it, and it would likely have to be done in full sight of others. She smirked ... it would be a literal 'kiss of death'.

Turlock was getting more and more frustrated. There seemed like hundreds of bars all over Kardern, and his garb was not exactly conducive for gathering information – everyone avoided him and only gave curt quick answers to any questions he asked. So he walked from bar to tavern to bar moving through one dockyard section at a time, hoping his path would overlap with Gaeten. Even the Alterians had come up short ... until just today. This afternoon two had caught up with him and delivered the news that a merchant ship had arrived and had been escorted into the harbor and docked over in the naval area ... which had been heavily cordoned off with special soldiers. Rumor had it that some extremely important and special cargo was aboard, which had been immediately hustled off to the castle in a shroud of secrecy.

Now the Alterians were also on the lookout for a white haired blind man who might be frequenting the local bars and taverns. At least with the several pairs of additional very watchful eyes it should not be overly long to track down Gaeten. Turlock worried that they might not have much time. An Overlord either had already arrived or was due any day ... and from what he knew of them, rescuing Ethan before any meeting was extremely important. There were credible accounts of grown men leaving such meetings incurably insane, or even dead.

From what he could recall of the demonic presence that had been within his own mind, he could only shudder at the thought of what might inhabit or associate with an Overlord. Apart from direct Divine interference, Ethan would not stand a chance. And from what Turlock had been told about Ethan's behavior prior to the abduction, he was not so sure the boy could ... or even would ... call for help from the only One who could possibly provide it. Even as that thought went through his mind, Turlock stopped in his tracks and bowed his head within his deep cowl and prayed earnestly.

Gaeten walked quickly in the twilight toward a tavern where he had heard officials from the castle often came to unwind. It was not the type of place he had been regularly attending, the down and gritty joints that sailors were more commonly frequented. He was dressed better than normal as befitting his intended location, though this was certainly not a classy restaurant. Gaeten expected a place where staff would come to unwind, and that was exactly what he wanted ... where the real behind-the-scenes kind of talk might flow more freely. There had been considerable commotion a few days previous, yet none of the sailors he had talked to or listened in on seemed to know what it was really about … just some loose talk about some VIP arrivals that was muttered oh-so-quietly.

He paused at the entrance and adjusted his clothing slightly before entering. Gaeten wanted to project the image of a once important staff person who was now down on his luck and too old for anyone to take much interest in. He had Nimby help to pick out some clothing that at one time … maybe 20 years ago … would have been quite stylish and proper for a man-servant to wear at the manor home of some lord, and which appeared quite well worn and faded.

Gaeten strode into the tavern, his walking stick making slight tapping sounds. Slowly maneuvering forward, he soon found an empty seat at a long table and carefully sat, holding his back straight and his head held high. He knew from experience that his entrance was always watched with curiosity – it was not very common for a blind person to have such practiced mobility, and staring was much easier to get away with when the recipient could not see you. As a serving girl moved by he stopped her with his raised cane and affected an accent more common to the islands off Alteria to the west. "Lass, I'd be obliged if you could serve me a tankard of ale and a piece of that fine roast I smell cooking at yonder fire." He made a show of patting down his outer pockets until he found one in particular and fished out a coin.

"Yes sir, right away." The coin he had given her was a bit much for what he had ordered, but it did ensure he would likely get an actually decent cut of the roast, away from the burnt end his sensitive nose identified. It also would more likely attract the attention of others who may then try to befriend him.

In a few minutes his food and drink arrived, and shortly afterwards one of the other patrons sitting further down along the table shuffled up closer. "So … you look new around here."

Gaeten turned his head toward the voice and spoke in a slow cadence, "Yes my good man. I came in yester night. I'd heard there might be some hiring going on hereabouts, and thought I'd try my chances in a sizable city like Kardern. I understand this is the region's biggest city and the seat of government – is that the case?"

"Well, as a matter of fact, it is indeed both of those. But I think you are too late, old-timer. There was a slew of hiring last month in preparation for the arrival of … of …" The man's voice lowered conspiratorially. "… of the one 'no one may speak of.'"

Gaeten assumed a very real look of puzzlement. "I'm afraid I am not following you." He edged closer and lowered his own voice. "And who just might that be? I've served under some rather important Lords before, and some had mighty important … and secret … guests. Governors, princes … even once a rather high ranking Dark Magician!" At that last one Gaeten scowled most darkly. "That one gave me the creeps, it did. When he walked into a room it was like a cold chill swept in. And the other servants said that the shadows in any room he was in … it was like they followed him, like there was something there that you could never quite see. I had to air out the place for a week before it seemed back to normal."

Gaeten waited to listen if that would get any reaction. He had picked up some of these stories from his time here in Kardern, and he half believed them himself. A couple of times Nimby mentioned they were near a Dark Magician on the streets and he could feel the spiritual evil emanating from them. He had made sure to keep his distance – if he could feel the evil, it was possible they might feel his own spiritual light, and that would not do, not for his current mission.

The man sitting next to him only nodded absently in agreement and then, realizing the condition of his audience, quickly spoke up. "Aye, you have been near one then. I've heard it does not pay to examine those shadows none too closely … you may not exactly like what you find. One of the servant blokes at the castle said he had to clean out a room where one of them had stayed. He said there was one corner that was in shadow, and no matter how many candles were brought in, the shadow stayed put. So he said he got up his nerve and put a candle right in the corner and swept it out good and proper. He swore that for the next several days that shadow followed him … I think he may have been off his rocker, or maybe filching a bit of the whiskey … but two days later I met him right here, and he was acting crazy – looking around this way and that, never turning his back to any dark corners. Poor bloke. They found him the next day, jumped from the window in the very room he claimed had the shadow. Cursed he was. Now I hear they canna' get any of the servants to clean up the rooms after the Darks stay there, at least not after they hears the story. But that is nothing like what is going on now … you must be pretty new not to have heard who just came to town."

"Who?" Gaeten said this in a low whisper.

"An Overlord, that's who! A real Overlord! Here! And I hear that anyone who comes near him says he is ten times worse than any Dark Magician."

Gaeten was stunned. An Overlord? Here is Kardern? Why? He had been told they never travelled out of the far South where the capital of the Dominion was located … and was shrouded in mystery. What could be so important to bring an Overlord this far north … except for the war on Freelandia? "My God, man!" Gaeten chuckled inside … His God indeed! "I suppose it must be the impending war up north."

His companion looked quickly left and right and lowered his voice even further. "Surely that must be part of it, but that's not all. I work up at the castle myself, I do. And they just had a mighty peculiar visit a few days back. I was pressed to tidy up some additional rooms real quick-like. Some big procession came up from the dock yards, all really important folks from what I could gather … and a prisoner. I don't knows who he may be, but there are more guards about there now than I ever seen, and I am not even allowed near those rooms anymore – no one is unless escorted by a pair of guards. And even more Darks have come. Seems whoever that prisoner is, he is going to be getting quite some attention – and supposedly he will be questioned by this Rath Kordoch, the Overlord himself!

Poor wretch. And I hear the bloke is pretty sickly to start with, being tended by several of the best healers around." The man shuddered strongly. "He may be an enemy of the Dominion, whoever he is … but I would not want my worst enemy subjected to what he is going to get. Some big meeting is happening in a couple of days. All us servants have to get the main audience hall all spruced up … the Overlord himself will be there with his top Magicians. I hear that is when the prisoner will be brought in."

Gaeten's mind was running at full speed. Who could this be? It had to be someone awfully important. Could it be … someone from Freelandia? He had to find out more.

"Say, my good man – you said they were having trouble getting someone to clean up rooms? Shadows don't mean a thing to me … my whole world is one big black shadow."

"Say, you're right on that one, mate. And a blind feller might just be considered higher security, seeing as you can't, well, see. You might just indeed be the ticket! And me finding you ... there might just be some kind of bonus in it for me too! Hmm. We gotta move fast on this before someone else comes along to fill the position. Can you get yourself to the castle tomorrow at dawn? Wait – you'd never get in, not even near it. Tomorrow I will check to see if the job is still open, and suggest that I just may have someone who would fit the bill. My shift starts late the day after – so meet me right here by noon two days hence and I will walk you up there – how 'bout that? Try to dress up a bit better if you can ... maybe I can bring you one of my old coats to wear ... but if you keep it I expect you to pay me for it!"

Gaeten smiled. "That is very kind of you. I would really appreciate the job. My name is Goshen. What's yours?" He held out his hand.

The other gentleman took it in a firm shake. "Barth. I'm one of the head butlers for the east wing of the castle, so that makes me a pretty important bloke among the servants. You picked a might good friend to find in me, Goshen!"

Oh, I didn't do the picking, thought Gaeten. *But my God did!*

Chapter 4

Ordained Meetings

aeten walked slowly with a frown of deep thought carried on his face as though it were a heavy weight. He had nearly arrived at his modest apartment across town, when Nimby, out for a walk of his own, sidled up and greeted him.

"Say, just what did you find out 'grandfather'?"

"Well, the good news is that I may have a more regular job in two days, up at the castle. That would occupy my days anyway."

"Oh." Nimby looked downcast and his voice conveyed his concern.

"Now that does NOT mean I still don't need a good set of eyes and ears to scour the city for information while I am out, and I still plan on visiting the local taverns to supplement my … our … pay! You have been a good helper, and good companion, Nimby. You are not out of a job yet."

That brightened the boy up considerably. He certainly did not want to go back to the life he had had scouring the streets and always one slip-up away from a beating … or worse. "Right! I'm glad ta' hear that, old man. But you said that was the good news – and you sure don't look none too happy."

"Yes, you are observant – that is one of the reasons I chose you. The castle is full of Dark Magicians, for one thing."

"Ugh! That is enough to deflate anyone's sails. And you in particular seem to steer very clear of them … like you got's more ta' hide than most."

Gaeten considered this a moment. Nimby had proven trustworthy so far, but he was none too keen to let on more than the lad absolutely needed to know … loyalty only went so far, especially if confronted by the point of a knife. "Let's just say that I really don't like those cowled wretches, and they probably really wouldn't like me much either."

"I can imagine that … what with your keen interest in Dominion war efforts especially relating to Freelandia." Nimby let that out while closely watching Gaeten's face for the slightest twitch of surprise. In a movement far too fast, Nimby was lifted off his feet and carried into an alleyway they were crossing. Gaeten pinned him several feet above the ground against a wall.

Through gritted teeth Gaeten asked, "And just where did that foolish notion come from, boy? Answer carefully now, the full truth, or your feet will never touch the ground with life in them again."

Nimby's eyes bulged out of their sockets and he gulped as best he could in his decidedly awkward position. "I … I've been watching and listening to you … you told me to keep my eyes and ears open to everything going on! You always seem to come around to talk about Dominion warships, armaments, troops … that sort of thing, and especially about any news of expected troop or ship movements. And …"

"And what, boy?"

"And … and I've watched you pray. You don't do it like the magicians do, or commoners, or even … or even like I've heard people do at the Southern temples. You do it like you are really talking to someone … someone who you think is really listening. And sometimes you stop and seem to be … to be listening like you was listening to someone answer you back. At first I thoughts you was crazy. Maybe you are. But you can do more than any sighted person I know. And there is something … something more real about you. I don't know. But when I sees you pray and sees what you do … it makes me think I want to know more about this God you talk about … and seem to talk to."

Gaeten stood very still for a moment, then began to slowly lower Nimby with the arm that held him, while reaching into his tunic. Nimby watched that hand with fear building in him … he knew that was one of the several secret pockets that held a knife. He knew the often shambling old man was actually quite well armed at all times, and that he seemed extremely proficient with those weapons. Furtively, he held the suspicion that the old man was not a former circus performer at all, but was instead a Freelandian spy. Yet he never, ever voiced even the slightest hint of that. Not that he had any love for the Dominion or Freelandia – which of course he had only heard distorted comments about – but he held the old man in very high regards. Was this to be the end, now, here in this alley?

"Caught a pick-pocket, did you?" The voice was low and deep, muffled by the heavy hood hiding all of the man's facial features.

Nimby stared and his fear grew in bounds. He gasped quietly. "A Dark Magician!"

Gaeten did not turn yet, though the knife was now mostly out of its hidden sheath, ready to be hurled with deadly accuracy at a moment's notice. He spoke with a rickety old-man's voice "Yes I did, and I was 'bout to give 'im what his kind deserves, trying to steal a coin from an old blind man like me."

The deep, quiet voice continued. "Yes, I saw you walking with a cane out in front to feel your way, though it did not seem like you had any problems moving with great speed into this alley. And your pick-pocket seemed more like a companion than a true thief."

Nimby was free now, and he backed around Gaeten as though to put some distance between himself and his attacker, curving his path to the other side of the narrow passage and toward the freedom of the mouth of the alley.

Gaeten assumed he could never pass a close inspection by a Dark Magician – at least not one with any significant spiritual sensitivity. He turned slowly, one hand at his chest hiding the knife, the other fumbling down on the ground for his dropped walking stick. Finding it, he slowly rose, keeping his back bent over as though that was his normal full stature. He took a few steps closer toward the voice at the mouth of the alleyway, centering in on the breathing that betrayed the man's exact position. "And who might you be, sir?"

The hooded figure took two steps closer and began to raise his hands. Gaeten of course could not see that. He could only discern that the man was moving toward him and was doing something with his hands and arms. For a keenly trained fighter operating well behind enemy lines, already tense from an unexpected encounter, that was more than enough incentive. Gaeten spun the rest of way around toward the stranger, crouching at the same time, willing his hand to throw the knife with deadly accuracy and force.

Taleena was furious. She had been interviewed several times now by what she considered low level administrative assistants who barely even registered when she mentioned her vast knowledge of Freelandian defenses. And to make it worse, she was completely denied access to Ethan, so she could not administer the final lethal dose of poison to silence him and increase her own value immensely. She had tried coercing the guards, bribing them, seducing, even demanding that she see him – to no avail. Only the doctors were allowed in, under close supervision of high ranking guards. Even the Dark Magicians were kept out, though it seemed like one or more were nearly always nearby in the hallway. They gave Taleena the creeps.

So instead she spent her days getting familiar with the castle and with the local administrators. She was working her way up the political ladder rather skillfully, and she figured that within another week she likely could have an audience with the regional governor.

And then there was the Overlord. Everyone spoke of him in whispers, though none had actually even seen him. One wing of the castle was his alone, and only top ranking ministers and Dark Magicians could enter – and then only on request. She glanced at the piece of parchment paper left on her bed ... while she was out someone had actually entered her room! It was a good thing her potions were carefully hidden with her perfumes and other similar items – though it was highly unlikely anyone would know what they were, unless that person was trained in looking for such things.

The notice was really a command to appear before Rath Kordoch the next day. It appeared that finally there was to be a formal introduction of the Dominion spies to the Overlord, and it also inferred that Ethan may be in sufficient health to be brought out from his sickroom. Well, if she could not come to Ethan, perhaps Ethan would be brought to her. Taleena smiled. Wouldn't it be nervy to poison Ethan right in front of the Overlord himself? Who would ever suspect? She did not believe in the stories told about Overlords to scare the simple minded. No, they could only be just men, albeit very, very powerful men. She began to practice in her mind how she would pull it off. Yes ... it would work!

Murdrock was also impatient. They had been essentially held at the castle without ability to leave since they had arrived and there had been no formal debriefing of their activities in Freelandia. The waiting was infuriating. He was satisfied that his prisoner was being well taken care of, and he himself was not lacking in anything ... in fact, he was being treated with deference and respect. That was a good sign; it meant the Overlord had understood the audacity and importance of bringing the son of Freelandia's chancellor here. Surely he would be well rewarded. More than any immediate benefit, Murdrock wanted a position of his choosing in the invading army, one that would allow him a top choice of the spoils. He had come to like aspects of the country of Freelandia, and surely someone of his stature and talents would be allotted a prime slice of territory to run as he wished ... or maybe even the whole country. Yes ... Governor Murdrock ... he could get used to the sound of that. And he would take immense pleasure in subjecting the oh-so-gentle and weak populace to heavy Dominion rule. He smiled.

And it looked like he would get his first chance to impress the Overlord tomorrow. Murdrock ordered a new set of clothing, one that seemed more befitting an army commander with political aspirations.

Chancellor Duncan looked over his paperwork for the day ... it seemed that the war efforts required far more paperwork than anything else. He wondered if they could just make big bundles of it all and fling it from catapults at Dominion ships – surely they would never run out of ammunition! Yet for all of the decisions that required his attention – mainly settling prioritization disputes and funding ... always funding ... it was actually rather amazing how smoothly it was going. He was pushing decision making down upon his hand-picked subordinates based on their skills and abilities, and encouraging them to do the same. God was behind it, that was for sure.

Yet even in the midst of the work, he worried. He knew he shouldn't, but he did. He worried for his country, for his people ... and especially he worried for his son Ethan. But he could not and would not let that distract him long from his responsibilities. He prayed again for Ethan's safety, and for wisdom in his decisions.

Master Oldive came bursting into Robby's office/conference room, his clothes disheveled and wet with perspiration.

"Whoa there Oldsy … no need'in to rush about … or did you start another fire in one of yer workshops?"

"Actually, I've just come from a fire … an extremely hot one at that." Master Oldive fished out a handkerchief to mop his balding pate, but the bright gleam in his eyes did not change. "We've got a young metalsmith who just won't follow the normal rules … keeps trying out wacky ideas … sounds rather like a young engineer I once knew." That was said with a pronounced wink. "Seems like this fellow got hold of some of that swamp gas from Arianna's crew and brought it to one of the metal working furnaces."

Robby's eyes went wide and he flung his arms wide apart in agitation. "What! He could'a made the whole place go ker-blewy with that stuff!"

"Well, I will give it to him that he is careful and thought this out. He piped in the gas from a pressure pot with several of those new-fangled valves that Arianna invented, and trickled it into one of the furnaces. Seems he figured it might change the heat output … and boy was he right. He was working with some new ore in a small caldron of tile and sand. He used a dipping ladle made of sillarium to stir up the mix and pull out the melted samples. We have found that sillarium can handle quite a lot hotter furnace temperatures than steel or iron, so we use it with the unknown ores to take 'em out once they have melted."

"Wait a minute – don't you usually have to add other ingredients to the pot to help convert the ore to metals, and then sometimes need nickel, copper, charcoal or other ingredients to make useful alloys? How can you do all that kind of testing on every new ore someone brings in?"

"You are correct, Chief Engineer. We have a procedure we use to screen the new ores, and if any look promising we run them through a broad battery of combinations and tests to see what we might get. Back to my story – this new ore just would not melt or change, even with some of the standard processes we use. The metalsmith cranked up the furnace as hot as he could make it, and still nothing. Why he did not stop there, I do not know – he says the thought just 'came' to him. He begged off a small pressure pot of swamp gas and fed it into the furnace. Talk about heat! That gas made the furnace so hot we couldn't get near it! He let it roar for 20 minutes or so, then shut off the gas and tried to reach in with the sillarium ladle to get out a sample – but it was so hot he couldn't hold onto the metal handle, and we had to let it cool for several hours before we could remove the caldron with the sillarium cup still inside. Look what we found." Master Olidve held out a piece of dull white metal about the size of his fist. "We polished this up a bit, but it gets dull- looking rather fast – but then does not seem to change anymore. Here, catch!" With that he tossed the sizable chunk of metal toward Robby's sitting form behind the desk.

"Hey, watch it – are you crazy?" Robby scrambled to get his hands out to catch the block of metal, pushing backwards on his chair so he could sling his arms with the metal to catch it without straining his wrists from the expected weight. As his hands closed around it and stopped its downward momentum his face lit up with amazement.

Without a word Master Oldive watched as the Chief Engineer gingerly tossed the hunk of metal back and forth between his hands, gaining confidence and speed. He looked with questioning eyes at Oldive. Then he took a small hammer off a shelf behind him and whacked at the metal, wincing and shielding himself with his free hand as though the object might shatter into a million fragments. Nothing happened, aside from the dull metallic 'WHANG' sound.

"Oldsy … what is this stuff? Is it truly metal? I've never, ever felt anything metallic be so light weight – is it full of air holes, or hollow inside?"

Oldive smirked. "No, we thought that too and dissected the first one, and the second too." He said that carefully, watching for a reaction.

"So you've gone 'an repeated it then … it's no' some kinda fluke?"

Oldive smiled. "No Robby – it is repeatable. You are holding what has to be the lightest weight metal we have ever seen, lighter than anything we have even dreamed of. And it is not brittle like iron nor rusts like steel. Now, truly it is not nearly as hard as those two either – you wouldn't want to make a sword edge with this stuff. But it is stronger than you might think, and once made it is pretty easy to work with."

Robby turned a critical eye toward his elder engineer. "An' justa what're you thinkin 'bout for practical applications then?"

Master Oldive smiled broadly. "Now just what might we have a use for with a super light weight, strong and easily worked metal that does not seem to rust? I am certain just the very same thing your mind is racing toward. Armor."

Gaeten's hand would not move, even as his fingers grasped the knife he was determined to throw. Something seemed to be staying his hand. The hooded figure before him slowly drew back his cowl, unaware of the mortal danger he faced. "If I am not mistaken, we have a mutual friend … Aunt Lydia."

For a split second Gaeten's mind froze, mimicking his hand and arm. In that moment he realized he had not noticed the sense of evil that seemed to accompany the few other Dark Magicians he had come somewhat near. He willed his taut muscles to relax … at least a little. He did not recognize the voice, but this person knew one of the few code phrases designed for quick acceptance among Freelandian undercover agents. And though he could not see, Gaeten had learned to rely on his spiritual discernment to help distinguish friend from foe when he took the time to listen. And he was not detecting what seemed like an enemy, even though Nimby had named the newcomer as a Dark Magician. Come to think of it, every one of those had a distinct aura of evil about them, and there was none of that here. As his mind told his fingertips to loose their hold on the knife, motion suddenly returned to his hand and arm and he slowly let them drop … a move that could be reversed in an exceptionally short time if needed. "Oh, and who might you be?"

"That is a longer story, one you are due but which is not terrible important immediately. My name is Turlock, but what is much more important is that Auntie's young nephew is missing and I have good reason to believe he may have arrived here at Kardern."

Gaeten literally staggered. That code phrase could only refer to one person – Ethan. But how could that be? Could somehow that be the prisoner lodged at the castle? No! Even with his considerable control Gaeten could not help but gasp, and he stumbled backward a step as if from a blow.

A sudden sharp intake of breath from the man before him brought Gaeten back to the reality of the moment. "No Nimby, it's alright … whatever his appearance, this man appears to be a friend."

Nimby had quite stealthily worked his way behind the imposing robed figure as if to escape, and the point of his dagger had made the man take such a sharp breath. "Are you sure, grandfather? If he so much as twitches again I can slide this dagger past his spine and tickle his heart."

"Thank you Nimby … you show remarkable courage … and loyalty. I am certain. Please let him go."

Nimby took a step back and stared at the old blind man. Had he really said "please"?

The trio made their way back to the apartment Gaeten and Nimby shared, though it would not do for the hooded figure to be seen walking with them. Turlock kept to a discreet distance following behind, and a few minutes after they arrived he quietly slipped in. Once inside he removed his heavy cowled robe and dropped down into one of the few chairs in the sparsely finished quarters. "Ah, that is much better. I really don't like wearing that costume."

Nimby was staring at the vivid tattoos that ran up and down his now bared arms. He looked up. "But you sure look like a Dark Magician! I've seen those tattoos before."

"Yes, lad … I once was a Dark Magician. And I did unspeakable things, horrible things. And worse, I even let a demon control me, though once possessed I no longer had any say in the matter. I even …" He looked up at Gaeten, and though he knew the elder man could not see him, Turlock still looked him square in the face. "I even attempted to have the Chancellor of Freelandia assassinated. I helped plan the attack and it very nearly succeeded, both in getting Chancellor Duncan and also Master Warden James. We did poison several others and kill several innocent bystanders."

Gaeten's hands were gripping the table at which he sat with whitened knuckles and his voice was a deadly whisper. "Nearly, you said. You once were a Dark Magician, you said. Kindly fill in the rest … now!"

Turlock could see that Gaeten was constraining himself with some difficulty, and knew that he was utterly helpless to defend himself before the very senior Watcher – and so he hurriedly continued. "The Chancellor's son, Ethan, thwarted our actions, which led to his becoming a kind of national hero. I was captured and in a highly ironic twist of fate … er, I mean of God's plan … I … well, I poisoned myself with what was meant to kill Lydia, the Chancellor's wife. But a remarkable thing happened at the Ministry of Healing. A missionary to the Southern lands, Minister Polonos, was led by God's Spirit to come with an antidote, saving the lives of James and the others. And he healed me too, but much more, he cast out the demon that controlled me and then, bless his heart and God's grace, he led me to a loving relationship with Jesus and with my creator, the one and only true God."

At that Turlock reached over slowly and touched Gaeten's arm. "You have every right to hate me, to despise me … and even to kill me here and now. I will not stop you in the least. But Duncan himself told me you have a high level of spiritual discernment. Look at me now in the Spirit. See me for what I have become, not for what I once was."

Gaeten sat very still for several minutes. Then he loosed his tight grip on the table and gingerly held out a hand to Turlock. "I welcome you in the name of our God. I welcome you as a fellow believer and as a brother in Christ."

Turlock looked relieved and Nimby, listening to it all, looked bewildered. He blurted out, "But wait a minute! There has to be more to it than that. You … you almost killed the top people in Freelandia and now you are forgiven and accepted, just like that? You are guilty! You deserve to be punished! Surely God would want to exact some penance from you – is that it? You have to come back here to the Dominion territories and turn yourself in to be tortured to prove your worth and pay back for all your … your sins?"

Gaeten chuckled. "It does not work that way with the true God, Nimby. He does not want your penance or punishment. He wants your obedience and love, and has a boundless, endless supply of His love for you. He has told us to forgive our enemies, just as He has forgiven us. But you are right in that there must be a payment, a punishment for sin. But God's only Son Jesus paid that for us with His own life, which God His Father gave back to Him. Because Jesus paid the penalty, we are already forgiven. Being forgiven means there is no longer any punishment, no penance and no guilt anymore. What you did before was done by someone else, your old self. Once you become a believer your old self is, well, it is like that person died and you are a new person … having a brand new start. And if God can totally forgive and accept someone, even a former Dark Magician, well then I can try to also. I can forgive – and I would even if his former self had succeeded in killing those I dearly love."

Nimby shook his head. "I don't understand. It goes against everything I ever heard or believed. It don't make much sense."

Turlock nodded. "That is what I first thought too. When I was first freed from the demonic influence I was overcome with grief over my awfulness and wanted to destroy myself. Yet Minister Polonos told me that God would truly forgive me; that it was a present from Him to all those who would accept Jesus His Son as their Lord and turn their lives over to Him. And there is so much more to this life with God than there ever was trying to live without Him. So, Nimby – if God wants me to be captured, even tortured for my faith, then so be it. I will do it without regret. I owe Him much more. You … you don't ever want to know what it is like having a demon inside you, controlling you." He shuddered.

"I think I'll just take your word on that! But I don't know about the rest. This is a whole lot to think about. You could almost convince me to believe in your God," Nimby looked worn out from the heavy thinking.

Gaeten turned toward the young man. "Nimby, I do not want to rush you into anything you are not ready for. This is not a light decision. It is the most important decision of your life. But don't put it off either. We are in a dangerous business, you and I. With the information you now have, it is tremendously more dangerous for you – like it or not, you are a spy working against the Dominion. If you are captured and this is found out … you would likely come to have much more intimate knowledge and acquaintance of Dark Magicians. And, of course, you could cause great harm to come to me."

Nimby had shrunken down in upon himself with the thought, but he stared defiantly up as Gaeten mentioned his own vulnerability. "I wouldn't rat on you … you been gruff with me, but kinder than anyone ever treated me. And now you be saying you trust me? Tell me, if I get up and walk out right now, will you stop me … will you kill me?"

Gaeten shook his head. "No, Nimby. You are free to leave anytime. I have been bluffing with you, figuring that kind of talk and behavior is what you would understand the easiest given your prior life. But I hope you will stay … and I hope you will accept the offer to become a believer in the true God.

But I cannot wait for you to think about it. I am not sure how much you may have picked up from our conversation so far. Turlock here has information that the son of the Chancellor of Freelandia – Ethan, a boy only a few years older than you – has been kidnapped and brought here. And …" he turned toward Turlock "…and today I learned where he was taken – to the castle on the far side of the city. What's more, I have an appointment there the day after tomorrow for a job as a servant to clean up rooms – in particular, rooms occupied by Dark Magicians. It seems there are some rather jittery servants there now who won't go near those rooms. And one more thing; an Overlord showed up and came to the castle just days before Ethan arrived. If they have not questioned him yet, it is only a matter of a short time – so we will have to act quickly."

Nimby was the first to speak. "Act quickly to do what?"

Turlock had gone quite pale, which of course Gaeten could not see. "Did you say an Overlord is here … and may question the boy personally? Do … do you know what they do? What they … are? Pray that it has not happened yet … pray that we can rescue him in time!"

Nimby's eyes stood out of their sockets. "Rescue a prisoner from the castle? Filled with Dark Magicians and a Dominion Overlord? Are you both crazy?"

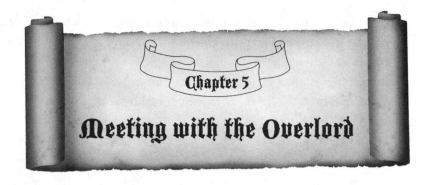

Chapter 5

Meeting with the Overlord

The next day Turlock went out to find the Alterians and let them know he had found Gaeten, and to communicate a request. He had to move about the town carefully – there were many Dark Magicians about and he had no desire to be tested … or for someone … or something … to notice that his spiritual existence was far different than any other cowled figure. He found the Alterian ship within a few hours of walking the docks and relayed the message. Then he went about securing some of the items suggested by Gaeten.

For his part, Gaeten had Nimby take him to some of the nicer second hand shops and help him select updated butler-type clothing. They had picked up some lunch and were slowly walking back to their apartment. Nimby was still incredulous about what they seemed to be planning. "You're going to work up at the castle, and try to break out a prisoner right under the nose of an Overlord and his guards? And even if you get out of the castle, how you gonna get through the town and to the docks with him? The city is filled with soldiers! Even if you got to the Alterian ship you talked about, how would they get-away from all the naval ships? Since the last few days everyone in town is as tense as a pig at the meat market … a ship leaving suddenly would attract a whole lot of bad attention. Patrol ships would shoot for sure if it did not stop."

"Nimby, you have that thought through fairly well, but you don't know the whole plan … and quite frankly I don't know all of it either. God is going to have to help, without doubt. We could never succeed without His intervention. Now, before we get much further I need to know something. You are coming to a decision point, my boy." The two had been walking down a street and had come to an intersection. "You must choose if you are going to risk it all with us, or go back to your gang and what may actually be a safer life, at least for the next while. I am not going to force you to go along. If you leave now, you will likely never see me again and you can blend back into the street gangs. When the authorities start looking for an old blind man they will hear about some young boy with him, but you will be one of several hundred that are around these parts. It may be difficult for all of you for awhile … it may be better to even relocate to another city for at least a few months. I will give you some money to tide you over.

If you stay, I can only promise great risk, maybe even torture and death, and surely a life on the run for awhile. I will be heading back to Freelandia with Godspeed. I expect rather shortly afterward the Dominion will launch its invasion, so even there life will be in great peril. It is yours to choose. I have grown to be rather fond of you … and to trust you. And if you stay, you can be of tremendous help. I have a plan where you would play an instrumental part in helping us get out of the castle grounds and the city – but it would be better for both of us if you did not know the details unless you were staying. Now is the time to decide."

Nimby was wide-eyed listening to this, and a tear began to form in the corner of one eye. He jutted his chin out and brushed it off roughly. "Can I at least think and decide on a full stomach?" Not long after lunch, Nimby departed, alone, and with a rather full money sack.

Gaeten walked slowly toward the tavern where he was to meet Barth and be taken to the castle. He was dressed in his finest … or at least the finest Nimby had found for him when they shopped the day before. The outfit was more restrictive than he liked, but it did have lots of pockets, including a few he had sewn in himself this morning. As he neared the tavern, he began to somewhat straighten out his back from the old-man shuffle he had adopted. Now he assumed a role of a dignified if somewhat down on his luck former senior steward and strode forward, his thin walking stick lightly tapping out in front of him. He reached the tavern just before noon, and the smells made him a tad hungry.

"Why, there you are! I was wondering if you would make it." Barth looked around curiously. "But where is your grandson who was helping you? How ... how did you make it here alone?"

Gaeten smiled. "Once I have been somewhere I rarely forget how to get back. I may be blind, but I am far from helpless."

"That is good, Goshen. I had been having some second thoughts – how will you get around the castle, and how could you possibly clean and straighten a room without being able to see? At least it appears you can find your way around pretty well."

"You may be surprised at how 'able' I am. For instance, you had bacon for breakfast, and on the way here you stepped in something ... a bit is still on your left shoe. You stand five feet eight inches – about average – and by the feel of your hand when you shook mine I'd say you have not had particularly hard labor for quite some time. You have a short mustache – you brush it lightly after you eat – and you are careful about your appearance – you inspect your clothes after eating and brush off any crumbs before you leave the table. Today you are wearing a light wool coat with a vest underneath it and likely matching pants. You wear sensible shoes but the right one squeaks slightly, so it has not been oiled recently. Your wife uses lavender soap. You were late in getting here and hurried the last several hundred yards by the slight smell of sweat I detect. Would you like more?"

Barth looked amazed at the old man, then began to chuckle. "No, that is enough. I don't need you to tell me how often my wife does the laundry! I think you just might be exactly what the Master of the servants is looking for. I spoke to her yesterday, and while she was doubtful she did see the beneficial points I made about you. And if you can repeat what you just did for me, I think the job will be yours. Tell me, can you start immediately? There is some big event happening late this afternoon in the big audience hall, and I am certain they will want some of the rooms cleaned and straightened while the VIPs are out."

"Yes, I am available right now. I am sure I could start on those rooms immediately."

"Oh, it would not be right away, not while they are still in the rooms. You will get shown around first, introduced to the important servants, and shown where the cleaning supplies are located. They won't let you near the rooms until the guests ... and the prisoner ... have left."

"Prisoner?"

"Oh yes, we have several of those too, and one is considered a real VIP – though he must be awfully sick with all the doctoring he has been getting. I hear he is a young man too. Anyway, today there is some big meeting with the Overlord Rath Kordoch in the audience hall. All the servant masters are in a stitch to get everything perfectly prepared. We'd best get along over there promptly."

The two walked the half mile to reach the outer grounds of the castle. "This is the first check point coming up. Don't worry, I am well known here. The guards will get used to you; otherwise you need a pass from the head servant. I am sure they will remember you, though."

Gaeten listened carefully as he was led through the checkpoint, and noted that there was a low wall in what amounted to be an outer Keep of the castle. From the sounds of all the people coming and going, it must have been a rather busy entrance, and the speed at which they passed through indicated that real security was not a high priority … though of course that could change. The gate through which they entered appeared to be rather large, easily wide enough to allow the nearby two horse drawn wagons he could both hear and smell to both enter and exit simultaneously and still allow them to walk through also.

Barth gave him a running commentary on the sights as they walked on. Inside the castle keep was a large open area that they hurried through. "Normal folk typically enter through the main gate, which is straight ahead. They get checked out more thoroughly. The servant's gate is off to the left side."

"So they just let the servants come straight in?"

"Nah, well, not really. Now I recall years back when we even had a tough time entering, even though we have to do it every day. That got to be rather old. Seems the administrators did not like the fact that their servants were taking too much time at the gates, so they relaxed the rules. Same for the food carts and kitchen help – we wouldn't want none of those high and mighty rulers to have to wait for their lunch or dinner, now would we?"

Gaeten just smiled absently as he noted every sound and smell and feel along the entire way, counting his steps carefully.

"Here now, this is the servant's entrance."

Barth turned to address the gate guard. "Tis alright Dorian – this is gonna be our new butler for the … the 'special' apartments."

Gaeten heard a grunt and snicker from what sounded like a single guard at the entrance. "Guess that would be 'bout right for those quarters! Ha. The last fellow that worked on them … he got rather weirdly. I kept my distance from that one, I did. Wanted 'im to pass through right quick too. Now git along w'ya!"

Barth led the way through a series of passages and doorways, meeting no further security checkpoints. "This is the main common area of the castle," he explained. "Here now, we are at an important junction." He turned Gaeten slightly. "Straight ahead of you now is the wing where most of the administrators and the regional governor have offices." He shifted Gaeten to the right. "In this direction is the wing taken over by …" here his voice lowered to a whisper "… the Overlord and the Magicians. And over in this other direction," he turned Gaeten still further, "is where the kitchen and eating areas are located, and where most of the servants work. Got that?"

Gaeten nodded and pointed unerringly toward each direction and re-peated what his guide had told him. "So where is the main hall where the big faluting meeting is supposed to be held … I want to make sure I stay well clear of that!"

Barth nodded. "Good idea there, Goshen. It is between the servants' area and the wing where those 'other guests' are located. There are several passageways so the servants can bring in food and such without getting in the way of the royalties. Come along now, we need to get you to see Miranda, the head of the general staff servants. If you pass her muster, you are in."

Gaeten spoke a silent prayer, asking again for special favor with the authorities here, and for clear guidance on when … and how … to rescue Ethan. He had no doubt that this was what God had brought them to-gether here in Kardern for, but he only had rudimentary plans on how to accomplish the goal. He hoped it could occur before the Overlord brought Ethan in for an audience. That, however, did not seem overly likely. Per-haps it was best that way anyway … everyone will have likely calmed down afterwards and be more at ease. And besides, what was the Overlord likely going to do but be told who Ethan was and what they may hope to get from him? From what Gaeten had heard, Ethan had been or even still was quite ill – which seemed strange, since Ethan normally was the epitome of health – and there was limited information you could trust that was obtained from someone very ill.

Barth led him down several more passages and finally rapped on an already opened door. "Excuse me ... Miss Miranda, I have the gentleman here I was telling you about."

Gaeten took quick note of the size of the room by the echoes of sound and of the number and location of various people in the large work area. A lot was going on and it took a moment to isolate and identify it all. After that very brief pause, he strode forward and unerringly held out his hand directly in front of the person who had moved slightly in response to Barth's introduction. "Madam, I am Goshen ... at your service". He said the last with a slight bow while keeping his sightless eyes directed straight ahead.

Miranda was a gruff woman of perhaps 60 years of age, with a head full of whitened but carefully arranged hair, who held her head high with her position of authority over this section of the castle servants. While at first slightly rebuffed by the audacity of such a direct greeting, she noted the accuracy of his extended hand and of his neat appearance. She took the proffered hand and held it up, looking first at the back side and then turning it over to the front. "You are not unaccustomed to hard work I see. Your calluses have been earned for many years, though I cannot exactly tell from what kind of labor they have come from."

"Ah, madam, you are very observant. And you run a tight ship, with only a few in the room here who have paused to listen while the rest have stayed true to their tasks."

Miranda's eyes grew to slits, and without even turning she snapped the fingers on one hand. It was as if a whip had cracked: everyone in the room redoubled their efforts at their tasks, though all tried to tune in their ears all the harder. "So, Mr. Goshen ... what you lack in sight you appear to more than make up for in hearing. Are your other senses so finely tuned as well?"

Gaeten smiled genuinely. He made a show of sniffing the air before him. "The girl there," he pointed with his reed cane, "needs a fresh bandage for the cut she recently had. Whoever bound the cut knows what they are doing, the alcohol that was used on it should keep away infection, but it has opened again. If she is not careful she may stain the cloth she is working on … mending perhaps?"

Miranda swiveled abruptly and strode over to the girl in question who was sewing. At a questioning glance the girl proffered her left hand up for inspection. Indeed, a spot of red was forming through a thin bandage covering one finger. The girl looked up, frightened, but saw a gentle smile. With a nod she was sent to the infirmary to get a new bandage. Miranda returned to stand in front of the two men. "Well, you seem clever enough. But I am not so sure how well you could tidy up rooms – you need eyes for that. Perhaps if you had a younger helper … hmm … I think we could get one of the children to work with you."

She looked off into the air for a moment as if considering something. "Ok then, I'll hire you – but only on a trial basis for now until we see how you will work out. I want you to start now … there are a number of rooms that will be vacated this afternoon and it will be an ideal time to tidy them up. The guards in that section have been assigned to do up the rooms, and all the guests have been complaining. Well, all but the prisoner. Anyway, the guards wouldn't let anyone else into that area to do the cleaning – as though one of the servants would even try to approach a prisoner! But given your condition, I think they may allow you. No offense intended."

"Well, thank you, madam, and no offense taken. May I ask what my wages might be?" There was something about this woman that he liked, and his impression so far from her actions and from his spiritual discernment was that she could be trusted … as far as anyone who worked directly for the Dominion could be.

"That will depend on how you work out. If you can last and keep up for the next three or four days, then we will talk about wages. That is my rule here."

"Alright. I am ready now."

"Good. Go with Barth to get a cleaning apron – all the cleaning staff here wear them so we can keep tabs on who is who."

Gaeten smiled inwardly – that meant anyone in the proper apron would not be questioned. Security was rather lax … at least in this area of the castle. As Barth led him away he wondered where Ethan might be, and just how ill his young friend was.

Ethan moaned as the Dominion healer forced him to drink down another awful herbal concoction that he was told should make him feel better. How could something that tasted so bad possibly be good for him? He knew he was still quite ill – he was very weak and his head often seemed to be swimming. Even so, he knew he was not on the ship anymore, but in some sort of … well, he expected a prison, but he was on a rather comfortable bed and was being well cared for. Yet he also heard the heavy metal bar lifted off his door whenever anyone came to enter, and several times he saw armed guards waiting outside his door the few times it was opened. Still, he was doing better than when he was on the ship. Though in his present predicament he was not sure if doing better was truly for his ultimate benefit.

The healers said today was supposed to have a big event … he was to be dressed up in new clothes and presented before some important Dominion dignitary. One doctor had mentioned it was an Overlord – Ethan had only even heard of them a couple of times. None would tell him anything about what was to happen to him, and indeed, they tended to tut-tut under their breath and look at him warily and even with some sympathy whenever the topic was brought up.

While Ethan knew by all rights he should be scared, instead he had considerable peace about his situation. God had reassured him that He was with him and would help him through it, and he was clinging to that as one of the few truths that was forming the bedrock of his sanity. Ethan was sure God would use even this for His plans and purpose, somehow. It may go very badly for him – but then again he figured he deserved whatever was coming for his own stupidity. He would try to take it calmly and look for God's hand … and pray for the grace and strength to stay true to his God and his country.

The time must have come, for he was helped up out of bed and, under the watchful stare of guards, washed and dressed. He was still considerably light-headed and had to be held vertically by one of the healers, but even in this helpless state his arms were roughly pulled behind him. A four foot long pole was thrust between his arms and back and lifted high to fit in his armpits, and then his hands were pulled forward and tied together in front, effectively locking in the pole. A guard stood on either side and could, if needed, readily control or even carry Ethan by simply lifting the pole. Then, to emphasize his helplessness, a metal band was fitted around his neck and chained quite tightly to a ring on the pole, forcing his head upright and even bent backwards slightly. It was highly uncomfortable and meant to both constrain and humiliate the prisoner. To Ethan, it was just uncomfortable. He actually smirked inwardly as they were fitting him to the restraints … in his mind, blue ribbons indicated directions to follow to escape and red to indicate actions to incapacitate everyone in the room – had he any energy to do so.

Instead, the guards began to half-walk, half-drag Ethan down a hallway, with the ranking Master Healer in tow behind them. As they passed by a window the bright sunlight made him wince and stumble, and the guards jerked him back upright roughly. Even though he did indeed try to walk, he could only shuffle and ended up being dragged a good deal of the way to the audience hall. As he neared the entrance, Ethan could see Murdrock glaring down at him from a few yards away.

The guards supported him on either side, keeping his head looking straight forward and upward, but Ethan could hear other people moving about nearby and the hushed whispers of attendants. Before him was a large double door with several finely liveried guards standing before it.

"Where is that little flea bag we dragged in with us? She was supposed to be here for our entrance." Murdrock was pacing before the door. "It is so like her to be late and make the rest of us wait for her. She would like that – us waiting upon her majesty to grace us with her presence. It won't happen." The last was said with a dangerous low growl.

"You may enter shortly." The voice was a hiss of sound and made Murdrock and Ethan jump – well, Ethan would have jumped if his restraints would have let him. No one had heard the Dark Magician come down a side passageway but as he stepped forward everyone nearby drew back. It was as if a cold dank wind had entered the room, and even the torches flickered and shadows seemed to lengthen and darken. For most present it was both eerie and discomforting, but with Ethan's heightened spiritual senses it was much more. The figure reeked of evil and hatred and darkness.

The Dark Magician came up to stand near Ethan, but off to one side so that Ethan could not quite see him out of the corner of his eyes, and the guards stood at stiff attention, not letting him move. The foreboding presence became a heavy weight around him and a sense of fear and terror began to flood into his mind. He tried to resist and shake it off, but it deepened and closed in on him, thoughts of despair and guilt rising. Resolutely, Ethan focused his attention on the bright light of God's glory he had experienced on the ship, walling off the terror that was nibbling around the corners of this thoughts. He clung to the deep knowledge that God loved him, accepted him, and had forgiven him. The battle did not last long, and the darkness seemed to withdraw.

"This one is strong, stronger than his physical weakness would suggest. It will be especially enjoyable to break him." The robed man scanned the others in the entourage. "They are harmless – they can enter now."

At that pronouncement Murdrock swelled his massive chest and began a low growl but the Magician raised an arm, displaying heavily tattooed skin. The growl transformed into a gurgling cough as Murdrock felt something restrict his throat. He raised a muscular arm to find what was choking him and found … nothing. His eyes bulged and as his breath came in as a thin gasp the Dark Magician lowered his arm. Murdrock sucked in gasping breaths as the tightness lessened and then disappeared.

A more subdued Murdrock stepped aside and the entrance guards opened the tall heavy doors and the group was ushered into the audience hall, with the Dark Magician following behind them. Ethan tried to step forward with dignity, propelling himself forward under his own weakened strength.

Ethan did not know what to expect. He had wondered if the hall would be filled with all sorts of dignitaries to watch the spectacle of the son of the Chancellor of Freelandia paraded forward in chains. He was just as glad that was not the case. Instead, a small group of people stood around a raised platform near the center of the room, on which a large throne had been set. The hall itself was quite large, making him feel all the more insignificant. He was marched forward and brought to a low stand with tall vertical posts, to which his pole was attached. It was uncomfortable, surely purposely, but at least he did not have to support his own weight. As the guards latched him to the posts, Ethan's weak knees gave out and he sagged against his restraints. From his vantage point, he was dizzily looking directly up to the dais and throne … and onto the Overlord.

Rath Kordoch did not dress like the Dark Magicians, though Ethan had always been taught that these mysterious figures rose up through the ranks of the Magicians to attain this highest position within the Dominion. He had no cowl to hide his shaved head, which was adorned with vile looking tattoos of murderous creatures in various acts of destruction. The Overlord was dressed in black clothing with a red cape so dark as to be almost black itself, and its color somehow reminded Ethan of dried blood. His looks were not really what you noticed first however. As dreadful as the Dark Magician had been outside the hall, this man seemed to have a cloud of evilness swirling about him. Indeed, it did appear to the onlookers that strange shadows crept and crawled about the Overlord. His malevolent eyes took in Ethan as though examining a small fly one was about to swat.

"So, whom do we have here? The son of Chancellor Duncan? He does not look like much." The voice was sickly sweet and its contrast with the spiritual darkness pervading the man tended to catch one off-guard, as it was designed to. "Well, do you have a voice, cur? Or has someone already removed your offensive tongue? I think …"

He was cut off by the unannounced and rather brazen entrance of Taleena, who despite her diminutive size could indeed make a rather grand and gaudy entrance. The guards at the door were still arguing about letting her in, and other guards inside were moving to more aggressive stances. Taleena, arrayed in vibrant blues and purples in a rather revealing dress that left no doubt that she was far more advanced than the little girl her height might warrant, strode with supreme confidence into the audience hall. The guards glanced at the Overlord for direction, and he raised one eyebrow but assumed a quizzical smile that truly was more of a sneer. They stood down.

Taleena knew she had to pull this off grandly or not at all. She barely glanced at the rather astonished onlookers, breaking from the slightly haughty, arrogant, superior expression only when she passed Murdrock – then her eyes flashed with fire and her lips parted as though to show fangs. She swept up to the edge of dais and curtseyed most formally, bowing low before the Overlord. She was well aware he would have been thoroughly prepped as to who was present, their roles, and why they were here. She was also very aware that her deep bow and curtsey would leave only the slightest amount to the Overlord's imagination as to her womanhood. He was just another man to be manipulated, after all, and she wanted him distracted but with full attention on her. Of course, he likely had not been made fully aware of her importance ... importance that shortly would grow significantly.

She had the full stage for the moment, and knew she may never get another chance. Taleena had anticipated this and pushed her acting further. As she rose from her curtsey, she made a show of taking in the whole room in a sweeping look. "Ah, poor boy Ethan, there you are!" She sidestepped rapidly over to his small platform and stepped up before him. The guards assigned to Ethan began to move forward, but they were rather slow, as surprised by this woman's actions as the rest.

In a fluid movement Taleena lifted her hand and gently parted Ethan's hair and caressed his face. "It was fun, while it lasted, lover!" Ethan's slumped form was a bit high for her, and for just a moment Taleena feared she would not be able to reach his lips ... and that would be disastrous to her plans. She rose onto the very tips of her toes and planted a full lip lock kiss onto his unsuspecting and helplessly immobile form. She smeared as much of her tainted lipstick onto him as she dared, then sunk back down and waltzed back to the line standing before the Overlord.

For his part, Rath Kordoch was looking at the performance rather curiously, with one eyebrow arched. *What was this insignificant flea up to?* he wondered. It made the affair slightly more interesting ... and especially so with what he planned for her. "So, you betray your lover with a kiss? How very appropriate! Human love is so often such a short step from hatred, so easily manipulated over reason."

Murdrock's face was a mask of fury and he was shifting weight from one foot to the other, barely containing himself during the showy farce just displayed before him. Rath Kordoch watched the play of emotions on the Dominion agent's face with some amusement and motioned Murdrock to step forward. This one was useful to him, though the spy needed to learn better patience. Yet impatience had its purposes too, when it could be sprung in a purposed manner.

"Murdrock – your record has been impressive ... at least before going to Freelandia. It looks as if you went soft there. I have heard life is pretty easy up north, especially when you are fully funded by the benevolent wealth of the Dominion." The Overlord held up a hand and studied his nails. "You failed miserably for quite awhile, even lost a team of our best assassins, and even lost one of our Dark Magicians! That must have taken some exceptionally poor planning and execution. Do you have an explanation for your appalling ineptitude?"

Murdrock bristled with defensiveness, almost taking the bait. Then he noticed the sly and careful look given him and recognized he was being goaded and provoked. He took a deep, drawn out breath, stalling to gain greater emotional control and then smiled over gritted teeth. "Their magic is very strong in their homeland, far from the protection you and the Dark Magicians provide in Dominion territories. I am no magician, just a warrior. Their magic is also much more subtle than ours … yours … and much more difficult to recognize. Yet I can attest that it is quite powerful – as I am sure you have heard from the naval force sent northward. My sources say our fleet was badly mauled, though they far outnumbered and outweighed the Freelandian forces. Perhaps that shows what I was up against."

Rath Kordoch nodded without acknowledging either the veracity of the statement nor Murdrock's seemingly intimate knowledge of what very few in the Dominion yet knew about – or would ever hear of. Inwardly, he moved his ranking of this soldier up a notch or two, both for controlling his anger after such an overt provocation and for how smoothly he integrated recent battle knowledge into his own account to appear all the more credible. He might make a decent territorial administrator, once the cursed Freelandians were crushed.

"Don't suppose your failures relate to whatever ill fortune happened out at sea. Your reports singularly spoke of success and your own prowess, yet you somehow did NOT assassinate the Chancellor, or his wife, or the Master Warden. Nor did you even manage to incite rebellion beyond a few hoodlums. If it were not for yonder boy standing here in chains I would have enjoyed watching you flayed inch by inch for my dinner entertainment tonight."

Murdrock grimaced at that thought. Then he straightened his back and looked at the Overlord eye to eye, as unpleasant as he found that to be. The man's eyes were … were not 'right' – there was something in them that was malignant and malevolent just below the surface, something that did not seem …totally human. He swallowed hard and continued. "But this plan worked perfectly. I planted a female spy to get close to the Chancellor's son. This boy …" He gestured dismissively toward Ethan, "was largely responsible for interrupting the assassination operation. I have had mixed reports on how this was accomplished, but all appear to involve some strong magic. As a result, he became a hero figure to the ignorant populace. I reasoned that if the Dominion could capture this 'hero' who also was the son of the popular Chancellor, we would control something of very high value both to the leadership and the populace of Freelandia. In addition, this resource has considerable personal knowledge of much of the defensive preparations going on in Freelandia and may have insights into the decision making processes and the individual personalities of the main players.

In all, I think it was a highly successful operation, with the prize presented before you here today."

Rath Kordoch nodded, but had a deep frown on his face. He rarely gave out praise and always wanted his minions to be off-balance and wondering if they had really pleased him. "But, you bring me damaged goods. Obviously you did not take very good care of my 'prize' – at this point he is more valuable than you are. He should have therefore been treated as the most important person in your presence and taken far better care of than you took even of yourself. Tell me, were his quarters better than yours? Was his food better than yours?"

Murdrock's eyes went to slits and he looked down in answer.

"I thought not. Your operation appears to have been mildly successful, but if the boy dies he is far less valuable to me." The Overlord looked over at Ethan, who for some reason now looked far worse than when he had entered, hanging from his chains, his eyes having a vacant, unintelligent stare. The healers had said the boy was doing better, though there was always the potential for a relapse. They had not been able to identify the malady, nor had any of their standard cures proven very useful. At least one senior healer had brought up the possibility that the boy may have been expertly poisoned. That was an interesting potential.

Alive, the boy was the most valuable, but even dead he would still be useful … since only a select few would know of his demise, and a look-alike substitute could always be found. He would need to get that selection process started, maybe even with half a dozen candidates chosen for advanced training. That might be the best solution anyway, since those substitutes would be much more controllable.

"You said he has intimate knowledge of defenses and leaders. Do you have proof of that? He is just a boy."

Before Murdrock could speak, Taleena took a step forward and curtseyed again with a deep bow. Rath Kordoch smirked – did the woman think he would be influenced by the obvious display of her flesh? He would enjoy what was coming all the more, destroying this one's pride.

"Most esteemed Overlord, I was with the subject nearly every day for the last month we were in Freelandia. He showed me nearly all of the defensive works and discussed in detail with me the startling new technologies they were developing. He even described how many of the leaders thought and how they reached decisions. I estimate I have heard and observed perhaps ninety percent of what the boy knows. In addition, I have been absorbing this information with an eye for attack, rather than his mindset of defense. So I am the only one who has seen it personally from both sides – and as you said, Murdrock did not take very good care of this highly valuable resource – it appears the boy's knowledge may be inaccessible in his present state, or of questionable value … will you hear truth or a delirium induced fantasy that sounds like the truth? How will you know for sure?"

The Overlord sneered loudly. "I have ways of extracting information that is far beyond your comprehension … at least momentarily."

That threw Taleena off and she stammered into silence as Rath Kordoch continued. "In fact, let us see what really is known, what really is the truth here."

A Dark Magician who was standing behind the Overlord strode forward to stand before the bound and now fully slumped Ethan, hanging nearly lifeless from his bonds. As he reached up to touch Ethan's head an arm became exposed, showing an exceedingly life-like serpent tattoo with yellow eyes and red tongue. As he reached up, Taleena, who was closest to Ethan, gasped. It looked to her like the serpent's tongue began to flick outward into the air. Just as the fingers were about to touch Ethan's face, the Dark Magician's hand jerked away with considerable speed and force. Though none could see the Magician's face inside his deep cowl, they could hear the raspy voice. "This one is sealed from us! We cannot enter."

The Overlord frowned deeply. "Then influence him. Read his thoughts, disturb his body and mind."

The Dark Magician's hand again approached Ethan and a dark shadow seemed to emanate and wrap around the outstretched arm and begin to curl around the chained boy's neck. Taleena stifled a scream.

Ethan's mind was a swirl of foggy colors and lights. The poison administered to him was both potent and fast acting, and his mind was nearly totally detached from his surroundings and body. Yet even here, a core part of him moved to the source of white light deep within him. The light seemed to envelop his core being and he felt protected and at peace.

When the darkness coiled around him, Ethan's body jerked within his constraints and the shadowy serpent form moved this way and that over him, looping coils around his head again and again. The voice of the Dark Magician changed, taking on a soft eerie hissing. "His mind is confused, his thoughts only meaningless dreams ... deeper ... deeper ... his soul is sealed from us ..."

Ethan had few coherent thoughts, but it seemed like the lighted bubble around him was being pushed upon, contracting slightly.

"Waaiitt. There is something in his body that does not belong ... a sickness? I cannot reach him, I ..."

The light in Ethan's mind coursed with power and a rainbow of colors spun through it. It began to pulsate, growing brighter and larger with each beat. It pushed back against the suppressing evil, expanding the pure white light area that shielded Ethan's mind from the attack.

"I am trying to ... ahhhhhgggg!" The dark shadows of coils suddenly withdrew upon themselves, withering back to the arm of the Dark Magician. The hooded figure himself stumbled backward and nearly fell.

The Overlord was furious, and his darkened visage was indeed terrible to look upon. A feeling of hatred and doom spread out within the hall, overwhelming the senses of everyone. The guards readied their weapons even as they trembled in fear.

The Dark Magician gingerly rose to his feet. "The boy's supposed knowledge is useless to us in this state! The best we can do is wear him down, but if his mind is mush we cannot even glean information from his thoughts! Who … poisoned … him?" The last was thundered out, making everyone in the room cringe, even the other Dark Magicians.

Rath Kordoch scowled most darkly and looked over to the Magician. "Do what I had planned … now."

The Magician slowly rose fully upright and shuffled over toward the group of people standing before the Overlord. Everyone stood transfixed, nervous eyes on the moving figure. He stopped and turned swiftly, reaching out that awful arm toward … Taleena. Stark fear overtook her, rooting her in place as the serpent tattoo once again seemed to come alive in a dark shadow. This time it coiled slightly on the Magician's arm and then swiftly struck outward. Taleena loosed a blood-curdling scream of terror and would have fallen right away, but the smoky black coils transfixed her in place. Again the hissing voice emanated from the deep cowl. "Ahhhh … this one we can have, easily! Can we take her, master?"

Rath Kordoch grunted. "She is yours."

The dark coils grew thicker, more substantial, and then seemed to dive straight into the stricken woman, disappearing completely from view. The Dark Magician collapsed to the floor in a heap. Taleena's body convulsed violently, thrashing to the floor and flopping about several times, her arms and limbs flailing. Then as quickly as it had started, her body grew quite still. Slowly she rose, unnaturally stiff and wobbly, and looked up at the Overlord with unblinking eyes. She glanced about, as if searching for something.

"We do know much! We have seen much! But this mind is not well organized and is filled with petty schemes and fears. It will take some time to search it all out." Taleena's head turned slowly to look at Ethan. "She liked this one, she did. But oh, she is highly deceitful! She used him, she tricked him and then she … she … SHE POISONED HIM!" Taleena's body jerked to one side as though struck and then was thrown to the ground with great force.

Rath Kordoch roared in anger, leaping to his feet. The guards around him all drew their weapons and held them ready, unsure of what really was happening.

Taleena – or more accurately the demons that now controlled her body – rose up from the floor, face bruised and bloodied. She made no attempt to wipe away the blood that slowly trickled down her face to slowly drip onto her ruined dress. "She tricked us ... she wanted fame and fortune all for herself! She even ..." a horrific scream curdled the air before her and her eyes rolled back into her head. "No! The deceit! The arrogance! She ... she just gave the boy a final dose of poison ... just now ... with her kiss! Ahhhhhhh!" With that, the demons began to thrash her body about this way and that, oblivious to the broken bones the actions were certainly causing. With a wild leap, Taleena's body was thrown through the air sideways, twisting at the last moment to land facing the Overlord.

Unfortunately, the demons had not been paying much attention in their crazed abuse of the small female body. Taleena had landed directly before one of the guards, who was standing with sword drawn outward at low ready, her body impaling itself upon the sword with such force that it went completely through her. A look of astonishment became frozen on the once beautiful face of the now very dead Taleena.

The Overlord screamed in anger and lashed out with the small metal scepter at his throne, crushing the guard's head and adding a second dead body to the growing mess on the floor. Everyone took several steps backward in stark terror. Dark coils began to exit Taleena's still body and a shadowy shape slithered to the comatose Dark Magician from whence it had come. The Magician stirred sluggishly and slowly made great effort to stand. "Master, we did not see ..."

"SILENCE! You will be punished most severely for your incompetence, worms!"

"No ... don't send us to the arid places, not to THE PIT!"

"Of course not, foolish ones. I will not be divided like that. The place of eternal flames is not for you ... yet. But you will have the least important, worst possible position I can imagine ... and I can imagine much! Now go, crawl back to your lair until you are called for and grovel in despair until I decide exactly what to do with you."

The Dark Magician slumped and shuffled off, exiting the hallway, while everyone else trembled in fear over what they had just witnessed. Murdrock was the first to shake off the terror; his anger at Taleena's scheming overcoming all other emotions. With minimal control over his own fury, he spoke: "Overlord, with due respect ... may we take the boy back to his room and immediately call the healers back to see if they can save him? I believe he has some value left, if he lives."

Rath Kordoch's own anger was white hot on the inside, but he would let that simmer and address it later. He sat back down on his throne and turned malevolent eyes toward the master assassin. "You allowed this all to happen. The boy was under you watch, your personal care. That … that woman …" he pointed dismissively to the still figure on the floor, "was under your supervision. You did not control her. You did not perceive this treachery and prevent it. You allowed her to poison the most valuable prisoner in the entire Dominion not once, but twice – and this last time right in front of your own face … and right in front of your Master. You are a disgrace and a blight in my presence. Take the boy and see to it he receives the best care. If he dies, you have precious little left to offer of any value to me or to the Dominion … other than entertainment." The last was said in a low guttural growl and Murdrock's face went white. He spun around, ordered Ethan to be unshackled and had the guards follow him out of the hall.

The Overlord dismissed the rest and retired from the carnage scene to his working quarters. His dark visage caused all manner of servants and Magicians to scurry out of his way. Once inside his private room, the deep scowl vanished and he sat to think. It was indeed a loss to not have the detailed description of Freelandian defenses and personnel, but he had reports from other lesser spies that filled in most of the important information as he saw it. Some of the reports certainly were curious – what did exactly happen at the naval battle anyway? Most Dominion people were highly superstitious – they had strong reason to be so – and therefore their reports tended to blend fact, fiction and fear into a less-than-totally-coherent documentation of events.

Still, whether it be human or angelic, it would not do to underestimate Freelandian strength. And just recently he had felt some spiritual movement to the north – that did not bode well for the Dominion either. However, he had the means to weaken their resolve. The Chancellor's son would play into that nicely. It would be best if he could be healed and questioned – and paraded around the Dominion as a hostage. But it was not essential. The Freelandians, and for that matter his own people, would not be able to discern the real Ethan from an imposter. He would get trusted servants to work on that immediately.

Now, what to do with Murdrock? The assassin had shown considerable control and quick thinking to want to get the boy to the healers after what he had witnessed. Of course he needed to think he was close to final failure – it would give him greater incentive to prove his worth. He would likely be quite useful back in Freelandia before the invasion began, and so he would need to ship out relatively soon. The Overlord made a few notes for his underlings. There was much left to do, and not an abundance of time remaining.

Chapter 6

Room Service

aeten moved his way down the corridor, the cart's wheels squeaking as they went. That provided him echo feedback of his surroundings and gave advanced warning to others that room service was coming. A young lad of perhaps 10 helped to steer, having assumed to be 'in charge' of the old codger who would clean the rooms. The boy, Ardan, did not like going into Magician rooms either, but he led Gaeten to them and pointed out anything he saw amiss that Gaeten did not get quite to the boy's liking. They had been directed to work on a specific VIP wing of the castle, which they were told would be empty for several hours at a specific time this afternoon. Gaeten had noted that a few guards were present based on the noises they made and the whispered description from Ardan, but they did not challenge mere room cleaners.

Gaeten pushed the large cart ahead of him. It had various cleaning supplies and a large deep bin for depositing used bedding, which later they would bring down to the main washing area. Gaeten was surprised at such amenities … he did not normally change his own bedding until the smell became quite noticable.

Ardan steered them to the first room in the hallway, just a few feet down from a guard. They entered and Gaeten smelled several things immediately that roused his curiosity. The resident was a man who had recently been at sea – though that covered a lot of people in a port city. But … there was another odor too, diluted and masked by many others, but it reminded Gaeten of something. He could not quite put his finger on it. Ardan and he busily cleaned. Gaeten found several shapes within various clothing items that were undoubtedly weapons, and several were quite cleverly hidden both in clothing, in boots and even around the room. Whoever was rooming here was a warrior, and an uncommon one at that.

They finished rapidly and moved to the room directly across the hallway. That room had not been used, and the guard indicated one several doors down that was in use. They entered and the contrast with the former room was startling. This was unmistakably a woman's room, heady with perfume and flowery odors. Yet Gaeten detected something else too, something much more disturbing, reminding him of several rather toxic compounds used in … assassinations. As they cleaned, Gaeten scoured the room, finding several hidden trinkets – likely gold or jewels that he left in place – and finally found the source of the offending odors in a small satchel under a false floor panel of a trunk. While Arden was busy elsewhere, Gaeten opened the satchel and verified his suspicions – he recognized several of the odors that even though being quite rare, were not unknown by the Watchers. Gaeten closed the satchel, replaced it and finished cleaning the room with Arden.

The next room down was also unused – it appeared that the guests here were being kept separated. At the next the guard acted strangely – he would not get too near the doorway. Gaeten could feel the reason … there was a spiritual oppression about the room that told him it was the dwelling place of a Dark Magician. Arden entered, pointed out a few things and then mentioned that the room was making him feel quite ill and therefore he would wait outside. Gaeten heard the boy's steps move further down the hallway. Gaeten did not like the room either. It was as if it smelled of dank evil and sulfurous demonic influence. He tidied up, but there was actually little in the room itself, a few clothes but nearly no personal effects. Gaeten thought that rather odd. He was most of the way done in the room when he heard footsteps out in the hallway and a high sing-song voice that seemed to be babbling to itself. The door to the room burst open and Gaeten sensed the presence of not only a man … but also of a demon. He could feel a cold breeze and what seemed like darkness enter the room, even though he could not of course see anything. Gaeten had the cleaning cart close to the door but not in the walkway and he pressed up against the wall as the man stormed into the room and slammed shut the door.

The odd thing was, it appeared the Magician had not even noticed someone else was in the room. The babbling continued, and Gaeten could only pick out a few odd words and phrases. It appeared the Magician had not had a very good day, something about being banished and sent to his room without supper. Gaeten eased off the wall and moved to his cart. He figured it would be best if he could just quietly exit, hopefully before the man or demon recognized that Gaeten was not really a Dominion person at all. He silently reached the cart and began to shove it toward the door when the telltale loose wheel let out a loud squeak.

Even without sight, Gaeten had a picture in his mind of the room, where everything was in it; the cart, doorway and of course exactly where the magician was – he was standing over near his bed, muttering about someone dying, it not being his fault, and of being told to remain in his room indefinitely. When the wheel squeaked, Gaeten could hear the robed figure whip around to face him.

A cold hissing voice replaced the high sing-song. "What is thissss? Who are you? ... what ... are ... you? Sooo bright! You are of God's elect! What are you doing here? Wait, I can make up for killing the female by finding you! Yes! Guar ..."

The Magician's – or demon's – voice ended in a stifled gurgle as Gaeten's hand clamped tightly over the man's windpipe. Futilely, the smaller man struggled at the arm that held him in a choking vise, and Gaeten could not see the tattooed snake began to grow and fill out in a dark ominous shadow and begin to coil, with its head rising into a striking posture.

But what he could not see, Gaeten's sensitive spiritual sense registered. He squeezed harder, and in a steely clear low voice spoke out, "In the name of God Almighty, whom I serve, and in the name of His Son Jesus, I cast you out to the Pit!" Though not a wisp of air could possibly escape through the man's voice box, a hissing "Nooooooooo!" echoed as the shadowy serpent totally disengaged from the Magician's arm. Even as it started to strike the dark smoke dissipated into a faint fog and disappeared. The form in his hand slumped, and Gaeten let the lifeless body drop to the floor. He was sweating, but the stench of evil was already fading.

Gaeten had to pause to think of what to do next. If the body was discovered before he found Ethan, his ruse would be up. He did not relish the thought of trying to fight his way out of the castle, with or without his objective.

Gaeten lifted the body and carried it to the bed. He dumped it under the covers, but then thought better of it and removed the smelly heavy robe first. He dropped it into his dirty linen cart, then found the single spare that matched it and stuffed that down into the bin too, making sure they were well under some of the other contents. Then he maneuvered the cart to the door and exited the room.

He moved down the hallway toward Arden, who was telling him he was feeling better now and could help him with the last room just a few doors down. Just then there was a ruckus of several people coming from the other direction.

Murdrock was in a particularly foul mood. The day had not gone at all like he had hoped, and instead of showing himself to be a hero, the Overlord appeared to think he was a bumbling fool. How could that dratted Taleena have done this to him? He should have strangled her long before! Instead he now had to babysit the boy, who was obviously delirious, far worse than he had been before. At least they had found one of the healers waiting outside the audience hall, and they pressed him into an immediate examination once the guards could carry the boy back to his room.

The troupe rounded the corner in the hallway to see that the house cleaning staff apparently had not even finished yet – was everything to go wrong today? This was intolerable! "You!" Murdrock pointed at Arden. Get the room clean this instant! Can't you see the prisoner is very ill?"

Arden hurriedly opened the door to the final room and Gaeten pushed the cart inside. "Wait!" Murdrock closed the distance and Gaeten moved a hand to one of the pockets where he had hidden several throwing knives.

"Boy – let the old man finish that. You go get me some food – and it had better be top quality, I am in no mood for the slop I have been fed lately." Arden took one look at the impatient scowl and scurried off, and Gaeten moved completely into the room.

"You, guard!" The guard who was stationed in the empty hallway jumped to attention. "Go find the other healers – get them all here, and you had better be quick about it – but you had also better not forget any! If that boy dies, I will personally see that you follow him … slowly!" The guard gulped loudly enough for Gaeten to hear it and ran down the hallway, figuring the imposing and demanding VIP guest surely outranked his commanding officer who had assigned him to this hallway.

Murdrock turned to the two carrying Ethan. "You, put the boy in his bed, regardless of whether it has been cleaned up or not. Healer, start your healing and you had surely better hope you can do more for him now than the bunch of you did before hand. The Overlord will boil you in your own medicines if he dies. Get to it!"

The two guards carried Ethan's limp form into his room and gently placed him onto the fresh sheets Gaeten had hurriedly put onto the bed. Then they promptly left, not wanting to be anywhere nearby if the boy suddenly died. They moved down the hallway, unsure of what they should do next. Murdrock was pacing back and forth, and whipped about to open his own door and stomp inside. The frame shuddered at the strength of the slam the door made. One of the guards poked his head into Ethan's room.

"Hey, old man – the woman's room can be totally stripped – she won't be coming back … ever."

Gaeten grunted in assent. The guards looked at each other, then shrugged and began to walk back to their station at the audience hall. Gaeten heard their heavy footsteps retreating, leaving him alone in the room with just the Healer between him and the boy prisoner who could be none other than Ethan. He had nothing against the healer, and for a moment as he cleaned he wondered if this was truly the best time. But God had given him what appeared to be a golden opportunity. Gaeten prayed a quick silent request for direction, and even as he finished he felt he knew what actions he was to take.

The Healer was bent over Ethan and never heard Gaeten move up behind him. A blow to the head or neck would have dispatched the man easily, but could have hurt him permanently. There was no need for that, and Gaeten rarely expended more force than necessary for a given circumstance. Instead he slung his right arm around the man's neck from behind in a classic choke hold, while his other hand grabbed the Healer's left arm and twisted it behind the man's back. Gaeten held the man quite firmly until the struggling stopped and he went limp, and then he gently lowered the unconscious form to the floor.

Gaeten moved over to Ethan and gently stroked the boy's face. Even in his obvious delirium, Ethan responded to the light and comforting touch. "Oh God, you led me here, you orchestrated the events to bring me to Ethan's side. I don't know what has happened to him, but God, I need your help now. Blind the eyes of the enemy, protect us with your mighty hand and guide my steps to escape. Thank you for your mercy. I am in your hands … as always."

Gaeten sighed and then arranged his cart, removing some of the items in the dirty laundry bin. He checked and found that the guards had not chained Ethan to the bed itself, and so with little effort Gaeten lifted and lowered him into a nearly upright sitting position inside the bin, with his legs folded under him. After arranging the linen contents as best he could over the still form so as to allow easy breathing, he put the healer onto the bed where Ethan had been, then adjusted the covers to disguise his handiwork. He wheeled the now heavy cart to the door, listening intently. Then he took a deep breath and opened the door, ready for quick action.

No one was in the hallway. Without acting like he was in any hurry, Gaeten began to wheel the cart down the hall. He stopped for a moment outside of the woman's room and retrieved the satchel he had investigated earlier, knowing now it would never be missed. On a second thought, he also collected up the various stashed coins and jewelry, figuring he may well need additional funding sources very shortly. The whole stop was less than a minute or two, and then he and his precious cargo began moving again, wheel squeaking its way along.

Murdrock grunted in his room. Finally that decrepit-looking servant had finished and was leaving. Good riddance. And couldn't he get that blasted wheel fixed?

Turlock felt something – he did not know what, but his inner spirit just felt like there was something going on that he should know about. It was rather frustrating until he finally figured out the one and only recourse available, and so he prayed for guidance. He had planned to meet Gaeten near the outer castle wall, but now felt prompted to enter the grounds proper to wait.

The Alterian captain was preparing his ship, stocking up on the few items he needed and submitting to a departure inspection, which of course was passed without incident. He was supposed to leave within a few hours, and someone was posted to ensure no additional cargo was taken on board. A small purse of coin convinced the dock guard that a tavern on the other side of town was more to his liking.

Gaeten lifted Ethan from the laundry bin. "Ethan … Ethan! I need your help. You need to get up and put on this robe."

With no coherent response from the boy, Gaeten prayer, "Oh God, you have shown mercy to get us this far … please show your mercy on Ethan now and give him the strength and clarity of mind for us to escape. Please continue to blind the enemy's eyes and give us time. Amen,"

Ethan stirred. "Gaeten? Gaeten is that you?"

Gaeten would have loved to stop and chat, but this was not the time and the cramped closet they were in was certainly not the place. "Ethan, try to stand up. Here, give me your arm." Gaeten took the proffered limp arm and struggled to slip the Dark Magician robe onto the boy. It was about his size, which was a blessing that he silently thanked God for. Gaeten slipped into the other robe, though his shoulders stretched the fabric considerably. Even so, he hoped they could pass reasonably well for Dark Magicians. Now if he could remember his way correctly to get out through the servant's entrance to the Castle keep. It certainly would not do if he stumbled into a guard room – or worse, into a convent of Magicians – or the Overlord!

They were as ready as he could be. With an arm around Ethan, he half-carried, half-guided Ethan out of the closet and down passageways toward the exit. At least no one wanted to talk to Dark Magicians, and so no one was about to question them. Even so, it was not easy going. Gaeten could not use a walking stick and it was difficult to support the weak Ethan without it really looking like that was what he was doing. At the same time he was on ultra-high alert. He was not sure how far he could go like this. *As far as God allows me*, he thought.

Turlock paced back and forth within the castle compound, weaving in and around the various officials, guards and workers who seemed to constantly stream through. Everyone seemed in a hurry, though none jostled against a hooded Dark Magician. Even within his cowl he could occasionally catch nervous eyes darting his way for a brief moment. His costume was hardly inconspicuous, though never challenged. He had come much earlier than he expected Gaeten to finish his first day's work, so why had God seemed to impress upon him a sense of urgency? He made his eighth or eighteenth loop and was just about to turn back when he noticed a pair of Dark Magicians seem to semi-stumble out of what appeared to be the servant's entrance from the castle. That was odd, but not particularly noteworthy – Dark Magicians often acted quite oddly. Turlock began to turn when one of the figures thrust out an arm to steady himself in the doorway. The flash of white skin caught his attention … Dark Magicians were always highly tattooed.

Without seeming to race, Turlock took long strides to reach the two robed figures. Gaeten heard someone approach and tried to shift Ethan's weight so he could let the boy slide to the ground if he needed to move into action. As Turlock came near, he spoke out "Ah, brothers! I did not expect to see the two of you so soon! I see Brother Thane is a bit under the weather. Here, let me help."

Gaeten took a deep breath … they were not out of the woods yet, but Turlock's presence was literally a Godsend. "Yes, Brother Tock, let's get Brother Thane out into the fresh air, maybe by the docks – that may help him."

Turlock came alongside and wrapped Ethan's other arm over his own shoulder. He tried to stay a half-step ahead to better lead them without it being too obvious. The crowd parted widely and as they came to the exit the guard acted as if he did not even see them. They passed right through and two walked, one stumbled, down into the city. They could only go so far, as Ethan's legs began to give out. Exhausted, they stopped at a bench a few hundred yards away from the castle entrance, down a side street that was out of sight from any guards or officials.

Both Turlock and Gaeten were breathing heavily, while Ethan seemed oblivious to everything around him. "There is no way," huffed out Turlock, "that we can drag him all the way back to your apartment. Maybe you could do it, but I cannot – and it would surely be noticed if a Dark Magician walked through town with another Magician slung over his shoulder!"

Gaeten nodded, and then realized that within his cowl that would be invisible. Scowling, he pulled off the robe, first listening to determine that no one was nearby. Turlock took both Gaeten's and Ethan's robes and stuffed them into a nearby fire pit, spreading ashes and coals over the top. "Best place for that, if you ask me."

Gaeten cocked his head to one side as if listening to something no one else could hear, then rose and walked past a small merchant's horse and cart. He felt his way until he found a door and lightly knocked. The door opened immediately and a short, burly woman looked out at the old man in servant's garb. Gaeten smiled as best he could. "Madam, our Father has need of your horse and cart."

The woman looked wide-eyed, gulped, and whispered "I just woke from a dream, where someone came and said that, and I knew I was supposed to give it. I don't know why, or who you are. But if our Father sent you, the horse and cart are yours. When you are done, loose the reins and I expect the horse will return here – but that does not really matter I suppose. Oh … and know that there are other children of our Father here … I was supposed to tell you that."

"Thank you kindly. May God richly reward your service. Please, I can pay for the horse and cart."

"No sir! I will not take payment … do you wish to rob me of our Father's blessing?" She smiled, and her tones showed it. Gaeten thanked her again and walked back to his companions.

Turlock was flabbergasted. "Do you always go up to strange doors, knock, and be given such things?"

Gaeten grinned. "Only when I am escaping with a very sick son of the Chancellor of Freelandia! … or when God tells me to. Now hush up and help me load him in!"

In less than half an hour Gaeten was helping a very weak Ethan stumble up the steps into his apartment as Turlock drove off to the dockyard to talk to the Alterians. They could not stay for long – by now an uproar surely must have started at the castle and it would not take long before the whole town would be on the alert for a very sickly youth and an older blind man who seemed remarkably adept at finding his way around. Gaeten doubted it would be long before the authorities connected this to the blind 'circus performer' who had been frequenting the local taverns and asking many questions about the docks and ships. And who had a young boy with him that someone will have recalled was named 'Nimby'. It was decidedly not safe to stay. Yet traveling this night – for it was already twilight – would not be safe either. Within the hour every exit from the city would be either closed altogether or heavily guarded and on the lookout for anyone even close to their description trying to leave.

It might have been possible to escape from Kardern if they had immediately ridden out of town. But though Ethan seemed to be strengthening he was still semi-delirious and in his heart, Gaeten was worried that he would be far more of a hindrance than a help during a sudden escape. And the physical exertion might sap what little strength Ethan seemed to be clinging to.

Besides, that would have left Nimby unaware and unprotected, and Gaeten would have none of it. The Alterians would have been fine on their own, but Nimby was another matter. He would likely have been caught before he knew he was even being searched for, and every tidbit of information would have been extracted from him ... probably in the most painful way imaginable. No, that would not have been right. Yet they could not stay at the apartment since a thorough investigation would surely find them.

Gaeten gathered up all of his belongings – what few of them there were – and was waiting for Turlock to return when he heard the light footsteps of several people coming up the outside stairs. He moved near the door, and all pretenses of a mild mannered old servant left. There was no way he was going to have gotten this far with Ethan to be easily taken in. If somehow the authorities had found them already, then they had better be well prepared. Extremely well prepared. Exceptionally and extraordinarily well prepared. After the stresses of the day so far, Gaeten was REALLY in the mood to break things ... or someone, or maybe even a group of someones.

The latch to the door opened and in walked Nimby with two others. Though there was no way for Gaeten to know, it did not look like it had gone so well for Nimby. He had a black eye and bruises that were beginning to show on his arms, and the two larger boys nearly threw him into the room, none of them seeing Gaeten, who now was hidden from view by the mostly open door.

"Where is the rest of the money, scumbag? You said there was more than what was in this bag ... who'd you rob to get so much coin? Half now and half later? No way – all now, none later, and none for the likes of you!" The larger of the two shoved and Nimby tripped down to the floor, but rolled into a low crouch, hands ready for action. It was not particularly needed.

Gaeten slammed the door shut. Even as the attackers registered that they were not alone, both of their heads were smacked together with a sickening thud. Both collapsed unconscious. Gaeten just smiled with satisfaction.

"Aw, I coulda' taken em, I could. I was just getting started."

"I take it your business proposition did not go over so well with them?"

"Well, I started with the younger ones like you said, and my old gang was all for it – especially when I gave 'em each a coin and said more was coming. But then some of the older gangs got wind of it … I think they caught one of the smaller kids and forced it out of him. Anyway, those two tracked me down and jumped me when I wasn't looking. I figured it would be better to lead them here, biding my time for the best way to whack 'em. I was just about fixing to do that too, when you startled me and didn't let me finish them off."

Just then one of the boys on the floor moaned and Nimby jumped back. "I guess so," chuckled Gaeten. "It appears it was fortuitous that I happened to be home. I am glad you made the arrangements with the others – we are going to need it … tomorrow morning!"

"What? I told them in a few days, maybe a week! What happened so quickly that …"

Ethan moaned from the other room and Nimby dashed off to see the source, grabbing back his knife from one of his assailants. "Who's the kid?"

Gaeten pondered a moment before answering – how much did Nimby really need to know? "Nimby, you risked your life today for me, and it is only fair that you know the whole reason. That is the one and only son of the Chancellor of Freelandia, Ethan by name. I rescued him from the castle about an hour ago. The Overlord who came to town a few days back is going to turn Kardern upside-down and inside out looking for him, and it shouldn't take long before the hunt will be on for an old blind man and his young grandson. By tomorrow night I suspect every tavern will be crawling with soldiers and Dark Magicians, and they will have a quite good description of both of us.

We need to work on some disguises, but regardless, we have to leave this apartment as soon as Turlock returns, and find somewhere to hide for the night. I suspect the town is effectively shut down tight already. We will need the diversion I talked to you about to help us escape, and the sooner we can do that the better. I think very early tomorrow morning would be best – it should be less expected than at night. As I recall that is high tide, when many ships will be trying to leave the docks and plenty of merchants will be coming in and going out of the city. Do you think your recruits can be ready?"

Nimby cocked his head sideways as he pondered the question for a moment. Then he smiled broadly. "Well … sure, the money will still be burning a hole in their pockets, and I have a second cousin who is reasonably trustworthy – he will hold the remainder for me and dole it out per instructions. But I will need to get back out to tell everyone and make sure they get everything ready." Nimby paused and looked down a minute. "But one problem … well, maybe two. First, you said the authorities will be out looking for us, and likely will even have a description. Now I know the back alleyways of this here town better than anyone, but even still, I could get caught. And second … maybe worse … the older gang knows I was passing out money, and if they see me, others may have the same idea as those two on the floor."

Gaeten smiled. "I think I can help with that, my boy." He pulled out both Taleena's satchel and one of his own that he had been stocking with odds and ends from shops around town. "Go get me a pot of hot water. By the time Turlock returns he may not even recognize us!"

Chapter 7

Spiritual Warfare Training

inister Polonos and Chaplain Mikael walked slowly down one of the cobblestone streets of the Keep, deep in conversation. They had been charged with developing the spiritual defenses of Freelandia, and that was a mighty tall order.

After a few minutes of silence, Mikael spoke up. "Well, so far I have begun to organize prayer teams that will include every chapel and church in the country, divided up by regions. We are seeing a remarkable cooperation among the various churches … I think all can see this is the Spirit of God's doing. Prayer cards are being prepared that list the various leaders of Freelandia and specific needs. We formatted them on a ring so that there are two or three per page, and a page for every day of the month. People can flip over to a new page every day. We are also asking each church to organize the members who have special spiritual gifts, and especially asking them to forward any specific relevant prophecies up through their reporting structure. A team of discerners will review these each day and direct those on to the appropriate people if they feel so led." Mikael smiled. "So you see, I have been busy!"

"Wow, it sure sounds like it! I have been busy too, though the results may not seem quite so dramatic. I have been away from Freelandia many years, serving in the Southern Dominion. Before I first left Freelandia, do you know what I had done?"

"No, Polonos … what?"

"I was a scholar of the history of the church itself. My favorite study was of revivals. In fact, that is what I have been reviewing again. And I come to one of the same conclusions I did back then, one through which God profoundly spoke to me to go into missions." They walked on for a few moments in silence.

"Well, don't leave me hanging!"

Polonos chuckled. "Patience, my young man!"

"Young man?" It was Mikael's turn to laugh. "I have not been addressed that way in several decades!"

"Well, you are young to me! I concluded that while God of course showed up and showed off – if I may use such a phrase with no irreverence intended! – anytime and anywhere He so chose, nearly always He did so with a specific starting event. Some special happening seemed to be the catalyst or at least the initiation point for most spiritual awakenings. As I realized that, God showed me He wanted to use me as such a catalyst in the Dominion. Over the years I experienced multiple times and places where God's Spirit seemed to come down on people with power from on high. Some lasted for hours, a few for days, and one for several weeks. Whole tribes would come to God during those times."

Polonos beamed with excitement. "Unfortunately they were relatively few and far between, and I don't recall one happening in the last several years, at least not in the area I was working. Still, they were exciting times, with effects that lasted a lifetime in those converted. There are still pockets of believers, even among the Southerns, though they are ruthlessly dis-criminated against and often killed outright once it becomes known they have turned to our one true God.

Now to the task at hand. I especially reviewed the revivals in the history of Freelandia. While in other places an awakening often comes with star-tling miraculous happenings that demonstrate God's power and might, in Freelandia such demonstrations are fairly normal occurrences – of course those are outpourings of Spiritual gifts that are used every day. But even still, people's faith sometimes has stagnated and the giftings have dropped off – without faith and ardent belief we know such manifestations of God are more rarely seen.

Now I have a few things in mind gleaned from this study, but before I go into that, I want to ask you about the recent revival events that have been happening here, especially in the Keep. Mikael, when did these awaken-ings first start? What seemed to be their trigger? It seemed to me that when I arrived at the Keep the stage had already been set – well before what seemed like the entire capital walked out to that beautiful lake to be baptized."

Chaplain Mikael looked thoughtful. "I have wondered about that myself. Before the Lake Front revival, I heard there was a miraculous event at the outdoor auditorium near the Music Academy. Grand Master Vitario said it was profound, and said it correlated exactly with the defeat of the Dominion naval fleet. The way he described it, God used their music directly to fight against the dark evil empowering our enemy, and people from all over felt led to pray, and that seemed to combine with the musical worship somehow. Let me see … before that … well … I guess I am thinking about a concert. Have you heard of Sir Reginaldo?"

Polonos began to laugh. "You mean the pompous, ill mannered lout with the golden voice?"

"Well then, I guess you have heard of him! Anyway, he came here nearly two months ago to give a concert, the highlight of which of course was his Masterpiece. Even I was invited – and what a performance!"

"Yes, I have heard he can sing like none other – though I myself think I have better things to do with my time than listen to an ungodly singer, regardless of how well he can perform his very own virtuoso."

"But Polonos, that's just it … it was performed as a duet!"

"A duet? I thought that no one had ever figured out a satisfactory accompaniment to either the song, or for that matter for Sir Reginaldo either – and especially not one he would ever recognize."

Mikael stopped walking and turned to the older Minister. "Yet Reginaldo himself requested it … and even broke down in the midst of the song, leaving it all for a little blind girl to finish."

Polonos turned a flabbergasted face toward Mikael, but before he could speak the younger man continued, his face turned away now, looking off into the sky with eyes starting to water and a voice that deflated into a whisper of awe. "God's Spirit came down upon us right there. It was as if heaven had opened a window and we were listening in to the angels singing before the throne of the Almighty. There was not a dry eye in the place. It was so much more than just a song, than just a performance of a highly skilled singer. We all felt it … we all were touched by the Spirit in a way I have never felt before. And when it was done, God was given the glory – even from Sir Reginaldo himself!" Mikael looked back down to this reality and focused on Polonos. "That was the start I think. The trigger event was that concert!"

Minister Polonos looked thoughtful. "One of the conclusions of my research is that true heart worship is a sure sign of an awakening, though repentance is more often the first consequence of a personal meeting with our holy God. And in a number of cases it has been some worship event that seemed to be a leading indicator of revival coming. But usually there is a focal point to the event, a person that God seems to use there and throughout the spiritual outpouring. Mind you, the person of course has nothing personally to do with it – they are not the cause, it is all from God. Yet God seems to find an instrument to do His work. I just cannot believe it was Sir Reginaldo. I can believe it was that little blind girl though. Wasn't her name Maria? Wasn't she at the start of the Lake Front Revival? I met her there, just for a brief time."

Mikael considered that just for a moment. "Yes Polonos – you must be correct. Could it be that God's chosen instrument, as you call it, is a blind orphan? Albeit one with an extraordinary musical talent – from what I have been told the likes of which no one can ever remember being in one person."

He pondered silently for a minute and the two began to walk slowly along again. "I think we need to make a visit to the Music Academy … and soon."

Grand Master Vitario looked up from his desk. "And to what do I owe the pleasure of two so eminent visitors?"

Mikael grinned and came around the desk to embrace his friend. "Vitario, I don't know if you have met Minister Polonos. He has for many years been a missionary in the Southern Dominion regions and has just recently returned, just ahead of a brutal purge the Dominion undertook of foreign followers of our God."

"Welcome, Minister Polonos! I am sure you must have many stories from your adventures … maybe some would be worthy of a ballad or two?"

Polonos smiled. "Oh, I don't think any were so dramatic as to put to song. But we do have something rather important to discuss with you."

Vitario cocked his head to one side. "That sounds serious. How may I be of assistance?"

Mikael charged ahead after a nod from Polonos. "First let me explain our mission. Master Warden James has asked us to lead a whole segment of the defense of Freelandia." At the very quizzical expression from Vitario he continued. "It was recognized at the highest levels that the upcoming confrontation is as much or more of a spiritual battle as it is a physical one. So we were asked to organize our spiritual defenses."

Vitario nodded in thought. "And you two have come here to see how the Music Academy may fit into such preparations and how we may fit into the spiritual 'battle plan' – correct?"

Mikael and Polonos both dropped open their jaws and stared first at each other and then at the Grand Master of the Music Academy.

At their obvious surprise, Vitario continued. "We have had a significant change here within the Academy … I guess you could call it an awakening of God's use of music, of significant spiritual power God can wield through music. There is no question in my mind that members of the Academy were very specifically used in the defeat of the Dominion navy. I do not understand it, and even have a hard time describing it well – but it surely happened. I was there; I was part of it."

Polonos had a question. "So you felt led by God to intercede musically within the spiritual realm, and God used that in part to influence the physical world?"

Vitario looked excited. "That is a great explanation! But my part was much smaller. I was one of many who felt pulled by God to come to the amphitheater and to join with the others instrumentally in musical worship of our Creator. That worship was then somehow crafted and directed against the Dominion forces."

Mikael looked at Vitario with puzzlement in his expression. "But Vitario, when I heard of this before I presumed you were the one who somehow led this, brought everyone together, and in some way used it against the Dominion evil."

Vitario shook his head. "No, I just joined in. But I felt the power; I felt the worship push back the evil darkness. But you would have to talk to someone else here for greater detail – to the one who God specifically used to blend our music and prayers into a spiritual weapon."

"And just who might this 'worship warrior' be?"

"One of our new students, actually. A young girl named Maria."

The three men climbed a set of stairs and walked down a hallway amidst a disconcerting array of sounds coming from various rooms. Vitario lead the way, continuing a discourse he had begun down at his office. "Maria has really not been the same happy young girl she was when she came here. After the naval battle she has seemed more distant, withdrawn and, well, driven. She felt she was unprepared for her role, that she did not have the skills and repertoire needed, and that somehow she either failed or at least caused some of the Freelandian losses. She said she has felt God has a significant use for her in the coming conflict, and that she therefore must 'get ready' for it. After the revival I thought Maria was past feeling so burdened. She certainly seemed so for a short time, but then it seemed to come back. This has frankly consumed her ever since. She has been furiously learning different styles and instruments and trying to write new pieces, all with a theme around war and marching and standing against an enemy.

I have tried to counsel her to lighten up somewhat, to get back to enjoying music and to worship – but to no avail. She is absolute in her focus and driven by a tremendous weight of responsibility she has imposed upon herself. I support her efforts and zeal, but this is unhealthy. Yet she will not stop."

They reached a doorway and stepped into a smaller room that had a table and chair along one wall and a mixture of instruments and stools seemingly haphazardly scattered about. A young girl sat on a stool, intently plucking strings on an instrument while a young woman sat at the table before large sheets of paper upon which were many scratched markings of musical notes.

Maria did not even look up, but with intensity played a short piece through. "There … that is what it should be – make sure you get that down correctly! Now we can work on the next score."

"Maria …" began Vitario, "I have two gentlemen here who would like to meet you."

It did not at first even appear that she heard him as her brows furrowed in concentration. Distractedly she barely turned her head as she spoke in short clipped words. "Not now. I'm in a difficult passage. I just can't work it through right."

"Maria! I insist. Please stop for a few minutes."

Polonos looked over at Mikael. "Do you also feel the Spirit's touch on her?

"Yes, but she is not letting it flow. It is almost as though she is bottling the Spirit up."

That got Maria's attention and she put down her violin. "Huh? What do you mean? I am creating the music we will need to fight against the Dominion! Who are you to say I am not letting the Spirit move and flow?" Her voice had gotten brittle and all could see her physical exhaustion.

"Maria, this is Minister Polonos and Chaplain Mikael. They have recently been appointed by the Master Warden to assess and organize the spiritual defenses of Freelandia against the Dominion. They wish to talk to you about what God has been doing with you and through you in this area."

"Oh … then you must recognize the importance of this work! For some reason God has put on my shoulders a huge burden. When we …fought … against the Dominion Navy I had to gather together all this music, all our efforts and shape it into a cohesive whole and direct it toward the blackness of the Dominion. I could barely do it, and it just did not seem 'right' somehow, like we did not have the correct kind of music or skills. The evil almost overtook our navy … I could see it in my mind … and … even though I … even though I did the best I could, there was still a great loss of life. We still lost many ships, many sailors … many fathers. I cannot let that happen again! I will not!"

Mikael looked kindly at the stricken girl, feeling her pain and frustration and thought he also heard fear and perhaps even despair behind much of it. "Maria – do you think God would allow His own people to die just because a young woman did not know enough songs? Is He so very limited that He would not have known that ahead of time? Did He make such a poor choice in choosing … you?"

Maria had stopped moving and stood very still as Chaplain Mikael spoke. Her head jerked with his words, as though they were blows. At first she was filled with indignation ... but then the softly spoken words of truth began to break down her defenses and sink in. Tears began to flow and Maria sank to the floor in quiet sobs.

Mikael came over and put his hand on her head while Polonos squatted down and took her hand to get her attention. "Maria ... I don't know you at all, but I sense a beautiful spirit within you ... God's Spirit. You have such an indwelling that it brings tears to my eyes." He lifted her hand and gently brought it to his own face. "Come, my girl. Know me."

Maria cocked her head to one side, her own tears drying up. She gingerly brought both hands to his face and felt the weather-hardened skin, the many wrinkles from age ... and a few tears as he had acknowledged.

"Listen with your spirit, down deep inside. You will know I speak the truth then. Listen with your spirit as well as your ears. Let God's Spirit who is in both of us communicate beyond mere words. God is sovereign or He is nothing. He KNOWS you – better by far that you even know yourself. He fully understands your weaknesses and strengths, abilities and ... inabilities. And he still fully loves you. One of the great mysteries of the faith is that the Almighty chooses to use such frail, leaky vessels as us. One of the most important things to realize though is that He only wants our obedience to what He shows us to do ... the results are totally in His hands. He does not judge us based on the outcomes of our actions – and that is a mighty good thing, since we all fall down and fail regularly. You are striving against what seems like an incredibly heavy yoke of responsibility – yet God has told us that His yoke is easy and His burden is light. If you are so incredibly burdened as it appears, something is amiss. It is commendable that you are taking His calling on your life so seriously. But you must leave the responsibility of the outcome to Him."

Mikael piped in. "Yes Maria. Here is a check you may find useful. Have your efforts helped you to feel closer to God? In your striving, how has your relationship and closeness to God and His Spirit faired?"

Maria had lowered her hands, her respect for the old Minister raised considerably. She turned her head toward the standing Chaplain and grimaced. "Ah ... well ... He seems to be further away, at a distance. I have not understood that – if He wanted me to work on all this, why does He seem far away?"

Mikael smiled, even though he knew she could not see it. "And be honest now … who moved? You or God?"

Maria started to speak, then stopped short and hung her head. She whispered, "It must have been … me." Tears began again and she brushed at them absently.

Apprentice-turned-Master Ariel spoke up for the first time since the men had entered the room. "Maria, where has your joy gone? Where is your sense of awe that was so apparent when you first came here and which you so wonderfully showed to all of us at the Lake Front revival? You used to be so vibrant, and you seemed to make others around you sense the wonderment of God and His creation. Now …"

"Now I am a pain to be around?"

Ariel laughed in a light, musical way that was highly contagious. "Well, I certainly did not say that! I have been honored to work on writing down your music, and I definitely understand that creative types can be moody … but it has saddened me greatly to see you so knotted up, worried and even scared."

Polonos took up the thought. "Maria, when was the last time you remember being close to God, really close? What would you notice first if you started moving back closer to Him?"

Maria thought about that for a minute. "When I … when God used me to weave together the music to fight the Dominion evil and its navy I felt so very close. And when I played for Him at the lake … it was just God and me, and it was as if His nature itself was joining in. It all blended together into a marvelous symphony and dance of life in the Spirit that spilled over into the physical …. " Her voice trailed away into a tiny whisper. "… It was so awesome, so joyous … my words are totally inadequate."

"So what were you doing, besides playing an instrument or singing or doing physically – what were you really doing before your Maker?"

"I … I was worshiping Him!"

"Yes. You were. And what was God's response back to you?"

This time Maria was quiet for much longer, and when she spoke it was in a still small voice, but her face lit up like the sun. "He … loved … me! I felt such an immense love and acceptance and peace! I wanted to just stay right there and curl up in it and have it go on and on and on forever!"

Everyone in the room had tears now. Vitario had been silently listening the whole time, but now spoke in a hushed low voice. "I wonder if that is a glimpse of heaven?"

Everyone was silent at that. Mikael was the first to speak. "So, Maria, what do you think you need to do to get back closer to God?"

She let out a tremendous sigh. "When I am tense and upset it is hard to feel God's presence. Yet if I believe it is all my fault for the death of the Freelandian sailors, and all my own responsibility to be fully prepared for the next onslaught – whatever "fully prepared" means – then I cannot help but be nervous and scared. But … if it is not MY responsibility for the outcome, only for the obedience … then I really just need to be able to listen to the Spirit's leading and follow that … right?"

"Right," came two voices in unison.

"So I mainly need to be listening to God's Spirit. That comes easiest when I am thinking about God and playing an instrument, or sometimes when I am singing. It is when I am worshiping."

Vitario spoke up again. "And when you are doing that, you have a remarkable gift of bringing everyone around along with you into God's presence. And when that happens, it sparks a revival, such as happened at the lake, and which has happened here within the Music Academy.

Minister Polonos, Chaplain Mikael … our Academy is at your disposal and service. We have had a major reorganization lately, and our entire focus now is on bringing God glory and bringing His people closer to Him. I fear we had largely drifted away from that and were following excellence in music as an end of itself. Now we realize the entire purpose of music is to glorify God … and so now, here, it is all for Him and all about Him."

Polonos and Mikael looked at each other. "That should make our jobs easier!" said the older man.

Master Ariel led Maria by the hand down one of the corridors in the building of the Academy where Maria had her first official class. They could hear all sorts of instruments sounding, some not very well. "We are near the beginner's classes, right?"

"Correct you are, Maria. Do you remember your first class?"

"Oh yes! It was wonderful! Everything seemed so new. Was it really only a few months ago?"

"Well, now that you mention it, yes – it was just a couple of months ago. You were enthralled by all the new sounds."

A bell sounded and at that warning both Maria and Ariel pressed themselves up against the wall as young children disgorged out of their classrooms at the end of the day. After a minute the hubbub died down.

"Oh – hi Maria!"

"Kory, is that you? Are you teaching a class now?"

"Yes, it is a good experience, and it is a lot of fun to see the faces as the younger children learn."

Master Ariel spoke up. "Kory, would you like to go to dinner with Maria and me? I thought we would just have something simple at one of the café's right nearby."

"Sure, let's go!"

The three walked out into the early evening sunshine. Though Maria could not really see it, she could sense shadows and light and could feel the warmth on her skin. They chatted and Kory noticed that Maria was smiling – something that had been in short supply lately. The two others filled Kory in on their recent discussion as they approached the café and found an outdoor table to sit around.

"Wow – that is sooo awesome! What are you going to do next, Maria?"

"I really do not know. I feel like a weight has been lifted from my shoulders." She felt around for the crystal water glass in front of her, a hallmark of this particular café. "While I am so very relieved, I still feel like I do have responsibility … just maybe not to single handedly defeat the Dominion with a song!" She began to absently play with her glass. "I do need to concentrate on worship though. There are so many things to praise God about – all around us. Even here!" She giggled. "Listen – listen to the sounds all around us."

Kory and Ariel stopped eating and listened to the soft clinks of silverware, scrapes of chairs and murmuring of low voices. Kory spoke first. "It is almost like a symphony … well, maybe more of a cacophony since it really isn't coordinated at all. And that is funny, since nearly everyone here is from the Academy."

Maria dipped her finger and swirled it in her water. "It does have the makings of music though." She turned her face into the slight breeze, feeling the familiar tug to go to her 'special place' which had been absent for several weeks. She brought a finger to the lip of her glass and without even thinking wiped it around the rim. A shimmery pure tone sounded out, loud enough to startle several people nearby and the three girls themselves.

"What was that, Maria – how did you do it?" Master Ariel was very attentive now, and tried to mimic Maria's movements. In a moment her glass sounded too, though at a different pitch.

Kory grabbed her glass. "Your two glasses have different amounts of water in them. Mine is nearly empty – let me try!" Her note sounded out and then all three toned. Sounds around them died away as apprentices stopped eating to watch … and listen.

Maria laughed joyfully. Ariel and Kory began a simple two toned duet and Maria took her metal fork and began to lightly tap out a beat to their notes. Others noticed and began to join in. At first the sounds were somewhat haphazard, and then Maria stood and held out her fork like a baton and tapped her glass for attention. All noise stopped and all eyes turned to her. She pointed at a nearby table and cocked her ear their way. Each diner chose an 'instrument' at their fingertips and made a short sound. Maria smiled broadly, nodded, and then turned to another table. They followed suit and Maria pointed table to table. Some copied the water-glass notes while others chose whatever was at hand to make a sound.

Maria tapped again for attention, and then pointed accurately to one diner. The lad smiled and began tapping his plate with his knife as he had done the first time that Maria had requested a sound. With another point from Maria, a water glass note joined in. Maria took her fork in her other hand and began to tap out a simple beat, then pointed to others, one by one, at the various tables. A melody took shape, though quite unlike anything any of the diners could ever remember hearing.

In a mental rush Maria was standing in her special place, the unusual sounds making ribbons of sparkly light that while jagged and irregular, were somehow beautiful all in their own way. Even without consciously realizing it, she began to hum and then to sing – no words, just lilting notes that swayed with and somehow tied together all of the various sounds being made.

The song – if you could call it that – grew in volume and intensity, with various diners adding what they could based on their own skills and imagination. Master Ariel assembled nearly a dozen water glasses and was somehow playing them all, each producing its own note based on the water level within it. The sounds blended and folded, ran here and there, all in a joyful ensemble that had everyone grinning ear to ear. A few waiters joined in, mostly tapping their feet to the sound and then one of the cooks came outside with a big empty kettle and wooden spoon and with a huge smile began to drum along. Passersby stopped in their tracks, and several began to whistle or snap their fingers to the beat. Others began to add their voices or hum and soon it seemed the entire block joined in.

Maria drove them all, a simple little maestro with a fork baton and a voice like an angel. It grew into a crescendo and in a rush ended triumphantly. Everyone stood and cheered and hugged each other, and Maria's joy was evident as her face pointed upward and her hands rose toward heaven.

Maria sat back down, her face flushed with excitement. Master Ariel giggled, then added, "Maria – what are you feeling right now?"

"Oh, I don't know. Wait … I feel happy, excited and … somehow satisfied. And I feel closer to God too – this was all done for Him."

"Yes – I feel that too, though I don't really know why. In fact, every time I have played music with you I tend to feel closer to God, that somehow the music we are making is purposed to glorify Him. I don't always feel that way when I play an instrument on my own. There is something so very, well, so spiritual and Godly about your music. And when it ends I feel invigorated and encouraged to do my work. It is as though the worship unleashes energy to do good!"

Kory joined in. "I play better too, it is like the best is brought out in me. Worship must be pretty strong medicine, and seems to link me stronger to God Himself. Maybe we tap into God's power when we worship like that."

Master Ariel looked thoughtful. "Maybe so, Kory. And if we feel so refreshed and stronger, maybe others would too. And if God uses worship as a spiritual weapon against the enemy – as we saw the other day with the navy, then perhaps we are indeed a vital part of the defenses of Freelandia against the Dominion as Minister Polonos and Chaplain Mikael have said.

Say, I have an idea of how we can start helping. You know how tense everyone is getting with the defense preparations – it seems like few people smile anymore. Maybe we can help with that ... can help revitalize the worship of God here at the Keep. I think the whole Music Academy can be part of that ... and to launch it all off I am thinking about a rather special concert we could prepare.

Maria, some of that new music you have been working on is rather somber and strident ... but I think it could be modified to bring the triumphant worship to the forefront. We could use it like this..." Ariel continued for a several minutes. "What do you think? You too, Kory."

Both girls enthusiastically agreed. Ariel continued, "Come, let's go spring the idea on Master Vitario!"

Chapter 8

Escape from Kardern

urlock looked both ways up and down the street before he entered the apartment building. So far, it did not appear any alarm had sounded, at least not in this area. The dockyards had been another story though – grim faced soldiers were running this way and that, and foreign ships were being boarded at sword point and searched.

The Alterian captain had met him on-shore and acknowledged and agreed to the requests that Gaeten had sent. He was just as glad he could lift anchor in the morning with the tide too – Kardern was getting decidedly unpleasant, especially if you were not from a Dominion controlled territory.

It would not be very long though before a house-to-house search would get underway. Even at the dockyard rumors circulated about a white-haired and bearded old blind man. Turlock came to the apartment door and rapped the prescribed pattern. The latch was lifted and he quickly scooted inside, turning to close the door behind him immediately. When he turned again to the occupants he did a double-take.

"Wo-ah! That is quite the transformation! If I didn't know, I would surely not recognize either of you!"

Gaeten chuckled. "It is rather amazing what some pigment and hair dye can do, and a change to much younger looking clothes."

Turlock began to laugh. "My good man, you've lost 20, maybe 25 years since I last saw you!" The man who stood next to him had short dark hair atop a neatly trimmed thin black beard and was dressed as a blacksmith might, complete with a leather apron that left his bulging muscles very noticeable from under a short sleeved work shirt. Turlock looked at him closely, and under scrutiny he could see the age wrinkles that belied a much older man than first impressions gave – yet even those could readily pass for someone who spent long hours under a hot sun and hot forge. Gaeten had even added a few reddish scars on his arms commonly found on blacksmiths, and perhaps most ingenious was a black patch over one eye. Gaeten was sightless in both eyes, but from a distance the patch looked convincing, and with a wide brimmed hat the other would be far less noticeable.

Nimby was likewise transformed, though perhaps the change was not quite so dramatic. He too had on a blacksmith apron, a tad too big for his lanky frame, with hair dyed to match Gaeten's and cut very short in contrast to the longer curls he had sported. They looked like a very ordinary master and apprentice blacksmith.

"I had Nimby's help of course with the hair dyeing and clothes, and with the trim – how did we do?"

"Perfect! You look nothing like an ancient stooped over grandfather figure with a street urchin side-kick. You now look downright presentable!"

Gaeten swung an arm toward Turlock in response, slowly enough so the younger man could dodge out of the way. "Good. We should look totally plain and commonplace and therefore be able to go undetected – unless they post Dark Magicians at every outpost to peer into the spiritual identities beyond just the physical. We would still likely draw attention together though."

"Not to worry, Gaeten – I can readily escape the city by other means. I presume you will take the horse and cart?"

"Yes, I think so. We will stop and collect a few odds and ends of scrap metal to load into it to be even more authentic. My only three worries are, what can we really do with Ethan, will we be able to get word to Nimby's street irregulars in time, and will they even recognize him in this get-up?"

"Ah, I thinks I can take care of that …'papa'."

"Ugh! That will take some getting used to … son!"

Ethan somehow staggered into the room, looking barely alive. Turlock rushed to catch him before he collapsed. "Well, we can disguise ourselves relatively well, but it is rather more difficult to hide a very sick, very Free-landian-looking youth – even with a change in hair and skin color."

Gaeten sighed. "Yes, I think the best we can do is make him sleep, stash him under our things in the cart, and pray that God will blind the eyes of the guards. At least he does not seem to be getting much worse, though I am very concerned with how weak he seems."

"But what if he stirs or cries out? It would alert the guard to us in a heartbeat," Nimby warned.

"Well then, I will just have to make sure he stays asleep." Gaeten dug into the satchel of potions and poisons. After smelling each one he began mixing a few items. Turlock recognized a few things, but was lost on most of what Gaeten was doing. In a few minutes a concoction was ready.

"Ethan … I am going to give you something that is going to make you sleepy. Trust me, it is for our safety right now if you sleep." Ethan rolled his eyes and tried to focus on his old friend.

"Alright Gaeten … But pray also for God's help. I can feel Him, Gaeten. He is with us."

While Nimby looked around the room nervously, Gaeten smiled. "He is always with us, Ethan. He will NEVER leave us or forsake us. And I believe He will see us safely back to Freelandia. His protecting hand has been upon us the whole way. Now just breathe deeply." With that Gaeten poured some of the powder into his open hand and blew it into Ethan's face.

Ethan screwed up his face at the acrid odor and taste, but dutifully inhaled deeply. He coughed a couple of times, and then slumped forward peacefully.

Turlock surveyed the sleeping form. "How long will that last?"

At the dosage I gave him I think he will be out for at least 24 hours, maybe longer. I am mixing these up totally by smell and texture, so I am guessing at the exact make-up and potency … but it is the best we can do for now. Nothing I used is particularly toxic, so there should be no long term harm. My bigger concern is the poison that was given to him. I found a mixture in the bag that was very fresh – still in a wet paste – and by its smell I think it was a highly lethal combination. But I am not familiar enough with it to even hope to prepare an antidote. Ethan seemed to have revived somewhat from when I first found him, but unless something changes – unless God heals him – I doubt he has more than a few days."

Nimby gulped. "You mean … he is dying?"

"Yes, Nimby. Pray for a healing."

Turlock surveyed the two older youth sprawled out on the floor. "I take it these two came home with Nimby?"

"Yes, and despite his arguments otherwise it was much to Nimby's favor that I was here when they arrived. Now we need to get rid of them ... I don't want to give the authorities any additional time to find this place, though I think we have scrubbed it down pretty well."

Nimby piped up. "We could always cart 'em down near the river and dump them in ... with some stones in their pockets. I've seen that done enough times."

Gaeten shook his head. "No, Nimby – killing them is not the answer – that is a far last resort only used when absolutely necessary. But we could make it difficult for them to coming forward quite so fast to any authorities. Let me see what I can concoct." He dug around in the bag he had taken from the room at the castle.

"We should be ready to go very soon, while there is still a little bit of light out. We need a different place to stay overnight, one that will be beyond question. I have a place in mind, if God is willing to go before us and work it out. On the way we can tip off Nimby's friends to set their actions in order for the morning. Now, let's load the wagon and prepare our guests here."

The light was growing dimmer as Nimby drove the cart away from the apartment, with Gaeten sitting next to him. Turlock began walking in the other direction – with the stops the two would make with the cart, they all should arrive at the place Gaeten had in mind at nearly the same time. And who would ever suspect them of staying so near the Castle?

The cart creaked more now that it was loaded with scrap pieces of metal they had purchased here and there. Nimby had even found an old cracked anvil someone was using as a base for a flower pot – the owner said it was too heavy to move without three big men and so he had just shuffled it out to the front of his shop. Nimby had mentioned it to Gaeten, who had them stop. When the owner said they could have it if they could move it, Gaeten had Nimby move the flower pot and had squatted down next to the anvil. Onlookers saw him mutter under his breath, but Nimby's sharp ears picked up a few words from the softly spoken prayer. Then to everyone's amazement the burly 'blacksmith' wrapped his arms around the anvil and with a grunt lifted and walked it over to the sturdy cart. He carefully lowered the massive piece of metal onto a thick plank they had previously picked up and placed on the floor of the wagon near a large roll of carpet that once had adorned the apartment floor. The carpet seemed bulky and lumpy, but no one noticed. Then they were off, creaking as they went.

The light was getting dim now, and Nimby steered the wagon toward the city center. He did not want to go into any of the alleyways when it was truly dark – he knew all too well what happened to unwary strangers in such circumstances. Instead, they parked the cart at a shop, browsed inside for a few minutes, and then went back outside and ducked down a nearby alleyway while there was still enough light to be reasonably safe.

Once they were out of sight from the main thoroughfare, Nimby raised two fingers to his lips and let out a whistled cadence. He waited perhaps half a minute and then repeated the odd notes. A moment later, the sound was repeated from some blocks away and within a couple of minutes Gaeten could hear the scampering of light feet coming closer. He stood back in a doorway, hopefully out of sight but close enough to assist if the situation warranted it.

The closing footsteps stopped perhaps a dozen yards away down the alley and a low whistle was given, slightly different than the first. Nimby duplicated it precisely. More careful soft treads came closer. "Who is you – and who is you friend there hidin' in the doorway?" The voice was high pitched and wary.

Nimby, mindful of his highly altered looks, responded with a deeper than normal voice. "Nimby sent me with a message." He recognized the young street ruffian, but made no show of it.

"Ho, Nimby, eh? What might that message be then?"

"He says to tell everyone to start banging up the place just before dawn tomorrow."

"What! He said we'd have a few days at least! What is this?"

"I'm just the messenger. Nimby said to tell someone called 'the Boss-boy' to make it happen tomorrow, startin' just before dawn. He said the extra money is with 'Banker' for safekeeping."

"Banker has it, eh? Maybe I should just go a-vistiting 'im myself tonight then and help me-self to some of the treasure! Or maybe I should'a see what you might be carrying your-self!" The boy approached slowly, a small knife held out in front of him.

Nimby-the-blacksmith's-son laughed. "Come closer an I'll break you in half with me bare arms." The boy took a further step, then saw the leather apron and the muscles on the bigger boy's arms, helpfully exaggerated with the colored makeup Gaeten had directed him to apply.

The smaller boy took a step backward and the point of the knife sagged. "Oh ... well then ... if the message is from Nimby then it should be good enough."

Nimby tossed the boy a coin. "He said to seal the deal with this." The lad caught it in a flash and pocketed it.

"Right then, tomorrow morn' it is." He grinned ear to ear. "I wouldn't ta' missed it even without the pay, heh heh. Specially since all 'dem soldiers and creepy magi ... magicy .... majiccally persons are all over the dockyards and moving into the city and startin' to grab us little fellers for questioning. Somethings got the castle folk all stirred up worse than a bear in a bee's nest. Poking their nose with a stick is gonna be fun!" The boy turned and began walking away. He stopped after a few paces and turned back. "Say, how did Nimby get away from them older boys who'd grabbed 'im?"

Nimby smiled. "Let's just say he had a little help – and those two louts were far the worse for it and won't likely be showing off their ugly faces round here for awhile."

Back at the former apartment, the two rough youth moaned nearly in tandem and very groggily lifted their heads off the floor. They wrinkled their noses at the strong odor, wondering what it came from. Each licked their lips to try to remove the crusty film that seemed to be present, and both immediately tried to spit out the vile taste that gave them.

The first to awaken staggered to his feet and took a few shaky steps toward the front door, but his vision blurred and he stumbled in a circle instead. His fellow ruffian blinked twice and tried to laugh at the supposed drunken stupor he was witnessing, though he too felt rather like he had just finished a bottle or two of strong drink.

"What are you laughing at?" The first youth was trying vainly to reach a wall to steady his legs which were barely obeying his will to move. In great irritation and without any thought he swung one foot out toward his companion. The instability was more than enough to send him crashing to the floor without ever connecting to his intended target.

Both tried to rise again, but the herb mixture Gaeten had smeared on their lips was taking hold. Both fell to the floor heavily and passed out. Gaeten had figured they should get enough from a few lip licks to keep them either unconscious or in a heavy enough stupor to stay in the apartment for at least a day. If they were dumb enough to lick their lips again when they awoke, their stay could be even longer.

Gaeten and Nimby pulled up to the small house near the castle where they had acquired the horse and cart the day before. They had passed through several checkpoints along the way, where Gaeten-the-blacksmith had nonchalantly held the reins to drive them through. Along the way they had practiced small signals that Nimby could silently give to Gaeten to direct the steering, and Gaeten's wide brimmed hat effectively hid his unseeing eyes. Though not expressing any outward concern, both Nimby and Gaeten had fervently prayed their way past the guards. The guards had eyed them suspiciously, but since they did not match the descriptions of who they were looking for, they had allowed the pair through after a quick look over the obvious blacksmith equipment in the back of the cart.

"We are here, 'father'." Nimby held the reins while Gaeten carefully stepped down from the cart. "That was not too hard – you sure fooled those guards with your driving!"

Gaeten scowled. "Nimby, if God had not protected us I don't think we could have ever passed those guards. I fooled no one. God blinded them to let us by. And we will need even more of His help to get through the checkpoints to leave the city."

Nimby shrugged. "If you say so. But I still think your acting and my expert directing helped." He climbed down and walked up to the house and politely knocked. The door opened to a warm, well-lit interior and to the older woman who had impressed the cart and horse upon them in their time of need. "Ah, I see you came back with God's gift. I've been expecting you. Dinner is just about ready, and I have bedding in the back room for all of you." She peered around past Nimby and Gaeten. "Where are the other gentlemen … I saw four of you in my vision seeking lodging for the night."

Gaeten stepped up. "May our heavenly Father bless you for your service, ma'am. One friend should be coming shortly – he had to walk a fair distance. The other is asleep in the cart."

"Ah, the one who is ill? Please bring him in, I have a bed prepared."

Nimby stared at her, then at Gaeten. He wondered if he would ever get used to this God-stuff! Gaeten and he turned back to the cart and released Ethan from the carpet roll and carried him into the house and to an upstairs room. Then they stabled the horse and were led inside to a hearty pot of stew behind shuttered windows. "The soldiers have already searched this place thoroughly, attic to basement – oh, they were in a foul mood. The Dark Magician who was with them made 'em even do it twice, but he would not enter himself. Heh heh, I guess doorways anointed with prayer-oil scares the likes of him away! I am sure they won't be back – I was told to offer you safe haven for the night and Godspeed on your journey in the early morning."

A gentle knock on the door made them all jump up, but in a moment Turlock joined them at the low table. "You have the attire of a Dark Magician, yet I do not sense a whiff of evil about you, only light. There must be some story there! Here, have some stew and tell a widow servant of The Most High how I may be of further service. I don't get vision visitors all that often you know!"

"Kind lady, I do not wish to give any reason for the Dominion authorities or Dark Magicians to question you – the less you know, the less you could be coerced to tell them." Gaeten shook his head sadly.

She nodded wisely. "Then tell me nothing of yourselves you think is not prudent – but do encourage my heart with what The Almighty is doing in your lives, of how He has shown His greatness and majesty and grandeur to you. It brings me great joy to hear how His children are doing and how He has shown Himself to them."

"Well that, dear lady, is something we would be happy to do … if only you also would share likewise! And let us not forget to pray – we dearly need God's protection, and the young boy upstairs desperately needs healing."

"Hmm. There is a Man of God in these parts – we are not all Dominion puppets. There is a considerable resentment of the Dominion in this area. The man is a prophet who is filled with the Spirit and with power. I could try to find him tomorrow …"

A slow knock sounded on the front door. Turlock and Gaeten moved quickly to either side of the door while the old woman called out, "Who is calling on an old widow this time of the evening?"

"Just an equally old and tired prophet, madam."

She unhesitatingly threw open the door and in strode a wizened white-haired gentleman, holding a stout walking stick which he leaned on rather heavily, dressed in a roughly cut tunic with an animal hair vest.

He strode in with surprising strength and confidence, looking straight ahead as he made his way into the house. Without ever even looking, he spoke out, "Well, gentlemen, is that the way to greet someone on God's quest? Put away your daggers, for while I am far from harmless I pose no threat to you. I do have a few messages, and a couple of actions I was sent to do."

"Would you dine here then, Elgan?" The hostess obviously recognized the man.

"No, not today Elly. But tomorrow and the day after, yes."

Elly – now they knew her name – looked rather confused.

Elgan looked at each one in the room slowly and carefully. "First the message." He turned to Gaeten. "Our Father said you will leave Kardern tomorrow, and you will arrive back to Freelandia with the boy, for He has much left for you both to do. But the way will not be without peril. But be of good cheer, for if God Almighty is for you, who can stand against you?"

He turned to Turlock. "You are a chosen vessel, set apart from your former ways to now walk in the light … and to show others the way as well. You will reap a great harvest, but you will never set foot in Freelandia again." Turlock looked downcast, but then raised his chin high.

"As the Lord declares, so I will follow. I've committed my life to Him, so wherever he sends me, there I will go gladly."

Elgan moved to the next person in the room. "Elly, the Lord has heard the prayer of your heart. You will no longer be alone in your walk with Him." Elgan reached for her hand and gave it a squeeze. Then he came to Nimby and stared long and hard into the boy's eyes. He seemed to be seeing something that confirmed a thought.

"Few may have chosen you, but the Lord does not look on the outside or judge as a person would. He looks inside, at the heart. He sees not what you are today, but what you will be tomorrow, what you can be if you let Him have His way with you." Elgan looked up. "Where is the Chancellor's son?" At Elly's pointing hand he nodded. "Come, Nimblefoot. You and I have work to do upstairs, and you will be a different man when you return."

Nimby's eyes were wide as he uncertainly followed the old prophet across the room. Elgan rather spryly took the stairs two at a time, silently and rapidly rising out of view. Nimby turned back to look at his companions, unsure. Gaeten sensed his caution and confusion. "Go ahead Nimby, do whatever he says. Trust him, and have faith in God. Faith is doing what it seems God wants, even when you don't have a clue as to where it will go or what will become of it. Living a life of faith is never knowing for sure what will happen tomorrow, but knowing our heavenly Father does, and that He is preparing us for that future even now."

Nimby did not understand all of that, though his faith and trust were growing daily. He headed up, each ancient step creaking as he went. He found Elgan in the bedroom, standing over Ethan's sleeping form. "Come Nimblefoot, give me your hand." When the boy proffered his hand, Elgan placed his staff into it. "Now we will pray. Place your other hand onto the boy's forehead with me." Nimby did, feeling rather odd and a little bit foolish.

"Oh Lord, fulfill the Word which you gave to me. Heal the Chancellor's son; breathe your life of health into him. Let the boy exhale the poison and inhale your breath of life."

Ethan coughed violently, and Nimby saw a dark red cloudy mist seem to flow out from the boy. Nimby could smell a vile, pungent odor. Elgan looked over at him. "Now Nimblefoot – breathe into him with God's very breath. Have faith and act on it."

Nimby gulped, but then bent over Ethan and with a quick look at Elgan, he took a deep breath and blew it down over Ethan's face. Nimby nearly leapt aside as what seemed like particles of white light exited his own mouth and settled down over the still body below him. Ethan took in a breath, and the light was sucked into his lungs and body. His limp body began to spasm, but his head was held in place with the hands of Nimby and Elgan on his forehead. Elgan himself removed his hand but motioned for Nimby's to remain. A warm glow seemed to begin at Ethan's forehead and began to migrate down, spreading over his whole body. Nimby watched in awe. At one point he moved his hand and lost contact, and the glow began to fade and stop its spread. He quickly replaced it and firmly held it down, and the glow resumed its spread. As it finally reached Ethan's feet, Nimby felt a weight settling onto his shoulders that was both incredibly heavy yet also light. He did not understand.

When the glow seemed to have fully infused Ethan's body, Nimby lifted his hand. The glow faded and Ethan's eyes opened, looking around in confusion. "Let me help you up, boy." Elgan held out a hand and with effort helped pull Ethan vertical. Nimby quickly reached for Ethan's other hand and effortlessly pulled him the last bit up. He looked over at Elgan and marveled, not having noticed before how ancient, wrinkled and tired looking the old man appeared. Elgan smiled warmly at him. "Come, let's present ourselves back downstairs."

Elgan moved to the stairs and gratefully held onto the handrail. The others downstairs heard the creaking stairs and turned to see the old prophet easing himself down, with a somewhat dazed Ethan following on his own strength. Nimby glided down silently behind them, with a mantle over his shoulders and carrying a staff.

Turlock ran forward. "Ethan, you … you look great! How do you feel?"

"I … I am fine, I guess. I really don't think I know yet. It is like I just woke up from a very long sleep. Where are we anyway?" He turned to look past Turlock and saw his long time mentor. "GAETEN! I thought I dreamed about you, but it seems like I have been in a rather bad dream for quite some time." Ethan reached up to touch the now dark hair. "Either time has not only stopped for me but actually reversed many years, or …"

Gaeten had tears in his eyes and held the boy tightly. "No, my boy, it is just a disguise … but we can discuss that later. For now it is enough that you are back with us!"

Elly, though, had eyes only for Elgan. "What … what happened? Why does the boy have your vest draped over his shoulders? Why does he have your staff?"

Elgan came over to her and held both of her hands. "The Lord knew it was time for a change, my lady. A change for both of us individually … and together." He looked deeply into her eyes. "Elly, the mantle of prophetic service has been passed on to another. It is time for me to settle down – I am not sure I thought I would ever say or think that! But before I say another word, what has God been showing to you?"

Elly smiled a wide grin. "Yes, my Elgan. I would gladly be your wife."

Elgan grinned himself and turned to Turlock. "You will become a priest here, establishing a secret church for God Almighty right in Kardern. It may be slightly premature, but not by very much. Will you do the honor of marrying us?"

No one was looking at Nimby, who was staring at everything and everyone around him. Everything seemed to look different now. The people here had a white glow to them which he recognized as the presence of God's Spirit. Elgan turned to him. "Nimblefoot, you now wear my mantle. You will be a prophet here in Kardern and elsewhere within the Dominion, standing boldly for the truth. The authorities will hate you, and persecute you for God's sake, and you will need to stand firm and persevere. God will use you with great power. Use such power all for His purpose. Heal the sick, resist evil, and proclaim the truth of our God."

Nimby had a flash of scared-little-boy come over his face, which was rapidly replaced with a more confident nod toward the old prophet. Elgan smiled back, knowing that life was suddenly far different for the boy who just a few weeks before had been a street urchin. He chuckled inwardly – meeting one's God had a way of doing that.

The pre-dawn morning promised a bright and sunny day ahead. The dockyards were unusually quiet. Even with high tide, only a few ships were being allowed to leave, and only after a very thorough inspection that included a high level Dark Magician. The Alterians were stoic as they waited for their final approval. The opening of the small harbor on the river had a heavy chain across it to completely close it to ship movement, and a small flotilla of Dominion warships patrolled inside the harbor itself. The plan appeared to be that groups of ships would be inspected and approved to leave, and then the chain would be lowered and only that convoy would be given passage out. So they waited, watching the soldiers and inspectors working their way down the line of ships. Several other sets of eyes were watching too.

Gaeten and Turlock had transformed Ethan's appearance to closely duplicate how Nimby had looked the day before, and both of them had loaded a few extra supplies into the wagon and hitched up the horse. Elgan volunteered to join them, both to further confound any soldiers, who surely would be looking for just an older blind man and one or two teenage boys, and to bring the horse and cart back after this little adventure. Nimby and Turlock would stay with Elly at least until Elgan returned. They left the house just before dawn broke.

The dockyard was crawling with soldiers. The Alterian captain watched with interest how inspections were carried out. A dozen soliders would board, along with several naval sailors pressed to help search the tiniest nooks and crannies aboard every ship. Several squads were also nearby on the wharves, ready to bring a lot of hurt to any resistance that might surface. All of the Dominion inspectors were tense, as one mentioned that the penalty for allowing the escape of the prisoner was a particularly horrific death. That and the presence of so many senior Dark Magicians made everyone's skin itch and seemed to bring a pall of doom over the whole area.

Once his and a group of nearby ships were thoroughly inspected, a signal was given and the chain across the harbor began to be lowered. The captain was told he could weigh anchor when that happened, but he hesitated, waiting. The captains of the other inspected ships wasted no time and their crews began to scurry all over the decks to cast off as soon as possible. That was when a commotion began to break out near the first ships that had been inspected. Soldiers began to run toward the hubbub, and those who were supposed to watch and guard each inspected ship approved for departure also had their attention distracted. Several soldiers were on the ground, obviously injured, but by unknown assailants. As more soldiers and Magicians congregated, a hail of small projectiles rained down on them. A few soldiers pointed to the rooftops of surrounding buildings, but before a contingent could charge forward the projectiles changed to bottles filled with very flammable liquids with burning rags attached. A wall of flame sprouted up and rapidly spread.

Few sailors feared anything more than fire, and as the first tongues of flame began licking their way across the dockyard, nearly all captains immediately began to cast off and try to pull away. People ran back and forth alternating between trying to help or to escape, causing considerable confusion. The Alterian captain finally gave orders and his ship was one of the last to pull away. Most of the captains figured this was a good time to exit the harbor entirely and they put up sail, gaining speed as they approached the harbor exit.

The crews of the Dominion warships out in the harbor saw the flames start up and their captains barked orders to close in to block the fleeing ships, but with the harbor chain down there were just not enough warships to prevent the mass exodus, and no captain wanted to be anywhere near the billowing flames whose sparks could easily be carried by the wind well out over the water. As such, Dominion crews were none too fast to comply. The Alterian captain saw the warships changing course and he also altered his own direction and slipped past the nearest Dominion vessel into the river mouth and thence into the ocean proper.

The soldiers and their superiors quickly moved to contain the flames, but the orderly dockyard was in shambles. The Port Director fumed as he saw several buildings engulfed by flames and he turned away from the window where he was watching them in disgust – just in time to see the last ship slip out of the harbor. His face went white and his eyes bulged from their sockets. "STOP THOSE SHIPS!" he bellowed, realizing that the confusion of the last few minutes would have made a nearly ideal cover for one of those ships to pick up un-inspected cargo … or passengers.

Signal flares were shot skyward to instruct the warships to give chase and the race was on … just in the wrong direction. The Port Director realized he wished he was on one of those outbound ships leaving Kardern … remaining here would almost certainly cost him his head once the Overlord discovered this mishap. He assigned underlings to direct the fire fighting and restore order, and then told everyone he was going out to inspect the damage … alone. Once out of immediate sight he slipped away from the dockyard. He never really liked his job anyway, though with the graft he could take in he had become rather wealthy. Perhaps it was time to retire … maybe somewhere far away.

Elgan nudged the cart forward in the line going through the checkpoint on the exit of Kardern nearest the castle. It was a quiet checkpoint, though it was well-manned with soldiers and a couple of Dark Magicians. Gaeten breathed another prayer of blindness to be upon all those they were passing by. Ethan was sitting between them on the rough cart bench, and slouched with head bent forward, as though sleeping.

As they neared the head of the line, a shout rang out and several people lifted their arms to point to the rising black smoke coming from the merchant dock area. At the same time, they began to hear a din start up at the next checkpoint further to the east. The soldiers were pointing and nervously shuffling, wondering what was happening. They distractedly passed through the next few wagons, and then peered at the occupants of the blacksmith's cart. The Magician stared hard at Gaeten, and began to mutter something to a soldier next to him. Gaeten turned toward the two and nodded, as though greeting them. They were waved through.

As they slowly pulled away there was added commotion at the gate and the heavy portcullis rattled loudly as it was lowered, blocking all further exit. The city of Kardern was now closed, sealing everyone – including the soldiers – in.

❦

Late in the afternoon Elgan drew the reins up in front of a tavern in a small town situated at the crossroads of three well traveled roads. All three dismounted from the wagon and stretched their tired legs and rather sore bottoms.

"I suspect a town like this probably gets a steady supply of horses, what with all the travelers through here." Elgan scratched his head and looked around. "Ah, there is the stable, down the way, and I see a blacksmith there too. Why don't you two rid yourselves of those aprons and I will take them and the scrap metal and anvil to the 'smith and see what he will take for the lot. Then I can see if the stable has a couple of sturdy horses and gear for you."

Gaeten nodded. "Great. Thanks Elgan. Make sure you don't let them see all the coin I gave you or they will steal you blind."

"Oh, that is why I am doing it and not you – you already appear to have been taken in!"

"Ha – I'd cuff you good if I didn't need you for a bit longer! Ethan, let's rustle up some grub and hope Elgan doesn't get caught rustling up some mounts."

Ethan laughed – it felt good to do so, after such a long time where absolutely nothing around him had seemed humorous. "It's a good thing we are travelling by land and not sea – when you put that patch over one eye I figured for sure someone would mistake you for a pirate!"

"Arg ye matey, let's find us some grub before I run ye through or make ye walk the plank!" Gaeten grinned. Their travel so far had been quite uneventful, and he looked forward to making good time by horse. Ethan seemed to be growing stronger by the hour, and would need to start eating more heartily and exercising to work the obvious flab from his under-used muscles. He figured they might be at least a full day ahead of any news coming from Kardern, and he would like to keep it that way for as long as possible. Surely an alert would be issued, and from this point onward they would more closely fit the description that may have been put out.

If they could make it further east before they turned north, he figured they could reach one of the larger coastal cities where they could more easily hide amongst the crowds. A bit further north could also take them into some of the more recently conquered Dominion territories, where perhaps some of the more wealthy and important people might just have rented out a Freelandian Watcher. By now all of the Watchers should have gotten word to be on the lookout for Gaeten and Ethan, and he would not mind the extra help at all.

Ethan led the way into the tavern, with Gaeten close enough behind to get clues so as to act properly for a sighted person. They ordered enough for themselves and extra for Elgan, who had told them to eat without him – he had a long ride back and could eat along the way easily enough. There were many travelers, and the two blended in with the others and ate without speaking much. Ethan paid with money Gaeten had given him, collected a small wooden box with extra food, and they walked out into the early evening.

"I'd rather get a few more miles between us and Kardern while we still have sunlight – how long do you reckon we have of that left, Ethan?"

"Oh, I'd say at least three more hours. Do you think we should try to pick up any other gear like …" Ethan's voice lowered to a whisper "weapons?"

"I am not so sure about that – we don't want to raise any suspicions. But we could use a small axe, and I wouldn't think people would look too askance at you picking up a hunting bow and some arrows. We should get a small tent, rope and other gear too, since we likely will sleep on the trail for awhile. Let's see what Elgan has found first, and then acquire anything else we need."

The two walked down to the stable, finding the old prophet busily haggling over two horses and riding gear. Not wanting to disturb his deal making, Gaeten and Ethan found a hardware store and purchased a few other belongings, including an old horn bow that looked well worn. The store owner had given them a great deal on it, with an extra string, saying it was just too difficult to draw for most of the travelers that came through here. When he observed Gaeten draw it to its full extension without showing the strain he was eager to rid his store of what he considered a dust collecting item. Ethan selected a dozen hunting arrows, and another half dozen field points – explaining both he and his 'dad' needed some practice and did not want to ruin any of the good tips. The proprietor nodded in approval and threw in a beat up but serviceable quiver and some old worn fletching materials. In all, they had a good armful of items by the time they were done.   Elgan was just walking two fine looking horses up the street, complete with saddles and bridles. "He drove a hard bargain, he did. But most travelers here want carriage or cart horses. Just last week someone traded these two in for a nice carriage rig and mare. I even have some change left over." Elgan fished into a pocket and began to give over a handful of coins.

"Keep it, Brother Elgan. I doubt you saw many of those during your ministry."

"Well, that is true enough ... but let me tell you, God is so very faithful. I never went hungry – well, not too hungry anyway, and truly never felt in need of anything more than what He would provide. I somehow don't think He is going to stop either – and I think you are much more likely to need these than I am." Elgan thrust the coins into Gaeten's hand, and the two hugged.

"It has been an honor meeting you, Elgan. May God richly bless you. I do have a few things that I doubt will be useful to me, but which are perfect to give you and Elly as a wedding present."

Elgan looked quizzical as Gaeten fished out of a pocket the small bag of jewelry he had removed from Taleena's castle room. He handed it over. When Elgan opened it, he stuttered in surprise. "But .... But Gaeten ... this is ... this is worth a small fortune!

"Oh, is it? I could not tell if they were real or fake. Either way, they don't really go with my outfit! I have no use for them, and even trying to pawn them out in the poor countryside would raise too much suspicion. I am certain in Kardern you can find ways to convert them to more useful currency ... but do keep one or two as a special gift for Elly."

"I ... I don't know what to say except thank you, brother."

"Thank our Father, He provides in the most unusual ways."

Elgan turned to Ethan. "It was a pleasure to meet you, Ethan. God has great things in store for you, I saw that plainly. But your travels will have great dangers before you return to your mother and father, and you will have little time for reunion before the Dominion arrives. But you will see God's power and might – and the world will too. I do not know if we will meet again – God did not show that to me one way or the other. But I send you off with God's blessing, and Godspeed."

The older man turned away, waving as he walked back to his cart, the lunch box in his other hand. He was not sure if he would be able to re-enter Kardern immediately, though getting in should be easier than getting out. Regardless, Elgan knew a number of believers of the true God out in this region, and knew that he could therefore find safe lodging for as long as needed.

Ethan and Gaeten loaded up their mounts with their additional items, and Ethan adjusted the stirrups to fit both him and Gaeten. They climbed up and rode out, heading out on the road to the east.

The tavern proprietor looked out the window at the two as they left town. As he had served their meal he had noticed some scars on the older man's arms. They had looked faded, but in a few places some darker coloration appeared to have been smudged off and more distinct shapes had shown through. The scars did not look random. He was sure he had seen similar markings once before, when some rich land baron from one of the northern cities had been traveling through. That fellow had seemed to keep a rather heavily muscled man of his entourage close by at all times, a man who did not seem to miss a single thing that happened around the baron. The tavern owner had questioned a few people about that – it was not a normal sight – and had discovered that the baron had a rather expensive bodyguard from somewhere or another, one whose arms bore similar scars to what he had just noticed.

It was odd, remarkable really. Something unusual to file away in his memory. *Who knows,* he mused. *Maybe it will be useful to remember it someday.*

Chapter 9

A Surprise for Arianna

ot so fast there, mister high faluting Chief Engineer! You've been avoiding me the last several days and I will not stand it another minute!" Arianna was fuming, her eyes sparking dangerously and her wild hair whipping about.

"Now hold on there, lassie. You know I had to go out inspectin' some of the coastal defenses, and ye yerself said you were too busy here to come along."

"That is entirely beside the point. You had promised that this week we would set a date and the week is essentially over. Pay up, mister!"

Robby cocked his head to one side and grinned. "Well now, if all this fuss is just over goin' out on a date n' all, well fer sure I kin take you out fer lunch to Maggie's diner. They make a mean grilled cheese sandwich after all."

"Oh you thick-headed, weasel mouthed infuriating tower of cheese mold! I oughtta …" Arianna had no chance to finish her tirade as Robby adroitly avoided her exaggerated round house punch, stepped inside her next swing, grabbed her in his long gangly arms and planted a massive kiss over her fussing mouth. She squirmed most enjoyably and nearly bit his lip, but then melted into his arms.

"There now, lassie. Did I ever tell ya how gorgeous ye are when you're all aquiver like that? And don'tcha think makin' up is far preferable to ranting and raving and carrying on so?"

Arianna tensed and Robby held her tighter to avoid a close-quarter kidney punch. She changed tactics and affected a slightly hurt tone. "But Bobby, you promised we'd set a date for our wedding this week. I've tried to be patient, but … you … promised." The last came out with a hint of pout and a slight stiffening of her shoulders in his arms.

"Ah, now you've done it again lassie. You know ye twist me 'bout your pretty little fingers when ye start to pout. Ach, an' I betcha ye got those great big woeful doe-eyes trained in on me too." He pulled back and confirmed he was being targeted by one of her most devastating weapons. "Ouch! Ye got them turned up on full power too I see! I don't suppose I stand much of a chance of resisting now, do I?"

Arianna shook her thick long hair, just hard enough so it partially covered her face to look even more doleful, if that were possible. It also helped to hide the sparkle that was now in her eyes. Robby groaned. "Heaven help me, yer pulling out all the stops now, aren't ya? Ye best be careful … some young apprentice engineer may saunter by and be caught in the crossfire an' be ruined for the rest o' 'is poor life!"

She smirked coyly and held his hand, absently playing with his fingers. "Pleeeaaassseee? You prooommmiiisssed me, Bobby."

Robby began to laugh ruefully. "I surrender! I surrender already! Much more o' that I'd likely get burn marks on me exposed skin! But could ye at least wait until the dinner I already had planned for tonight?"

Hair whipped back sharply and eyes flashed fire again. "You mean you made me go through all that and you had already made plans! Why you lanky lard-head lout! You exasperating engineer of entrails … I … I oughtta …"

Robby grappled her in close again. She was a wee bit less dangerous up real close, least-wise from punches and pokes, and he rather liked burying his head into her lightly scented hair. And besides, she really was gorgeous when she was all afire like this, he thought, especially with no heavy blunt object swinging in her hands.

"Oh, just wear any old thingy! We are not goin' to the Silver Chalice ya know. Just something a wee bit nicer-like than a work apron will do fine."

"Robert, you can't just expect me to throw on any random outfit! Do I need a formal dress, something to dance in, something understated or colorful, very conservative or more relaxed and casual …what?"

"Argh, ye make life so complicated, you do! I just grabbed a relatively clean pair o' slacks and a nice shirt – and I even combed my hair and trimmed me beard. All set. Ten minutes tops." He rolled his eyes standing outside Arianna's apartment. "And the carriage is awaiting, deary."

"Men!"

"Just slip on something not too formal, but not too casual either after all ...colorful, that brings out the hues of yer doe eyes, or of yer pretty hair, or of the flowers along the way – you look great in anything anyway."

"Well, that is a world of help! Just dandy!"

"Well yerself … if ye cannot decide, ye could always just do without anythin at all … that would surely get ye even more attention than you normally draw when ye saunter down the street." Robby snickered and put his hand to the doorknob and began to twist it. "Now if yer want'in me to come on in and help ye out, I'd be mor'n willing to do the right proper manly service for ye." He opened the door an inch or so, just enough to catch a glimpse of long smooth legs disappearing under some shiny lacey material.

"Oh no you don't! If you want a look your going to have to get that marriage date set right quick and then wait until it is all good and proper! Now scat!"

Through the crack of door opening he saw her flash a big grin his way and he grinned back. "Are ye sure now? You know I just might turn out to be quite the connoisseur of fine ladies clothing, quit me engineering job outright and becomes a master tailor, or purveyor of fine fabrics." He opened the door just a hair wider. "I think I like the yonder one on the left there, the pinky silky number that nicely matches the color o' your cheeks right now!"

"ROBERT!"

He laughed uproariously and closed the door. A few minutes later Arianna breezed out and twirled in front of an appreciative Chief Engineer. "Whoo hoo! I be thinkin twas worth the wait'in … and that pink blousy sure 'nuf looks right fitting for a gorgeous princess … or a future Mrs. Chief Engineer of Freelandia!"

"Do you really like it, or are you just flattering me? Tell me what you really think."

Robby had been around Arianna long enough to know he was now faced with one of those questions … the supremely dangerous kind with few right and many, many wrong answers foisted upon husbands and husbands-to-be around the world. He winced and then grinned and held her hand. "Arianna, I have come to love ye. I like yer outfit – it looks absolutely super on you and I'll surely be the envy of all the male-folk for miles around. You are the most gorgeous engineer in the world, and I be absolutely honored that ye would'a want to be with the likes of poor old me. You could be wearin a soggy gunny sack and I'd be proud ye'd be seen with yours truly. How's that?"

"Pretty good, for a beginner. I especially like the first part … can you practice that again?"

Robert looked deeply into her eyes – he felt he could get pleasantly and hopelessly lost in there – and softly murmured, "I love you, Arianna."

"What? I don't think I could hear you very well. Did you say something?"

He sighed and rolled his eyes heavenward – then pulled her into a close embrace. "I … LOVE … YOU!"

"Right smart of you too, once you finally caught on."

"Arrrgghh! Ye gots me good, that you do. Can ye please escort yer prisoner o' love out to yonder waiting paddy-wagon?"

The carriage pulled up to one of the nicer restaurants near the concert hall. They disembarked and were escorted to a private table conspicuously empty in the center of the otherwise rather busy establishment. As they walked by, both waved at Master Oldive and his wife, who were seated off to one side. The waiter pulled out Arianna's chair, and as she let herself be so formally seated she noticed Chancellor Duncan and Lydia at a table nearby. Both rose when they saw the newest guests and skirted around the tables to greet them.

"Hello Robert, Arianna!" Lydia beamed at each, and then laid a hand on Arianna's arm. "My, that is a lovely silk blouse! You know, you have not stopped by since our evening at the Silver Chalice – and the invitation is still open … and it isn't particularly polite to not accept!"

Arianna blushed lightly at the slight rebuke. "Well, Mrs. Chanc ... I mean Lydia," she corrected herself as she saw the stern look appear on the older lady's face, "We have been awfully busy. Robby here runs a tight ship and works his engineers to the bone. Build this, blow up that, make the explosion bigger! It's a wonder I still have all my fingers and have not singed my hair."

"Oh, you poor thing. Men can be such taskmasters."

Robby looked annoyed at this sudden turn of conversation, and Duncan was quick to his rescue. "We are all busy, that is for sure. And you engineers are at the forefront of building our defenses. We are all very appreciative of your hard work. And, I must say, Arianna you look stunning ... if that is what overworked looks like then I recommend it for everyone!"

They all laughed and Arianna's blush became a shade deeper. "See, me girl picked out just the exact blouse shade she knew her face woulda' turn when she was with the likes o' me." Robby smirked.

"Robert!" whispered Arianna fiercely as her face went ever darker and her eyes widened at the attention being drawn their way by the other patrons. It was bad enough having the Chancellor and Chancelloress standing right at their table!

"Oops, there, I've done it now ... I went too far and now she be not matchin' her blousey exactly. I guess I need to practice that better ... but I got all evening now to work on it proper-like."

Somehow Arianna blushed even harder, but now her eyes were flashing dangerously and she gripped the edge of the table with white knuckle intensity. Duncan smiled and gave Robby a look, then a nod that was lost on Arianna as she glared at her companion. Lydia leaned over and patted her arm. "There, there – I will pray for you. Do try to control yourself though ... otherwise it may be a rather long evening."

They left, and Arianna glared suspiciously at Robby. "And just what exactly did Lydia mean with that last comment?"

"Ya know, lassie, I donna think I had ever noticed it quite be'fer, but even yer pretty little earlobes get all pinky when ye blush hard 'nuf."
Arianna tried to keep her voice down, but he was sorely pushing her and she eyed a large-tined fork on the table, wondering just how far those tines might sink into unprotected male flesh as she icily hissed out "ROBERT!"

He just grinned and motioned for the head waiter to come over.

"Yes sir … it is Chief Engineer, isn't it? And therefore this must be the lovely Arianna. You two are quite the talk of the social circuit in the Keep you know."

Robby rolled his eyes, and Arianna had yet another chance to practice her coloration, just as it had been starting to return to normal.

"Everything is just as you desired it, Chief Engineer. And the Master Chef sends you his compliments. I'm sure he will be out to greet you in person later. I've heard," the senior waiter lowered his voice conspiratorially, "that the modifications you suggested for his stove have worked a wonder in the kitchen. Our owner believes it will move us up to a full five star rating in no time, with the most technologically advanced stove in all of Freelandia! Oh, here comes the owner!"

A plump and very distinguished gentleman approached their table and began to vigorously pump Robby's hand. "Thank you – thank you Chief Engineer! In the last two days we have had to shoo out several chefs from other restaurants who have tried to sneak back into the kitchen to spy out the new designs you created. We have had to hire a guard for the back door! And the food critics have already marveled at our new dishes our Master Chef says were inspired by your work. I know of only one way to possibly repay you … anytime you are in town, please stop by here for your meals – on the house – at least for this year! Sorry, I cannot stay longer – I have an architect in to look at expansion ideas – I cannot thank you enough!"

Robby smiled and nodded as the man scurried off toward the back rooms. The head waiter nodded again to Robby, looked over at Arianna appreciatively, gave a short bow, and snapped his fingers before moving off. Another waiter hurried over with tea and water, while yet another readied their table. A third waiter came right out with appetizers in an artful arrangement. Arianna grinned, but then scowled at Robby. "Ok buster, you obviously have been planning this for awhile now. Just what else do you have up your sleeve?"

"Ah, me lady … that is for me's to knows and ye's to yet find out … but all in good time. Let's just say I've planned a wee bit o' surprise for you."

"That is what I am beginning to be a wee bit afraid of."

"Never ye mind. For now, just sit back and enjoy."

Arianna leaned back in her seat, suspiciously eying her companion, with a wry grin creeping over her face. She could not hold the look for long though and quickly enough flashed a full smile with her famously sparkling eyes.

Robby forgot his surroundings. It was oh so easy to get lost in those luminous eyes. He swallowed hard, thinking, *steady there now fella. We gots to stay in control … leastwise for a wee bit longer now!* Outwardly he grinned back, watching her face.

The head waiter appeared again, this time at the front of the establishment. He loudly and conspicuously cleared his throat. "Ladies and gentlemen, attention please! Pardon me for disturbing your meal, but I wanted to introduce to you something really, really special for tonight. For the first time ever, we are pleased to offer some accompaniment for your meal, straight from our acclaimed Music Academy. We are sure you will enjoy what we have in store for you, and most certainly you will all find this to be a night to remember!"

He bowed. From a back entrance soft music began to play as five musicians in black and white formal wear entered the dining area, each playing a different stringed instrument. They slowly fanned out over the room, pausing at each table for a few moments, all playing the same beautiful orchestral piece in harmony. Many patrons clapped with surprise, and Robby glanced over at Duncan and Lydia, who beamed back at him and nodded toward the back entrance where the others had entered.

As the musicians filtered out along the outer edges of the room, two younger girls entered, dressed in royal blue and black. One had a particularly elegant violin and the other a viola. The girl with the viola stepped a pace ahead, with the violinist following, and they made their way to the center of the room, playing as they went in perfect tune with the others. The two came to a halt quite near Robby and Arianna's table. At that close range they noticed that the violinist was blind.

As the latest musicians drew near, a noticeable auditory change rippled through the room, almost as if the eatery had transformed into a grand concert hall. Many diners looked around in astonishment … the acoustics of this place were obviously not designed for orchestral playing, yet the sound quality they were hearing was astounding. And yet there was more to it than just that. Somehow the music was not just sound; it was energy too. And it was not just pleasant; it was …gripping and focused, and inexorably drew in your mind and heart. Somehow, even without words, it reminded all of God and His majesty.

Everyone was enthralled, food forgotten. Even the waiters had stopped in their tracks, and no one noticed. The instrumental score went on for several more minutes, and then ended grandly. Everyone clapped with joy and appreciation. The servants snapped back to their duties, quickly delivering main courses and removing finished items.

Arianna stared first at the musicians near them, then at the widely grinning Robby. "Bobby … that was … was wonderful! Did you … did you somehow arrange all of this?"

Robby just smiled. "I wanted this to be an extra special night for us. But just you wait, darlin' … there is still more to come!"

Their meal arrived and as they ate the musicians started up and played a light airy piece that swirled and looped around the room in whimsical gaiety while not forcing such attention that the first score had. When the main course was finished, the waiters whisked all the plates and silverware away and disappeared for a few minutes while the musicians rested. Then a group of waiters burst into the dining area carrying arrangements of red and white roses, which they placed with great flourish around Robby's and Arianna's table.

The owner reappeared, grinning widely as he personally carried an ornate crystal vase with three long stemmed roses over to their table. Arianna gasped in delight. The rose stems had been intricately woven together into a living green braid. A pure white rose, with edges dusted with gold stood above the other two flowers. The rose nearest Arianna was pointing in her direction with deep pink petals lightly variegated with blue and white while that facing Robby was an incredibly bright blue with the same white variegation.

"Bobby … how did you … where did you ever … what …" Arianna's voice trailed off as she stared dumbfounded at the exquisite floral arrangement before her.

"Well, what do ye know … I finally found what it takes to make thee wordless!"

Arianna was too lost in wonderment to take the bait. "But Bobby, I have never, ever seen such colors in roses! And how did they get the stems to braid together like that? It must have cost a fortune!"

The proprietor beamed. "It is a gift, Miss Arianna, from the Chancellor and his lovely wife."

Arianna turned to stare wide eyed at Duncan and Lydia, who in turned smiled at her and Robby and raised their goblets in salutation. A thought crossed Arianna's mind and she quickly turned with a suspicious look back to her companion. "Wait a minute! " She held her arm out to the pink rose and it nearly perfectly matched her new blouse. "Robert ... you bought me this blouse two weeks ago; you said it was a present to commemorate my Master Engineer rank approval. And yet it somehow perfectly matches this rose ... quite a coincidence, wouldn't you say?"

"Oh, most undoubtedly, me love."

"That means you have been planning this behind my back for at least two weeks! And probably more! Oh, you are a chief rascal, Chief Engineer!" Her eyes spoke much louder than her words however, and Bobby barely registered she had spoken as he gazed into them.

With conscious effort he broke contact from those mind numbing magnets. "So, does ye like them?"

Arianna's eyes grew wider as she leaned forward and turned her full attention onto him. "Bobby ... they are beautiful and you are adorable! But I am not sure I understand there being three roses, with the central white one being higher than the others."

"Ach, I thought ye'd pick that one up in an instant-like. The top rose represents our Father above, over all of us and we being intertwined around Him. Likewise it can remind us of God the Father, God the Son and God the Holy Spirit."

"Bobby, I do believe there is a poet hiding somewhere within that calculating engineer's body of yours!" She beamed at him and he nearly lost all resolve, barely holding in his final surprises for the night.

Arianna saw him struggling, and smiled slyly at her man. "But what are you really doing here? And that girl musician ... the blind one ... isn't that ... I mean, I've heard a lot of rumors about a young blind singer and musician, one that sang at Reginaldo's concert." Robby grinned for an answer. Before Arianna could query again, the two girls came up to their table.

"Hi, I'm Kory."

"And I'm Maria." Maria came forward and held her hand out. Arianna took it lightly and Maria smiled. "You must be Arianna. Lydia has told me about you." Arianna turned toward Lydia, who beamed back. Maria turned. "And you must be Chief Engineer Robert. Lydia has told me about you too. I may not be able to see you, but I can sense God's Spirit in both of you. That is what counts anyway. Especially for what you are about to do. I think love for one another must be a picture of God's love for us – only His is so much more immense and never ever ends. I've been told that God IS love – He defines it and is the source of true love. So if we first love God, and we know He loves us, I think then and only then can we truly love one another."

"That's beautiful, Maria." Arianna looked sideways over at Robby, who smiled broadly back in agreement.

"I'm glad you think so."

Kory nodded at the restaurant owner standing nearby. He raised a hand for quiet before speaking. "Good evening everyone! I hope you have had a wonderful meal and enjoyed the music so far. Now I would like to introduce to you Maria – and yes, she is The Singer who accompanied Sir Reginaldo for the very first time ever in his Masterpiece. She has a few words to say before the next number. Maria ..."

Maria smiled warmly and swiveled her body to address the room full of diners. "Good evening, everyone. I trust we have pleased you so far with our accompaniment to your meals – this is the first time I have tried to play an instrument while salivating over all the wonderful smells!"

That got a twitter of laughter from those listening. "I hope you will enjoy the next piece too, but I must make a confession ... well, two I guess. First off, I wrote this next piece, so you won't recognize it and I just hope it works! Next, it is not really for all of you. It is only for two special people here tonight. You get to listen in, but this is all for the Chief Engineer here and Arianna. I wrote it for them, for this special night."

A scattering of applause sounded and Maria did a simple curtsey. Arianna's mouth hung open and Robby was about to comment about that in his usual oh-so-somber and serious tone when he thought better of it. There was a time for jokes, but also a time for seriousness. Well, a little time for that anyway. He reached across the table to hold her hand.

Maria lifted her violin and began playing a solo piece that started out quiet and simple. In the complete silence of the dining room the perfect notes had a vibrancy that reached out to capture everyone's full attention. The sound quickly went beyond their mere hearing, beyond the physical and into the spiritual dimension, stirring and lifting everyone's hearts.

Maria played with an incredible intensity, obviously lost herself within the sound ... or was she really not lost – just somewhere else? After several minutes the others joined in, and a minute later Maria stopped playing and began to sing.

It was like Reginaldo's concert all over again, but this time much more intimate. The song spoke of God's love and beauty, of consuming His people within that love and acceptance and peace, and of God pouring out His love into their hearts to overflowing. Then it moved on to the love between a man and a woman, each displaying a reflection of love's source, like a diamond facet that is unique but part of the whole, and all reflecting God's astounding beauty and light. It was awesome, in the truest and fullest sense of that word.

There was not a dry eye in the house, and Robby could hear soft crying coming from multiple tables. He thought it was the most beautiful song he had ever heard.

The last sounds lingered, slowly fading out in a purity of stillness. A profound silence settled over the room. After waiting several minutes, into that awe-struck silence Robby spoke softly. "Arianna, me love. Will you marry me? With the invasion coming and all, I don't think I can wait to plan some big fancy wedding ... we can do that later ... but right here, right now, will ye marry the likes of me?"

Arianna was dumbstruck and dumbfounded. The song had moved her more than she thought possible, and tears were streaming down her cheeks. She used her free hand to wipe at them and give herself a moment to think, but she already knew without a shadow of a doubt that this indeed was what her heavenly Father wanted for her, was preparing her for, and now was giving to her as a most special gift.

"Bobby, my love ... I would be most honored to be your wife, right here, right now."

The room erupted in jubilant clapping and cheering. Duncan and Lydia were suddenly at their table congratulating them, as were Oldsy and his wife. Then Chaplain Mikael strode forward and after having them repeat solemn vows, gave them his official and heartfelt blessings on the union. He turned and declared all present to be witnesses, and then officially presented to the cheering crowd Mr. and Mrs. Robert Macgregor. Arianna barely heard or saw. Her heart stopping doe-eyes were turned full force on her new husband.

Chapter 10

Unexpected Friends

Gaeten had directed Ethan to lead them east by northeast. In the dimming light they made their way off the main road in a remote area, letting the horses pick their way as they walked upstream in a small creek for several miles. With no tracks showing their exit from the trail, any potential followers would have a quite difficult time tracking them. Ethan observed a small hill near the stream and Gaeten agreed it would make an ideal campsite.

Gaeten figured they could afford a small fire tonight – and he was not sure if that would be the case for the next several days. Even so, he had Ethan gather only very dry wood and they worked to dig a fire pit and built a rock ring around it to further hide the glow from the flames and coals. They had plenty of food for the next several days from the town, but it would not keep fresh after that – so they ate heartily. When that was gone, further sustenance would have to be gathered or hunted from their sur-roundings. Such skills were basic instructions at the Watcher Compound, and neither had any concern over going hungry.

Ethan related his adventures, or perhaps more appropriately misadven-tures, to his long-time friend. As he related Taleena's seduction, Gaeten grunted.

"Whenever your attention is drawn away from God, you should exam-ine most carefully the cause. Even when whatever it is seems desirable, take great caution. Does this thing or person build you up in – or bring you closer to – God and holiness? If the answer is a solid affirmative, then be blessed and enjoy it. But if you cannot with good conscious say 'yes,' then you really have to question yourself about it … and for sure implore the Holy Spirit to show you most clearly, to give you a discerning heart and mind for His truth. Many a young man has been turned from his God-given vocation, and even from God Himself, by beguiling vixens. And sadly, some of the women do not even realize what they are doing. Others seem sent by the devil himself to tear down the faithful."

"Gaeten, have you ever been tempted by a woman? Have you ever married, or at least dated?"

"Well now, those are several very personal questions, my friend. And because you are my friend I will tell you. Married? No. Have I had female friends? Surely – and still do. Are any close friends? Certainly – Lydia and Suevey are two. Have I ever felt more than a brotherly love for a woman?" Gaeten was silent for a few minutes and Ethan waited patiently.

"Yes, Ethan. When I was a young man – not much older than you – I was a far different person. My eyesight was getting dim, but by that time I had long left the orphanage where I had grown up and struck out on my own. I was tough as nails and had an even tougher attitude, and that helped convince the Watchers to take me in. I don't think I am being prideful to say that I was excelling at my studies, both physical and mental. But it had gone to my head, and I was a very prideful, stubborn youth who felt he was better than most of his teachers and nearly all adults. Already I was a level 4 apprentice, and in reality my skills were likely a level or two higher – though my maturity certainly was not. And I had essentially no relationship with God at all."

Ethan suppressed a surprised cough. He had difficulty imagining Gaeten without God.

Gaeten sensed the surprise. "Yes, Ethan – with no parents and living by myself, I had no rules but my own, and I did whatever seemed right in my own eyes. I hid much of it from the Watcher Masters above me, knowing they would disapprove and maybe even expel me for the worst of my antics. But among my peers I was rather popular. And among the young women, I guess I was highly desirable. I would show off my prowess in front of them, and several began to show me quite a lot of attention. The Masters frowned very strongly on young apprentices having any relationships between males and females outside of total professionalism – rightly so – but it chaffed me to no end. Yet that rule saved me from taking any of the female relationships beyond the flirtation I engaged in.

Then I noticed a young woman in the Keep, the daughter of a local official. She was impressed with my muscles and skills, and I was impressed with her … well, with her body, mainly. She liked to flirt, and it was like a game to us, getting heavier and going further between us, each of us seeming to dare the other on. We were playing with fire without even acknowledging it – but we both eventually realized where it was headed physically … and that was not marriage; I had no intentions of settling down."

Ethan squirmed in his seat. "But I hear and see that sort of thing regularly. Well, maybe not so much from Watcher apprentices, but from young men I have met when traveling with my mother and father. It has never seemed right to me, but it seems pretty commonplace."

Gaeten paused. "Commonplace? Maybe. But as God's chosen people we are not called to be 'common'. We are held to higher standards, and those standards are to please God in all that we do. I wish I had done that. In hindsight, I praise God that we did not take it further. Had she become pregnant, our lives would have been far different, and not along the lines which God had wanted for us.

I was quite the rebel. I tried to avoid going to chapel whenever I could, but the Watchers were pretty strict about that. I tried my best not to listen. But one day the chaplain's message got through, and it was as though it was written specifically for me. I began to wonder what I was really doing, what my purpose was for even being alive. Right then, my existence seemed like quite a waste. But then I heard that God had a plan and purpose, and I could either join His plan or work against it. There was no middle ground." Gaeten was silent for a moment. "I surrendered my life to His will right then and there. From that point on I have purposed to view every female as a sister, and God has made it clear to me that His purpose for me was to be celibate and focus my entire life on pleasing Him. That is a calling, I believe – a calling to not work at nor worry about pleasing any spouse or the cares of this world, but to focus only on pleasing God. I can say that with time I no longer had any sensual desires for anyone, and now have so very many sisters in God that I can spend very enjoyable time with – without any sexual tension.

So, was I ever tempted – yes, certainly so. Young men at your age are full of such thoughts and desires. It takes a disciplined mind and faith to keep pure. But tell me, would you have gotten into such trouble if you had considered this Taleena … what did you say she called herself? Oh yes, Kaytrina … if you had only considered her just as a sister?"

Ethan chuckled. "Well … probably not in quite the same way … ok, very likely not. Though I think the poisonous perfume she wore did help break down my resolve. And she was really cute, at least on the outside."

Gaeten grinned. "Especially then it is important to keep your mind clear, focused and pure! And you later saw how ugly and evil she was on the inside! Poison in a pretty package is just as deadly. And impure thoughts are a poison within us, if they find a place to grab hold and stay. At your age in particular, random impure thoughts will come unbidden. But it is your responsibility to ensure they don't take root. Dismiss them promptly. Practice praising your heavenly Father for whatever beauty you see. The more you infuse your thoughts with God – talking to Him and listening all the time – the more you will see the world as He sees it, and respond accordingly. Purity is not easy or common – but that is why it is so highly valued, whether in gemstones or people."

Ethan looked puzzled. "But I don't think I had much choice! She poisoned me right from the start – I couldn't think straight!"

"Ethan, the drugs she used on you weakened your defenses and made you more susceptible and gullible – but they could NOT pull you away from your parents or God all by themselves. You cannot put the blame on anything or anyone other than yourself. Even Taleena's lies could not take root unless they were allowed to – unless they found some willing soil to get planted in."

"But I love my parents and God! I would never … I didn't really want to …" Ethan's words stumbled into silence. "Oh Gaeten, I was so … so …"

"So childish and immature? Yes, Ethan, you were. And proud. You probably thought that you would never fall into temptation, that you were beyond that. Am I correct?"

"Yeah, I guess so."

"Pride goes before destruction and a haughty spirit before a fall. Whenever you are thinking pretty highly of yourself, you can be sure you are not truly thinking about God, how He views you, or of others more highly than yourself. Remember, we are called to be servants. Servants first to God, but then also to each other."

"I guess I have a lot yet to learn, my friend."

"We all do, Ethan. We never should stop. God is the ultimate Master Teacher, and He never stops teaching us! And that, my friend is a very good thing. We need to pray to be willing students!"

Gaeten stretched and yawned. "We have a lot of riding to do tomorrow, so let's get some sleep."

"Thanks. Goodnight Gaeten." Even though he was tired, Ethan had a lot to think about.

The next day dawned mostly overcast, according to Ethan, which was to Gaeten's liking anyway since it could reduce the likelihood of being spotted from a long distance. He wished they knew if pursuit had started or not. He figured that even if it had, they likely had at least another half day or so before anyone could possibly get this far out of Kardern after them.

Ethan ensured the fire was out and that they left nothing behind, even burying the fire pit hole and scattering the stones. Then they saddled up and made their way back to the main road, figuring to make the best time possible while pursuit was likely still far behind. They went on at a steady fast walking pace for their horses all morning, and at noon departed the well worn trail again. They were in countryside with rolling hills and patches of fairly dense woods interspersed with occasional open fields. Gaeten had a good sense of direction, unhindered by eyesight, and he directed Ethan to take them a mile or so off the main road but to stay approximately parallel it. From then on it would be too dangerous for them to stay directly on the main thoroughfare.

From what Gaeten recalled being taught of the geography of the area, in another day they should turn north by north east, leaving the road behind and going cross-country to more directly head to the city of Cisteria. He had been told there were several Watchers there on assignment with a wealthy merchant named Matthias.

The afternoon travel was uneventful, and after fording a small stream they turned to follow it northward. A few hundred yards off the main trail they topped a small hill that overlooked a valley ahead and they stopped to rest the horses and themselves.

Ethan looked carefully in both directions. "For this being what looks like a main road, there don't seem to be many travelers on it. We have only had to stop in the woods twice so far today to avoid being seen."

"Yes Ethan. As I recall from my briefing before traveling to the Dominion, this area is generally not well travelled – it really is in-between the important coastal towns and too far inland for good trade. The more frequented trade routes are further to the north. We have only passed by a few farms. There are few here to see us, but then again those that do may take more notice. I think … wait! I hear horses – many horses – running hard!"

Ethan cautiously moved to the crest of the hill, where he could clearly see the road as it headed down into an open field. "Yes Gaeten … I see a dozen, no, more like a dozen and a half of riders, and they are pushing their horses pretty hard. And … yes, I see sunlight glancing off weapons. They must be soldiers."

"Then I think we have to assume that word is out on us. I wondered about the tavern where we ate – I sensed that the proprietor seemed to pay us extra attention. They probably are sending word out to all the major cities, and I expect they will start patrolling all the major roads and trails. They may send out real search parties too, trying to pick up our tracks. We will need to keep a very careful watch from here on out. There are several smaller towns we will be near, and we may need to supplement our supplies. That could get tricky. I think you should keep your bow strung and ready from here on out, and be watching to take down a deer or wild pig for food. I don't think I will be of much help there, though I can set out a few smaller traps wherever we camp tonight. Are you pretty sure we were not spotted?"

"I am sure, Gaeten – they were all focused on the road ahead and travelling too fast to pay attention anywhere else."

"Good. Let's get going then. I'd like to put some real miles between us and this road before nightfall. I can only guide us by dead reckoning to go in the approximate northerly and easterly direction – you will need to take the lead on our exact route."

"Sure enough." Ethan removed and with effort strung his bow and shifted some of the supplies to more easily access it. He slung the arrow quiver over his shoulder, then both mounted and continued their journey. The going was now much slower.

Murdrock was not particularly happy with his assignment. He was used to working alone or in small groups, and not to being under someone he considered so very his inferior. At least he had been given his choice of which patrol team to join. After pouring over maps of the region, he chose the team heading to Cisteria. If he were a Freelandian looking to escape Kardern on foot or horse, that would be the direction he would go.

He would have far preferred staying at Kardern and helping to set the final invasion strategies, but with the mood the Overlord was in, Murdrock felt it was much better for his long-term health – and life expectancy – to get out. And at least this had some potential for action. So he had given as much detail of the Freelandian defenses as he could and left.

Now he was actually more excited. That tavern owner truly had skill in observation, and had given them a great description of an older man with dark hair – that was easy enough to fake – and of a youth who had left on horseback on the eastern road. There had been no mention of the second man who witnesses said had helped the two other robed men in the castle courtyard, nor of the street urchin who was well known to have hung out with a blind former circus performer who asked too many questions in the local taverns … and who apparently had considerable knife skills. Murdrock also wondered about the boy, the Chancellor's son … the description given had been accurate enough, except for one glaring point. The boy the tavern keeper saw appeared overly thin, but otherwise in fine health. The last time Murdrock had seen him, Ethan had been one short step away from death's door. Somehow the old man must have had an antidote … or maybe found one while cleaning out that blasted Taleena's room.

Too bad the tavern proprietor had been so cooperative though – Murdrock would have enjoyed relieving some of his own stress by taking it out on a witness who needed proper encouragement to talk. Nevertheless, he was reasonably sure they were only a day to a day and a half behind the fleeing duo. And how far could a blind old man go with a youth who until recently had been terribly sick, especially when neither likely knew the local territory?

He checked himself at the thought. That blind old man had somehow gotten a job in the castle and had singlehandedly taken out both a Dark Magician and a much younger healer, and he had escaped the castle with a very sick young man with little apparent difficulty. And the tumult in Kardern was masterfully planned and carried out – when he left, the authorities were still trying to track down a supposed group of Freelandian spies that must have been behind the rioting – as reported by several street youth that had come forward with the information.

Murdrock chuckled – the Overlord had been sure that the prisoner was spirited out by ship from the dockyard, and the entire Dominion fleet was alerted to stop and inspect any Alterian ship, as well as a few others that had left Kardern that day. It had been a great ruse, which even he had believed was the likely escape route, until he had heard of additional rioting at multiple exit gates. If he had been planning an escape, he might have done something similar. He would have tried to leave from a gate near the castle, which all else would think the least likely. And Murdrock felt no particular need to inform the authorities in Kardern of their new-found information about a very suspicious twosome riding out to the east. He had convinced the patrol team leader to continue on in pursuit – no sense in giving a false alarm back in Kardern in case it turned out to be a wild goose chase.

Now if he could only be the one who re-captured that dratted Chancellor's son … now that would surely get him back into good graces with the Overlord! They would reach Cisteria in another two days of hard riding – it might kill the horses, but there should be plenty of new mounts available in a city of that size. He was pushing the patrol leader to go as fast as possible to cut off any possible escape route. Once they arrived and relayed the message, Murdrock planned to usurp the patrol leader's position with his seniority. Then he would take several of the best scouts and any other reliable soldiers and head back on patrol. From the map he had memorized, he already had several small towns and crossroads in mind to stake out. With any luck, he'd have both of the escapees within a week – one to send back to the Overlord safe and secure, and one to exact his frustrations on before delivering. He wanted a piece of that old man before Rath Kordoch finished him off.

Yes, this could still work out in his favor.

The cross-country route they were travelling was slow going. The horses had to pick their way around deadfalls, across small streams and up and down hills and valleys, often while contending with thick brush and trees. At least they had found some food – Gaeten's traps set out the night before had captured a rabbit and they had found wild leeks and tubers which tasted remarkably like potatoes. It was difficult on the horses – the country did not offer much forage. They had passed over several smaller trails, carefully watching to ensure there were no travelers passing by, and they had skirted around one small village. Ethan had wanted to ride in and replenish supplies, but Gaeten desired none of it, at least not yet.

So it was that as they exited a dense forest into a very secluded small empty glade that Gaeten called a halt after Ethan described their where-abouts. They dismounted and allowed the horses to forage in the succulent grass.

"Ethan, I need your eyes. Before we left Kardern I applied darker color-ation to my hair and skin, and to yours as well. I suspect that is wearing off by now – how do we look?"

Ethan chuckled. "Your hair is a brownish-blackish color with gray-white streaks showing through, and you have many light patches on your face and arms where the dye has rubbed off. From what I can tell, it is probably the same with me."

"Well, it was only meant to last a few days. We could reapply it, I sup-pose, but there is always the risk that it will get washed off at an inopportune time and make it look like we are trying to hide something. Besides, any descriptions that may have been given on us by now would likely include our darker hair and skin. There was a stream just a short distance back. Grab some moss we can scrub with, and we can take out most of the color-ation. Besides, we could both use a bath." He wrinkled his nose comically.

They left the horses and Ethan led the way back to the small creek. They found a slightly deeper pool with perhaps a few feet of water and proceeded to clean up. The day was bright and sunny, so it only took a short time to dry off. By the time they got back they figured the horses would have had enough and they could continue their slow-paced journey.

Gaeten and Ethan walked out of the bushes at the edge of the field and began to cross the open glade. Ethan was just a step ahead of Gaeten as they neared their horses under one of the few trees in the little meadow when he felt a hand touch his arm and heard a low whisper. "Someone is here, Ethan. Over past the horses."

Ethan tensed and stared, but could not see anything out of the ordinary … and no red indicators of danger had gone off in his mind either. Nevertheless, his hand whipped out a knife from its sheath and he warily moved forward toward the horses where the bow was secured. The horses were unaware of anything amiss, though they were starting to pick up on Ethan's tension.

Gaeten was concerned, and more than a little. His hearing was far more acute than the average person, and something had triggered an alarm bell in his head. It had taken a few moments to even realize what was wrong … the absence of insect noises from a small patch of ground ahead of them. He was not even totally certain of danger, but his sense of "wrongness" was now in full alert, and while he knew his own fighting abilities, he did not expect Ethan was in shape for hand-to-hand combat. His right hand was already on one of the throwing daggers he had stashed into his clothing and he was just about to throw first and ask questions later when a voice quite close behind him softly whispered, "Hold on that knife, most honorable Master Gaeten. I think Miguel De La Rosa will be of more use to us unventilated."

Gaeten was NOT an easy person to sneak up on. Very few had the superb stealth skills required. And very, very few might survive his startled response. Even as the first whispered syllable was uttered he was spinning sideways with a stiffened hand slashing through the air that should have terminated in an impact a few inches below its source. A leg sweep followed in milliseconds which should have flattened the by now choking culprit. Yet both hand and leg met no resistance as Gaeten spun through the air. Undeterred, Gaeten landed and was about to commence quarter-

ing the area around him for an undetected assailant when the words, and particularly the accent, finally registered.

Ethan had swiveled at the sound and movement behind him, dagger ready. A blue ribbon in his mind suddenly sprang up to direct his path away, and he heard a betraying rustle from the direction he had previously been looking toward. Without time slowing, Ethan was not fast enough to respond. Even as he was turning toward the new threat very strong arms clamped down, pinning his own arms in place.

"If you would be so kind to pause? Pardon my manners, but I must insist you cease from struggling." The words seemed nearly musical as they flowed in a strong accent different than the whisper he had heard behind Gaeten. It was not as if Ethan seemed to have any choice; when one's arms are pinned from someone close behind you there was only one real defensive option. As Gaeten had taught him, Ethan forcefully leaned backwards into the tight grip bringing him closer to his captor. Then, with as much speed and power as he could muster, he doubled over forward, thrusting his hips and buttocks out backward.

The maneuver was difficult to defeat, even for an experienced Watcher, and doubly so when one had no expectation of it coming from a relatively young man. Miguel let out a surprised "Oooofffhhh." His grip loosened as his tall frame suddenly bent over awkwardly. Ethan had learned well from his older teacher. As the hands loosened on his arms, he grabbed the one on his left, intent on bending it backwards as his own body swiveled and took a step sideways. The result should have been that his assailant would be forced to the ground and captured by the awkwardly bent hand and arm.

However, this was less likely to work on a highly experienced senior Watcher. The hand and arm were pulled back with more power than Ethan had anticipated, pivoting the boy off balance and back into the waiting engulfing arms. "I perceive the 'nephew of Lydia' has had some training, no? Perchance from none other than the most esteemed Grand Master Gaeten himself?"

Ethan struggled for a moment, but as he glanced up he could see Gaeten with his hands on his hips and a rueful smile on his face as he chuckled lightly. Ethan felt the hands holding him in a vise suddenly loose, and he took two steps sideways, watching Gaeten for a clue and then turning to finally get a look as his captor.

The man before him was tall, at least six foot two inches and thin, but with obviously well developed musculature. He had jet black wavy hair that even here in the wilderness looked nearly perfectly in place. His most distinguishing feature though was an impeccably manicured thin pointed mustache and matching goatee, which he thoughtfully stroked with one eye cocked skyward. Ethan turned back toward Gaeten and hid a smirk behind a hand.

Just outside the range of Gaeten's reach stood a bush ... well, it looked very much like a bush that had legs and arms, with a camouflaged face peeking out of the squat form. Ethan stared in wonderment. He and Gaeten had walked right by just such a bush before entering the meadow ... it couldn't have been ... He looked past them and saw there was no bush in the spot he would have sworn one had been a few minutes ago.

Gaeten stopped his chuckling and, sensing Ethan's confusion, introduced their new friends. "Ethan, God has blessed us with companions, I believe. The gentleman before me who is rustling like a tree is Master Watcher Chu Tang. He has been on assignment to an Alterian embassy in the northern Dominion ... though I last thought it was quite a bit further north and east from here. He used to teach at the Watcher Compound in the Keep years ago. Back then he was the only person I knew who could hide so well that I could only discover him about half of the time. I think I could have stepped on him just now and not even known it. It appears he still has that skill!

And the other gentleman who apprehended you is Miguel De La Rosa, senior apprentice Watcher, loaned out to a very prestigious art dealer who travels freely around the world making deals ... and a lot of money as I recall hearing."

"At your most distinguished service." Miguel bowed low with a flourish of his arms.

Chu spoke up – but his voice still seemed like a loud whisper. "I am glad we found you so quickly. The whole countryside seems stirred up. You must have caused quite the ruckus leaving Kardern."

Ethan was catching on rapidly, but still had questions. "But how did you find us? How did you even know we would be here – and what was that about 'Lydia's nephew?'"

"If I may, most honorable Master Chu? Yes? Alright then. In reverse order, if you please. Chancellor Duncan and Lydia sent a note out to all Watchers – worldwide as far as I know – to be on the lookout for her young male nephew – a reference we all realized was to you. The note also suggested that Gaeten here needed to be notified if any of us spotted him, and we had been alerted before about his undercover travels around Dominion port towns. It appeared probable that the Dominion had somehow spirited you off.

It seemed most likely that Master Gaeten would be in Kardern since it is the most important naval port of the Dominion in this entire large region, by far the closest to Freelandia and therefore the most logical pre-invasion base of operations. Master Chu and I both considered that the Dominion would probably bring such a prominent prisoner to a large, well fortified military city like Kardern, especially with the rumors of an Overlord visiting there.

As there are no Watchers in Kardern, Chu and I were working on a way to convince our principals – those we work for – to take a visit to Kardern shortly. That was proving troublesome, especially since my principal was instead planning an extended stay at his villa in Rhoditian. But then an Alterian ship stopped into Cisteria a few days back and its captain gave us a detailed run-down on the events happening in Kardern – seems they had left that port a few days prior and mentioned you might be heading in this general direction under hot pursuit. The stakes appeared rather high, and so Chu and I took a leave of absence with our principals and set out to find you to offer our assistance.

And lastly, how did we find you? Well, if we were leaving Kardern and wanted to find the quickest way back to Freelandia, then the port city of Cisteria would be the most logical destination, and there are only a few logical routes from Kardern to there. It was a rather simple task to check the various trails and roads that you would have had to cross, and look for the tracks of two horses going north easterly and avoiding any of the main pathways." Miguel looked rather pleased with himself as he pronounced the ease with which they had found them.

Chu spoke up in his soft voice. "And if we found you so easily, others with adequate tracking skills will too. We saw evidence of several sizable patrols on three different trails. I would bet that your markings either have already been picked up, or will be shortly.

Our horses are a short ways further. I suggest we get moving rather quickly. We have several days of travel yet. As we get closer to Cistern there will be far less cover and more small towns and villages to navigate around. If we move quickly enough, we may be able to outpace the patrols and trackers, and be out of this region before a sizable part of the Dominion army is sent out looking for you. We need to get going, now."

Gaeten and Ethan retrieved their horses and double mounted with Chu and Miguel. They rode off at a slow canter to recover the other horses, and then all four moved out. Chu took them further to the west to avoid a larger village, but they had to cross several main trails where Chu could only lightly cover their tracks – there was too much danger of stopping for more than just a minute once they had passed. By nightfall they have covered only half the distance that Ethan and Gaeten had done the previous two days, but it could not be helped. Being circumspect was more important than speed when they were desperately trying to avoid detection and especially so as they were likely moving directly toward a large body of enemy soldiers.

They made a camp with no fire. As the light dimmed Master Chu slipped out of their makeshift camp, explaining that he wanted to backtrack a few miles to see if there was any evidence that they were being followed. None slept very soundly, and when Chu returned a few hours before dawn all drew weapons at the sound of his entrance.

Gaeten spoke first. "There must be trouble – otherwise we would have never heard you come back."

"Yes, I hurried. As I suspected, at least one patrol has picked up our tracks. I climbed a tall tree at the edge of the field we crossed late yesterday, and spotted a campfire several miles further back. They are no more than half a day behind us. With daylight they will be able to move faster, and perhaps send scouts out to the main thoroughfares to alert others. By nightfall we could be easily surrounded within a widespread noose. We may be able to slip through with great skill – and of course God's mercy … or …"

Gaeten finished for him. "Or we turn the tables and bring the fight to them when they least expect it. I like your thinking, Chu!" Gaeten even rubbed his hands together in anticipation. It had been WAY too long since he had broken anything.

Miguel picked it up. "But we mustn't endanger our young charge here – at least not unnecessarily. Perhaps it would be best if we tucked him away somewhere safer while we spring our 'Freelandian Special' surprise?"

Gaeten chuckled. "You had only a small taste of his skills. Let me assure you, Ethan gives me a good challenge when we spar – though he has been quite ill recently and is still recovering. You saw he has a bow, and I rather expect one or both of you do as well? Ethan there is one of the most skilled archers we have at the Compound. He stays with us and will be a very valuable asset. Perhaps we could arrange for our pursuers to meet up with us at a location of our choosing, one where each of our skills can be best put to use against our enemy?"

"My thoughts exactly," whispered Chu.

They mounted and carefully made their way in the darkness back the way they had come, riding slowly for an hour until they reached the edge of the large open grassland they had crossed the day before, sparsely dotted with trees and clumps of low brush. Chu pointed out a particularly thick growth of chest high scrub that sprouted up in a dense cluster perhaps two dozen yards out into the grassland on a slight rise. He described it to Gaeten, and all agreed it was a near perfect position for archery sniping. Ethan was about to go explore it but Chu held him back.

"First, you must become a bush."

Miguel began to laugh. "You will most surely itch for the next week. Just make sure Master Chu in his immense wisdom does not wrap you in poison ivy or poison oak, or with leaves infested with ticks!"

Chu gave the innocently smiling Miguel a dark scowl. "At least I will not try to convince him to try to talk the soldiers to death!" He removed some fabric bands from a saddlebag and began to attach them around Ethan with small buckles. The bands had fuzzy yarn dangling all over, along with numerous small loops and what looked like netting. Once multiple such bands adorned him, Chu began to fasten small twigs, brush and leaves into the loops and snagged into the dangling moss-colored yarn. Satisfied with that, he next smeared mud and soot mixed with a few drops of water over every visible patch of skin Ethan figured he possibly had, and even some onto his clothes in jagged, irregular streaks.

It had only taken a few minutes, and the transformation was complete. "Now Ethan, this camouflage only helps you to stay hidden – you are hardly invisible! Instead, you must look like you belong as part of your surroundings, so that no one ever gives you a second glance. If you appear exactly like what someone looking your direction already expects to see, to them you are essentially invisible."

Ethan grinned. "Oh, sort of like what you did yesterday. It was totally expected that a bush might be where you were hiding, and so I did not even see you … I just saw a bush."

"Exactly. That is the art of going undetected in plain sight. But looking like a bush is not enough. You must also move like a bush. Your movements must be identical with your surroundings. When a breeze moves the brush, you must move in the same way – slow, steady, never rushed or jerky. Try to move and be as quiet as possible. Pretend you are part of the very brush you will be standing in. Be one with the bush."

Miguel could not help but comment. "Oh great bush-god, save us from the fearsome brush-beast our misguided Master Chu has created … let us not be pricked with a thousand thorns!" He barely ducked in time to avoid the rock chucked his way. Undaunted, he continued. "And bushy-god, may yonder boy-bush not become lost in his bushy-ness and become so one with the twigs that he takes root and we must transplant him when it is time to move along!" This time two stones were airborne while Miguel was still speaking, and though their aim was dead-on the senior apprentice Watcher adroitly ducked under one and neatly deflected the other with the dagger he held.

Gaeten restrained Chu from further launches. "While I may be spared from seeing your latest creation, I likely could use your talents as well – but I need a great deal of freedom of movement, much more so than our archer Ethan. I was figuring on staying just outside the tree line, with plenty of unrestricted space in front of me. We should spring our little trap just as they near the trees. A few will likely surge ahead … they will be mine just before they reach the apparent safety of the tree line."

"Mine too, sir Gaeten. If I know Master Chu, he will want his biggest sword and try to be right in their path, no? Between your young friend there with his bow and Chu, there may not be many left – but we would prefer none to remain to tell of our little adventure. I will be the rear-guard and dispatch any that may have the audacity to get past you. So … with great reluctance … I will succumb to the ministrations of our mossy friend here. But be gentle with me – I don't want to spend hours washing it all back off! Just a dab here and there, if you so please."

Chu grunted, mainly ignoring Miguel. When Chu had finished with the others he gathered some of the grasses and brush from the field and added them to the collection he was already wearing. They moved the horses well out of the way and brought their weapons back to the edge of the field. Chu and Miguel gave Ethan the quivers of arrows they had removed from their mounts.

"I think we have perhaps an hour. Maybe more, possibly a bit less," spoke Master Chu in his normal soft voice. "It is getting rather light out, and so I suggest we get settled into our positions – especially Ethan and I since we will be more easily spotted moving out in the open."

"Good. And perhaps Miguel and I may have time to rig up a few other 'surprises' for any of our forthcoming guests who do make it into the woods."

"Very good, Grand Master Gaeten. It is my honor to work with such a distinguished Watcher as you." Miguel turned to Chu. "Please be a good sport and let at least a couple through for us? I promise to save any ivy I find for your collection!"

Chu snorted derisively and walked out into the field, a short sword strapped to his side and a quite long slightly curved sword in his hand, which he had freshly blackened with his soot and water mixture.

Gaeten turned toward Miguel. "Do you always spar with him like that?"

"Oh, no Master Gaeten." Miguel had a contrite expression that only Ethan could observe. "Usually it is much worse, I'm afraid. You see, Master Chu …" Miguel and turned to point to the figure who had just walked out into the field, and Ethan's eyes followed his pointing finger ... but there was no one to be seen. Ethan stared intently at the tall grassy landscape. Surely the Watcher had to be right ... there ... but nothing at all looked amiss or out of place. Ethan tried to spot the outline of human shape, but to no avail. Master Watcher Chu had disappeared.

"Ah, there he goes again, evaporating like mist in the morning. I can be discussing most urgent, important matters – like where to have lunch – and he just ...poofs ... and is gone. Oh well, it has saved me from buying his lunch on more than one occasion. Now then Ethan – do be careful and make sure you don't stick any bushes with your arrows? No?"

Murdrock made his base camp at one of the more central small villages, requisitioning the best room at the local inn, which also served as the area's tavern. He organized patrols of all the major and minor roads and held a small contingency of soldiers with him, ready to ride out at short notice. He also sent a request to the garrison at Cisteria for additional troops. It was nearly certain that the blind man – likely a Watcher spy – and the boy were close by. He felt he could nearly smell them. A scout had already found tracks leading this direction that appeared to be a few days old, so it would only be a short matter of time and he would have them. Even now, one of the patrols was hotly following their trail, and by the day's end may even affect the capture. And if not, the added pressure of avoiding hot and close pursuit would make the Freelandians take greater risk in their flight, charging forward into an almost certain trap as all patrols and extra soldiers were now tightening their noose around the area.

He had appointed a secondary team to ride hard to join the first patrol, and they should rendezvous ... he estimated ... around noon. In the best case, they would provide additional security for the triumphant ride back, or perhaps join in on the capture itself. Murdrock wondered if he should plan his victory speech for the Overlord for when he presented the re-captured prisoner and would-be rescuer. Well, maybe not just yet.

The lead tracker rode perhaps fifteen yards ahead of the others, picking his way carefully as he watched for the telltale signs of the two horses he had been following now for two days. Only for the last few hours it had been four tracks. So either this was not the two they were searching for, or they had met up with assistants … it made his work all the easier and allowed even faster movement. The tracks were not overly difficult to follow – for the last full day he had not seen any real attempt of the subjects to mask what they were doing, except for a few fairly well done road crossings. He knew it was rather difficult to hide the passage of four horses, especially cross-country unless the ground was very rocky.

He broke through a tree line into a field, which the tracks clearly crossed. He could have let the others catch up and confer with their patrol leader, but he had no intention of getting another tongue lashing for not keeping them moving at the fastest possible speed. And these tracks were clearly from the previous night, so they still should have at least several hours of hard riding to catch up to their quarry. He shrugged and urged his horse on into a fast loping canter. The field was several hundred yards across and they had to be traveling several times faster than their prey … and so they would catch up to them all the sooner.

Gaeten heard the single horse hoof beats and a few moments later the thunder of many charging steeds. This was really not his best element. He was far surer of himself in closer quarters where eyesight might only give his foes a split second benefit. Out in the totally open grassland he would be at a very distinct disadvantage. At least here with the woods to his back he should be able to fend better. He had considered moving inside the tree line, but there it was much too easy to trip on some unnoticed root or crack his head on any low limbs. He had walked the entire area twice in the last hour, including the immediate woods, familiarizing himself on everything he could touch and feel with feet and hands. He had also found a stout pole of about seven feet in length as a hefty staff. Between that and his knives he was ready … not that he really needed those either. They just made it more … interesting. Gaeten was kneeling, looking to a distant onlooker like a natural part of the grassland merging into woods. Once the riders were close it would not matter what he looked like anymore … he would look like death coming for an intimate visit.

Ethan both heard and saw the first rider emerge from the far tree line, and a moment later a group of nearly twenty horsemen broke out and began to gallop across the grassland. His location was no more than twenty or so yards from the trail of their tracks. Bow in hand and arrow nocked, he slowly rose to stand, reaching just under the highest branches of the bushes to his side and behind him. He craned to see all of the riders, looking for the straggling few that would be his first targets. Already faint blue lines were forming in his vision, though the only solid line was to the scout far ahead of the rest. He was the only enemy within range yet. The trouble would not be finding a target, it would be in choosing which to start with – in what shortly would become a very target-rich killing field.

Then he remembered his instructions, and began to slowly sway in the faint breeze. Think like a bush … I'm a bush … don't look over here; it's just us bushes ….

Miguel leaned against a large oak near the edge of the field. He had noticed the scout coming at them quickly, but the rider was still quite a ways out – at least 100 feet …no need to hurry. His hands reached for the hilts of his matching long swords, after he first ensured his mustache did not have any leaves stuck in it. It just would not do for his enemies to think they were getting perforated by a stray tree branch!

The scout was losing his advanced position as the remaining riders thundered across the field at full gallop. The tracks he was following were clear enough in the soft soil, and so he urged his steed to greater speed to reach the tree line. Once there he saw the hoof marks to follow and at a much slower pace he began to push on through the outer tree branches. As he was brushing aside a few of the branches he turned to look back just as the other riders were starting to slow … and just when the world erupted into violence.

Ethan had already taken out the three furthest back riders at the very outer edge of his bow range, no one even noticing as his shots advanced forward. Vibrant blue lines glowed brightly and the horses were charging forward at what seemed more like a slow stately walking speed … at least in Ethan's reality. His hands and arms were a blur as he began to rapid fire at the mounted soldiers. He was moving so fast that even had any of them been looking his way, the motion would have appeared to be just a blurred … bush.

Those toward the front of the pack did not realize what was happening behind them for several moments. As more bodies fell though, it rapidly became obvious something was very, very wrong. Six more bodies fell from their mounts, falling out of the way for clear shots at yet more riders. Horses began to whinny in surprise and fear as the charging soldiers stopped just outside the trees in total confusion. Two horses suddenly reared upward as an apparition rose from the ground right in front of them and a long black blade began to flicker back and forth. Men and horses screamed in terror and pain as the blade bit again and again and again.

What had started as a fairly orderly double file of riders disintegrated into a melee of churning dirt and whinnying horses with wild shouts of disarray. Soldiers and steeds whirled about and began to scatter, looking for an enemy that only a few in the center of the pack could even see. Three more men fell with arrow shafts sprouting from their bodies.

Several riders wheeled to their right to escape the slaughter. One fell after only taking a few steps forward, clutching a knife hilt protruding from his chest. Three others drew swords and charged forward at the white-haired man that had suddenly appeared only a few yards before them.

The first was just raising his sword for a brutal downward slash when a stout wooden pole lifted him right off his saddle and flung him backwards. The second came a step closer when his steed plowed nose first into the ground as its legs tangled with the same pole that seemed to be in two places at once. The third was having second thoughts and was turning aside and beginning to gallop off when the staff-turned-spear crashed into his back to cause an unplanned and unwelcome dismount.

Gaeten heard the first unhorsed soldier pick himself up and come charging even as he was flinging the staff forward with great velocity. Gaeten dived aside to avoid the first sword slash and came up as the second soldier came stumbling forward with his own sword up. The third was not rising, having broken his neck during his wild fall.

The two soldiers moved to corner Gaeten in between them, sword points held low and ready. For Gaeten, this was almost easier. There were now no horses to get in the way, and at least he had some challenge with the two of them. Not a lot, but at least some. His opponents looked warily at each other and then back to the obviously blind old man standing before them with no weapons in his hands versus their swords. Gaeten grinned widely. Breaking time!

The patrol leader had been out in front, and as he turned in confusion the only thing that registered immediately was that the large majority of horses he could see were rider-less. He made a command decision. A wrong one as it turned out. He spun back forward and dug his heels in, charging ahead and away from whatever demon nest had been stirred up behind him. The scout had already concluded that forward appeared a much better route to take, and one of the two remaining soldiers followed suit. The last rider in the now decimated line turned and bolted sideways at full gallop, away from the bush demon whose demonic sword had decimated every solider within reach just ahead of him and the strange white haired man to his right who was even now leaping into the air with a twisting kick that downed his last opponent.

With another soldier and his horse pressing in directly behind him, the patrol leader could only surge directly forward along the hoof-marked trail. He only made it past the second tree when his lieutenant, directly behind him, ducked under the first branches and looked up in time to see a heavy log come swinging down in a tight arc directly into his hapless leader. The change in command did not last long. The lieutenant drove his mount to the left and before his eyes a leaf-and-twig-festooned man suddenly appeared in front of him. The soldier did not even have time to lift his drawn sword as two bright metal blades drove into his chest. The last conscious sight was of a dark-haired man with an annoyed expression brushing a leaf out of his trim mustache.

The scout had swerved further to the left and had stopped for just long enough to see the patrol leader come face to face with a log swinging down on a rope pendulum. He turned and dug in his heels hard and gave his mount full lead to exit the death scene as quickly as possible. His horse only took a few strides forward before it reared without warning with a whinny of pain, dumping him unceremoniously onto the ground. He landed reasonably well, rolling and avoiding banging into any tree trunks. As he righted himself he drew his saber and watched in horror as a second rider just off to his side tumbled from his steed as what looked like two swords stabbed the life from him. He recognized the form as being a man, covered in some sort of camouflage that made him blend into the trees and shrubs quite well. In his periphery vision the scout could see his own horse gyrating on the ground a short distance away, and he thought he could make out a knife hilt projecting out of its hind quarters. The scout only made two steps forward before the prey-turned-predator turned to face him, two swords wide apart at low ready position, tips ominously pointed at his own heart.

The bolting rider in the field had turned away from Master Chu and Gaeten, and in half a second was beyond throwing reach. Both rider and horse were terrified and moving away at great speed, but great speed was a relative thing … at least to Ethan. An arrow lifted the soldier clean off his horse and even before the body tumbled to the ground a second arrow struck, though it had hardly been really necessary. Ethan looked down. He still had a small handful of arrows left, but there were no more targets … and for sure he did not want to hit any moving bushes.

Ethan, Miguel and Chu gathered as many of the horses as they could, and added to their collection of clothing, supplies and weapons. Then they roped together sets of four horses each and sent them off in different directions across the field. Anyone following would not know which set of four tracks were actually theirs. Less than an hour after the trap had been sprung, the four travelers were heading across the field and into the far tree line for several miles before turning north again. Master Chu had taken some of the collected clothing and wrapped them around the horse's hooves. It was not for long term, but between that and his ministrations as he trailed behind the others, stopping now and then to even further disguise the tracks, it would make following them much more difficult than before – but there were only so many places they could be heading toward.

Chapter 11

Finishing Touches

Lydia nearly ran into Duncan's office. "Something has happened with Ethan – I can feel it!" Duncan's face first went pale, but on seeing the smile on her face he forced himself to relax. She continued. "The Spirit has not yet shown me what, but he is safe ... or at least safer than he had been. I ... I admit I was beginning to lose hope. I was getting resigned to ... to ... losing him. But something changed. It is like a tiny pinprick of light in a vast black darkness ... but it is there and growing stronger and brighter."

Tears formed in Duncan's eyes before he closed them in prayer. "Thank you, God for saving our son. Please bring him back ... show Your glory and might to the world. The Dominion has set itself against You, declaring that their gods are more powerful than the true God. Don't let your name be tarnished! Bring about Your will. And, if it is within Your sovereign will, let us have our son back. Yet we will praise Your name regardless." Duncan looked up, tears in his eyes from his prayer.

Oldive looked with pride at his latest creation. While general armor was being cranked out with the new metal as fast as it could be produced, he had grander plans. Before him was a masterpiece, if he said so himself. It was a whole suit of armor, from head to toe – but with at least twice the maneuverability and at a fourth the weight of any suit of armor he had ever seen. He had it hanging alongside of what was considered the top-of-the-line Dominion armor, supposedly the most advanced design available that Master James had procured from who-knows-where. From that he had copied various features and tested different attributes, and then, being the Master Engineer that he was, he began to tinker with and improve on the basic design.

From his testing, Oldive knew what kind of projectile had the best probability of penetrating the Dominion armor, at what velocity and shape, and where its weakest points were located. Spring guns were adjusted accordingly, for whatever could defeat this armor would likely work even better against lesser versions.

When the new metal alloys had become available, his tinkering had gone into high gear. He originally wanted to know how to best copy an improved design for Freelandian use. Now he could do far more – he could do far better. Of course, static testing could only do so much ... at some point the first such new suit would have to be made and tested. That was now finished – and it fit him perfectly. After all, someone had to try it out ….

The total weight of his metal suit was only about twenty pounds, not unnoticeable but easily managed. However, even with his adaptations it was still awkward to move about in it. Yet, with some practice, he found he could walk and actually even run in it. It may not be for the dance floor, and he surely would not want to be in the water with it on, but on a battlefield? Well, that he was ready to test.

CLANK … CLANK … CLANK … CLANK. Master Oldive walked across the testing grounds in loud footsteps. He'd have to oil a few of the joints better, and it may be worthwhile to try adding something to the soles of the metal boots to give better grip ... and make less noise. His assistants looked dubious, though they were not the ones in any particular danger ... except possibly from splinters. The first swung a hefty stick at him. Oldsy tried not to cringe, though it took considerable self control. Instead, he raised one arm and angled it so that the staff struck a raised ridge, where it splintered on impact. Some experimentation had shown that while smooth curves used less metal, weighed less and were less likely to catch on anything, they also tended to transmit a lot of blunt force onto the skin beneath. At best it caused bruising, even with padding. At worst it could allow broken bones. However, the new metal was so light he could incorporate reinforced ridges to stiffen strategic areas and which could disperse the force. He had also found that thin layers of certain clays packed into flat sheets and pressed into woven fabric seemed to dissipate impact force when placed between the armor and skin in strategic locations. It added slightly to the weight, but made the suit far more comfortable – the clay tended to absorb much of the copious sweat worked up within minutes and it definitely softened the sting of a hard blow.

Another apprentice approached apprehensively. He swung a light weight sword, wincing as it struck Master Oldive across his ribcage. Too bad for the sword, its edge was ruined while barely scratching the armor. This new metal alloy was light, hard and quite tough. "Harder boy ... swing it harder!" His voice was muffled considerably, though he had fabricated an array of small slits in the helmet over his mouth and nose. He had added other small holes and slits as vents in other places, and he was particularly proud of the work for the visor. Not only could the front of the helmet swing upward and hold open, but he had fabricated raised metal ridges over the eye area and fastened a hardened wire mesh over each eye hole. His vision was still obstructed and limited, but it was a far, far improvement over the Dominion visor which just had a very narrow slit to peer out of.

The apprentice shrugged – he worked directly for another Master Engineer, so if he accidentally ended up killing this one he would not be out of a job anyway. He reared back and swung hard.

It was incredibly difficult for Oldive to not jump aside or even raise an arm to ward off the blow ... but he had done this himself to the suit hanging on a rack and he had to trust his own pre-testing. But what if there was a weak point he had not noticed? What if the metal had cracked in just the wrong spot? What if ... CLANG! The sword hit squarely and ... bounced off harmlessly. Oldsy looked at the impact spot, and could see a barely discernable dent in the metal. He had felt the impact, but doubted it had even caused a bruise. Ok, that had worked.

The apprentice picked up a much larger, heavy scimitar. A strong blow from that could easily cleave off whole limbs ... or one's head. Oldsy steeled himself as the apprentice swung. His only real mistake was in not setting his feet wide enough apart. The force of the blow bowled him right over and he landed with a metallic crash.

"Ho there, it looks like the metal man fell ina heap. Maybe you shoulda built in some of your springy-thingys so you would bounce!" Robby laughed at his own joke, and he assumed the horrific cackle he heard from the motionless metal mess on the floor was chuckling noises – otherwise it was someone being rather sick ... not at all a pleasant thought if one was inside a closed suit of armor! "Here now, let me helps you up, me goodly friend Oldsy. A suit o'armor can weigh a ton. I've heard say that few Dominion armored riders can barely pick themselves upright if they are unhorsied if they have their heaviest and strongest suits on, and even their lighter suits take a mighty strong man to move about in."

Robert reached down and grabbed a proffered gauntleted hand. He put his back into it and pulled hard – and nearly had Master Oldive crash right into him as he came up easily from the floor. "Great God Almighty! That suit hardly weighs a thing! Are you sure'in you're all in one piecey – that light o'metal could hardly have protected you from such a sword strike!"

Oldive lifted up his visor and grinned at the Chief Engineer. "Take a look." He turned so Robby could look at the chest piece where the sword strike had impacted. A narrow crease and scratch in the metal was all there was to show for it. "It can take a quite strong hit. I was finally able to get through a similar thickness sheet of the stuff with a heavy axe after five or six blows. I suppose if you had a weighted axe or war hammer that came into a point – like a nail point – that you could probably puncture through it. But we have not been able to breech it with any arrow except from the spring guns we've prepared for the pachyderms, or any of the bigger mounted versions. I think it would even survive a hail of rocks and nails from one of the catapults or maybe even from one of Arianna's bombs ... though I have no intention of letting her try one out on me!"

"Aye, that's a smart 'nuff move there, me friend. And I'm none too sure it woulda survive the tongue lashing I got this mornin' either for that matter."

"Oh, you and your lovely wife have a spat did you?"

"That's just the thingy, Oldsy. I went and married the woman as she wanted ... even planned a special night of it, even asked the good Chancellor and Lydia for help and all ... and now she's complaining that it went all too fast and none of her girly friends or kin were present for the nuptials! I told her, I did, that with the war an all we 'ad no time for a fanciful grandy wedding … that if that was stuck in her craw I supposed we could go about it sometime later … but I says to her that this way was much lighter on me pocketbook, combining the marriage thingy with a nice dinner, and that me much preferred to have a good meal in me first off anyway."

"Oh, you told her all of that, did you?" Master Oldive was laughing hard by now.

'I canna see what ye think is so awfully funny now. I tells her that this mornin', right after asking her ta fix me a nice breakfast like a goodly wifey should. I'ma thinking I needs a suit like yours Oldsy, 'fore I be asking agin tomorrow 'morn!"

"Oh … oh Robby! Stop already, will ya? I never build this suit to laugh in it so hard!"

"Hmmph. Women!" He looked down at his good friend. "I tell ya man, I love her like the sun rising in the morning, like nothing and no one else in God's creation and I thank me heavenly Father for bringing her into me life, but I canna say I understand her very well yet, leastwise not about this fanciful marriage thingy … or maybe not just in the early morn!"

Oldive had straighten up from his laughter and now stood stiffly. "Well, you will learn to … probably slowly, knowing you. But you really should be asking for things, not ordering!" Oldsy jutted out his chin and darted his eyes back and forth a few times.

"Ach, but I was expectin' me bride to wait on me at least a wee bit, specially like the first few days of martial bliss."

"Robby, I think you meant 'marital' bliss." Oldive's eyes continued to dart back and forth.

"Oldsy, did ya pick up some type o' twitch from wearin' that suit? It seems to me …"

Master Oldive nodded his head to one side while jutting out his chin again. Robby looked perplexed, but then shook his head and rolled his eyes and gave out a huge sigh. "She be right behind me now, is that it?"

Arianna grabbed one of her husband's arms and spun him around. Her eyes flashed with fire, but her smile was genuine and warm. "Bobby, if you were not such a romantic … the sun rising in the morning and all … I would just bean you with one of Oldives hammers here. As it is, I guess

I will just have to keep working to take the rougher spots off you. Maybe Oldsy has a file around here I could use for that?"

Robby smirked. "You can rough me up anytime you want, me sweetie!" He spread his arms out wide in mock surrender. Arianna rolled her eyes and Robby took that split second of inattentiveness to wrap her into a tight hug. She squealed in surprise, causing Robby to laugh uproariously while Arianna sputtered but made no great effort to get away. If anything, her squirming brought her into his embrace even further until she stifled his laughing with a kiss. Just as his attention was fully consumed, Arianna gave him a not-so-light sucker punch to a kidney.

Robby gasped, released his spitfire wife and took two quick steps backwards, with eyes wide in surprise while Oldive roared. "Now why'd ya do such a naughty thing!"

Arianna jutted her chin out in a pouty look. "Because you took entirely unfair advantage of me, Chief Engineer. I would have expected more professionalism from you. Now at least one of us has serious work to do today." With that she spun around and began to march off.

Robby stared in near total confusion, first at Oldive and then at his retreating wife. He whistled, partly in disbelief and partly at her disappearing shapely figure. As she turned a corner to leave, Arianna looked back with a sly smile, winked and gave a wiggle just for him. "Ach Oldsy, I dunno 'bout that woman, but I surely aim to do lots of homework to figure her out!"

"It will take the rest of your life, my friend … and you will still be wondering."

Robby sighed and turned back to look at Master Oldive, who was removing his helmet. "So Oldsy, it looks like your armor ideas were successful. How soon do ya think we could be rolling out such suits for our army?"

"Oh my, Robby! This is the first full prototype, and I already have a few modifications I think I want to try. And we have just begun making quantities of this new alloy – I commandeered most of the world's supply to make this, and it took four or five apprentices nearly two full weeks to get to here. With all of the other weaponry we are working on, I cannot spare more than a dozen apprentices tops on this right now. I figure on perhaps a dozen suits in a month, mainly for further testing and refinement. Then in, oh, let's say three or four months we could consider a low level production like, maybe getting a suit out every other day or so, if we do not run into problems."

"I donna know if we have that kind o'time."

"Maybe so, but that is the best I think we can do. Even if you doubled my apprentices I doubt we could go much faster."

"Ach, then do whatcha can, me Amour Master." Robby spun about and walked out of the engineering shop.

Oldive removed his gauntlets, pondering how he could produce more suits. He had limited options. Therefore he would have to prioritize, and he had just the first two test subjects – candidates he corrected himself – in mind. He figured he probably should speak to Master Warden James to see who should be next in line, and get them sized up as soon as possible. He did not personally really want to get into production details; he was more of an inventor of new things. Still, he needed to get a larger batch of prototypes made, since that was typically when you discovered missed flaws, and when you still had a chance to correct them. It would be awhile before any real production could be up and running – and he had several ideas to incorporate into the next models that he wanted to try. And something the Chief Engineer had just said had gotten him thinking … yes … it just might be worth a try.

The concert was by invitation only, stating it was only for senior Freelandian leadership and senior Music Academy apprentices and Masters. The invitations came from the office of Grand Master Vitario himself, and Chancellor Duncan had also signed them … so it was really a "command" performance.

The concert hall began to fill, with the tickets being collected and younger apprentices ushering people to their seats. Minister Polonos looked out over the crowd from where he stood on the main platform. He was rather excited by what was about to occur … and to think that God had given the idea to three young ladies responsible for an impromptu "café band" that had spawned numerous copies throughout the city!

The various leaders were greeting one another and striking up conversations with the many interspersed senior Music Academy apprentices and Masters. Quite a number of the non-academy guests seemed agitated, and from several areas about the hall Polonos could hear complaints from people who felt their schedules were much too busy to be bothered with, of all things, a concert. In a few more minutes the hall was filled and curtains were drawn closed over the windows, leaving the hall dimly lit except for the stage.

Minister Polonos walked out to the center of the lit stage to address the seated crowd. "Citizens of Freelandia, welcome! I thank all of you for coming to this special concert. We realize it takes away from your busy and very important duties of preparing our country for the inevitable war. And we too are preparing for war ... yes, even here at the Academy of Music. For our battle, both now and upcoming, is not just with the Dominion forces we can see. No, our war is also in the heavenlies, with the spiritual forces of darkness and evil.

Therefore our defenses are not just those we can touch and feel and see. The defenses you are preparing are important, but only one part of what our real DEFENDER will use. This is God's battle. Our prayers are certainly part of our spiritual defense. There are others too, and tonight with God's grace you will be more formally introduced to another – one Chancellor Duncan, Lydia, Master Warden James, Grand Master Vitario, myself and many others believe is vitally important. We are about to do something our spiritual enemy HATES, hates with intense passion. And before we are done, Lord willing, we will be doing it with overflowing passion ourselves.

Interested? Skeptical? I suspect both. So be it. I only ask you to open your heart to God – ask Him how He wants you to respond. Please don't resist the Spirit tonight. If you do, the enemy wins."

Polonos paused and there were scattered intakes of breaths as his words sunk in. "Yes, you heard me. If you sit here tonight with hard hearts, thinking that you should be elsewhere, that you're much too busy to be here tonight – then YOU are letting the devil win in your own hearts. Your leadership does know how important you are ... and that is precisely why you were requested to come."

He allowed another, long pause. "Gentlefolk, prepare your hearts and minds for war ... of a different kind, and in a different arena than you are used to. You came here tonight as leaders ... but Lord willing you will leave as warriors!" Polonos smiled graciously and backed away from center of the stage.

From the dark shadows behind the stage several big kettle drums began a steady beat, starting very slow and then gradually picking up into a marching tempo. Fifes joined in, staying with the marching beat in a very simple tune. Master Ariel stepped forward, guitar in hand, smiling at the audience. "Greetings, warriors of Freelandia! Yes ... warriors! Our enemy is truly the devil and his minions. Everyone who calls on the name of the True God is the enemy of evil and at war with wickedness! Now we do not fight spiritual forces with sword and bow. We have far more powerful weapons and defenses than those – weapons each one of you possess. Tonight, we have a training session – boot camp if you will! But it is more than just practice. Tonight, we stand against the enemy! Tonight we launch an attack ... we fight together!

Now some of you are likely thinking ... how can I fight? I am too old, too weak, unskilled in warfare! Ha! That is what the enemy wants you to think. We are here to prove that wrong. So to lead us, we have one of our most potent warriors coming out ... a giant warrior already proven in spiritual battle."

Ariel stood to the side and a thin tall screen was illuminated from behind by flickering torchlight. A huge shadow was cast onto the screen, easily identified as the outline of a person walking toward the front of the stage. As the figure neared the screen other torches lit up and the first extinguished, making the shadow grow enormously until it stood just behind the screen, rather menacingly. A few people in the audience actually gasped and pushed backwards in their seats. Ariel giggled and pulled on the screen edge. It was on wheels and rolled easily aside. Out stepped ... Maria, with the Diamond Violin in her small hands.

Maria was nervous, but very excited at the same time. This felt like what she was here for, at least a partial fulfillment of her God-ordained destiny, what her gifting was given for, the culmination of her entire life ... to lead people in worship warfare. She smiled, waiting a few moments for the chuckles to subside, as well as the few gasps and murmurs of "Isn't that The Singer from Sir Reginaldo's concert?"

With the backdrop of the now more softly playing fifes and drums, Ariel reached over and held Maria's hand, guiding her forward to the very front center of the stage. Maria took a deep breath to calm her nervousness and smiled when Ariel gave a last squeeze of her hand. "Hello everyone, I'm Maria. You may have heard that I am an orphan, and I am blind. God does not hold that against me, and I hope you will not either. Because standing before God, what I mainly am is a worshiper. And so are you! Tonight, we begin in earnest our worship warfare. I don't think our enemy is going to like it one bit … and I sure hope not! But I think … I truly think God will like it – that it will please Him. That makes it worthwhile to do all by itself. If it pokes the devil in the nose, all the better!"

The audience chuckled again. "Oh good, you are out there! I was a bit worried that the other apprentices had me all set up to sing in front of an empty hall – I would not have easily known the difference!" More laughter erupted, and now the audience was both at ease, and rather curious as to what was about to happen next.

Maria smiled and lifted the violin to her chin. Inside she prayed. "Oh God, open the hearts of your people to your Spirit. Let them feel your power in this music. Let them lose themselves in love for and in worship of You. May my actions, words and thoughts bring You and only You honor and glory. None for me, all for You." She took a deep breath, and then drew the bow across the strings to join in on the simple melody.

There was just something so … so very captivating when Maria played, thought Grand Master Vitario. It was palpable, like something reached right out and touched you, grabbed your heart, and brought you closer to God's presence. And it was as though his own spirit was joining into something far bigger, far grander. He was joining with God's Holy Spirit, and that part of God's Spirit that resided within him vibrated in tune with the worship.

Maria began to sing, both in the theater and in her special place. It was a new song, one she and Kory had been working on the last week. It was an adoration of their heavenly Father, but while most such songs they had sung before were soft and gentle, this one was much more strident and forceful, flowing with the marching drumbeat. Ariel joined in, with guitar and dulcet voice, and soon other instruments located behind them, out of sight, added their accompaniment. The lyrics shifted to proclaim God's might and protection of His people, proclaiming Him to be the conquering King of Kings and Lord of Lords and ending with a triumphant shout of God's victory.

The audience was dumbfounded. They had never heard such a stirring, rousing rendition of worship. Some began to weep, others leapt to their feet in applause, while still others sat in silent awe. Some were rejoicing that they had indeed attended rather than made some excuse to stay at work.

Maria waited a few minutes. She could hear the effects the praise song had engendered, and she rejoiced. When the noise subsided, she spoke up. "Leaders of Freelandia … this is worship warfare. This is the type of praise we are preparing." She paused again. "We have just begun."

She began again on her violin, this time in a more complicated score but with a similar marching tempo. She was back into her special place – well, she really had not left it since entering early into the first song. Somehow, she could be in both places at once. And the special place was different today – it was brighter, more joyously vibrant than ever before and the musical ribbons seemed infused with extra life and energy. It was even more welcoming than ever and her audience of One seemed even more majestic … and close. God's presence was so very real.

As the other musicians joined in, Maria began to blend the sounds and energy together once more, creating an integrated whole that burst out from the stage in both the physical and spiritual dimensions. The very air seemed joyously alive. Kory and several other singers came out onto the stage and Maria joined their voices. Her violin playing became simpler while her voice more complicated. If spiritual passion had a sound, it could hardly be sweeter than what flowed and circulated around the auditorium.

The concert went on in like manner for perhaps another hour of charged worship, quite unlike anything the audience had ever experienced. The large majority of the people in the theater hall had tears running down their faces as they stood, kneeled and sat. It was exhilarating, energizing, encouraging. Master Ariel came forward again and the music died down, all except for Maria and Kory playing a soft duet. "Gentlefolk of Freelandia, you have experienced a part of what we believe is our – the Academy of Music's – contribution to the war effort. We have two songs left, but now it is your turn to join with us – not just in spirit as you have been, but with your own voices. We realize you may or may not be gifted vocalists – if you were, you most likely would be part of the Academy here already! But you all can sing, even if you cannot carry a tune. God wants your worship in spirit and in truth – singing in tune is just a bonus! You have now felt for yourselves the power there is in praise and worship, but there is much more to it than vicarious listening. You need to join in. There is something special that happens when you join your voice with others ... there is a multiplication of spiritual blessing and power.

Now some of you may be getting nervous – you won't be asked to come up on the stage to perform! Sit, or better yet stand, where you are and join us. The first song will be the one we started with. We will go through it a couple of times, and we have a surprise to help you feel more comfortable. Let us start, and then join in. After that we will conclude with our national anthem, *Freelandia*. Let's give our God and Father the praise He deserves – with everything we have within us. No one will be noticing you. You are not performing. You are worshiping God – this is just between you and Him." Ariel turned as several ceiling to floor banners began to unfurl with huge block lettering which said: Truth – You are Worship Warriors! She smiled. "Don't forget this truth. You ... each one of you ... have a warrior role in our fight with evil."

Other banners unfurled, displaying the song lyrics as she stepped back and joined the small ensemble with Maria at its center. The drums began their beat and in a moment, the senior Academy 'guests' scattered about the auditorium – who were all talented singers themselves – began to join in one by one. The acoustics of the hall were designed specifically to direct sound from the stage outward ... not in the other direction. But the building's designers had not really counted on the gift God had bestowed on Maria. The volume of the singers grew as the hundred or so assigned vocalists strategically placed throughout the audience stood and added their richness to the swelling song. Somehow, the sound was magnified, spread and returned in a perfect whole. Without further prompting, the rest of the audience began to pick up the words and add their voices.

No one at the Academy of Music ever remembered doing anything remotely like this. The closest comparisons would be to singing at a church, but those tended to be slowly played hymns with great theological content but which often lacked much emotion or energy. Comparing that to what was happening within the concert hall, on the other hand, was more like comparing a small campfire to a volcano. The intensity grew as every person stood and sang with all their heart, mind, strength and soul.

Grand Master Vitario looked upward, partly from the coursing joy that filled his very being, and partly out of wonder. The power of the volcanic praise soared, swelled and threatened to lift the very rafters. Vitario for a moment wondered if they were literally lifting the ceiling, but then instead realized the very ground upon which the building stood must be shaking. For a split second he felt a panic rise at the thought of an earthquake that could wipe out the entire top tier of Freelandian government. But then a warm blanket of peace settling down over him. This was no ordinary earthquake.

He wondered what sort of quaking was going on in the spiritual realm that was spilling over into the earthly. Just what power, what warfare, were they truly unleashing here tonight?

Way across the ocean, Rath Kordoch trembled violently as if the firmament upon which he rested was coming apart around him. Something … something dreadful was happening in the spiritual realm up north that sent shivers up and down his spine and for the first time since he could remember he felt … fear. What was happening up there? His spies had told him the population was weak and unorganized. They had said the people were a superstitious lot, though not in the same demons and demigods, spirits and sprites and witchcraft that had long ago been spread and taken root within the Dominion's conquered lands. No, the people in Freelandia claimed to serve the one true God, but what did they really know of Him? He was weak and feeble – the demons of the Dominion had proven that their leader was more powerful and was truly the Prince of the earth. No, this was their hour. They would become stronger while His children would become weaker. It was their destiny.

Rath shook himself forcibly. He had a splitting headache, no doubt related to the spiritual reverberations emanating from the north. This could not be allowed to continue or grow! The Dominion wanted their enemies to be filled with fear … not with spiritual strength.

He rushed out of his private quarters to find a large gathering of very agitated Dark Magicians and administrative authorities. Several of the Magicians had hands held tightly to their heads as if in agony, and a few even writhed on the floor in near convulsions. All were cowering.

The Overlord steeled his outward appearance even as he inwardly winced in actual spiritual pain. The Dominion army and navy were not prepared to the level he desired and his plans called for waiting at least another month. But this … this changed things. He had to regain control and look strong! Rath swelled his massive chest, drawing in a deep breath, the better with which to bellow fiercely. "You cowards! Stop your sniveling! Our Master is stronger than the Freelandians and their so-called god. Work your witchcraft and magic to even greater depths. Whip our people to a frenzy! We must begin immediately. Send out the orders! The Freelandians are growing stronger – we cannot wait or delay as they build strength! We begin to sail north a week from today!"

Chapter 12

The Road to Rhoditian

The Four from Freelandia – at least that was what Miguel had begun to call them – made their way northward but at a westward angle, hoping to confuse their pursuers. It had been several days since their ambush, and the enemy would likely be much more cautious now … and crafty. They would have preferred to travel exclusively at night, but in the wooded areas that would have meant slow progress indeed and time was against them. The longer it took to leave Dominion territory, the more troops would pour in, reducing their options. That meant they could not go too far out of a given pathway. There were only two ways to leave Dominion lands now. One lay to the east, where they could hope to cross the easternmost border of the Dominion into one of the semi-neutral nation-states whose meager natural resources and rather inhospitable terrain had not made them prime targets for acquisition. Gaeten and Chu seemed to prefer this option, feeling that they could more readily lose pursuit in either the swampy coastal lowlands or the mountainous crags further south.

The other was by sea. They were not far from the coast now, and the shoreline was littered with both larger cities and smaller fishing hamlets, all with ample opportunity to be picked up by a speedy boat and whisked northward to Freelandian freedom … if only there was some way to arrange such transportation. Surely Dominion warships were even now prowling the territorial waters to seal off this escape route, and undoubtedly troops were being stationed at every likely port. Yet, for a reason he would not yet reveal, Miguel adamantly insisted that they travel slightly westward from their original destination of Cisteria.

"All in good time, my esteemed comrades," he would say. "Trust me in this, I have a plan." Gaeten grumbled about 'blind trust' but after a time of prayer they all felt this was the direction God was leading.

Even so, there was getting to be rather meager cover to hide their passage, and finally the forested tracts gave way to rich open farmland. Chu called a halt late in the evening and they made a sparse camp while he continued on. After perhaps a half hour he returned and dismounted. "I rode ahead, and the woods give out in another few hundred yards. There is a small creek that meanders toward the sea, cutting through a valley ahead. I propose we walk as far as we dare tonight along the creek – there is ample cover along its banks – and then ride to the nearest small town. Perhaps we can join some merchant caravan or at least find other disguises to blend in more with the locals. Miguel, now would be a good time to let us in on that plan of yours."

"Gentlemen, we of course cannot fight our way through the entire Dominion army in this area. We must escape with subterfuge if we are to escape at all. If my navigation reckoning is correct, two days journey ahead of us lies Rhoditian, a city I know quite well as my principal lives there part of each year."

Chu had screwed up his face into a scowl. "Rhoditian! That worthless place! You mean to take us there? No wonder you have held back on telling until there are few options left!"

Gaeten had a puzzled look on his face. "What is the matter with this place, Chu? I take it you have heard of it?"

Master Chu turned aside and spat onto the ground in disgust. "Oh, I have heard of it. The city fathers there long ago decided that they had neither natural riches nor a strategic location and so went about the task of finding something, anything they could do to put their city on the map – to attract visitors and merchants. They had no significant craftsmen, nothing really notable save for one eccentric retired banker who for some undisclosed and likely rather shady reason had chosen that out-of-the-way forsaken and forgotten town to settle in. Am I correct so far, Miguel?"

"Oh, most honorable Master Chu, your knowledge of such history is amazing! I for one never thought you would have deemed Rhoditian worthy of such scrutiny!"

"Ha! When I heard about it I learned at least a bit of its history – learned enough to know I'd stay clear of it if possible! Why don't you fill in the rest – I am rather interested to see how you will convince Gaeten not to skewer you with one of your own swords when he learns just where you intend to take us."

"I am aghast at your maligning of such a noteworthy and fine cultural center! Really, Master Chu, I think you must spend considerably too much time with moss and leaves on your head – it has clearly begun to affect your judgment. Or maybe one of those creepy-crawly bugs you seem to enjoy rolling around with in the dirt and mud has infected you with some nasty parasite ... if you stopped and thought about it you could probably even feel a few of them slowly crawling around under your clothing even now!"

"I might prefer such companionship to the human parasites that abound in Rhoditian. Anyway, go ahead with your history lesson for Gaeten and Ethan."

Gaeten snickered and Ethan smirked while rolling his eyes, but the lad leaned forward to hear the rest.

"Very well, I am certain they will have a broader cultural awareness and appreciation than you." Miguel rolled his eyes and gave a stiff nod in Chu's direction before he turned to address the other two. Without the slightest change in his cadence his eyes widened as he realized that Chu had completely disappeared. One moment he was there and the next he wasn't. Miguel had not heard or seen a thing. In the fleeting second before he continued he wondered if the departure was due to the topic ... or to something more sinister. Either way, he continued gamely, while slowly adjusting his seating to more easily access weapons.

"The officials from Rhoditian sought advice as to how to reshape their little port town into something that would attract investment. They finally sought the advice – and financial backing – of the retired banker. With his wealth this banker had created a villa just outside of town and filled it with art he collected from around the world. He first proposed to put much of this art into a museum – if the town would pay him to build it and would allow him to collect a royalty on admission fees. The town leaders were desperate and this sounded like their only hope.

The banker himself was a shrewd character. He knew he could have made a mint while ruining the city's finances, but instead he desired to create something far bigger ... something that would be lasting and that could be passed on to his children and their children. This is not to say he did not profit from the work. He seems to have acquired and assimilated all of the local construction businesses into a monopoly which he controlled, and then his business was selected to build the museum, then expand the port and then reconstruct the entire dockyard and city center. It was all part of a grand plan. To lure in visitors he hired musicians and other entertainers from far and wide, and in a masterly touch he also staged grand contests for painters, musicians – really any form of creative art."

Ethan raised his eyebrows. "Really? Are there that many rich people in those parts that would squander their money on such things?"

Surprisingly, Gaeten spoke first. "God reveals his beauty to us in many forms, Ethan. We need to recognize the reflection of God's own beauty in the various arts, as well as in His natural creation. It is not squandering to appreciate such artistic talent as long as it does not take away from other purposes God has for us. At the same time, if the art is not used to remind us of God and assist us to worship Him, then it may truly be squandering a God-given gift."

Miguel nodded. "Yes ... yes you have it exactly, my friend! But let me finish my story. It took a few years, but the idea caught on and now any artist worth his salt within a thousand miles knows he will never hit it big unless he gets noticed in Rhoditian. Some say that the musicians there rival even those from the Academy of Music in Freelandia in skill. Some of the most widely known and successful artists of various kinds have come from Rhoditian, including one of the grandsons of the banker himself. A few even studied as youth in Freelandia. You may have heard of one, he was even knighted by a local king for his outstanding singing voice ... Sir ..."

A rustling in the undergrowth interrupted Miguel's discourse and both he and Gaeten had drawn weapons when a dark shape burst out of the woods and into the fading light. Chu had a long dagger in his hand, and something wet was dripping from it. "We must leave immediately. I caught two soldiers who appeared to have spotted us. A third got away. Only one was close enough to have heard anything, and he will not be talking to anyone again." Chu wiped his blade on some wet grass and dried it with a cloth.

Gaeten spoke up. "Then we have little choice. The Dominion noose will tighten considerably in this area. We need to get out of these territories and back to Freelandia. If Rhoditian is the nearest city where we can likely find a ship, then so be it."

Chu shook his head. "I think, my friends, that I may be of greater service to you now if I were to provide a form of diversion for our party. I propose to take the horses and turn due eastward, skirting the forest as though we were trying to sneak back toward Cisteria. I believe I can give a plausible deception for at least several days, by which time you may be able to make your way into Rhoditian, and may God help you with whatever further plans Miguel has cooked up. If possible I will rendezvous with you there – but of course do not wait for me – escape as soon as you possibly can."

Gaeten pondered that for just a moment. "I believe you are right, my friend. Such subterfuge may give us the time we need to reach the city and disappear within it. I fear that out here in the countryside we can be encircled and caught far too easily unless we were to give up heading to Freelandia anytime soon. God will have to show us a means of escape from Rhoditian. Go with Godspeed and protection, Master Chu."

Gaeten found the smaller man and embraced him as a brother. Ethan shook his hand and Miguel looked at Chu with misted eyes and finally brought him into a powerful hug. "I will miss you, Chu. Perhaps one day a minstrel from Rhoditian will sing of your adventures!"

Chu groaned and gave Miguel a good natured shove. "I think I am leaving none too soon! Now, all of you please remove what you will need from your saddle packs. I will leave immediately."

Miguel finally called a halt to their forced march in the dark, taking them out across the open fields under the patchy clouded night sky. They stopped in a small stand of fir trees near the creek they were following and took shifts sleeping. Early the next morning they set out again, following the creek until they observed an old farm house and barn that was built close enough to use the creek water for household needs. They were just to the barn when the back door to the house slammed open and two obviously drunk soldiers staggered out, laughing.

"Come on, Brin … let's see if those old coots had anything valuable stored in the barn … they won't be needing anything again!"

Ethan's blood went cold and he was already nocking an arrow to his bow and acknowledging the blue trajectories in his mind when Miguel boldly walked right out to confront them.

"Hold up there, my not-so-good friends. Just what has become of the farmers who own this place?"

"What … where did you come from? And what's it to you anyway? … you don't look like their son or anything." The lead soldier peered out from alcohol blurred eyes. His buddy had already drawn his sword, which was conspicuously stained, and was beginning to move out from the first man in an encircling path.

Miguel seemed to ignore him as he approached the first soldier. "I asked you a question, soldier. Where are the owners of this farm?"

The harsher tones made the man stand straighter and he eyed the Watcher warily while his friend made his way behind the intruder. He smiled with a sense of superiority that came both from the alcohol and from what he figured was now a tactical advantage. "They refused us the hospitality and deference due us as Dominion soldiers. And they paid their price for it. And so will you." With that he lifted the knife he had quietly drawn and lunged forward even as his partner in crime swung his blade from behind.

Neither had time for a second step before Miguel had drawn both of his swords and run them through while adroitly sidestepping out of harm's way. He wiped his swords off on their clothing carefully and then arranged the bodies closer. To even a skilled observer it would appear like the two must have had an argument and done each other in. The three checked out the house to find the owners slain, as unfortunately expected. They acquired clothing that would look more appropriate in these surroundings, though they were big on Ethan and a bit tight over Gaeten's muscles. Miguel waved them off, preferring his own more fashionable woodsmen clothes that somehow still seemed remarkably clean.

Perhaps most importantly, they found an old cart in the barn and hitched up the equally tired-looking horse. Lightly loaded with odds and ends from the barn and house, it had the appearance of down-on-their-luck farmers heading into town to sell off items to make ends meet. With God's mercy, they could make it to the next town without drawing undue attention. They added a few hay bales and covered an area with an old rug, under which Ethan could settle in without being seen but with fast egress, if they felt the need for greater concealment. It was not to Ethan's liking at all and he insisted this arrangement was only for emergency use. For some reason, Ethan had developed a strong aversion to being under rugs.

Chu was wondering if he should have gone with the others. He had narrowly avoided two patrol teams already, and by now for sure they had to have picked up his trail. In fact, it was likely they had sent riders ahead and were already preparing a trap. A faint sound registered and without conscious thought he kicked the lead horse very roughly into a frightened gallop as he rolled off his saddle to the left and launched himself upward and outward as hard as he could. He had already taken to wearing his most important gear about his camouflaged body. His hands closed around a small sapling and he used that to pull him even faster and further away from the immediate danger his unconscious mind had somehow recognized.

The lead horse whinnied in fear and bolted when the brush ahead exploded as a dozen soldiers leapt out with spears, bows and swords swinging. A shout behind Chu indicated both the frustration of the attackers of not finding their intended prey and possibly of someone noticing his flying departure. He hit the ground in a hunkered low dead run, turning sharply to his right to circle around toward the ambush, figuring it unlikely they would expect that of him. Chu only ran a dozen yards before he dropped to the ground and began a surprisingly fast scuttle to put more distance between him and the now charging soldiers. He spied a spruce tree with low branches and ducked underneath their canopy, while spreading a few branches slightly to observe the enemy's movements.

Most of the soldiers recklessly ran in a slowly widening fan in the general direction he had come from, but one was studying the ground near where Chu had landed. Chu removed a narrow metal tube from its leather holder and inserted a very thin dart with a fuzzy duck down plug on its end, being very careful not to touch the green goo on the needle sharp tip. The soldier came closer, still not having alerted his patrol group since he did not immediately recognize the tracks to be from his prey – the sticks Chu had attached to the bottom of his boots gave a confusing print and the slight delay was all he really needed. When the soldier closed to within fifteen feet Chu raised the tube to his lips and blew hard. The dart sped out and flew true. The soldier had stopped to examine the tracks again, and the dart struck the side of his bared neck. Even as he slapped at the supposed biting insect, the poison took hold and he stiffened before falling to the ground. Chu cautiously left his cover after seeing no others nearby. He retrieved the dart, and returned it to the small leather pouch where its tip stayed protected in a tiny sleeve. He rolled the wide-eyed soldier to his other side to hide the small wound and then scuttled away even as the paralysis took its final toll on the hapless … and now dead … soldier.

In ten minutes most of the patrol began to circle back but by then Chu was well away, now heading north and west. It was a long way to the city of Rhoditian … but first he needed to get away from this area – and it would now be crawling with Dominion soldiers who had fallen for his ruse. Perhaps he could cause more trouble for them before he finally left. After all, causing trouble was one of the things he did best.

Miguel had fashioned some old clothes from the farmer's house into make-shift minstrel's attire, complete with a beat-up lute whose strings he worked carefully to not over-strain them. The disguise, he confided to his travelling companions, would fit perfectly for their journey toward the artistic center of the region. Ethan thought Miguel's singing was actually not too bad, and it did make the time go by faster. At the slow walking pace of the old mare it was going to take nearly two days to reach Rhoditian, but the road was well maintained as it was a main thoroughfare connecting the many farms along the trail to the well paying markets in the city. As they travelled further, the farms began to slowly transform into country estates and small villages. Though several other travelers had passed them without comment, their farmer guise was beginning to draw more attention than desired since their cart did not have the produce nearly always accompanying people with such clothing. Miguel was just mentioning that even though he could not see any other travelers behind them for several miles, they would still need to change into different garb soon. Just then they rounded a corner right into a Dominion patrol which had blocked the road.

"Ho there in the cart! Pull aside. We want to take a closer look at you and whatever you have there." The six soldiers looked bored, but as Ethan turned the old horse to the side of the otherwise empty road, he noticed the sergeant looking at them quite suspiciously. Even as Miguel was putting down his lute, the leader grunted and began to draw his sword.

Ethan watched as the man's hand inched backwards, ever so slowly drawing his saber from its scabbard. His men were barely moving, most not having caught on yet that this set of passersby may not be just like all the others that streamed along this road every day. Bright blue ribbons festooned the air before him, and from long experience he knew this meant immediate action was needed. He did not wait. One soldier to the side of the sergeant had a short bow, and though it had only been held loosely, the soldier who wielded it appeared somewhat competent – at least he was reacting faster to the sergeant's movements than any of the others. Since the archer appeared to be the most imminent threat, it was to him that Ethan's primary attention went.

In a fluid motion Ethan dropped the reins and leapt forward. One foot landed squarely on the old horse's back, giving him a springboard to launch himself forward. He careened through the air, hands outstretched directly before him. Ahead, the bowman was slowly raising his nocked arrow and beginning to draw back the string.

Gaeten had been sitting slumped on the buckboard seat. Without even straightening his hands flew outward, each flinging a knife, and both dove back into folds of his garment to retrieve additional projectiles. Miguel was the slowest to react, but even as Gaeten's knives were reaching their intended targets he was leaping off the wagon toward the remaining soldiers, drawing both of his long swords from scabbards at his feet.

The archer looked in astonishment at the apparition flying directly toward him. His bow was up and the string half pulled back when Ethan's left arm deflected the curved bow sharply sideways while his right swung in a shallow arc with fingers bent back in an open fist. Ethan's fist smashed into the man's throat while his left hand slapped the bow sideways, causing the arrow to be released at half-power. Then the rest of his body slammed into the bowman and both tumbled backwards off the horse the man had been seated on. Ethan was twisting as he fell, and landed on his feet, taking two steps forward to regain his full balance. He looked up to see the totally surprised sergeant toppled slowly from his horse, the errant arrow protruding from his side. Time came back to normal as all red and blue ribbons faded away – the fight was already over.

The three loaded the bodies of the dead soldiers into the wagon, after first removing clothing of two of them that appeared closest in size to Gaeten and Ethan and that were not too bloodied. They collected the horses and chose three that looked most rested; for the rest they removed the saddles and all trappings and drove them off. When everything was loaded into the wagon Miguel drove it forward, with Ethan and Gaeten riding just ahead. Miguel had said the road would very shortly meet with a river, and in less than a mile they could hear the sounds that indicated they were nearing such an obstacle. A bridge lay before them over a rather deep chasm. Halfway across the bridge Miguel stopped and unhitched their tired old horse, adding its harness to the rest of the wagon contents. Ethan retrieved the small axe they had picked up back at the farmer's house and proceeded to chop through two boards that made up a short railing along one edge of the bridge. Then the three pushed the wagon, with considerable effort, until the front two wheels edged over the side of the bridge. With great creaking the wagon plunged off the bridge and down into the fast moving river below. They hoped the staged "accident" might confuse pursuers at least for a few hours, and every little bit of extra time could help.

The three mounted their new horses and rode on – just two Dominion soldiers escorting some minstrel toward Rhoditian – now only a day's cantering ride ahead.

The intensity of the search was greater than Chu expected, and his progress was slower. He found a large balsam tree shortly after evading the ambush and climbed high into its thick branches. In spite of the prickly branches and pitch, Chu strapped himself to the trunk and slept as best he could. This was one of his favorite ways to sleep in the wilderness anyway, since he was invisible to anyone and everything, unless some bear decided it wanted a look-out perch. He was thankful too that he was never invisible to God. With a prayer of heartfelt thankfulness, he drifted off as the wind gently rocked him to sleep.

He had hoped to get a good sleep, and that he actually did. He woke to the waning light of late evening and unstrapped himself from the tree trunk. He waited ten minutes to let his ears get re-accustomed to the wood noises and ensure no patrols were nearby. Chu slowly shimmied down through the covering branches and spied about for a taller tree he could use to get better bearings … and to look for the smoke from patrol camp fires. He saw a pine that towered above the main tree canopy, and since he was already sticky with pitch figured he might as well rub in some more of it – anyway, a quick roll or two on the ground afterwards would give him even better camouflage, and save him several minutes of having to touch up what he already had. You rarely could have too much camouflage, and it always could be touched up to make it even better. He removed his climbing spurs from the small pack he always carried and quickly scampered up the tall tree.

What he saw at first was discouraging. From the high vantage point he could see over two dozen wisps of smoke curling up in a random scattering all around – though directly to the northwest there was a conspicuous absence. Chu thought about the maps of the area he had long ago memorized and realized that marked a large swamp that eventually drained into the ocean. No one could travel through that, at least not with any kind of speed. Maybe not directly through it, but perhaps along its edge …

As he cataloged the various locations of the patrols he realized they seemed truly randomly distributed … they were not evenly spaced out in any kind of logical search grid pattern. That meant there was not a solid central organization of the patrols. As he reflected on that Chu made another realization – the uniform of the patrol that had almost ambushed him had been slightly different than others he had noticed. Perhaps there were several different soldier groups involved, each under different authority structures. That would fit with the random locations of the patrols he was seeing now too. Hmm. That might just be rather useful information.

Back on the ground Chu did roll about a few times, collecting quite a mix of debris that stuck to all of the pitch he had accumulated. The light was fading away as he made his way straight toward a nearby patrol camp fire, one that was actually only half a mile or so away from another camp … and Chu doubted either knew of their proximity to one another. Chu hoped to change that, in his own special way of course.

Master Chu slowly crept forward near a patrol group of a dozen men. He reflected that the patrols had grown in size … perhaps in response to several of them disappearing? There were two sentries who were staying within eyesight and earshot of the fire. Chu had fashioned a crude sling-shot and gathered a handful of small stones. He used one to careen a shot off into the woods 30 yards to the left from where he was, just outside the camp. The sudden pattering movement noise startled several of the soldiers who had just finished their evening meal and were about to bed down.

"What was that?" The speaker was a young man, who nervously glared out into the shadows.

"I dunno … it came from over that way," another voiced piped up.

A second rock pattered through the leaves and undergrowth, sounding like rapid movement. Several soldiers jumped to their feet, drawing weapons and peering out into the darkness. With attention focused elsewhere, Chu moved in closer and drew one of the knives he had liberated from prior Dominion owners. He chose the soldier that appeared to be the leader and threw. No one saw the movement and the blade flew true. The big man cried out, clutching the handle that now protruded from his side as he collapsed to the ground writhing. Even as it had left his hand, Chu had moved behind a larger tree and brought up the slingshot again.

As expected, the sudden attack broke the soldiers into a wild panic, and in the resulting chaos of the camp Chu shot several larger rocks off into the woods, progressively further out. Soldiers were a rather predictable bunch, and the fight or flight response was right on cue.

"They went that way!" shouted the younger soldier and he charged forward in that direction, sword in hand and wild eyed. The rest followed, leaving the dying corporal beside the fire. Chu had already reconnoitered the area and now took off in a surprisingly quiet jog roughly parallel with the advancing soldiers. They were beginning to fan out, noisily crashing through the undergrowth as they looked for the supposed attackers. Chu let them go for a few minutes. Then as they began to scatter and slow he shot another rock off ahead of them. That galvanized the soldiers and they charged ahead once again in the direction of the noise. From a predetermined vantage point Chu could just make out the shapes of the soldiers in the faint moonlight, and this time he drew more carefully and released a relatively round stone. It struck one of the leading men solidly and he yelped with the sudden pain. Those near him yelled wildly and ran forward even faster, beating the brush as they tried to find the invisible enemy.

Master Chu laughed to himself. This was almost too easy. He raced ahead of groping soldiers, not caring if they saw his fleeting form since he has already determined his woodland skills were far superior to the bumbling antics of his prey. Several did see his shadowy movement and with great yelling they gave chase. Perfect.

Chu was perhaps a hundred feet ahead of them when he slowed and tucked himself into a small hollow in the ground. The sentries of the next camp should be pretty close by, and it would not do to run into one of them quite yet. The crashing and shouting of the other group was just muffled and incoherent noise from here. Chu took his bearings and could just make out a faint flicker of the other campfire. He drew his slingshot, aiming high arcing shots toward the fire.

The second patrol camp had indeed heard the tumult off in the woods and their sergeant had them all armed and facing in a semi-circle toward the noise. He had doubled the sentries, but not sent them overly far out into the woods ... the sounds indicated that whatever was happening, it was coming toward them. Better to let them come to us, he figured. Then some projectile came zinging down into the camp, and in a minute something struck the logs of the campfire itself, sending up a blaze of sparks. Something struck one of the men and he cried out, "I'm hit!"

Some of Chu's last few rocks whizzed forward only a few feet above the ground, striking and ricocheting off trees in the way. The noise seemed to pinpoint the source of the attack, and even without the sergeant's orders his men charged forward, several yelling as much to bolster their own confidence as to potentially create fear in their unknown attackers.

As the two separate groups of soldiers charged forward, Chu released his final stones to egg each group on toward one another. Then he settled down in his hollow, a dark shadowy bush among so many others. While professional soldiers may have avoided a confused clash, these had no such discipline. The last couple of rocks from the slingshot had struck leading soldiers from both sides and that pushed both groups over the edge. They engaged each other with drawn swords and spears, and Master Chu had a ring side seat, right in the midst of the battle ground. What fun!

The fighting only lasted a disappointing few minutes, but at least one of the Dominion soldiers had stumbled into the hollow to find that a nondescript bush had very long, sharp and decidedly lethal thorns. When the crashing of the few remaining standing soldiers indicated hasty retreats, Chu rose and collected a few weapons from the bodies to supplement his supply. He picked up a few spears too and began a slow lope toward another set of camps he had seen. By now all in the near area would have heard the unmistakable sound of steel hitting steel and would know a battle had taken place. The nearest should have sent scouts out to investigate, and everyone's nerves would be quite high strung. The night was still young, and Chu had had a decent sleep in the tree … there was much time yet tonight for more mischief. He would need to be careful and avoid over-confidence, but a master of camouflage and stealth truly owned the night … especially when his quarries were minimally trained and relatively unskilled soldiers.

By the time the morning light was just giving a level of real visibility, Chu was skirting the swampland and had left the destruction and chaotic confusion in the woodland far behind. He figured the survivors would have wildly divergent stories of scores of Freelandian attackers raiding the entire countryside. A few might even mention bush demons.

The uniforms that Ethan and Gaeten wore had an amazing effect on those they passed. Everyone seemed to give them a wide berth, looking rather fearful. Obviously, Dominion soldiers were not well liked in these parts. Several times they were passed by squads of troops who were riding hard in the other direction, but they were not challenged. Gaeten's riding was remarkably good for a blind man, and with a soldier's helmet on it was difficult to really see one's eyes anyway. Likewise, the garb effectively added years to Ethan's appearance. Perhaps most importantly, Miguel's theatrical appearance had taken on a tone of self-imposed importance, attracting attention like a moth to a light. No soldier would ever suspect the escaping prisoners to be in the company with such a flashy, demanding personality.

They therefore made quite good time and without incident came to Rhoditian, the haven for artists of all types. Miguel mentioned he hoped it would prove to be the haven for escape artists as well.

Miguel demanded they stop at a clothing store that obviously catered to the more successful artists. First they stopped at a corral on the outskirts of the city proper and sold their well worn-out steeds, fetching far less than they would have back in the farmland where they had been appropriated. Miguel had insisted they retain their soldier trappings and so the three walked for nearly a mile into the sprawling town before reaching a store that seemed to meet his requirements.

They had reached a rather well-to-do section of the town, though still a ways from the true heart of the downtown district near the dockyards. As the three entered the brightly painted building an attendant met them at the door, sniffing in disdain at their dirty and worn apparel.

"Wait – excuse me! We don't allow ... I mean ... soldiers are not ... we don't cater to the needs of soldiers in this fine establishment." The thin man looked over Miguel with an upraised eyebrow. "You certainly are in need of proper attire ... but I rather doubt you can afford our exclusive merchandise. I suggest you try the thrift shop back down the street half a mile or so ... they may be more ... accommodating of your types."

Gaeten growled ominously. What was it with these types of shops that made him instantly irritated? The attendant backed away quickly, sensing the very real danger and Ethan snickered under his breath.   Miguel turned away with his nose high in the air and pretended not to notice. "Well, this is Roberto's Wardrobes, isn't it? The most famous wardrobe masters in all of Rhoditian? If I have been somehow mistaken I will most annoyed. I am sure I followed Count Cristo's directions perfectly."

The attendant's eyes flew open wide and his stiff demeanor sagged ever so slightly. "Count .... Count Cristo directed you here?"

"Most assuredly my good man! We have just finished the last performance of 'The Singer and The Soldiers' – perhaps you have heard of it? We have had three weeks of sold-out crowds at the Emporium Theater."

"Ah, no … I only occasionally get to that prestigious theater."

"Tut tut. Too bad, it was a huge success. Count Cristo himself said we should take it on the road, but first we must celebrate. He suggested we stop here after the last performance to prepare for the reception party he has planned for tonight. He has given us a rather generous stipend but said we must charge it to his account. We will be seen by, well, by everyone who is anyone. So, if this is not Roberto's then my friends and I will just leave at once. If you could be so kind as to give us proper directions …"

The attendant nearly fell over himself to apologize profusely and show them the best attire the store had to offer. Despite Gaeten's adamant protests ("He is having some trouble coming out of character", explained Miguel), they left the shop two hours later dressed in the finest that Rhoditian could offer. Miguel had even insisted on picking up a few additional spare clothes, which of course had to be paid for out of their own pockets – and it was a good thing Gaeten still had some of Taleena's stash of coin. The attendant had even sent for a carriage, and the three men rode away in style.

Miguel directed the driver to bring them to Count Cristo's villa. Ethan looked questioningly at him once the carriage was under way. Miguel smiled back handsomely. "Count Cristo is my principal – he is the person I work for under contract."

That answered Ethan's question but spawned another. "But you have been gone for what, a couple of weeks? Didn't that conflict with your job?"

Gaeten spoke up. "We always write a clause into our contracts for Watchers that gives them temporary leaves of absence when an emergency occurs that concerns Freelandia. Many have already returned home by now, while others are considered more valuable where they are … to be called upon if needed."

"Yes, that is true." Miguel spoke softly. "I did show my principle the Count the official letter from Master Warden James, which left it to my discretion to take time off if I felt it appropriate. The Count has never questioned my loyalty to him – or to Freelandia. Yet I did not want to leave him without any protection. I have nurtured several promising men within the small security team I have developed to protect the villa, and gave them orders to see to all the Count's needs while I was away. I guess we shall see how well they have done, eh? And perhaps give them a bit of a test, no?"

The carriage arrived and Miguel left it to Ethan to pay the driver, much to Gaeten's annoyance. The villa was a lavish home of ivory colored stone. They walked up to a side entrance as the carriage rattled off, but a quick look around showed that they had not yet been noticed. Miguel led them around further to the side of the building where a servant entrance was marked by a well worn pathway. The door was simply latched. Miguel had it opened in seconds, and the three entered soundlessly. No one was immediately in view, so they walked through several work areas and then scooted into a closet when several staff workers came noisily down the corridor. By carefully ducking out of sight, they made it into the main section of the house.

Miguel gave a few instructions and directions to Ethan and Gaeten, and then he slipped off down one passageway while Ethan led the way in another direction. He and Gaeten eventually came to a back servant stairway that they slowly and silently climbed to reach a back room used to stage items needed when the Count was entertaining from his luxurious study. They could hear voices beyond the narrow door and both moved closer to listen in.

"I tell you, I want to see him. No excuses! I have arranged performances of nearly all of the other great artists – and this is a hometown man, after all!"

"Yes Count, but you know how temperamental he is – and when you greeted him at the King of Belladore's ball two years ago you forgot to address him by his newly knighted name – it seems that was a major offense for which he has never forgiven you."

"How was I to know he had just been knighted? So I did not say 'Sir' and bow before his non-royal highness!"

"Yes, Count – without doubt he can be an oaf and the only royal thing about him is his snobbery, worse even than many of the other top artists you work with. Still, he is considered the world's greatest singer, and if you could book a performance with him you know it would bring in significant income for you – and esteem. And he is here for only a few more days. Perhaps if you sent a formal letter of apology and invited him to a lavish dinner in his exclusive honor he might let bygones be bygones and accept."

"Apologize? Why, I would never ..." Count Cristo paused. "I suppose that might work. But while he is here he always stays at his father's mansion ... and what can I offer here that compares to that? I mean, his father virtually owns the entire town of Rhoditian!"

"You are right there. I don't know what we could really offer to get Sir Reginaldo's attention, much less his willingness to come here."

There was a bustle of noise that erupted in the room beyond the door, and loud intakes of breath from the two who had been speaking. Gaeten silently opened the door a crack and Ethan peered out. A hooded figure stood at the outer door, apparently having thrown it wide open without request. Through the crack Ethan could see a servant out in the corridor beyond the stranger, bound and sitting unceremoniously on the floor. A large burly man had been standing elsewhere in the room and was now resolutely barring approach between the stranger and two older men who were seated in recliners. Both the guard and the hooded intruder had drawn swords.

"Had you kept the servants on their toes I do not think I could have so easily come this far undetected." The hood was thrown back to show Miguel's smiling face and his sword point was lowered to the touch the ground.

"Ha! Even so, you would not have made it a step further, Watcher!" The big man had lowered his sword too, though not entirely all the way. If this was a test, he wanted to be ready for additional action.

"While I polished you off the good Count and his aide would have been defenseless from any other attack."

"What? You and whose army?"

Miguel turned to look straight at Ethan. "Please, my friends, enter."

Ethan pulled the door open and he and Gaeten stepped into the room. "May I introduce my army?"

Count Cristo began to laugh uproariously. "Miguel De La Rosa, you are back ... and with guests! Please, come in – but please, Orthello – will you untie my chief of staff out there in the hallway?" When the burly guard had left Count Cristo became more serious. "Miguel ... you have been gone nearly two weeks. While Orthello is a fairly capable bodyguard, he is not the caliber of a Watcher, which is what I have paid for. You left saying there was an emergency that you had to attend to. Pardon my directness, but it is difficult for me to see how these two," he waved dismissively at Gaeten and Ethan, "could be of more importance than my welfare."

"A thousand pardons, Count Cristo. I am not at liberty to introduce you to these two gentlemen properly, but you must trust my judgment on this."

"I don't know, Miguel. I am rather disappointed in you. Perhaps I need to reconsider our contract. I am not sure how you could make this lapse up to me. Perhaps your loyalty toward me is not what I thought. "

Miguel's eyebrows rose high in astonishment. "Sir, I have never faltered in my service to you! And I have always been totally forthright in saying that my loyalty is first and foremost always to my God first, my country second, and to my principal third. I have never ..."

Gaeten sensed this disagreement could rapidly spiral out of control and so cut Miguel off mid-sentence. "Perhaps if we could get Sir Archibald Reginaldo to meet with you?"

The Count and his aide both began to laugh. "I don't know who you are, sir, but what do you expect to do ... waltz right up to Sir Reginaldo and just ask him to meet with me? Even if you somehow made it past his nomal retinue he would not give you the time of day!"

Gaeten smiled. "Actually. I was thinking of doing something just about like that." Ethan grinned, but everyone else in the room, including Miguel, turned to look at Gaeten with wide eyes and a dubious expression.

Master Chu slept, but was too keyed up to get more than six hours. He had traveled along the edge of the swampland, roughly parallel to a well traveled road that likewise skirted that area. When the morning light became bright he had found a clump of thick marsh grass to bed down in, first having had to slog through thick mud to reach it and duck once down into the mud itself to avoid being spotted by a traveler. Still, he rarely was able to sleep out in the open sunlight when he was traveling like this, but the marsh grass allowed him to pat down a flat area and sleep undisturbed, except for the occasional frog that found its way onto him. The mud also appeared to be a great natural cleanser for the pitch, and while he was covered from head to foot with gray muck, at least he did not have any stickiness remaining.

He awoke with a start that sent a nearby crane wheeling off into the sky with flaps of its giant wings. Chu could hear voices, and he peered out between the marsh grass to see a somewhat small man with clothing that looked like a soldier, but which seemed from this distance to be in far superior shape to the three other soldiers in his company. He also had a prominent leather satchel slung over his neck and one shoulder.

"Aw, why do you couriers always get the best uniforms, the best horses, the best food ... the best everything?" That came from an unkempt portly soldier sitting on the grass just beyond the marsh edge. It appeared the group had stopped here for a light lunch.

"Maybe it's because we couriers are better than you dumb grunts! Anyway, hurry up – I've got very important messages and war plans to deliver and already am late because I had to take you all along as an escort for my 'protection'. Ha! It is more like me having to escort and protect you louts!"

Chu removed his blow gun and a dart from its watertight pack and slipped back into the water noiselessly on the far side of his grassy knoll. The group was only a dozen feet from the edge of the marsh and muck, so he figured he could approach unseen to a very close distance. Step by slow step he advanced on them, bent over double to stay just above the swampy water surface, slowly drawing one foot at a time from the thick goo and replacing it without making undue noise.

"You gotta big mouth to go with yer big head! There's word of a Freelandian army battalion working in these parts, and so our regiment has been assigned to escort all couriers. You don't have to like it - we surely don't - but you do have ta shut up!"

"Oh yeah? I'll shut up when I am good and ready to, grunt! I work for a major ... you probably have a corporal who is as fat and ugly as you! While I bet ..."

The courier did not have time to finish as the soldier could not take the insults any further and reared back with a roundhouse punch to the smaller man. The two began to wrestle ineffectively, but the soldier's two buddies joined in and together the three of them prevailed to hold the smaller man down.

"I says we should toss him into the marsh, get his uppity fancy clothes all muddy like."

"You wouldn't dare! Let me up this instant!"

Another spoke up. "I thinks we should cut 'im first, then ties his hands and feet and toss him in … the gators will finish him off within a few days once they smell the blood."

"Now that's an idea for sure! We could cuts his tongue out first too, so no ones will hear him out in marsh."

Chu was quite near them now, having found a deeper pool of water so that he could slide down with only his head showing. He still had his mossy hat on, which of course was coated with the mud and swamp slime. The marsh grass was thicker right next to the shore, and Chu was pressing through the outer layers to get even nearer. He had need of the courier – or more properly of the courier's clothing and horse, and not all bloodied or dirtied. The three soldiers manhandled the courier to his feet, holding him tightly.

"Let's just toss him in for now, that oughta tamp down his pride a few notches, and if he gets mouthy again we can always try the other plan." The three began to shuffle and drag the struggling courier toward the swamp edge.

A log jutting into the marsh moved and the courier suddenly slumped in their arms. With the soldiers' rough handling, the dart fell out without being seen but the effects of the poison were more evident. The nearest soldier was about to comment that logs shouldn't be able to move when he felt a sharp pain in his side and looked down to see the hilt of a dagger emerging from his torso. He screamed and dropped the stiff form of the courier, pulling out the knife and lifting it to show the others as his life blood pumped out. With an astonished glare he fell dead next to the other limp form.

The remaining two soldiers had no idea what had happened until one noticed a roughly man-shaped … thing … rising from the marsh muck. A look of horror stole over his features and he turned to run, only to drop with a knife blade buried into his back. The third soldier was either more skilled or more dimwitted, and instead of running away he charged forward, drawing his own knife. Soldier and bog monster fell backwards into the marshy water and began to thrash about in the mud. A moment later, only one emerged.

Chu dragged the bodies out into the marsh, watching for the aforementioned gators. He made sure the bodies were invisible from the shore, then stripped off his clothing and washed as much of the mud off as he could from a small pool of relatively clean water. The courier's clothing did not fit exactly, but it was serviceable. He used the canteens of the soldiers to wash out any remaining mud he could see on his hands and arms, and carefully wiped off his face and head as well. It would have to do.

The horses were skittish from the sounds and smells they had just experienced, but the courier's stallion looked to be a prize, especially compared to the others. Chu went through the messages in the pouch and grunted in surprise. They spoke of the launch of the Dominion fleet of warships and invasion troop carriers. All were to meet at an assigned island resupply depot and head for Freelandia, scheduling the arrival at the next full moon, which the Dark Magicians told them would be blood red. *This news must be taken to Freelandia immediately*, he thought.

Without further ado, Chu resealed the satchel and mounted the horse. He hoped his disguise would suffice. He needed to reach Rhoditian and his companions with Godspeed.

Chapter 13

Reunions

To say Murdrock was angry would be to understate the obvious. The scowl on his face kept the sailors as far from him as possible. Rath Kordoch had sent word to him in Cisteria that the Overlord was most displeased that the son of the Chancellor of Freelandia had escaped from under Murdrock's watch and not only had not been captured yet, but had put the entire north eastern sector in turmoil with outlandish claims of several battalions of Freelandian soldiers having staged their own invasion force. As though he, Murdrock, was at fault! It was terribly unfair and Murdrock was ready to lash out at anyone who dared come near him. The Overlord had strongly implied that banishing him to some far outpost in the deep south was strongly probable if he could not accomplish something useful for the Dominion. He was given one last chance; being sent as far away as possible … back to Freelandia to support the dissident teams that should be preparing to assist the invasion force … even now being assembled and staged for an imminent departure.

Instead of leading an attacking force of seasoned fighters, or being a consultant to generals, he was being sent back to work with ruffians and hoodlums who supposedly were to work as a cohesive sabotage team with timing synchronized to the invasion arrival. Well, they had better be ready. He was in no mood for slackers or incompetence. He would show that thick-headed Overlord who was truly important.

Murdrock had been ordered to take the first available ship out to Freelandia and so here he was, pacing the deck of a fat old merchant scow filled with some kind of special fabric that must be the latest fashion in that wretched northern country. Though why any lady would want to be dressed in a silken cloth that appeared to be airtight and not breathable at all was beyond him. Maybe it was for some form of fancy rain gear or bathing suits – who knew? The captain said merchants in Freelandia were ordering as much of it as they could get their hands on. Good – let them spend their efforts on fashion while the Dominion prepared for all out war.

For all his dark outlook, the ship was making good time, and he should arrive within the week. Now he just had to work on his credentials to pass as a ladies garment merchant … a garment merchant! The gall of it all!

Gaeten, Miguel and Ethan had been given the use of the upper meeting room after the Count and his aide left. Miguel was pacing back and forth. "Finding Sir Reginaldo should not difficult – he strikes a highly imposing figure and his propensity for the public spotlight means any dinner or party hosting the great singer will have loud fanfare and announcement. That will not be an issue. But knowing where he will be is not the same as being able to actually meet him! We can't just barge in with swords swinging to make our way to the guest of honor, Gaeten! How do you expect to get even close to him?"

"Well, knocking a few dozen heads did enter my mind … that would surely be my kind of party! But no, that would call undue attention to us. You say he will be at some form of formal dinner tonight in town?"

"Yes, my principle said there is some posh dinner in Reginaldo's honor tonight at the KingFisher. That is one of the top hot spots in a town known for its nightlife. It will be a very formal affair, invitation only, and they will have plenty of bouncers to ensure that only the VIP guests can enter. There is no way any of us could get close to him, at least not quietly. Besides, there very well may be dignitaries from elsewhere in the Dominion there tonight, possibly even from as far as Kardern. You and Ethan cannot possibly show your faces anywhere near the place."

"Oh, I think God can find a way, my friend. And I think He may have just given me an idea that will bring the exalted Sir Archibald Reginaldo to us!"

"Just what kind of idea might that me, Grand Master Gaeten … and how much will it cost me in time and coin?"

"Oh, I cannot imagine it will be too difficult for someone of your impressive skills and notable connections within a town full of actors and actresses."

"That is what I was afraid of. When you start buttering me up I start checking my coin purse to see if you have your hand in it yet."

"Miguel, now why would I ever do that? Besides …" Gaeten lifted a hand to reveal a small leather pouch "… I cut this from your belt nearly half an hour ago. It seems you have plenty of coins to spare. I may even be doing you a favor, lightening your load to improve your speed and agility."

Miguel's right hand dove down to his belt to discover the absent pouch now dangling from Gaeten's grasp. He rolled his eyes heavenward and then looked over at Ethan. "Is he always so impossible?"

"Oh no …" Ethan quipped. "Usually he is much worse."

Master Chu rode hard, entering the city of Rhoditian late in the evening. His courier status had allowed him to speed through the various checkpoints along the way and ensured he had priority status at a rather nice inn, but he needed to ditch this disguise quickly less some Dominion authority question him too closely. He needed to consider how he could best fit in with the crowds, to disappear among the normal population of the city. Chu checked into his room at the inn, stashing the revealing communications in the satchel behind the lone dresser. It would have to do for now.

He really did not want to walk out onto the streets in such a noticeable costume – he had already noted that couriers appeared to be relatively rare and people would stop to stare. He figured they were likely wondering just what important information was in the satchel. Chu disliked being stared at – disliked it with a passion. Well, maybe it was ok if the person staring thought he was some rare botanical.

Chu exited his room and took a back stairwell down to exit into an alleyway. The daylight was already waning, which made his task easier. Torches were being lit around the main streets, and as he came near the exit of the alley he saw a surprisingly large number of pedestrians strolling along the plank sidewalk. He stood slightly in the shadows, observing. There was a highly eclectic mix of people out. Most were rather well dressed, but in rather bright and colorful attire compared to what he was used to. The younger people were downright gaudy, but there was a considerable divergence in their fashions. And there were a significant mix of ... well, Chu wondered what he should call them. A threesome that fit into this 'other' category was coming down the walk now dressed in garish bright colors.

"I tell ya Fredrick, the tunes were fantastic down by the northern wharf last night! My ol' man finally coughed up the coin for a small set of thumpers like these," a young man held up two small bongo style drums. "We beat out a storm with a few blowers and strummers in along for the ride. We had the wharf on fire all right!"

A second young man – maybe Fredrick? – seemed to answer back in whatever foreign gibberish Chu thought they seemed to be talking in. "Fiery hot, that. Think we can cobble a corner, stack our stuff, and collect any coin for our eager efforts?"

Chu shook his head, which was starting to hurt trying to decipher their coded communication – or whatever it was. He was a bit sorry the third member of the party joined in.

"Embers! Sounds like a party that's hap'ning! Let's hoot and holler and see what legs might stroll by to be captivated by our artistry. What we wait'n for? The kindling is lit as of right now!" The three laughed and picked up their pace, heading off down the road.

Chu scowled. Fitting in around here just may be a lot harder than he had thought. He was about to edge out onto the street when another eccentric looking middle aged shorter man stumbled along. At first Chu thought the man had a disability, the way he seemed to somewhat randomly stagger, not going more than a few feet in a straight line. As he neared though, Chu caught the unmistakable odor of a plant whose leaves were commonly smoked by miscreants in the Dominion. It supposedly altered one's perception of the world around you. This fellow seemed 'altered' all right. But he was about the right size. The Watcher sighed. If he could crawl through fetid bogs and swamps he could bear with the pungent odor of stale snakeleaf smoke. He hoped that was all the clothing would smell of.

As the man stumbled right toward him, Chu reached out of the shadows and helped him along, murmuring, "Lights out for you, my fine fellow". The slight stumble became a genuine trip that ingloriously ended headfirst into a wall. Chu wondered if the man had even felt it as he dragged the limp body back further into the darkness and began to strip off the clothing and exchange it with his. The shirt was too snug and short, riding up out of the baggy saggy trousers. 'Just great,' Chu thought. 'I sure hope he didn't have lice.' He had room only for a short knife and added what little his new acquaintance had of coin to his own leather purse. It would have to do. At least the man had sandals that fit – the courier's tall boots were terribly uncomfortable.

Chu left the man where he was, loosely clothed in the former courier's attire and with a few of the coins acquired from the former soldiers … by morning he would not remember how he got there anyway, given the strength of the snakeleaf odor. Chu sincerely hoped the coin would go toward new clothes and a few good meals, rather than the next fix of mind-altering snakeleaf.

With another heavy sigh he picked up the man's odd stocking cap and headed back to his room to retrieve the courier satchel, and then exited the alley. He could have sworn he felt something crawling down his back under the bright lime green too-short shirt. Chu made a mental note that the next time he had Miguel out in the countryside he would ensure his friend bedded down over a termite nest.

Miguel was incredulous, but dutifully carried out Gaeten's instructions coupled with a description supplied by Ethan. In a city like Rhoditian, finding actors and actresses of any given specifications was not terribly difficult, though one that matched what Gaeten had required took most of the day. Then he had to charm the head waiter of the restaurant where Sir Reginaldo would be that evening. The man had thought Miguel was crazy but finally relented when told this was an advertisement of the latest and greatest play coming to the best theater in town and that Miguel could get him front row tickets. Since no guest was to be spoken to or disturbed in any way, the man finally relented.

"Gaeten, my good man, this is preposterous! How can your scheme possibly convince Sir Reginaldo to come here?" Miguel said with exasperation as he finally returned and slumped into a chair. "I think your time here in the southern latitudes has perhaps – with all due respect – made your head an eensy weensy bit mushy."

Gaeten laughed. "You just make sure everything is in place tonight for the dinner. Have you written out the message as I wanted it?"

"Yes, yes, but it makes little sense and why would it possibly influence the greatest singer in the world to come here?"

"That, my friend, is a longer story. Perhaps I can tell it when you return."

"Master Gaeten … a storyteller … that links to a famous singer like Sir Reginaldo? This I must hear. I'll bring popcorn."

Sir Archibald Reginaldo waltzed into the dining room with his normal grand swagger and disdainful look as if saying that royalty had entered – and everyone else most assuredly was not of the same status. He wore a condescending smile that could rapidly transform into a scowl if anything was not to his exacting standards and whims of the moment. But inwardly he wondered why. Why keep up the charade? A year ago he would have reveled in the attention he received the few times a year he traveled home to Rhoditian. Every night would see him at some event or another as the guest of honor and he would be wined and dined with everyone who was anyone. Yet now, it seemed both a bore and … a façade. He was not the same person he had been the last time he was here. He did not enjoy being the center of everyone's adoring attention anymore. Not since meeting Maria and hearing her sing.

Now he could only strive to capture a hint of that essence, which he realized in his heart was not as much Maria as it was Maria's God. She simply sang for Him, and not only did it show, but somehow it made you realize something about God Himself, recognize some wondrous aspect of His might and glory. It was profound. It was humbling.

And that, Reginaldo realized, was the real change in himself. He truly did not believe any more that the world did – or should – revolve around Reginaldo. He recognized it was not all about him, it was all about HIM – God the Creator.

So he came to these events, since many had been booked a year or more in advance and it would not do to disappoint his fans – his paying fans. Yet, he was still different. With that thought he dropped his veneer of a smile and began to genuinely smile at the others who had come to the dinner. If God could smile on him, it was the least he could do to smile at others. And who knows, maybe he, Reginaldo, could make a difference in someone's life – a positive difference, that is. Maybe today, maybe tonight, maybe here, he would catch a glimpse of God's hand at work, and have a chance to join in on what God was about to do. Reginaldo beamed. His host figured he must have done everything perfectly and complimented himself.

After he was seated at the place of highest honor at the front of the room, the dinner began to be served. It was a scrumptious multicourse affair with a few gratefully short speeches between the main courses. Reginaldo was just settling into a delicious meat pie, and it truly was one of the best he had eaten in a long time. He looked up with a very pleased smile at his host, and then let his gaze waver across the room. Just as he was turning back to the pie, his fork froze in midair and he looked back up quickly. The image he had scanned but that had not really registered until now had his complete attention.

Reginaldo's eyes bulged in their stare and color drained from his face. His host nearly sputtered in concern, wondering if somehow the cook had left some horrible little bones in the meat pie, but then his gaze shifted to what the great singer seemed to be totally concentrating on.

Across the room, next to the waiter's entrance a lone young girl stood dressed all in white, holding a single long stem red rose in one hand. In the other she held an unmistakable white walking cane, the kind exclusively used by …blind people. Even from a distance, it did indeed appear that the girl was blind. What was she doing in here? Who let her in? Certainly she was not on the invite list! Infuriated that the waif had interrupted Sir Reginaldo's meal, and apparently was causing him some consternation, the host began to rise, snapping angrily at a waiter to come at once. He felt a heavy hand on his arm and was about to snap at whomever had the audacity to touch him when he realized it was Reginaldo himself.

"Please … bid one of the waiters to bring that young lady to me." At the look on the host's face, the habitual scowl came back onto Reginaldo's face. "She will be my guest – open up a spot at the table – or better yet, offer her your spot." A horrified look overcame the host's face and he gave some rapid fire directions to the waiter, who nearly dropped the serving plate he was carrying as he listened while turning quite pale.

The waiter disappeared for a moment, then returned and went directly over to the girl. Meanwhile, half a dozen other waiters were scrambling to adjust the seating at the main table to squeeze in one more chair on the other side of Reginaldo, away from the host's seat.

Reginaldo watched curiously as the waiter slowly and carefully guided the obviously blind young lady to his table, and he stood and himself seated her next to his own chair. Curiosity was almost dripping out of him as he held her hand and asked for her name.

"I am Doranna, sir. Please, I must ask – are you Sir Reginaldo the great singer?"

"Yes dear, I am he. Did you not know the dinner here tonight was held in my honor?"

"Oh yes, I mean, of course. I just needed to make sure. I have a message for you." She reached into a hidden pocket and withdrew a small folded piece of paper and held it out. Reginaldo closed his fingers around it, marveling. If he had been curious before, now he was doubly or triply so. Who possibly would have positioned such a messenger for him? Who within a thousand miles would have ever dreamt that he would have the slightest interest or even notice a sweet young blind girl?

He slowly opened the folded paper. It was an invitation of some sort in rather elaborate scrolling letters, requesting his attendance to a private meeting at a local art dealer's … one he distinctly recalled having been insulted by a few years back. The scowl came back in full force. If by some sheer coincidence this dealer had thought to influence him in this way, he surely had another thing coming … Reginaldo surely would see to it that he … then the signature on the bottom of the page seemed to grow huge. It was simply signed, 'Gaeten'.

❧

Chu was a master at fitting into any environment inconspicuously. Any, that is, except perhaps for downtown Rhoditian. He followed the crowds along to the waterfront area, where a large number of restaurants, theaters and pubs seemed to crowd every street. He had hoped to find a place outdoors to sit where he could scan the crowds, hoping to perhaps spot Miguel or pick up on where his art dealer principal may be located, all without attracting undue attention. However, he was regretfully realizing he had picked the wrong snakeleaf head to bop.

"Hey man, burning duds hanging from ya shoulders! What flaming tunes you fire?"

The man and woman before him were dressed in similar lime green with stocking caps. One carried a guitar of sorts and the other some sort of wind instrument. He had only been out in the main park area for half an hour, and had noticed many groups of all ages form impromptu bands – of sorts – that played a variety of songs – of sorts. Frankly, he had no clue what kind of music they actually were playing, anymore than he knew what they were talking about. Chu was picking up a few of the phrases here and there, but now confronted directly by two of these … people … he had no clue what to say.

As he quickly considered whether to act like he could not hear them or perhaps knock them unconscious, a couple of Dominion army officers came walking by. Rats! He had been leaning toward the head bashing – it usually worked for him pretty well. Still, he could hardly carry on a conversation in whatever slang they were flinging. He thought they may be asking him what instrument he could play. Chu had not attempted to play music since a child. Maybe he could dissuade them with something they did not have. He made the motions of striking something up and down – anyone could play the drums anyway, he reasoned – and it was not too dissimilar to smashing heads with clubs.

"Totally on fire, man! Exactly what our group needs!" The girl grabbed one of his arms and the boy the other. It took most of his resolve not to part them of their appendages, but the Dominion officers were looking his way now and so he put on a comical dunce smile and nodded enthusiastically as they led him away. His next hopes of losing them in the crowds as soon as they were out of sight were dashed, as their group was immediately before him. Four people smiled up at him, all dressed in a version of lime green that he was wearing.

Chu felt like he could have stuck himself with one of his knives. "Try to fit in," he muttered under his breath. "Don't draw attention to yourself. Flow with whatever is going on around you. Right."

The group shifted to make room for him next to them on the grass and Chu noticed a pair of small portable drums amongst the equipment the group had brought and piled on the ground. One of them grinned lopsidedly and shoved the drums his way. Panic was almost setting in, but before he was called upon to show his non-existent skills the two people that had brought him over handed him a carton of food identical to what each of them had and gave him a pair of chopsticks to eat the noodles inside. They were laughing and fumbling with the chopsticks, often dropping more food than succeeding in getting it to their mouths.

Well, at least he could do one thing with the group well. His parents had come to Freelandia as young adults, and had taught Chu from as early as he could remember how to use the utensils common in their homeland. He picked up the chopsticks, adjusted his hold, and merrily snapped up long buttery noodles. In a minute everyone in the group stopped and looked on in amazement.

Chu figured it was now or never. "Uh … hold them like you were trying to write something, like this." He demonstrated. As one of the group semi-succeeded he complimented him. "Burning, dude!" Chu had to resist the impulse to gag – had he really just said that? – but instead just smiled in the oddest way he could. They all laughed and in a minute put down their food and chopsticks to pick up the various instruments.

"Time to flame, dudes and dudettes!"

One began to play and the others joined in. The fellow closest to Chu nodded at him and down at the drums. Chu groaned, though no one could hear over the din of the "music" being played. He scoured the ground before him looking for drumsticks, but it appeared none were brought. The thought of just banging on them with his hands was most unappealing. Then he spied the chopsticks. He grinned his kooky grin and picked one up in each hand. The musician (Chu really had difficulty in thinking of them in such professional terms) looked wide eyed and then elbowed the young woman next to him to watch what was happening.

Rolling his eyes before closing them, Chu listened to what they were playing, picturing himself listening to the wind and crickets and animals in his beloved woods. The night sounds had a cadence and rhythm too, he had long ago learned.

Tentatively, he began to tap out in rough time to what the others were playing. Several laughed, and then picked up the pace. 'Here we go' thought Chu.

The Dominion officers chose a restaurant with outdoor tables right across from what appeared to be a rather typical avant-garde street musician group. The drummer seemed peculiar – not from around these parts and he acted even more oddly than everyone else seemed to in this city. They sat in a position where they could watch and listen.

The group seemed to take awhile to really get going, but shortly they were playing relatively well – considering what went for contemporary music this year in Rhoditian. After a few songs they noticed the drummer really seem to be getting into the swing of things – one commented that he must be "really burning" and both laughed at the vernacular slang that seemed so prevalent among the younger and older "hip" crowd.

In fact, the group was getting better and better. As often happened, the best music started to attract more listeners, and within an hour there was a sizable group crowded around. The drummer in particular seemed to be the centerpiece of attention. He had two tiny drum sticks, which he twirled around and even tossed into the air to juggle, somehow never missing a beat. His dexterity was amazing, even with the silly look on his face and that ridiculous costume all the street musicians seemed to be wearing.

As the group began another tune, a disturbance broke out on the far side of the plaza. The two officers rose to investigate and helped the local police capture a middle aged man who had dashed out into the now crowded area, stark naked and babbling something about how a wall jumped out and hit him on the head. He reeked of snakeleaf, and one of the officers did everyone a favor and helped the fellow meet another hard object with his head.

The playing went on into the wee hours of the morning to a progressively smaller and smaller crowd. Finally, exhausted, they all stopped. "Totally awesomely burning, man! Did ya see the crowds? We like flamed them all out! We really sparked tonight!"

"Yea – our new matchstick drummer – he was like fire and the crowds like a moth! Say man, what's your signature?"

Chu was, well, burned out and his fingers ached. "My name is Hootchu. I'm new to Rhoditian, but hope to make a big burn here as a drummer."

"Well man, keep playing with fire like tonight and you will be the brightest new flame in the city!"

"Jalapeno Hot! I've heard there is a famous art dealer here I should try to meet …" Chu was interrupted.

"Jalapeno hot? … that is like, so totally burning! Spicy hot, totally cool! Say, that could be the name of our band!"

"Holy Hot Habeneros! I think we are really on to something dudes! This could really catch on!"

Chu rolled his eyes in exasperation. The last thing he wanted was to start some new craze! It took several more minutes to wring out the directions to Miguel's principal on the other side of the city. He would have excused himself and started heading off that way, but at this time of the night it would have definitely attracted attention. As though he needed any more.

"Come on, man – let's bunk out in the stable behind that tavern over there – that's where a lot of us burning artists sleep over – the proprietor says its ok, as long as we leave him a tip from our proceeds." One of the young men lifted up a hat that had a fair amount of coin which had been dropped in by those pleased with their music.

"Right-o, but who should keep the hat tonight? The last few times it was either gone by morning or a whole lot lighter."

"Hey, are you trying to spark with me? Somebody stole out of it during the night!"

The group started bickering back and forth as they carried their instruments over to the tavern in question. It was getting heated, and all Chu wanted to do was go to sleep. This did not seem too likely, not with the argument brewing. Then one of the young ladies suggested, "Hey, let's get our drummer to hold it tonight – he was the spark that ignited our flame tonight anyway!"

"Great idea – he's our … our …our chili flame-master!"

"Hey 'Hoot'… Hootch … Hooty … oh whatever – 'Flame-master' – will you hold onto our loot tonight? Make sure nobody douses your burn and leaves you burnt toast!" The group all laughed and surrounded Chu in the stable straw, settling down near each other to keep warm. Chu was the last to make a passable bed in the straw for himself. How did he get into this in the first place? It was a good thing Miguel and Gaeten were not here – he would never, ever live it down. With a sigh Chu nestled the hat full of money against him in the straw and drifted off to sleep, assuring himself that the itch running up and down his back was most definitely from the straw.

Only twice in the night did the chopsticks need to dissuade would-be pilferers from making a withdrawal.

It had not been easy. Anywhere Sir Archibald Reginaldo traveled within Rhoditian seemed to be news to some gossip reporter. Already his favorable reaction to the previous night's dinner was being whispered at the hotel where he had stayed the night after a very late final party, and rumors were flying around about Doranna, the young blind actress he had taken an interest in. Reginaldo suspected her career had just taken a steep upward trajectory. So be it. She had done her task well enough and he wished the best for her. However, he was having difficulty in escaping the gossip-mongers who watched his every move.

In the past he had adored the attention. Now he disliked it. Today in particular it was absolutely imperative that no one knew where he was going … or who he would see. Thankfully, there were ways. After all, this was HIS city and it was filled to overflowing with actors. Five were now standing in his luxurious apartment. He really did not think they looked all that much like him – obviously all had more pounds on their frames than he.

Yet clothed in fine woolen hooded cloaks, with identical apparel and some facial make-up, each could easily be mistaken for the real Reginaldo.

Now for the game. Four 'Reginaldos' converged on the carriage pick up dock simultaneously and were whisked away in all directions, chased by several galloping horses with spotters bouncing along on their saddles. Within minutes, another Reginaldo sneakily exited the rear of the hotel and went off at full gallop in another carriage. Not unexpectedly, two other horsemen had been watching for just such a move and set off in hot pursuit. A sixth and final caped person wandered through the hotel lounge for a few minutes and then exited a side door, flashing a heavily ringed hand as he brushed open the door and walked at a fairly good pace – for such an immense figure – across the street to a salon that catered exclusively to very well-to-do male patrons. Once inside that Reginaldo was ushered into a private bath. Several men took up positions surrounding the salon, while one pretended to be some important figure and tried to gain entrance. That imposter left the establishment rather unceremoniously by the hands of a burly bouncer, landing several feet out into the street in a pile.

Reginaldo's carriage – for the real Reginaldo – beat a hasty path to the dockyard. He exited and was immediately ushered aboard a private coastal yacht. As soon as his feet were onboard, the anchor was lifted, ropes unfettered and sail lifted, and the sloop began to pull away. Reginaldo disappeared below deck and peered out a window to see several horsemen come to a screeching halt and dismount, shouting and pointing toward his ship as it pulled out into the harbor. They would hear conflicting reports as to where it was going, and before another ship could be sent in pursuit they would be out of the harbor and around several shoreline points and out of sight. Within the hour he would endure the indignity of being lowered into a small skiff and rowed ashore to one of his father's many commercial wharves, where he would disappear from the public eye.

He sighed. Such was the life of the world's greatest singer. Or second greatest, he corrected himself. By lunchtime he should be at the prescribed villa. This had better be legitimate, he thought. Otherwise the slimiest gossip-monger would have an exclusive story told by him personally about a certain art dealer.

Chu had vainly tried to discourage the others from coming. He really had. But the thought of even possibly getting an interview with an important dealer who could become their benefactor had every one of the band members itching to come along. So, after brushing off as much of the hay and straw as they could, and after splashing some water on themselves at a public fountain, they marched off. Of course no one wanted to hire a carriage, so they walked … and walked. It took nearly three hours through the winding and crowded streets to reach the villa, and they were all in a rather foul mood after lugging their instruments that far. At least Chu had convinced everyone to disperse their revenue and he did not have to carry that as well.

Exhausted, they dropped to the street outside the entrance while Chu tried to figure out how to see if Miguel was present. He had just figured he may as well march up to the gatehouse and ask when a blacked out carriage charged up. Two burly guards came out and inspected the carriage contents, and must have approved the visitor since the gate was immediately opened and the carriage allowed entrance.

Before the gate could swing shut, Chu walked up to speak to the attendant. In hindsight, his timing was perhaps a touch too quick, as the guards appeared to think he was trying to sneak in.

"Hey, you there! Beat it before we beat you!"

Chu was not in a particularly patient mood, but figured it may not be in best form to knock these two senseless … at least not yet. "Keep your burning britches on. I am here to see Mr. Miguel – Miguel De la Rosa."

The other musicians looked up, startled. Chu turned toward them – he figured he needed to stay within disguise for a little bit longer. "I know this De la Rosa; he works here and said he could get me an audience."

The nearest guard smirked. "Sure you do. I bet he comes to hear you butcher songs every night in the park! Nice try. Beat it. Now."

Chu considered butchering something … or someone … else right now – this was getting very old very fast – but with considerable effort kept his hands from darting out to strangle the oaf in front of him. "As a matter of fact, De la Rosa has quite a flaming ear for fine music and thinks we may be the fiery hottest band to come along in quite some time. Will you please let him know that HootCHU is here to see him?" He hoped they would catch his emphasis.

The other guard came up closer. "De la Rosa ... a punk music fan? That's a laugh! You don't look like you could pluck a tune if it came up and bit you. Scram."

Chu sighed and counted to five inside. He sorely wanted to pluck something painfully out of the obstacle before him. *Patience ... it is a Godly characteristic, Chu* he said to himself. The band members had drawn up closer, looking to the guards like they might rush the gate. One of the guards pulled out a stout club while the liveried attendant back at the gate house grabbed a short rope and pulled, ringing a loud bell.

Chu sighed again ... did it have to go this way? Maybe it would at least get more interesting. But instead the leader of the little band had another idea. He tugged on Chu's sleeve and pulled him back. The others had already sat down on the pavement and had their instruments out and ready. "Hey man, let's show the dudes ... maybe this Delarotisserie guy will hear ya and come out on his own!"

Chu would have far preferred to dismember something, but his drums were thrust into his hands and the group started playing one of the tunes from the night before. If Miguel came out now ... But he had little choice if he was to stay in character, and Miguel may very well not even be here at the villa currently. So reluctantly he sat, pulled out his chopsticks, and joined in. This was SO embarrassing!

Reginaldo was greeted at the front door by a servant and led to the private upper room. The door was opened for him. Without waiting for a proper introduction, Reginaldo stormed in. "This had better be good ... I am in no mood for any trickery!"

Gaeten and Ethan had been in the room all day, and had just finished a rather long winded rendition of their past history with the great singer. Gaeten stood and turned. "How good of you to come, Reginaldo."

All pretense of pomp and arrogance fell away. "Gaeten, my friend! I never, ever expected to see you here in Rhoditian! And ... Ethan? What in the world are you doing here? It cannot be safe for either of you ..."

Reginaldo stopped, seeing that there were others in the room. "Pardon me." He looked earnestly first at Gaeten and then at Ethan, wondering if he might have already said too much.

Miguel stepped over and put a hand on Gaeten's arm. "Sir, it is a great honor to meet you! Please, do not be concerned. Gaeten and I go way back … he was one of my teachers at the Watcher Compound."

Gaeten nodded. "It is safe to speak freely. Miguel works here under contract, and I must apologize for my tactics in requesting you to come. We need your help. Freelandia needs your help."

Reginaldo took a proffered chair and turned serious. "It cannot bode well to see both of you here." He pointed at Gaeten and Ethan. "I must admit, your note had me very puzzled."

"I had to find a way to get to you without alerting any Dominion authorities, nor allowing anyone to see either of us. I hope you do not mind."

Reginaldo laughed. "Mind? No – I was able to have dinner with a delightful young lady instead of the stuffy old men who were surrounding me … and I was reminded of our mutual Singer friend. How I miss her! But you said you needed my help. I will do whatever I can."

"Thank you, Reginaldo. There are actually two things. One should be easy, the other quite difficult."

"Ok … try me."

"First, we really do need you to grant an interview with the art dealer – Miguel works here and it was the only way to bribe the dealer to both let us stay and to make up for taking Miguel away was to offer an interview with you."

Reginaldo rolled his eyes. "And the second?"

"We need safe and immediate passage to Freelandia."

The big man began to laugh, doubling over on his chair. Ethan looked nervously over at Miguel. "Oh my … what timing! I had planned on leaving in two days for a concert scheduled in Alteria. My father was lending me one of his own ships. I am certain we can slip you aboard without undue difficulty. Now you must tell me … which is the more difficult task?!" Reginaldo sobered up. "But are you sure no one knows you are here? Are you certain you are safe?"

An insistent bell sounded from somewhere out front of the villa. The effect was immediate. Miguel raced from the room in a flash, his two long swords in their scabbard on his back making slapping sounds as he ran. The others had no idea what was happening until a servant came up to the room. "Please, do not be concerned. That is just our gate alarm. There appears to be a few hooligans out front. We get them occasionally – usually they are trying to force an audience. I am sure it is nothing …" The strains of a tune wafted up through a window and the servant nodded with a scowl. "You see, just as I said. I am sure De la Rosa will dispense with them if the guards have not already done so."

Ethan and Reginaldo moved to the window, through which they could just barely see the front gate area through the leaves of several trees. As Gaeten joined them so he could hear more clearly, Reginaldo cocked his head to one side, listening. "They are not too bad. The drummer seems to be really flaming!"

The two guards at the gate were not impressed whatsoever. They had to disperse such troublemakers regularly, though usually they only came one or two at a time. And that drummer was making them quite nervous, for some odd reason, when he looked their way. Nevertheless, they had a job to do. Both swung their short clubs through the air threateningly and advanced on the squatters.

'This could really get out of hand in a hurry', thought Chu. He knew he had better stop it before someone got hurt. He stood quickly, swinging one of the two drums he had been playing out of the way. Unfortunately, the gate guard was closer than Chu had realized, and the swinging drum caught the guard on the wrist, sending his club spinning away. Naturally, they took that action as an attack. The second guard reacted instantly and swung a swift blow toward Chu's head.

Chu's training took over as it had so many times in the past to save his scalp. He ducked. Without the expected contact, the guard's swing overshot and it put him off-balance. Trying to help one of their own under attack, one of the band members stuck out a leg and the guard toppled to the ground.

"Great," whispered Chu. "Just great."

The first guard did not wait. He swung a massive fist in an uppercut that could have lifted Chu easily off the ground … had it connected. Instead, Chu pulled back the drum and the fist slammed through the skin cover and into the bottom which necked down considerably, effectively trapping the hand in the tight wooden confines.

By this time the second guard had regained his footing and charged at the only standing combatant, pulling out a knife from its belt sheath. Chu had no time to extract one of his own knives, even if he had wanted to. Instead, he had to use whatever was in his hand at the time. He rolled his eyes heavenward as he fended off the knife parry with … his chopsticks. It took some effort … admittedly it would have been a rather enjoyable challenge had not the person on the other end of the sharp implement seemed so determined to skewer him.

Now the guard with his hand caught in the drum charged forward, swinging that arm in a roundhouse, drum included. Chu still had a second drum next to him, and so he quickly grabbed that and used it to deflect the attack. So began a dance that was rather humorous to all onlookers … but deadly serious to the combatants. On one side, Chu blocked knife thrust after thrust from one guard with a pair of chopsticks, and on the other side he ducked, swiveled and blocked a drum-armed mutant guard with a second matched drum … with deafeningly loud percussions at every contact.

Just when it did not seem like it could get any worse, he heard another set of feet running up behind him. Adding a third, unknown attacker to the mix was certainly adding interest … and real danger. This could not be allowed. Chu felt he had to end it, fast – but without bloodshed or permanent damage to anyone … and especially to himself!

The drum mutant swung again. Chu leapt into the air, rotating an outstretched foot above the arm-drum 'weapon' so that it contacted solidly with the side of the guard's head. That spun the man directly into the path of whoever was running up. It was a forceful enough contact that the mutant should stay down for awhile. One down. Simultaneously, Chu's upper body spun in the other direction, and he stretched out the drum he was holding. Chu was rewarded with a very satisfying bass note thrum as it connected with the other guard's head. That guard's eyes rolled up into his head as he was knocked off his feet unconscious. Two down.

Chu still had not actually seen the body belonging to the feet that had just run up to join the fray. It took most of his agility and strength just to land reasonably well from his completed airborne acrobatics. Somehow he still had retained a grip on the drum and Chu brought this up as he heard the unmistakable sound of swords leaving scabbards. The drum

came up in perfect timing and Chu felt the impact of a sword thrust into the wooden base. He yanked and twisted as hard as he could, flinging the drum and captured sword away from the immediate conflict. He brought up his only other weapon in hand.

And so Miguel, one remaining sword in hand, faced the lime green coated, stocking capped middle-aged punk street musician who had just taken two of his best guards out of commission single handedly, had adroitly disarmed him of one of his two swords, and who now faced him with a pair of … chopsticks.

In the split second it took both warriors to reassess the tactical situation, Chu's worst fears – at least of the morning – were realized. Miguel recognized him. The ensuing laughter was so loud that Gaeten, Ethan and Reginaldo had no trouble whatsoever in hearing it, as did pretty much everyone else in the villa and the nearby neighborhood. Chu cringed. He knew he could never, ever, not in a million years live this one down.

An Alterian ship entered port at the Keep in Freelandia and a message was rushed to Duncan and Lydia – Gaeten had rescued Ethan, and they were trying to connect up with the Watchers Eyes network to escape from Dominion lands. The whoop of joy had quite a contingent of Watcher guards and James rushing into Duncan's office. Prayers of thanksgiving were lifted high … and more prayers for mercy and grace to get everyone home safely followed.

Chapter 14
Calm Before the Storm

obby sat down for lunch with Maria, Kory and Master Ariel. "I muchly appreciate the wee little dinner surprise ye helped me wit' the other evenin' for me Arianna ... ach, now I gets to call 'er me wifey! It shor'nuff was extra specially nice."

All three giggled and Kory spoke first. "Oh, that was so very much fun! Did it surprise Arianna? She is so pretty!"

Robby glowed. "Pretty? That just does not due me lady justice, my young friend! She is knock down, get up and be knocked down again gorgeous! And surprised? She was bowled over! I think she be so surprised she went 'an said yes before she knew what I had asked of her!"

Ariel smiled sweetly. "It was so obvious she is heads over heels in love with you, Chief Engineer. And with that setting how could she resist? The surprise was such fun to plan and bring all together. And as much as we were playing for you, we were also worshiping our Creator at the same time. I really do think the love between a man and woman must be some small aspect of the love God must have for us."

"Whoa! Me luv for that gal is mighty overwhelming. Do you really think that God gets all gooey eyed over us?" Robby smiled and laughed.

After laughing herself Maria added, "Well, He may not get dumbstruck like you do, Chief Engineer, but He is the source of real and true love ... so our love for one another and even for God Himself must be a tiny reflection of His love." She smirked. "When was the last time you got all love-struck for God?"

"Ach, ye have me there, missy. I guess the closest to that I've come recently is listening and joining in with the three of you singing the other night at the concert hall. I don't rightly reckon how or why, but worshiping like that brought tears to me eyes and set me heart to throbbing with love of my God like I had not felt in many a' year."

"Then we accomplished at least one of our goals," concluded Ariel with a big smile and gleam in her eyes.

"Then that ye have, my fine young ladies. But now I find meself in a wee bit of a pickle."

"Oh, you are just married and already you're in hot water?" Maria giggled again.

"Aye, and ye all have a wee part in the pretty predicament."

"Us?!" all three exclaimed at the same time.

It was Robby's turn to grin. "Aye, all three pretty little things that ye are, ya done helped me get into a bit of a jam. Ya see now, me lovely wifey figures the proposal was all fine and good, but that a wedding itself should be done right proper, with all kinda girly things like pouffery white dresses and a grand ole church and everyone that might have known her and her third cousin twice removed … whatever the likes that may be. Now, all the cakes and food might not be such a hardship for me, but the rest? What with a war on our very doorstep? I tried to explain it pure and simple like, but once an idea is planted in that pretty head there's no way to uproot it. I tried, I tell ye … but no fooling but she's awantin' to invite most of Freelandia, and maybe a goodly part of Alteria to boot!"

The girls were nearly in hysterics laughing so hard at Robby's speech and also from the most doleful sad face he had put on to match it. "But …. but what … what do we have to do with all that?" spurted out Ariel.

"Well now, it be nice you could find time betwixt your guffawings to offer a poor engineer bloke like me what you three highly talented artists could do. I was beginnin' ta think I'd have'ta be calling a healer, what with all your convulsionisms you be carrying on wit. Hmmph!"

Robby's face had transformed into a pouty miff that sent Ariel and Kory rocking back, holding their ribcages they were laughing so hard. Between giggles they described it to Maria who joined in with the infectious laughter. "Please …. Please stop Chief Engineer … my ribs huuurrtt!" Ariel gasped for air and tried … somewhat vainly … to control her giggling.

Kory took a deep breath to regain a level of control and between smirks and swallows was able to sputter out, "What could we possibly do to help you in your … your … delicate situation?" They all convulsed again in giggles.

Robby rolled his eyes skyward. "Argh … what have I done, Lord, to deserve all of this? Ah well, down to seriousness. If after the war we can indeed plan on such a mighty shindig – and of course the good Lord surely will see to that! – then sure as shootin' I'm gonna have ta top what you all done fer the proposal and wedding thingy. And I'm not all that sure such a thingy is even possible!"

The mention of the war broke the giddiness. Maria looked thoughtful. "Well, we could probably prepare a concert for you, or maybe a play? Do you know of anything in particular that Arianna might like?"

"Well, I be thinkin' 'bout that a wee bit. She said she herself knows a wee bit of musical making … that she learned to play the guitar as a girl, but has not done much playing like since."

"Oh – she could be part of the concert then … we could call her up on the stage and play with us!" Kory exclaimed.

Robby put on his doleful expression again. "No … no I don't think she would appreciate that none too well … I'd be in worser shape than before! No, I was thinking of using me engineering and inventin' skills in combination with your three musical abilities. I was watching you three play the other night, and I got to be wondering 'bout the way the stringy thingys vibrate and echo about in those wooden boxy thingys you were playing …"

"Chief Engineer! You were paying more attention to us than to your wife-to-be?" Ariel said with a sly smile.

"Ach – now donna you be telling my sweetie such outlandish stories! Where be I? Oh yes … those strings … what be they made of?"

Ariel sat up. "They are usually made of horsetail hair, sometimes from catgut." Kory and Maria grimaced.

"And I am suppos'in that they break every so often? And those different materials would make different sounds?" At her nod he continued. "We have some new materials we have been working with at the School of Engineering." He pulled a thin coil of finely braided wire out of a pocket. "Now most metals get rather fragile when pulled down this thin, they are only useful for fancy dancy necklaces and such. But our new sillarium, now it seems to be different." Robby pulled on the wire, showing that he could not break it. "Now watch … and listen … to this."

The engineer got up and moved over a few feet to a support post and wrapped the wire around a nail sticking out. He pulled out a pair of pliers and twisted it very tight. Then he strung out his braided wire to another post perhaps six feet away, looping the wire around it and twisting its end to make a circle. Then he grabbed a wooden peg lying nearby and inserted it in the wire loop close to the nearest post. He proceeded to start turning the peg end over end, tightening the wire cord. As it became taut, Robby plucked it. A deep, low chord sounded. He turned the peg another revolution and the sound was distinctly higher. A few more turns and the note was at a quite high octave. He turned it two more turns and would have strummed the very tight wire again, except that his peg could not take the stress anymore, breaking in half where the wire cut into it.

"See there? It is plenty strong, and yet thin enough to easily strum with your fingers. A regular guitar could not likely tighten the wire enough, but with some metal reinforcement it just might do the trick."

Maria looked thoughtful. "The sound was different ... sharper and unique. Several pulled at different tensions might just make some interesting sounds. So you want to become a musical instrument engineer now?"

Robby smiled. "I want to make something unique and special for someone who is totally unique and special to me! Will you help me?"

"Sure!" All three spoke at once, again.

"And who knows," the Chief Engineer said, looking thoughtful and stroking his chin. "Since this wire is so very much stronger than hair or gut, it might be able to be pulled considerably tighter – and surely could be made much longer ... into any length one might want. I wonder ..." He put the thought aside, for now. He figured he had to move on his ideas rather fast ... there was no telling when the Dominion might put a kibosh on longer range planning.

It only took two days of sailing from Rhoditian with a favorable wind to make port at Alteria's capital. Reginaldo and his guests were met by several Alterian warships well before they made harbor, making it appear that Alteria was taking Dominion aggression seriously enough to challenge incoming ships. It was surprising, perhaps, that the Dominion had not already taken over the small country, but it was not particularly strategic nor rich, and the spread of the Dominion horde had swept north and west first. If Freelandia fell, there would be no significant resistance from any other nation, and then Alteria would likely be swept over on the way to total conquest of the eastern countries.

In each case, when they were stopped for inspection, Reginaldo had harrumphed mightily and paced the deck scowling while the Alterian navy men looked on suspiciously. It was obvious they had neither particular interest nor knowledge of him, nor completely believed in his purpose. That, of course, made Reginaldo fume all the more. Miguel would come up on deck while the ship was being searched and the captain questioned, and he would slip a message to the boarding party's chief officer in one of the Alterian Command's own ciphers, as dictated beforehand by Gaeten for just such expected occurrences. The messages were met with considerable surprise that was hidden from the Rhoditian crew, and after a few minutes they were allowed passage. And so they docked without incident, though Reginaldo was now eyeing Miguel rather suspiciously himself.

He held his tongue, as so far the passengers had only been introduced to the crew as special guests of Reginaldo, albeit rather strange ones. Just before leaving Miguel had carried on board a sizeable drum and a pair of greatly oversized chopsticks which he placed in Chu's cabin with great ceremony … protesting to the rather irritated Chu that it would help him blend in as a fellow musician with the world famous singer … maybe even as a second or third string accompaniment. Miguel had barely escaped from the cabin before one of the chopsticks had been thrown at him with sufficient force to splinter when it struck the door closing rapidly behind him.

Reginaldo and his guests disembarked nearly immediately upon docking, and with great pomp the singer waltzed to the waiting carriage. The driver and attendant, however, did not open the door at his arrival but waited for the Watchers and bowed to them, offering them first entrance. That affront could not be passed over. As he lowered his large frame onto the carriage bench, tilting everyone over in his direction, he fumed "What manner of note were you passing to the warship officers … that you were princes of Freelandia come for a royal visit? I have not been ignored like that since I was an apprentice singer! And the audacity of that attendant … like I was YOUR lackey!"

"Actually," Gaeten responded before a somewhat flustered and defensive Miguel could rejoin, "it was a rather simple note. I just said I had a secret message that must be delivered to the Alterian High Command immediately."

Miguel looked perplexed. "But that is not what you had me write! You spelled out some gibberish words with extra dots and lines … I could not make out heads nor tails of it."

Gaeten smiled. "Ah, but the officer in charge of the boardings could. I had you write it in their most guarded naval cipher."

"But how … how do you know the Alterian naval cipher?"

"Oh, several mathematicians in Freelandia cracked it nearly a year ago. We were getting around to telling them, but with the threat of war and all we had not really … gotten around to it yet."

"Well, you surely have let that cat out of the bag."

"Yes, and on purpose. We could really use the Alterian help, more than just the behind-the-scenes minor things they do now. The vaunted Alterian neutrality has its uses, but when your friends are in need, it is not a time to be neutral. If you are not for God, you are against Him. There is no 'neutrality' with God when it comes to matters of good and evil. I am hoping that by being very open with them it may help sway them to take a side … to take God's side."

Reginaldo looked over at Gaeten with a frown and a far-away expression. "But taking sides involves greater risk."

"Yes, it does. In this case you risk not joining God's side. If God shows you what is right, what you are supposed to do, and you choose not to do it … what does that make it?"

"Sin."

"Correct. And there are ALWAYS consequences for our sin. We may humble ourselves and repent, and God will surely forgive – but there will be consequences to deal with. And even more, if we are not doing what God has called us to do, we lose out on His blessings too. I would rather be doing God's will and under His blessing and even face a Dominion Overlord than to miss the blessings and deal with the consequences of sinning against the Almighty."

"You make a powerful argument, Gaeten my friend." Reginaldo's voice was soft and thoughtful.

⚜

The carriage pulled up to the entrance of the Naval Command and they all disembarked. Reginaldo sniffed. "No audience with the King?"

"I doubt there is time for that. The Naval Commander is probably the only one who can see us immediately." Chu held the satchel with the Dominion war plans tightly. "But if we show these plans, will the Alterians confiscate them for their own use? Should we keep them to ourselves?"

Gaeten shook his head. "No, we need to be totally open and honest. The Alterians have been our allies for a long time – in action if not in actual treaty."

They were ushered into a teak wood paneled office. Behind a massive desk sat a dark-skinned surprisingly young looking lean man with short curly hair. "Freelandians, welcome. I am sorry there are not enough chairs here in my office – we had no time to prepare for your rather … abrupt … visit."

Gaeten took the lead as the senior Freelandian present. "Commander, thank you for taking time to see us. We have information of utmost importance to both Freelandia and our most noble Alterian allies."

"So your message implied. Pardon my directness, but there are a few things I must first ask you, sir." The Commander stared intently at Gaeten. Ethan, standing behind and somewhat ringed in by Miguel, Chu and Reginaldo, had an odd feeling that came upon him without warning or obvious cause … and time began its familiar slowing as red and blue ribbons came alive in his mind. Training took over and Ethan dived sideways between Reginaldo and Chu rolling into a ball on the floor and then launching airborne at the doorway. His movements alerted the others. Even as the first of several soldiers started to burst in, Miguel was drawing his swords and Chu had turned sideways and leapt back toward the door with a foot already flying out.

The first soldier never knew what hit him. Chu was closest and Ethan had already calculated what the Master would do. Chu's extended foot snapped into the first soldier's head, sending the large fellow tumbling to the right to crash into the wall with a startled expression frozen onto his face even as he slumped unconscious to the floor. The second soldier had no time to wonder why his captain had rather suddenly pitched sideways. Ethan's boots landed squarely in his chest, stopping and reversing all of the man's forward momentum and sending him stumbling backwards into his companions who were trying to enter directly behind him. Ethan rolled sideways as Miguel blocked the doorway, both swords held ominously.

Reginaldo had not moved at all, and had hardly registered yet what was even happening. All he knew was what was directly before his eyes – the Alterian Commander's sleeves somehow had knives pinning both his arms to his desk and a third was delicately being held inches from his face by a calm Gaeten.

"Have we passed your test, or do you need blood drawn?" Gaeten's voice was measured and slow, and his words caught the others by surprise. Chu had moved beside Miguel in front of Ethan, effectively blocking all access of any Alterian to the boy.

The Commander had a wry smile on his face as he cataloged each person and their actions. "Yes. STAND DOWN!" The soldiers out in the hallway who were just regaining their feet for another rush instead backed away. Miguel slowly lowered his blades, but did not sheath them quite yet.

In a calmer tone the Commander continued, looking across his desk. "You must be Grand Master Gaeten, and the lad over there must be the formerly captured son of Duncan and Lydia. Sir Reginaldo was expected here today, though not with such company! However, I do not know these other two, though they apparently are accomplished Watchers also … perhaps some of those loaned out for a fee?"

Gaeten had already sheathed the knife that had been so close to the Commander, and now pulled the other two out of the desk top, freeing the Alterian. "Yes, Commander. But that was a rather dangerous test. Your men could have easily been killed, not to mention you yourself."

"I had to know for sure that those who appeared before me were legitimate. And really, my men were not truly in mortal danger, now were they?"

Chu turned to face the seated man. "No, but then again it is somewhat a judgment call on how much force it may take to simply stop someone versus break their neck." He stepped over to the moaning soldier on the floor and gently felt around the man's head, shoulders and gingerly around his neck. "He will be quite sore for a few days, but I think none the worse for it." Chu motioned for two of the soldiers in the hallway to come in to retrieve their companion. Miguel stepped aside, but was still rather unsure about the tactical situation, though he did begin to sheath his swords.

Reginaldo finally had time to compose himself enough to be afraid, and he began to shake, his face turning red. Ethan grabbed one of the two spare chairs in the room and eased the large singer into it.

"Master Gaeten, your information must indeed be urgent – as is your apparent rescue mission – to disclose your knowledge of our naval cipher. We had not known you had decoded that one yet – it is quite a challenge to try to hide something for long from you Freelandians."

"Indeed, Commander – Ethan's presence alone would have been enough for me to request immediate assistance. Chu, the papers please."

Master Chu somewhat reluctantly handed over the messenger satchel he carried. The Commander opened it and quickly scanned over the main documents and maps, his eyebrows shooting upward and his eyes rapidly darting over the contents.

"Good God, man – these are the launch plans for the invasion of Free-landia!"

"Yes, Commander. Our God indeed has been very good to us – as He always is. We need your help – we must get both ourselves and these documents to Freelandia on your fastest ship. I also ask for something more."

The Commander stopped his busy poring over the papers before him and looked up. "And what might that be?"

"On behalf of the leadership of Freelandia, I ask you to come to our aid in our time of darkest need. You know what the world would look like if the Dominion was able to conquer Freelandia. You have had the luxury of independence and neutrality for a very long time. But I think the time is coming – and now is here – for Alteria to take sides. Stand for Freelandia and for our God, or stand for the Dominion and their gods, but do not try to stand in the middle."

The Alterian pursed his lips. "We have always taken a neutral stance on politics not directly affecting our country. It has kept us out of petty wars and has allowed us to profit from both sides – and to act as neutral ground for warring parties to meet and work out peace treaties. This policy has protected us for a century. And, I might add, it has benefited you Free-landians as well."

"Yes, there are aspects that have been … convenient. But will it truly protect you from the Dominion if we fall? Do you really think the Over-lords will allow Alteria or any other country to remain independent from their absolute rule?"

"No – I admit that. It would be highly unlikely our present form of self-rule would survive. But during the war itself it may allow us safe passage, and if a stalemate is struck Alteria would be a logical location to hold peace negotiations."

"Commander … no Freelandian believes there will be a stalemate. The Dominion will throw everything they have at us – you have now seen the plans yourself. They will either utterly defeat us – and by all human odds they should readily accomplish that – or their naval forces and invasion army will see the wonder and terror of fighting against the Living God Almighty."

"I am glad you have such clarity in the possible outcomes, my good sir. Our strategists give Freelandia very low odds of winning or of a stale-mate. If we did formally join you, and you are defeated as expected, then Alteria would also be utterly destroyed as your ally. As it is, being neutral, we anticipate a much less violent change of status when the Dominion is victorious."

"So, if evil wins, you will just roll over to display your belly before the dragon? You will capitulate as soon as the Dominion fleet enters your waters?" Gaeten took a step back. "Sir, the Alterians I have been close to have been some of bravest and most loyal friends I could ever ask for. They could hold their head high wherever they went. The Alteria you seem to be describing … is that a place you wish to live in? To raise your family in?"

"At least my family may still be alive."

"Hmph! Is that life worth living? What then, sir, are you really willing to die for? If you believe in our God – and I know a great many Alterians confess they are followers of the Creator – then you know death is not an end … it is a transition to a new beginning … a promotion of the most magnificent kind to an eternal life of joy spent in the direct presence of God Himself. With that hope before us, I would readily die in His service, taking a stand for God. And if I were you, I would not get into the practice of betting the odds against God. That would be a fool's bet."

The Commander had been looking thoughtful, but at that last comment his eyebrows shot up in shock. "So you take us for fools, then?"

"Not in the least, good sir. But it is much too easy to look at problems from a totally human perspective, to calculate odds and chances and then make decisions based on that supposed data. It is rather like seeing a problem and saying to God, 'Look at how big this problem is,' instead of looking at the problem and saying, 'Look how big our God is!' The odds of Freelandia winning are exactly zero or one hundred percent, if it is God's will for us to lose or to win. From our perspective, we fully believe God will deliver us from the hands of our enemies. All of the indications from Him lead us to that conclusion.   And there is one more benefit of fully trusting in God, one that takes effect now. When you are doing what God wants of you, He promises you will be under His blessing. I would far rather be under His blessing than without it. When you purpose to not do His will, you greatly risk being under His curse."

"That sounds like a threat."

"Not by me or by Freelandia. But God has said that you are either for Him or against Him. There is no middle ground, no neutrality. And any country or person who put themselves against God will most certainly be under His curse."

The Alterian pushed back in his chair. "I can make no decisions for Alteria – that is the role of our Grand Council. Under less demanding circumstances I would detain you until the Council could meet – but I fully appreciate your urgency … and I do not relish the idea of even trying to hold you against your will! I have made my decision. I will put my fastest ship at your service. It will need a few hours to prepare. That should be enough time for copies of this paperwork to be made, and for you to experience at least a touch of Alterian hospitality."

Gaeten bowed in acknowledgement, saddened that the man would not even seem to make a personal commitment to stand for what was true and right. Still, they at least offered a ship. In less than two weeks time they should once again set foot on Freelandian soil.

Chapter 15

Homeward Bound

rand Master Vitario closed the latest meeting of the Music Academy with a contented sigh. Not that there wasn't a ton of things yet to do before Dominion warships sailed into the harbor at the Keep. Even so, the Academy was more ... alive ... than it had been in, well, the last decade that he had been leading it, and even since he could remember when he was a lowly first level apprentice, now close to half a century ago. The sense of God's presence was so common now, and the wonder and awe of their creator seemed to permeate the entire school.

The organizational shake-ups had been difficult but entirely necessary, and their timing was so obviously God-ordained. The new leadership had just settled in and were re-vamping their priorities when the winds of spiritual revival had swept through the Keep and indeed the entire country. With that renewed attenuation to God and His purposes had come a focus on using music for godly purposes. And now an entirely new departure from their traditional formats and styles was sweeping through the Academy. It was not that the old styles were in any way bad, but the new forms of worship seemed so ... inspiring and inspired, so joyous and uplifting, and so full of energy and life. And so much of it seemed to have sprung into existence through the gifting God had given to a poor little blind girl.

Vitario smiled. Where was God taking his little Maria? What would become of all this energy and passion toward God? His smile fell. What was going to happen when the Dominion came? Would any of them survive? Vitario had no doubt in his mind that God had ordained that little girl to play some major part in the battle to come. He could not imagine how a frail little girl could stand up to the savage hordes that were expected to descend. Vitario resigned himself – as he had many times in the past – that this was thankfully not in his own power or hands, but in God Almighty's. He had to remind himself often that faith was particularly evident when no earthly solution seemed possible. God had proven Himself over and over, and he needed to trust that would continue.

He was the last to leave the conference room and he pushed himself up out of his chair, wincing. That dull pain in his chest seemed to be getting sharper lately. He'd have to go visit Mesha in the Ministry of Healing about it. After a few steps it subsided and faded away, and for the thousandth time his thoughts about it did likewise.

The Alterian sloop *Fa'lasha* was easily the speediest ship any of the Freelandians had ever been aboard. Coupled with the extensive nautical charts of ocean currents and trade winds that the Alterians had collected and refined for the last century it was easy to see why they were known as some of the very best sailors world-wide. The captain, fitting the stereotypical tall and thin profile of an Alterian, had openly discussed their options to reach Freelandia as quickly as possible. They could tack further eastward, skirting several chains of islands that were not yet under Dominion rule before heading north. That would very likely evade any Dominion patrols, but would add several days to the journey. Or they could veer slightly westward to catch a well-known favorable current and the northerly trade winds common this time of the year. That would bring them definitely well within Dominion controlled territory, and if their navy was indeed amassing as the captured documents suggested, they would run the risk of sailing right into a heavily armed flotilla at worst, and a gauntlet of navy patrol boats at best. The Alterian flag was still recognized as a non-combatant, and indeed the ship they were on had no obvious weaponry. Yet in the present situation it was not likely any Dominion captain would easily dismiss a fast Alterian sloop heading due north.

With prayers for protection it was mutually decided to risk the westerly route. Time was of the essence, and even a few extra days of warning could make a significant difference, especially to the Freelandian navy. So they departed, with no attention-arresting escort or commotion. The ship was made as light as possible and even had a skeleton crew, which meant the four Freelandian passengers – and even Sir Reginaldo – were expected to work right alongside the rest of the deck hands.

Once out to sea Captain Erkatan had produced a jar of dark paste. "We of course will avoid contact with any other ship, but there is always the possibility we may be stopped or passed by closely enough for someone to recognize light-skinned northerners among us. It would be wise if you could appear to fit in with the rest of the crew." Chu beamed, grabbed the jar and began to liberally apply the dark brown dye over every visible light skin on his body. In a few minutes he looked as dark as the Alterians and Ethan could not help but laugh at the transformation.

Chu's eyes narrowed, and before Ethan could dodge away he had smeared a dark brown stripe down his face. Ethan rolled his eyes and grimaced as he also was transformed into a sun-baked sailor fit to pass as one of the crew. In a few minutes the remaining fair-skinned Freelandians became honorary dark-skinned Alterian sailors.

Reginaldo had joined them on the deck, but now he took a step backward. "I think no face paint for me. I for one do not have such pale skin as you fellows." He looked over at Miguel. "Though I think poor Miguel here still looks rather pale, even with his skin darkened."

Miguel was holding his stomach and looked peaked, although he now had plenty of color to his face. "No, my friend, I don't think being a sailor is the life for me. Give me solid ground, or even better – the back of a horse – and I am much better. This rolling and rocking does not sit well with my stomach, I am afraid."

"A bit seasick? Oh, that is a shame. And this is such fine sailing weather too. Now if a storm came up, then the deck would be heaving up and down, up and down." Chu's voice followed his hand movements, imitating the large sways. Miguel did not look happy with the theatrics.

"Perhaps it would be better if I went below and rested. Maybe if I am not watching my stomach may settle."

"Surely Miguel. Just make sure you take an upper bunk."

"Why is that, Master Chu?"

"Oh, it is not really anything. I am sure this ship does not leak … much. I have heard that some ships leak rather steadily, and when everyone gets up in the morning the first order of business is bailing out the water they took on. In some ships it can get pretty bad, especially if people sleep too long in the lower bunks. Why, I've heard tell that a few passengers have even drowned, right in their sleep as the water rises. They just dream about water – rain, rivers, oceans, whatever – and that makes them not even notice when the water level rises up around them. Some even dream about fish and ocean creatures like the dreaded Walking Eight Arms ... and pretty soon the water comes up and they are breathing it in, under the waterline. With all those dreams of water and fish and monsters of the deep, they just go under themselves. And at least it would a better way to go than to have an "Eight Arms" sneak up on you during the night to steal your breath away." Chu scowled and shook as though bringing up some especially frightening thought.

Miguel looked pained. "Dreams of water ... and of fish? I ... I will see about a top bunk."

"Yes, my friend, that would probably be best. Just avoid being under any struts or overhangs, nothing that an Eight Arms could creep up and drop down onto your face."

"Wha .... What are you talking about?" Somehow, even with the dark face dye, Miguel seemed to be getting whiter.

"Oh – surely you have heard of the hideous creatures called the Eight Arms! They are rather prevalent in some parts of the ocean. Often they get dragged up in fishermen's nets, but before the fishermen can catch them, they pick themselves right up on their eight tentacle legs and walk themselves right up to the ship's rail and jump back into the ocean. And I've heard from sailors who venture up into the northern waters – like where we are going – that they have even seen whales as big as the biggest ships rearing up into the air, with monstrous Eight Arms covering their whole heads. Those poor whales, they must be no match – they try to gasp for air by lunging right up out of the water, but the Eight Arms have their mouths clamped shut tight with their tentacled arms and suck their breath right out from them. Oh, that must be a sight!"

Miguel looked even more peaked but Ethan looked curious. "Master Chu, is that for real? I mean, are there really creatures with eight arms and tentacles that attack even the whales?"

Chu glanced over at Captain Erkatan. "Surely the good Captain can confirm this?"

The Alterian captain was looking at Chu with an odd expression. "Er … why, yes lad. I have seen such a sight myself of a giant like that grappling with a mighty whale, arms wrapped all around the whale's head. And I have seen a few at fishermen's wharves, caught up in the nets with the fish. If the mates are not quick at it they can scoot themselves right off the shelves and head for the nearest water. They can go a surprising distance – and not just a' flopping about like a fish either – with real intelligence and determination to head back to the water, crawling along on those eight arms full of suckers that can grab onto things right strongly. And believe it or not, I have even watched one pull itself right up a wall, straight up the sides, just with those suckers on its arms."

Chu picked up the narrative again, with a knowing look at the captain. "And I'm sure the good Captain can also attest that his crew will regularly find a few ocean creatures mysteriously flinging themselves out of the very water in which they live, leaping up and sometimes even onto the decks of the ship – and especially during the darkest part of night!"

Captain Erkatan looked rather dubiously at Master Chu. "Well, yes, in fact that is somewhat common, especially on a ship with decks rather low to the water like this one, but …"

Chu interrupted. "And what is to say what might be chasing such poor creatures up from the depths to make them risk death in the air? And who's to say that some in fact lie in wait for passing ships, to fling themselves up on the decks at night, to catch unwary sailors and passengers while they slumber below? Perhaps they are just seeking the way back down into the ocean depths. Or perhaps, like the Eight Arms, they seek unsuspecting sailors.

I tell you, I have traveled on many an ocean going ship, but I always sleep light, and always with a knife close by, and I always choose my bed with care. But enough of that – have a good rest, my friend."

Miguel looked greenish-brown by now, though his eyes showed plenty of white as he stared at his fellow Watcher. He walked uneasily toward the door that led below-decks, and turned back with a questioning look just before he warily stepped down and out of sight.

Reginaldo began to laugh and even Gaeten began to chuckle. "Was all that really necessary, Chu?"

Master Chu put a hurt expression on. "What do you mean, Gaeten? The good Captain here confirmed what I said!"

"Well now, I would not go so far as to say that, Watcher." Captain Erkatan smiled. "Though much of what you said at least had some root in truth."

Ethan looked quite puzzled. "So Master Chu was telling a fable?"

"Not ... entirely. Erkatan looked Ethan over. "How much schooling of the ocean and sailing have you had?"

"I have studied quite a lot at the best schools in Freelandia, and of course the Keep is right near the best harbor in the Bay of Freelandia."

"Yes, I am sure you have had good text book learning. But have you ever done much sailing – outside of your protected bay?"

"Ah, well ... not really."

"That is a difference between Alterian and Freelandian royalty then. Our princes and princesses are expected to be just as at home in a ships rigging as in their own palace beds. When a prince reaches fourteen, he is traditionally given his first sailboat and is expected to captain it immediately. He cannot have the trust and love of Alterians unless he has proven himself on the sea, and he cannot be in line for succession unless he is an accomplished sailor and Captain of his own ship. What must you do to prove yourself a worthy heir to the throne?"

Gaeten chuckled again. "Captain Erkatan – you have not visited Freelandia before?"

"No, Grand Master Watcher, unfortunately I have not. I and my ship have not gotten that far north before, which is one reason I immediately volunteered when I happened to hear of your request. Most of what I know of Freelandia is from school books and is certainly colored by things heard in both Alterian and Dominion taverns."

Gaeten smiled and nodded. "Then much of what you have heard should likely not be trusted too closely."

"Oh, I have gathered that. The average person in the Dominion is quite ignorant of Freelandia and they seem to make you out more like devils, while in Alteria the children sometimes seem to think of you as angels. I figure you are somewhere in between, like the rest of us. I don't mind telling you that in Alteria we hold Freelandia and her people in very high regard – though I must add that some of the stories surrounding the

Watchers sound more like imaginative legends versus reality. You may be well trained, but my men on this ship have been all over the Dominion and in not a few skirmishes with them both at sea and on the land – even with their giant Southern Bashers. I would readily pit the best Watcher against any of my crew – and bet on my crew."

Chu pushed back his chair at that insult but Gaeten held out a steadying hand and smiled graciously. "Perhaps we can mutually learn from each other … I for one have never encountered a Basher and am greatly interested in knowing more about how they fight and any weaknesses you and your crew have seen in them. Perhaps your crew can also learn a thing or two from an old blind Watcher … or even young Ethan over there, though he is only a younger apprentice."

It was Ethan's turn to feel slighted, but at the smile on Gaeten's face he calmed back down – he may not have attained anything like a Master's level with the Watchers, but he knew he could give even Gaeten a good work out … and if anything he thought he was faster now than ever. His experiences in the last month or so had given him newly-found appreciation of the God-given gifting he had, and the desire to use it for God's purposes.

Gaeten returned to the original conversation. "But Captain Erkatan, you do have a few things about Freelandia wrong. Ethan may be the son of Chancellor Duncan, but he is not in any line of succession for future leadership of our country. We have no hereditary requirements for any position or job in Freelandia. Leaders must demonstrate their skill and ability publically. Those who seem the best qualified may be appointed or elected to positions of higher authority and power."

"But who does the appointing?"

"Our Chancellor, or a group he selects."

"But what about your Chancellor then? How is he selected?"

"The High Council chooses that person for a five year renewable term, and delegates some of their authority to the Chancellor to make decisions on a day to day basis.

"So the Council decides who it will be."

"Well, yes – but he does have a choice. No one is forced to hold the office, and all are asked to seek God's direction. The High Council also seeks input from recognized prophets and discerners, and the entire country joins in prayer over the selection. From what I gather, it has historically not been a particularly difficult task … God has given clear guidance in the process such that we have strong agreement from the large majority of the Council."

"But not total agreement? Does your God not point out the same person to everyone? Is your God somehow divided in His direction?" The captain was grinning, believing to have scored a point as he was not as certain about this God as his Freelandian companions appeared to be.

Gaeten sighed. "There have been times in our country's history that not all of the High Council members had true faith in God or sought His input. However, those have been the small minority and have not lasted in high positions of authority. Our God is such a very real part of our everyday life that those who do not believe are typically recognized as such quickly. While unbelievers can be fine administrators with great talent and skill, we do not think they make for very wise rulers – they rely solely on their own intellect, experience and skill rather than on the God who gave them those skills and whose knowledge is limitless."

The captain pressed his point. "So would you have me believe your rulers make no mistakes? And if they do, does that not show that your God is not trustworthy?"

"Not at all, Captain. Our leaders are just as humanly capable of making mistakes as others. Sometimes God does not give specific directions as clearly as we might like, and here are misinterpretations and mis-applications. Humor me for a minute. What if you had access to all the knowledge and wisdom you could ever want or need?"

The Alterian grinned widely. Gaeten continued, "But the knowledge was not accessible on your time table, and you could not control how much detail you could get? Would you thankfully accept whatever you got, or ignore the whole since you could not control it? God has His own reasons for what, when and how much He discloses, and to whom He chooses to give it to. And some people are more sensitive to hearing from Him – usually that takes some practice! For any major decisions, independent confirmation from multiple prophets and discerners are sought, along with each council member's own sensitivity to the leading of God's Spirit."

"Ah, so if someone wanted to 'pull a fast one' on your rulers they would just need to stack the prophet deck, so to speak – get several of these so-called prophets and discerners to agree to a story and present their idea in a way that pandered to the council members own interests. The idea would be agreeable to them, and they would assume it was 'a command from God on High' and figure they must do it. Surely that would not be so difficult to accomplish?"

Gaeten paused in thought. "Well, I suppose it is possible such a ruse could happen. I have never heard that it has. When you humbly seek after God, God Himself responds. When you practice listening to Him, He gives all the more guidance and direction. And when you surround yourself with others who just as actively seek after God's will, then as a group there should be relatively few mistakes. It sounds rather fanciful to those who have not had personal experience with God's direction and intervention in their lives, but once you have, life is never the same ... you never want to go back to just relying on your own intellect and senses again. In fact ...".

"SHIPS AHOY!" The lookout's voice rang out from the crow's nest atop the highest mast and all eyes followed the pointing arm.

Captain Erkatan wasted no time in snapping an order to the helmsman. "Fifteen degrees starboard, keep plenty of water between us." He looked up. "What flag are they flying?"

"I can't tell yet, Cap'n. But they looks like Dominion warships ... under full sail and heading northward. I count two ...no I see three of 'em now."

"Keep your eyes peeled – but not just on them."

The captain pondered something for a few minutes and then turned to his guests. "I was hoping to head further westward before turning north, but this will do." He turned toward his helmsman. "Point us north, Mr. Tankenkara. That should keep us many miles still to the east of yonder ships." He looked over to his First Mate. "Keep plenty of water between us and any other ship, and give her full sail."

He took a step away, then with a sly look glanced back. "I've heard that the record for the shortest journey from Alteria to Freelandia was set three years ago by the clipper Didyonous under Captain Sajkurin at five days, seven hours, twenty three minutes. At the time it was commonly said in Alteria that this record could never be broken. I have even heard that Captain Sajkurin has put up a gold coin for every man on any Alterian ship that can beat him – and he has publically said he would never have to pay up." He turned back and stepped away.

Reginaldo perked up. "I can do better. I will give three gold coins to everyone on board if we beat that record … and I will spread the news in my worldwide travels that I had the honor of being on the fastest ship known to mankind … if we beat that record!"

The captain continued. "Come, my guests. It is time for our lunch. For the duration of this voyage you are invited to dine with me in my quarters."

As he began to descend the rear stairs, he beckoned to what looked like a mere lad over to his side. "See if the other Freelandian gentleman is available for lunch – but go easy on him. I think he is having a touch of seasickness."

Chu strode forward. "Oh, I'd be happy to visit poor Miguel and let him know what a wonderful, sumptuous meal you surely have prepared for us. After all, it would be rude of him not to attend."

Gaeten chuckled. "Let him be, Chu. I hope he can rest … without worrying about some fish sneaking up on him."

Chu assumed an oh-so-innocent look and followed the others down to the captain's quarters.

Arianna brushed back her hair that was perennially falling over her forehead and refusing to stay bound behind her head. She had playfully suggested to Robby that perhaps she should cut it short – after all, it would be safer that way when working around all the fire and explosions that were part of her everyday life now – and had fully enjoyed the paroxysm of disbelief and consternation it had evoked. Arianna had no intention of changing something that she knew her husband found enchanting and that so obviously pleased him. Robby was so easy to tease. Of course, he knew all too well how to tease her back, as he so very often proved … and he seemed to relish in experimenting with new ways to get her goat. She frowned at that, but it dissolved again into a big grin … Robby also was quite skilled in making up!

But what she and Master Oldive were planning now … oh, this was sure to top anything he had pulled on her yet.

"So Oldsy, is it – or are they – finished?"

"I think so, Arianna." Oldive swept back a curtain in one of the back rooms where he had hidden his latest creations. "I started with the same basic parts but had to make … ah … certain adjustments for … ah … pronounced anatomical differences."

"Oldsy, you noticed?!"

Master Oldive turned a shade of red. "Kinda hard not to, my dear." He took a step backwards. "You do have rather large …"

"O L D S Y …!"

"… hips."

"Arrgh!" Arianna swung suddenly around, but her playful slap passed through now empty air. She glared at the older gentleman before turning back to what stood before her. She reached over and slid her hands over the curvature mentioned, then repeated the movement on her own body as if to evaluate if the proper dimensions had been used. "Oldsy, don't you think it is a bit big? I mean, my hips aren't really that big, are they?"

Oldive had been married long enough to see that trap coming a mile away. "Remember Arianna, you will likely want to wear rather thick clothing and maybe some of those clay wraps Robert has been working on. I needed to leave plenty of room for those and for sufficient freedom of movement."

Arianna turned toward him, arms safely now again at her side, and smiled. "Oh … that was a VERY good answer, Master Oldive!" She turned back to the suit of armor and rotated it to see it from the side profile. "And I suppose this area was … exaggerated … for the same reasons?" She said this with an almost sickly sweet voice that Oldsy knew meant he needed to tread extra carefully.

"Of course. And besides, I figured Robby would appreciate the … the accentuation better this way." He had almost made it out the door before one of the clay impregnated cloth wraps he had lying around connected with his rapidly retreating back. Oldsy ducked his head back into the room cautiously, checking for any further projectile launches, and in a moment Arianna joined in with his hearty laughter.

"Oldsy, that's two now. I suppose that's the payment I have to make for getting in on this before Robby."

"Hey, I don't get many chances anymore. Back when you were a lowly apprentice I could get away with a tease now and then. Now I have to first make sure that big hulking husband of yours is not in earshot or I risk a hard knock to my noggin!"

"Oh, come on now – it can't be that bad!"

"Really? The other day Robby and I heard two of the younger apprentices who had not noticed us yet make rather ... 'appreciative' comments about your hourglass figure. I had to hold him back from pulverizing them on the spot. He was so worked up I was not sure I could have held him for very long. Finally he settled down and said something to the extent that other men would be blind fools not to notice and appreciate that – his exact words – he had the best looking wife in all Freelandia. He gave 'em a strong lecture nonetheless that they can and should appreciate the beauty God created, including in members of the opposite sex, but that God would want them to look upon you and any other women as sisters in the faith ... and not let their minds or thoughts go anywhere beyond that."

Arianna turned with one eyebrow raised. "Is that what he said? Those were his words?"

"As best I can recall them. He told the two if he ever heard of them talking about their 'sister' inappropriately he would very personally educate them on proper respect, dignity and chivalry. I think he was absently bending a metal rod at the time into a tight pretzel. It was rather impressive ... especially to those apprentices of smaller stature than your lanky husband."

Her smile was a mile wide and her eyes danced. "No, not that part! ... the best-looking wife part!"

Oldive laughed again. "Yes, he said that too. And discounting my own wife I do believe he spoke God's truth. Now are you going to try it on so we can see if any adjustments are needed?"

Arianna beamed at her friend and mentor. "I surely shouldn't think any changes would be needed, what with all the measurements you made. If your wife had not been present I might have wondered a tad about your own 'sisterly' thoughts!" She said that last with a big grin, and then stepped in close and gave him a big – yet chaste – hug. "You know, you're the best, Oldsy. Someday I'm going to have to introduce you to my father. You two would hit if off for sure."

"I would be honored, Arianna, I truly would. You are surely an honor to your parents. Now let me help you get into this contraption."

Chapter 16

Sea Voyage

For two days now they had avoided nearing any other ships, though they had spotted over a dozen, all Dominion, and all seemed to be hurrying off in the same general direction to the west and now to the south west. That seemed rather ominous, as though they were all heading to some massive rendezvous site.

Captain Erkatan was pacing the deck. "I don't like it, not one bit. Every ship we have seen is scurrying off in the same direction. By this time we should have had two or three Dominion patrol ships heading our way to at least give us a look-over. They are preoccupied with something, and that cannot be good. I fear those plans you have there may be right ... the Dominion is preparing for their assault. It appears they may have pulled in their normal patrols, but I would bet they will have patrols further to the north, and those patrols may be just as likely to sink us as to let us proceed further northward. We will need to be on our toes for sure."

Miguel staggered up onto the deck. He looked pale and seemed barely able to stand. His bleary eyes gazed out over the water, and by shear will power he made his way over to where Ethan and Chu were standing.

"Ho there Miguel! It is good to see you up and about! But, my friend, you don't seem to be doing so well." Chu beamed in extra exuberance.

"I ... I have not been sleeping well. I did as you suggested, Chu, and chose my bunk carefully. But there are so many creaks and groans on this ship, and ... well ... the whole boat smells of ... fish. And last night, I could have sworn I heard something ... sort of a dragging, crawling sound. I could not see a thing, but I am sure I heard it. Did either of you hear anything?"

Ethan spoke up. "Not me, Miguel. I slept like a log. I think I like the movement in the bunk – it helps me go to sleep faster – you know, the rocking one way, then the swing back ... then swing again ..."

Miguel put a hand up to his mouth and swallowed hard, while Chu glanced over at Ethan with an approving wink.

Chu looked worriedly at his friend. "You say you heard something? A slithering, crawling kind of sound during the night?" Chu appeared thoughtful and concerned. "No, I slept very well too. Hmm. I wonder what it could have been. I would have thought our speed would surely have protected us from anything like those ... other things I may have mentioned before. Still, one cannot be too careful. I heard a sailor once say that putting a ring of salt around your bed can keep most any kind of crawling fish away. Maybe you can get some from the galley."

"Thanks ... thank you, Master Chu. I think I shall. Anything to get some decent sleep. I don't think I would be of much use to anyone as it is." He dragged himself off.

Chu smiled. "Poor Miguel. At least he has not mentioned anything about drums for several days now. Nothing like a good ocean voyage to clear your head."

Ethan looked over at the seasoned Watcher. He could not really tell if Chu was being serious or pulling his – and Miguel's leg.

Gaeten made his way carefully across the deck to join them. "If we do get challenged by any Dominion warship it would certainly be best if Miguel was in top condition."

Reginaldo had found a stool and was sitting out in the sun. "Do you think the Dominion is really starting their invasion – is it really going to happen?"

"Yes, I do. And not just because of the documents Chu obtained. I can feel it in my spirit too. The dark forces are gathering. This war will not be fought just with ships and men. It may well signify a spiritual turning point as well. If we win, the evil powers will be pushed back and weakened. Without a large navy and army to enforce their rule, a large power vacuum would occur, especially in the many territories the Dominion has conquered over the last years. The people in those areas have been under brutal rule, with no say in their own governing. Many will yearn for independence and self rule. A victorious Freelandia could help them

establish such rule – not as vassal states, but as truly free self-ruled countries. However, selfish strongmen could just as easily take over, vestiges
of the Dominion rule or home-grown dictators that can amass enough
armed men willing to put them into power to overwhelm a newly freed but
unorganized people."

Reginaldo looked puzzled. "I figured that if the Dominion lost that
would be an end of much of the world's problems and everything would
just … sort of … sort itself out." Even as he spoke he looked doubtful. "I
suppose that is not likely to happen, will it?"

"No. While there are most certainly evil spirits governed by the Prince
of Darkness, there is plenty of evil within many men without supernatural
intervention. There is a constant battle within everyone that pits what they
know is good, just, honorable and true against their own selfish desires for
power, riches and fame. There is an evil, selfish nature within all of us – just
look at very young children. Even if they are placed within perfect conditions of love, nurture and goodness, they will still show greed, anger and
rebellion. We all learn to suppress those desires, but even the best person
cannot truly conquer them on his or her own. Only with the transformation of your inner man that comes through acceptance of Jesus Christ as
your personal Lord and God and with His Spirit working in us can we
become close to truly being good – and it can be a slow and long process!"

"And if Freelandia loses?"

Gaeten's shoulders slumped. "If in the greater will of God it is His purpose that Freelandia falls? I fear the world will plunge into a much greater
darkness, at least for a time. God would of course still be actively at work,
and His people – including those within the Dominion even now – will
continue to work out His plan. The Dominion will be overturned, eventually. You cannot suppress good forever. But in the short term … it could
be a rather bleak outlook if evil runs loose with little in its path."

Captain Erkatan joined in. "But if indeed Freelandia does win, and let's
suppose the Dominion is badly defeated – then the Freelandian navy and
war resources may be the greatest remaining in the world. Would your
leaders not themselves look to expansion? I mean, think of the possibilities
if Freelandia controlled many of the island nations, or even some on the
Southern continent? Your wealth and resources would be vastly increased,
and so would your security."

"I am sure that thought has crossed some people's minds, mainly those who do not really know Freelandia very well. I suppose there may even be some within Freelandia that could entertain such aspirations. But no, that would not happen, not unless there were clear leadings from God that was dramatically different than what He has shown us in the past. We have no desire to expand beyond the lands God has provided for us. We certainly would like to have peaceful relations with other countries, and peace between other countries – there has already been far too much warfare in the history of the world. Freelandia would like open and fair trade with all countries, and unrestricted access of our people and especially of our missionaries."

"But wouldn't you want to rapidly spread your religion? If you controlled other territories you could stamp out worship of any other gods and ensure only what you say is your 'true' god is worshiped. You could set up a global theocracy controlled by your High Priests."

Chu spoke up on that one. "I can understand how you might think we would want that. Many other religions have forced their beliefs onto others, faith on the point of a sword as it were. There is no real benefit to that. Our relationship with God is based on love and faith, not on grudging obedience to a set of rules. We never force our God onto people. They must come willingly. God does want our obedience, but our willing acceptance to following His ways. Our religion is not a set of rules or ordinances that must be carefully followed. In fact, there are quite few rules. Jesus himself summarized them as to love the Lord your God with all your heart, mind, soul and strength, and to love your neighbor as yourself."

Erkatan was obviously thinking that one over. "That is far different than any other religion I know of. Most gladly force converts, and they keep a religious police to ensure everyone is kept in line. Most I have met are typically in fear of their gods and demons and all sorts of imaginative bad things. Yet I do not hear you speak of any fear … other than perhaps what you referenced about being under your god's curse."

Gaeten smiled thinly. "Yes, unfortunately that is the way many view their beliefs – a 'believe as I do or die' attitude. We don't do that. And while there is always something inherently somewhat scary about a totally pure, totally holy almighty God to whom we must ultimately answer for our deeds and beliefs, our God actually desires a friendly relationship with him. You may have heard us call our God our Father. He is a kind and loving father to us. Through our relationship with Jesus Christ, God has essentially adopted us into His own family – and that adoption is open to all … even to you, Captain."

Erkatan literally took a step backward at that thought. "Me? An Alterian? I would not have to become a Freelandian first?"

Gaeten picked up the dialog. "No, sir. God would gladly accept you into His family. All you have to do is believe on Jesus and surrender your life … your will to His."

Erkatan was spared further action … or distracted from it … by a shout from the lookout atop the mast. "Ships Ahoy! Captain – I see two masts off to the north, close to dead ahead of us."

Captain Erkatan scowled. "Are they coming or going?"

"Hard to say for sure, Captain … I think they are heading north like we are."

Erkatan looked at the sun, which was beginning to lower toward the horizon. "We have at best less than two more hours of light. At our speed we will surely catch up with those ships, if they continue on their present course. Then again, all of the other ships we saw were heading further west – like it was some gathering of whales for a feeding frenzy."

He paced the deck, deep in thought. "Helmsman – give us five degrees to starboard. We have some latitude; let's try to put some additional water between us. First Mate – double the watch tonight, and we run quiet with no open lights." He turned to the 'honorary Alterians'. "I suggest you stay below decks. From any distance you should be pretty indistinguishable from the rest of the crew, though you walk on the deck awkwardly compared to the rest of us. No need to draw any extra attention."

"Lookout – any flags visible yet?"

"Just barely can make 'em out, Captain. They are Dominion for sure. The masts and sails are configured like warships."

"Good eyes, sailor. If we can see them they likely can see us as well – those Dominion ships tend to have pretty tall decks and taller masts than we do."

As the passengers headed below decks, the lookout added one more comment. "Captain – it looks to me like one of those ships has changed course – she is tacking a tad to the starboard to match us."

"Well then, let them. There is only a short amount of sunlight left. We should be able to slip by them during the night."

A visitor to the Academy of Music would have been hard pressed to know that war was imminent and their very existence threatened. Instead, such a visitor would have been struck with the sheer joy and exuberance that seemed to permeate the campus, all focused on God. And at the center of it all were three young women.

Kory and Maria flitted from classroom to classroom, encouraging the apprentices and Masters alike. Master Ariel organized daily worship events and was even sending out groups on road trips to surrounding towns radiating out from the Keep. There had never been quite the contagious mood of celebration outpouring from the Academy ever before, and it seemed that nearly everyone exposed was infected and carried it like a contagion wherever they travelled within Freelandia.

So while the entire country was rather frantically preparing for war, they were also often doing their work with a song of praise for their God. Maria and the leadership of the Academy knew that this too was preparation. There was real power in worship.

Lydia arrived exactly at the time she had said she would and met Kory and Maria in the Commons at a picnic table. As usual, she swept into the area, all heads turning. Even when she sat at the low wooden table, her presence seemed to command attention, yet was not pretentious.

"Good morning young ladies! I must say, the sense of God's Spirit is strong in this place."

Kory was the first to respond. "Ever since we began focusing on WHO we were singing and playing to instead of the mechanics of just doing the music, it has been like this."

Master Ariel joined in. "And you know, I think the quality of our music has improved too."

Lydia nodded thoughtfully. "So how are your preparations going? Will you be ready for when the Dominion arrives?"

"Can you ever be totally prepared?" Ariel rolled her eyes. "But you said 'when' and not 'if'. Is it truly a sure thing?"

Lydia looked grieved, yet there was steel in her voice. "Yes, God has been giving a quite clear Word to many of us. We have less than two weeks. That is why I arranged to come over … I wanted you make sure you knew and would be as well prepared as the Lord directs you."

A bit of fear crept into Maria's voice. "Did … did God show you who would win?"

Lydia smiled, but there was sadness in her eyes. "Some things are hidden from me. I know we are called to fight, with both worldly and worship weapons and warriors. And I have seen … hordes of Dominion ships entering Freelandia Bay, and an overwhelming force landing on our beaches. It seems like a far greater force than we could possibly stop.

But even when it seems hopeless, yet I will trust fully in our God!" She smiled again and stood. "I have to run along, as there are many things to finish in the next two weeks." She came around the table as the others stood and gave each a large hug. "I do have a specific word from God for each of you.

Master Ariel: you have had great responsibility put on you recently, and even more will be coming. Hold fast to what you know is right and always keep going to God for answers.

Kory: you have been Maria's guide, assistant, and closest friend. She will need you more than ever in the next few weeks. Remain humble, have a servant's heart – and God will richly reward you – even more than He already has. And do not forget that you too are being used by God Almighty for His purposes … even in the small things."

Lydia reached out and held both of Maria's hands. "Maria – how short of a time you have been here and yet what a huge work God has done through you!" Then her tone and expression grew grave, and her voice had a far-away quality. "God is not finished with you yet, not even close. Hold fast to your worship – it is an incredibly potent weapon to be used both offensively against evil and defensively to protect the faithful. You will be sorely tempted to give up and run from the tasks set before you. Be of good courage and do not be afraid! The Lord Almighty is always before you, always listening, always your 'audience of One'. You will suffer severe personal loss and tragedy in the coming war. But remember – do all that you do as to our God. You are His chosen vessel, His chosen instrument. And in His sight you are not a small little blind orphan girl. You are a mighty warrior of worship! Stand firm then. Do not fear. Be very courageous!"

Maria withered inward as she listened, then struggled to stand more upright and set her shoulders back squarely. She took a deep, brave breath. "I am His handmaiden. Let the Lord do to me and with me as He wishes." She struggled to hold back a tear that had formed, and Kory took the cue and reached over to hold her close. Maria shivered, but then stood resolute.

Lydia had a tear in her eye as well. This poor little girl had gone through a great deal already, and what lay before her was a heavy burden and responsibility. Her part in the upcoming war was critically important, as she had been shown in the Spirit. Lydia herself had been given a responsibility concerning Maria – but that was not to be shared just yet. It added to the already heavy weight on her shoulders. At least her son would be returning within the next few days. That thought brought a big smile.

"I also have good news to share! Ethan has been rescued and will arrive here very shortly!" The three young ladies shouted out for joy and crowded around Lydia, showering her with hugs.

Everyone was on edge through the moonless dark night, and sleep seemed fitful. Sometime during the wee hours before dawn Miguel was startled awake. He could not detect what had brought him to consciousness, and he strained his eyes in the nearly black bunking quarters but could see no movement. But there was a noise. A soft rustling sound that he could just barely hear … a somewhat wet slithering sound like something dragging itself along the floor. Miguel sat up abruptly, pulling a dagger out of its sheath from under his pillow. Still, he could not see a thing. After a few minutes, he resheathed his weapon and lay back down. He was nearly asleep when he heard it again, closer to his bunk this time. He paused, then leapt off his bunk, landing on the deck with his feet planted widely … there was a faster movement sound and yet there was nothing to see in the nearly pitch blackness, though he could detect a distinct fish smell. Miguel stared into the darkness, only hearing the others sleeping soundly. Then he gingerly climbed back up to his bed. He eventually fell back to sleep, quite some time later, with one hand staying under his pillow clutching his knife ... just in case any Eight Arms were slithering about in the dark.

Captain Erkatan rose before the sky had even begun to lighten, and joined the double watch and night shift on deck. He strained his eyes, staring out into the darkness and listened for any telltale sounds that another ship may be close by. The wind had died down considerably overnight, and while they were in a northern current, they had not likely made as much forward progress as he would have wished. And though he had veered eastward as much as he dared during the night, the ship or ships that had spotted them during the fading light the evening before could be anywhere – long out of sight or right in front of them.

In a few minutes the pre-dawn glow of light began to penetrate the darkness. A low mist hung over the water, further obscuring sight. A breeze began to pick up and was just catching in the sails when the dark shape of a Dominion patrol ship loomed out of the night only a half a mile away almost directly to the north. Given the only slight wind and strong current, it would be difficult to stay out of catapult distance if her captain decided to challenge them. Even as Erkatan was deciding his best course of action, the other ship turned and began to close the distance. There was now no way to avoid the larger ship.

Word was passed along urgently but with no panic to the crew, and most hands came on deck, keeping busy with various activities but none far from stashed weapons. Captain Erkatan figured with luck perhaps they would just be hailed and allowed to pass without incident.

Master Chu worked on coiling an extra rigging rope that had been perfectly fine in its previous location. His movements mimicked perfectly the sailors around him, and the dark pigment on his skin was indistinguishable with the Alterians. He kept glancing up as the much larger Dominion ship came nearer, while staying as much out of the way and out of direct sight as possible. Gaeten was below in the galley, acting as an assistant cook while Ethan had scrambled up the rigging to the look-out's nest. Miguel, on the other hand, was no-where to be seen ... it appeared he had not come up from the sleeping berth. "Just like him," muttered Chu, "to be sleeping in when there's excitement afoot."

Miguel, for his part, was not sleeping. He was clueless to what was happening above; instead he was investigating some … well, he guessed they were tracks in the light dust left on the floor overnight. He was determined to discover the source of the slithering sounds he had heard. While there were many footprints obscuring the tracks, he could just make out lines here and there that appeared to correspond with something that had dragged itself across the floor toward his bunk. He heard some shouting above, but ignored it, intent on his pursuit. The drag lines seemed to keep going under the lowest bunk close to the slope of the hull. In the dark shadows behind the bunk he thought he saw something … something with a finned tail.

A voice shouted out from the Dominion patrol ship. "Prepare to be boarded for inspection!" Again Captain Erkatan considered flight, but the big catapults on the patrol ship were fully manned and he could not possibly get far before a burning projectile from one of them would take out his mast or set fire to his sails … or punch a hole through his deck and down through the hull and sink them on the spot. No, better to act totally innocent, but be ready for action just in case. He glanced at his First Mate, who nodded knowingly back. Their crew was handpicked not only for their sailing skill, but also for their battle experience both with a few skirmishes they'd had with Dominion ships before and with pirates … and in several cases they were quite sure both were the same. His crew, though acting busy about the ship's deck, all had weapons close by and all knew very well how to use them. He hoped the Freelandians stayed out of sight, and that word had been gotten to Reginaldo to especially stay out of sight … as much as that was possible for the rather large guest.

A skiff was lowered from the Dominion warship, now only about 30 yards away, and ten oars powered it quickly over to the Alterian sloop. A rope ladder was lowered and a total of twelve armed soldiers scrambled up and aboard. They assembled into four groups and began moving around the deck, with one group led by their Commander approaching Captain Erkatan.

For his part, Erkatan lifted his chin high and stormed forward. "What is the meaning of this outrage? We are a free vessel, from a neutral and free country! By what right do you claim to inspect us!"

The Dominion commander looked suspiciously first at the captain, and then, slowly, around the ship before answering. "First and foremost, Captain, my 'right' is those three catapults armed and aimed at your ship. It is well within my power to confiscate or scuttle this little scow of yours … with or without removing you and your crew first. Second, you seem to be in quite a hurry heading north. As you know, the Dominion has claim to all these waters. Third, we have had reports of various pirates operating nearby, and have been charged with inspecting all vessels we see to ensure their peaceful intentions. Fourth, we have heard reports of dangerous convicts trying to escape Dominion justice, and we are on the lookout for any of them that may be heading north. And finally, Captain … last evening we saw a ship veer away from their due north course once they saw us. That would not have been you, would it?" Erkatan showed no outward change, but on the inside his guard went up substantially. This might be a close one.

Miguel slowly and carefully approached the object of interest under the bunk, crawling forward in the cramped space with a short dagger held ready. Whatever breath-sucking monster from the deep might be lurking under the bed, it was certainly not going to disturb his sleep ever again.

Ethan crouched down low in the crow's nest high atop the mast. There was barely any room in the basket with the actual lookout standing next to him, and Ethan had to resort to actually hugging the man's legs to stay hidden. At least they had had time to stash two long bows and what must have been over a hundred arrows in quivers up in the rigging around them.

The three teams of Dominion soldiers spread out, looking at everyone and everything. One group passed by Chu without a second glance and headed for the stairs going below to the ship's hold. Another group went to the stern and another to the bow and commenced working their way back.

Gaeten cracked a few more eggs and added them to the large cast iron skillet heating over a very confined fire in the galley. He had recruited Reginaldo to act as the Chef's main assistant, and he was cooking – or rather beginning to burn – the bacon entrusted to him. Gaeten's keen ears had detected the boarding, and the Commander's loud exchange – giving everyone below decks fair warning that enemy soldiers would be soon arriving for an 'inspection'. This could be dicey. While Gaeten figured he could pull off his act as being a cook's assistant and likely even hide his blindness, he was not so sure of Reginaldo. The large man had protested greatly to having his skin darkened, though eventually he had been persuaded it was either that or being forced to stay below decks for the entire voyage. And Reginaldo could certainly act – any of his performances clearly demonstrated that. But could he act as a subservient assistant cook? Gaeten's nose wrinkled. And not a particularly good cook at that. He quickly suggested that the bacon was done and new strips should be added to the pan. Just as he was turning away to find more eggs, three Dominion soldiers entered the galley.

Miguel edged nearer the tail of what had to be some freakish denizen of the deep that was lurking in the deep shadows, probably sleeping by day to resume its nefarious nocturnal activities. His imagination conjured up hideous fangs and fins with sharp poisonous claws with which it might drag itself toward unsuspecting sleeping prey. But how to capture such a creature, even when it may be sleeping, and not inflict upon oneself some awful injury as it thrashed about seeking to escape … especially when one was lying prone, extended under a bunk with very limited maneuverability?

After a few minutes pondering this, while hearing some muffled yelling of some sort coming from above, Miguel thought the direct approach was probably best. He sheathed his knife and pulled close a towel he had procured. With one hand poised to drop the thick cloth over the creature, he tentatively reached forward and then rapidly grabbed the slimy tail and jerked it backward while instantly trapping the body of the creature under the cloth. Even though he was met with no resistance … and the creature was quite a bit smaller than he had feared … Miguel was taking no chances – after all, besides clawed fins, perhaps the creature has poison tipped tentacles! He wrapped the towel around and around while very rapidly scooting backwards out from under the bunk. The instant he was able to sit, he swung his toweled captive hard down onto the floor several times to at least stun it into submission.

There was still no movement. And as he peered down at the object wrapped under the towel he noticed something else … a thin black string trailing out from under the towel and back under the bunk. Perplexed, Miguel slowly and ever so carefully unwrapped his prisoner, with his dagger re-drawn and ready.

The three soldiers who had been investigating the ship's prow returned and made their way down into the hold. Chu noted that now only half were on the deck. The three at the stern were also returning, and they stood near their commander, waiting for further instructions. Chu was fiddling with some of the tackle along the side of the deck, and had an assortment of heavy wooden pegs in slots nearby that were used to tie down the rigging. The ones he was next to were unused. He absently seemed to adjust them, noting how easily they were removed and getting a good feel for their heft and balance. Chu also noted the crew's nervousness. Several had drifted closer to their captain and around the soldiers remaining on the deck. Others were keeping close to various chests and closed drawers all over the ship, likely where weapons were stored. Of course, most of the sailors had rather large knives in scabbards about their belts, and the captain had a sword buckled on.

A quick glance over at the Dominion ship showed several soldiers with bows aimed this way, but since no resistance had been made so far it appeared they had relaxed their vigilance somewhat. Master Chu began calculating the distance, wind and rocking of the ships.

"When I find the Freelandian who is responsible for this ..." The bellowing voice snapped everyone's attention to the stairs leading below decks. An angry, bleary eyed Miguel emerged, dangling an ocean catfish from a thin cord. He glared venomously around the deck, his long mustache twitching and his hairy brows knotted. Everyone froze in place momentarily as all eyes locked onto the dark skinned but not very Alterian-looking character who was rather comically holding a dead fish. The sleep-dazed Miguel himself glared at everyone, seeking his suspected nemesis Master Chu. His eyes instead locked first on the very near and very large Dominion warship just off their bow, next on the enemy soldiers on deck and finally on their Commander with his bright uniform. Miguel's eyes went very wide in shock, matching the astonishment which everyone else on Alterian deck was experiencing.

The Dominion Commander was the first to snap out of it. "Seize him!"

That shout broke the eerie stillness that had gripped everyone present and pandemonium ensued. Four of the Dominion soldiers immediately drew swords and made to rush forward to grab the fishy Watcher, but they were much too slow. Miguel was already armed ... well ... sort of. He twirled the catfish in a tight, very rapid circle while letting out more of the cord in his hand. The dead weight of the fish on the end spun in a sharp arc. Miguel let it loose not at the first of the soldiers coming at him, but instead at the fourth.

The catfish hit that soldier's head with a very wet sounding smack, while the other three combatants became momentarily tangled in the black cord attached to it. That momentary pause was plenty of time for Miguel to drive a foot up between the first man's legs and snatch his sword as the recipient staggered to one side. The second soldier was untangling and

turning to engage when Miguel's left knee caught his sword forearm while his left fist crashed down at the same spot. The bone shattered and before the sword could drop to the deck, Miguel deftly caught it. Now, properly armed with two swords – proper that is, to Miguel – he faced the third soldier and ran him through before the shocked fellow knew the tables had definitely turned on him.

Even as all that was happening the Alterian crew erupted into action. Various swords, knives, axes and other weapons seemed to instantly appear and the other soldiers on deck did not even have time to draw their weapons before they were felled. Chu had ignored them and instead had already sent four heavy rigging pins tumbling end over end in high arc trajectories toward the patrol ship. The distance and relative movements were considerable, but then again, so were Chu's skills. The Dominion bowmen went down.

Captain Erkatan instantly shouted out instructions for full sail and rudder directions even as several large multi-man mechanical bows appeared on the deck of the Alterian ship from hidden storage areas. In less than a second Ethan had stood and grabbed a bow. He already had several quivers of arrows clenched between his legs. Blue lines stood out clearly before his eyes and they seemed to compensate automatically for the movements and changing distance of the two ships. The Dominion catapults HAD to be made inoperable, and fast.

Everyone in the galley heard Miguel's bellow and the Dominion Commander's shouted order. The three soldiers had been very suspiciously eyeing Reginaldo, even as they 'confiscated' bacon samples as part of their official inspection. All three turned to face the exit from whence the shout could be heard. As they reached for the swords at their sides Gaeten hurled two bottles of spices that had been on the counter just milliseconds prior. Both dropped in their tracks. The third was just turning toward their assailant when he came face to face, as it were, with a cast iron skillet at the end of the arm of Reginaldo. "I burnt the bacon anyway," he muttered as the soldier flew sideways from the impact.

Gaeten raced for the door, catching the three soldiers who had been inspecting the hold as they scrambled deck-side. In the cramped confines of the narrow staircase, none of the soldiers could draw his weapon. Gaeten's were already out, attached to his wrists. His hands darted out in sharp strikes hard to even see and the three crumpled, tumbling backwards down into the hold. Several Alterian sailors rushed by to render the soldiers any extra assistance they might need to remain comatose.

In Ethan's world, there was always time to pray first, act second. "God, may the arrows of your servant fly true. Have mercy on us today and let us escape the grasp of our enemies. Thank you for your ever present protection and the abilities you have entrusted to me, and now use me for Your purposes, for Your glory and honor. Amen." The first arrow slowly left the string and Ethan had to remember to let it get past the bow itself before moving to nock the next. He was in his own element, his own kind of world that fit in between the seconds which rushed by everyone else.

In the past when he entered this time-altered state he mainly focused on the tasks at hand. Today he noticed something else. In his mind's eye he stood firmly planted in the physical world, but he could sense the presence of God Himself, as though God was right behind him. He had an audience. Instead of making him nervous it comforted Ethan greatly and he drew power from that infinite presence.

Never had he shot so fast and so true. To those below it was as if there were ten archers raining death and destruction down onto the nearby enemy ship. And to those on the Dominion warship it was as if the sky had opened and a steady stream of arrows with unerring precision was pouring down upon them.

The sailors manning the catapults were the first to fall, and in less than a minute everyone standing near one of the long range weapons was dead or dying. Next, the heavy ropes were targeted and after several strikes each catapult harmlessly launched its load into the sea behind the Alterian ship. By this time they were beginning to pull away, but the longbow had plenty of range. The Dominion captain went down next, followed by every uniformed officer in sight. The helmsman died next, and now utter chaos reigned on the enemy ship with all hands diving behind any solid object and many racing to go below decks. Some even made it.

Ethan ran out of arrows about the same time they passed out of range, and the Dominion ship's crew had been decimated to nearly half that had been present a few minutes before. The Alterian three man mechanical bows had also fired several times, though Ethan could not figure out why they had aimed so low … they had missed the deck entirely. As he came down the ropes he asked about that to Captain Erkatan.

"Did you not see where they struck?"

"No sir, I was … rather busy with my own aiming."

The captain began to laugh, even as Gaeten and Reginaldo joined them near the helm. "Never will I question the fighting worthiness or skills of

Freelandian Watchers … and particularly not when the son of Chancellor Duncan has a bow near about! Or …" he looked over at now very awake Miguel, "when one has a fish in his hands!"

Miguel smiled innocently and gave a short bow, even as he glared over at Chu.

The captain continued. "Master Chu, after dispatching those bowmen … by the way, I have never witnessed such throwing ability in all my life! … I am sure you noted where my men were aiming?"

Chu nodded. "Yes, Captain. Your men landed two of three heavy bolts directly into the rudder of the Dominion ship and the other stuck fast to the stern very close to the rudder itself. That ship will not be turned to a new course until they are removed."

"Yes, though now I doubt enough crew remains to try to follow us even if they do remove the bolts. But Ethan, I did not know it was humanly possible to shoot a bow that fast. It seemed like your arrows were nearly touching each other as they left the bow! You are not some kind of spirit … or angel … in disguise now, are you?"

It was Ethan's turn to laugh. "No Captain. Just someone to whom God has given a gift, to be used for His purposes."

Erkatan squinted at Ethan and shook his head. "You could nearly make me a believer, with that demonstration. If it was not a miracle I am not sure what else it could be."

Gaeten reached out to lightly touch the captain's arm. "Nearly, dear Captain? What would it really take to convince you to believe?"

Erkatan looked slowly around the ring of the Freelandians. Reginaldo spoke up. "You may as well start now, Captain. Otherwise you will get no rest. A miracle here and there, prophecy, strange happenings that seem just too coincidental to be pure chance … again and again. I tell, you, it is really, really tough to remain an unbeliever around these folks! It just wears you down! And then there's the gentle words and the integrity and genuineness of every one of these men. I finally had to give up!"

That brought a grin from everyone, but Captain Erkatan was grinning the most, and he had a soft look in moist eyes.

Chapter 17

Homecoming

There were no more encounters with Dominion ships, though they did see other vessels that all seemed to be heading in a southern direction. According to the plans Chu had obtained, the Dominion naval strategy was to first congregate most of their fighting vessels in one area. Then when the invasion troop carrier ships arrived the warships would escort them in two large flotillas, each with over two hundred ships and each larger than the entire Freelandian fleet. The first would have a larger proportion of fighting warships to clear the way for the troop carriers. It appeared the plan was to arrive with such a massive force that either Freelandia would capitulate, or be destroyed under the weight of the overwhelmingly large navy and invading army. At the spearhead of the fleets were the Dreadnaughts, the largest and most powerful warships the Dominion had ever created, ships so mountainous that the much smaller Freelandian vessels were not expected to be more than slight inconveniences to them – or so the Dominion planners noted.

Chu and Miguel appeared to have settled their dispute, and there were no further incidences of fish tracks during the night nor mention of certain drum-playing experiences.

On the evening of the fourth day, the northern coast was spotted, the fierce and rugged cliffs that were totally inhospitable to any possible landings. As they neared, several very fast Freelandian sloops came near to challenge their identity. The Alterian flag was raised high, along with a diplomatic signal flag indicating VIPs were aboard. The sentry boats allowed them passage and before the sun set the ship ran the rather harrowing narrow passage between the rocky crags and entered the much more peaceful inland harbor. Given the lateness of the day and the dangers of the rock pinnacles that jutted out of the water in several places, they laid anchor just inside the bay, out of the main shipping channel. In the morning they would arrive at the dockyard of the Keep.

Captain Erkatan ordered a bountiful meal to congratulate the crew on their successful voyage. Barring some unexpected incident they should nicely break the prior speed record and rightfully claim the title of the fastest voyage from Alteria to Freelandia.

The next morning dawned bright and fair, and at the earliest hour they raised anchor. By noon they were within sight of the dockyard. The Freelandians stood on deck, soaking in the sights and giving sight by sight commentary to Gaeten. They had diligently washed off the skin darkening pigments and all were anxious to set foot back on their homeland soil. None were more excited than Ethan, and probably none as apprehensive at the same time. He stood along the deck railing, staring moodily toward the approaching dock.

"Lost in your thoughts?" Gaeten had come up silently beside him.

Ethan looked down into the waves. "I suppose so. I don't know whether I should line up to be the first off the gangplank or go hide down in the back of the hold. I caused a lot of problems, didn't I?"

Gaeten chuckled softly. "Yes, Ethan, you did."

"I was so stupid. So very, very stupid! I put myself at risk, even put our entire country at risk by my recklessness. You and everyone else must think I am the stupidest person on earth!" Tears were now streaming down Ethan's face and he made no attempt to conceal them.

Captain Erkatan had overheard the last outburst and he edged closer circumspectly. He had heard that the Dominion had captured the son of Chancellor Duncan through some subterfuge and had planned on using both him and his knowledge against Freelandia.

"Well ..." Gaeten drew that out after a moment. "I guess you were in contention for that title."

Ethan's shoulders slumped lower. "See! I disappointed everyone. Especially those that I care for the most, and that care for me the most. And then you and Chu and Miguel risked your lives to rescue me, and even

Reginaldo and the entire crew of this ship. I feel like I have been a traitor to you all."

Gaeten put an arm around Ethan as he began soft sobs of remorse. "Ethan, you have learned a very important life lesson, one that most people never fully learn. You have learned about your own weakness – and yes, even stupidity. We all have our own areas of weakness, maybe especially when we think we are strong. God sometimes needs to break down our pride.

Let me ask you something. How do you learn best – by reading about something, or by experiencing it? Ok, so now you have learned much about yourself, and maybe about others too. But let me get to the heart of what I think is troubling you most. Do you think your parents love you any less? Do you think God loves you any less? Do you think I love you any less?"

Ethan looked up, tears still in his eyes. "You all would have every right to."

"Surely that is true! If we base our love on someone's actions, then without doubt at some point they will disappoint us and maybe even fail us, at least in our own perspective."

"But … you all must feel very disappointed in me, maybe even anger. You'd have the right to that too."

"Yes again. But if our love for one another – and especially if God's love for us were based on our feelings of the moment, where would that leave us? Our feelings are fickle. No. While our own love may be like that at times, God's love is certainly not. And the more we are filled with His love, the more we will actually love others His way."

"But …"

"But nothing. God's love does not depend on our feelings or on our actions."

"But wait a minute. How can God continue to love us when we sin, when we do something directly against what we know are His laws and wishes?"

"So does God's love flicker on and off like a lightning bug? Name a single person besides Jesus Christ who has not done wrong, who has not sinned? And even if you think there might be such a person, you cannot know what goes on in their heart and mind. No, God's love is constant because it is based on who He is. He does not change. And the truly awesome, almost incomprehensible thing is that He offers us eternal life with him with only one condition – that we accept Jesus as Lord. He does not say 'I will love you only if you always show love for me'. Nor do we have to become perfect and sinless before God will love us, or as a basis for His continuing love. He does not need us to love Him, nor does He force that … but God wants that from us.

God has said that He has chosen us since before we were born. And yet somehow He also wants us to choose Him, to accept and welcome Him in as King of our lives. And he does that knowing without a doubt we will fail him, again and again. It is rather like your parents, Ethan. Do you believe they still love you?"

"Well … yes, I suppose so."

"Suppose nothing. Of course they do. They will be the first to find you when we arrive. They have missed you terribly and have been praying for you many times every day. Did you disappoint them? Surely. Do they know you failed? Without doubt. Has that changed their love for you? Hardly!"

"But … won't they want to punish me for what I did?"

"I'd say the consequences of your own sins have been plenty punishing already – and that you have learned your lessons from them. The purpose of punishment is learning. Your parents – and God – do not punish because they somehow enjoy it. Do you deserve punishment? Yes – and so do we all. Every time we do something for our own selfish interests we go contrary to God's ideals and therefore we are guilty and fully deserving of the ultimate punishment – eternity apart from God in hell. But when we have accepted Jesus as our Lord, He declares us 'not guilty' … forever. He may still discipline us, but always for our good. He may still allow the consequences of our own actions to affect us, for our learning. And we are still His servants, and for the greater good – which we may have difficulty perceiving – He still allows evil to exist and to affect us. The Dominion is coming against Freelandia. God can use such actions to humble a people, to turn their hearts back to Him, and yes, sometimes to punish willful disobedience. But the goal is repentance, not retribution. God's plans are always to bring about His greater glory. And the real battle is not ours … it belongs to the Lord God."

Ethan still looked confused and Gaeten could sense he was still somewhat despondent. "Ethan, God still loves you incredibly, more than you can possibly comprehend. Your parents still love you. Your friends still love you. I still love you." The older man pulled the young man in close to put flesh onto his words, and Ethan gratefully accepted. "If you feel you have to prove anything to anyone, then show that you have learned from your mistakes – that you have matured and are stronger for it – a stronger and more humble man of God than you have ever been before."

Ethan took a step back, straightened his shoulders and stood taller. "I have, Gaeten. I truly have. And I am closer now to God than I think I ever was. He has given me gifts and abilities to use for His purpose, and that is what I want to do, regardless of the outcome."

"Good boy, my friend. Ours is to obey – the results are God's and God's alone."

Ethan turned back to look out over the water. He could just make out people standing on the wharf – a large crowd of people who were already beginning to wave. It looked like quite a homecoming celebration … though he wondered how they had known who could have been on this ship.

Captain Erkatan stood close behind them, having listened intently to the entire conversation. He had a lot to think about. A god who did not demand obedience and mete out swift punishment at the slightest misstep? A god who wanted our love? A god of … of LOVE? It was crazy! It flew in the face of every other god of the many religions he had encountered. And yet here was a Grand Master Watcher who believed it. Was it possible? What if it was?

He shook his mind out of his reverie and saw the crowd at the dock, who were closely tracking their approach. "What? They look as if they know who is aboard, and when we would arrive! How is that possible?"

Chu, Miguel and Reginaldo were just walking over to join the others. Miguel spoke first. "I expect they were told ahead of time."

The captain scowled and looked over at Miguel. "What do you mean? Who could have told them? We have just beaten the record time of travel between Alteria and the Keep. How could they have known to be here at the dock on the correct day, not to mention at just the right time?"

Reginaldo let out a deep, warm chuckle. "I told you Captain, you had better get used to it. I daresay you will discover that several of their discerners or prophets or whatever will have all come up with the exact same time that we would arrive, and I would not doubt they know exactly who is on board." Reginaldo had emphasized one word stronger than the others while fixing a stare with one raised eyebrow directly at the Captain, who blinked hard and then smiled.

"This has been a most … enlightening … voyage. By the way, Reginaldo, we both need to make good on our speed award for the crew. Let us prepare to dock." Erkatan nodded at his guests and began giving out orders to the crew. Chu turned to look quizzically at Reginaldo, who had assumed a quite innocent I'm-not-saying-another-word look. "Certainly, ah … Captain Erkatan. I am feeling in a most generous mood and will take care of both yours and my obligations to your most excellent crew."

To those waiting it seemed to take the ship a long time to finally come to a rest and the gangplank to be secured. Duncan and Lydia were barely able to constrain themselves not to run aboard, and Warden James put a hand on each of their shoulders to hold them back. Even so, when at Gaeten's urging Ethan was the first one down the ramp, Lydia broke free and rushed forward to seize her son in a massive hug, tears of joy streaming down her face unashamedly. Duncan was right behind her.

The crowd of friends, relatives and others began a loud cheer, embarrassing Ethan even further – who was already turning red at the expressive motherly hug he was already getting smothered with. As the others made their way down from the ship, Lydia released Ethan into the care of his father as she gave each of the Freelandians a hug for their service, and even Reginaldo found himself on the receiving end of a sisterly hug. Duncan and James followed suit, though in a manlier restrained fashion of course.

After the guests had all disembarked, Captain Erkatan stepped down onto solid ground. Lydia disengaged with Gaeten, and came forward. She curtsied as she spoke. "Your royal highness, it is so very good of you to bring our travelers back to us." Her emotions were running rather high, and a curtsy was just not good enough. She stepped forward and gave him a big hug too, then in slight embarrassment she stepped back. "Welcome to Freelandia, Crown Prince Erkatan. We are so very pleased you elected to deliver my son back to us! I trust your encounter with the Dominion ship brought no harm to you or your crew?"

Captain Erkatan bowed low. "No milady, no harm was done to us, in very large part due to the Watchers aboard and especially your son. He is simply amazing with a bow in hand! But tell, me – how did you come to know about that, and who I am, and when we would arrive? I am dumbfounded by your knowledge!"

Lydia smiled. "Dear Prince, it is rare that events of such importance would not be shown to us by God. I have had several dreams over the last week that clearly showed you coming, with Ethan and the others, and also that you would be stopped by a Dominion warship but safely escape. Nearly a dozen others had similar dreams and visions, and so it was very well confirmed."

Reginaldo was nearby and muttered under his breath, just loud enough to hear, "I told you so!"

One person on the outskirts of the crowd was cheering less enthusiastically than the others, and excused himself in short order to duck into a nearby shop. He hurriedly exited out the rear to his waiting horse and rode off. Murdrock would want to know of this, especially so close to the day – what a select few were calling Dominion Day.

Duncan sat back in his plush chair in the reception room where he and the Prince of Alteria had adjourned to after the arrival. "So, Prince Erkatan … how long do you intend to stay in Freelandia?"

Erkatan grimaced. "With the imminent invasion of the Dominion – which had been suspected of course, but which was solidly confirmed from the detailed communications that Master Watcher Chu obtained and shared with us before we left Alteria – I dare not delay. I would like to restock our ship and depart as soon as possible – even tomorrow or at most the day after."

"I suspected as much, and I have already given orders to restock your ship with whatever supplies your quartermaster desires. We count you as allies – even though Alteria has historically officially clung to its neutrality. It is hard for Freelandians to really comprehend that stance though, especially with the obvious evil the Dominion represents."

"I can understand that, Chancellor Duncan, perhaps better now than ever before. Yet we have a very long history of not taking official sides in political disputes, and that position has done well for us in past conflicts."

"Perhaps. But past conflicts were rather small in region and scope. The Dominion wants nothing less than to rule the entire world. And so far they have been quite successful on the way toward attaining that. Many believe that Freelandia is the last country that may be able to stop them. Many believe that if Freelandia falls, that Alteria will be swallowed up shortly thereafter and all other lesser countries will be mopped up. The world could be a much bleaker place. And both of our countries and our people could be slaughtered and enslaved."

"Such doom and pessimism, dear Chancellor! Where is your faith in the god you all seem to cling so tightly to?"

Duncan sat back and steepled his hands. "God expects us to obey, and to trust Him regardless of the outcome. I fully believe that God will save us, but even if it somehow was His will that we are defeated, yet still I will trust Him. I have absolutely full confidence in our God. If not now, then eventually the Dominion will be defeated. But Alteria has a historic choice to make, and our prophets have concurred that there are very significant consequences to your choice."

"You sound so dire! If as you believe Freelandia will win, then why should we have to take sides?"

"Alteria will have to take sides; you do have to make a choice."

"I don't see why that is, Chancellor."

"Prince Erkatan, choosing to not take sides is making a choice. When the issue is between good and evil, you are either for God or against Him. There is no middle ground. If Alteria decides to be 'neutral', it is akin to taking sides with the Dominion."

"Chancellor! Are you threatening us?"

Duncan spread out his hands disarmingly, but sadly shook this head. "No, I would never do that. Regardless of whether you remain officially neutral or not, Freelandia will not come against you. But God has shown us consequences that will come to you."

Erkatan frowned. "Consequences for our sin?"

Duncan looked up. "Well … yes, I guess you could call it that. You cannot be neutral about God, not to Him."

"So you are saying that Alteria is against your God?"

Duncan looked grave. "I have no diplomatic way of saying this, Prince Erkatan. But though I count you as allies in general … yes – your neutral stance is against God and His way. I am afraid we have seen rather dire consequences for you if Alteria remains 'neutral.'"

Erkatan sat back, strumming his fingers in thought. "So then, your God cannot accept us as we are?"

"God can and will forgive and accept – and show His love and mercy – if a people, or a person, will turn to Him. That means rejecting all other gods and subjecting yourselves to Him. It means turning away from your old ways to follow His ways – with all of your heart, mind, soul and strength. No half-hearted acceptance, no maybe, no 'neutrality'. And even still, there may still be some consequences from your former sins to that you would have to deal with."

"It may be of no real difference now. The Dominion warship will undoubtedly report being attacked by an Alterian ship and the Dominion will officially declare war on us anyway. I do not think we will really have much of a choice, Chancellor."

Duncan smiled. "Sometimes God does make it easier to choose His way! But you can be dragged into it against your will, or you can wholeheartedly place yourself for God and against the evilness of the Dominion. So, Prince Erkatan – will you return to Alteria and announce yourselves as full allies with Freelandia?"

Erkatan raised one eyebrow. "What, has not your God shown you already the answer to such a momentous event?"

"He does not show us everything, Prince. The crew of the Dominion ship has already reported the attack and the Dominion naval commanders are considering what actions they should take. Their attack plans for Freelandia are already set in motion, and taking on a new war front would significantly divide their forces. They have plans for this possibility, but would rather put them on hold for a few weeks if possible to focus on the northern invasion. One ship being attacked is not like a full declaration of war from Alteria. The Dominion will not force your hand ... not yet."

"So, do you know what we will decide?" Erkatan was both curious and skeptical ... yet these prophecies were proving uncannily accurate. It was somewhat scary to think Freelandia had detailed advanced knowledge like this. And where could it come from, other than their god as they claimed? Either they made exceptionally lucky guesses, or ....

"It is not as much what Alteria will decide, is it? But what you decide."

Erkatan's confidence and bravado crumpled and his shoulders slumped. "So you know that too, do you?"

Duncan's voice was gentle. "Yes, Prince Erkatan. God has shown that to us also. That your father the King requested you to be the courier of our people and Reginaldo, to listen and observe, and to return with what your decision would be if you were king."

"Well, what should I decide? Did God show you what I will tell my father?"

Duncan had a low laugh. "Oh no, Prince Erkatan. It will not be that easy for you. You must come to your own decision. No one here will tell you what God may have shown to us." Duncan stood and walked over, placing a hand on Erkatan's shoulder. "Being the leader of a country is no small matter. Decisions carry huge import. Yet they must be made."

"But you Freelandians have it much easier! It appears God tells you ahead of time what will happen and what you will do!"

"Only sometimes, my young friend. Yes, He does send prophets to speak to us what His will is – and we certainly listen and seek verification both within ourselves and by others with gifts of prophecy and discernment."

"But what if those prophets and others collude to tell you what they want, or what they think you want to hear? And what do you mean you seek verification within yourself?"

"Prince Erkatan, we don't only hear from God through those with special giftings. We do not have to seek out some 'oracle' or go to our priests to know God's will or direction. Yes, God does give special gifting to those He chooses. But we all have something far, far more valuable and wonderful. When someone accepts Jesus as their Lord, God not only adopts them into

His family, but He gives them a most incredible gift … a portion of Himself called the Holy Spirit. God's Spirit begins to reside within us. He is gentle, not taking over or shouting, but instead reminding us of God and revealing His will to us. But we have to learn to listen – and to obey what we hear."

"I don't understand, Chancellor. If I heard God speaking to me, how could I not believe and do whatever it was He told me?"

"Our God very rarely forces us to do anything. He wants us to obey out of love, not coercion. So He tends to whisper to us. In fact, the more we practice listening to Him, the softer it seems He speaks – rarely audible, more often as thoughts in our mind that are from Him, or a feeling that a certain way is His way, or in dreams and visions."

"But why would He do that? I mean, the closer you are to God, shouldn't it become easier and easier?"

"Yes and no. God wants us to listen, and the better at it you become, the easier it is to differentiate between your own thoughts and desires and His. But He wants us ever closer to Himself, taking ever closer steps to His will and His presence. And so we all need to be continually moving closer and closer to God. He draws us in. The softer He whispers to us, the more we have to lean in to listen. God is perfecting us, bit by bit, into His image."

Erkatan looked thoughtful. "It sounds rather idyllic."

"Oh, it is not easy. God has not called us to an easy life. Putting our faith totally in Him and setting aside our own wants and desires is never simple or easy. It is a choice every day, every hour. Our selfish desires seem to be in constant battle for control."

"But it is for the better?" That was really said more as a statement than an actual question.

"Yes, Prince Erkatan. And not just better for you personally. As the leader of our country, I have a duty to lead the best way I possibly can – to want the best for my people. The only possible way I can assure that is to listen and follow God's leading, to constantly be seeking the direction from the Creator of the universe, and to constantly request His help. I could not possibly be a good leader without God's guidance and direction."

The Alterian's eyes went wide as that sunk in. "But … my father … the King … is a good leader! He has said he believes in your god, along with others. He sometimes seeks input from the priests of various gods for direction."

"But do any of those other gods really have any power? Are they even real? Is your father the very best leader he could be? What do you think now, Prince Erkatan?"

Erkatan was in a quandary. The conversations, observations and events of the last week had shaken his long standing beliefs … or maybe lack of them. And now these last comments. If a ruler had the option of taking God's help, how could he truly be a good ruler if he rejected it?

In a very quiet voice he murmured, "I think you have convinced me, Chancellor Duncan."

Master Oldive approached the assembled Watchers with careful shuffling steps. He had asked Warden James to hand-select only a very limited audience, and so only James, a few of his senior Watchers and Chief Engineer Robby were present. Oldive was fully suited up in his new armor, with a few added refinements since Robby had last seen it. It was totally new to all the others.

As he came to stand before them, Oldive lifted his helmet and carefully removed it. He stepped over to James and handed it to the normally much larger man – though with the armor on, Oldive was nearly the same size. James hefted the helmet in his large hands, looking thoughtfully.

"This is remarkably light, Master Oldive. Robert has been telling me of some recent advancements in new alloys you have been working with, but he failed to mention you were so far along." With that he turned toward the Chief Engineer with a raised eyebrow.

"Master Warden, surely ye know a good engineer never lays all 'is cards on the table ahead o' time. We likes to hold back, just a little!"

Oldsy grinned mischievously. "I'm so glad you remembered that, Bobby!" He retrieved his helmet and addressed the small group. "Our new alloy is much lighter than any metal we have ever worked with. That allows us to make armor that is far superior to anything we have examined from the Dominion. And it lends itself to a few other capabilities, which we are about to demonstrate." Oldive donned his helmet and moved off with his odd shuffling steps to an arrangement of hay bales and wooden walls.

He lifted his visor as the guests moved in closer to observe. "First, let me demonstrate the movement capabilities." He lowered the visor and began a slow run around the obstacles. Then he began to run straight at three bales stacked into a four foot high wall.

James was ready to see Oldive crash through the bales, but instead, a few yards out Oldive's stance changed and he began to lean backwards onto his heels. Amazingly the figure in the armor began to make tremendously long bounding strides. When he approached the hay bales, Oldive planted both feet down hard on his heels and sprang upward, easily clearing the obstacle with over a foot to spare. The landing was not quite so graceful. After soaring perhaps eight feet, Oldive spread his legs apart as he landed, and immediately bounced upward again, landing awkwardly on the balls of his feet and nearly falling over.

"I am still working on my coordination – I have not gotten my landings down solidly yet."

James was dumbstruck, but Robby was grinning ear to ear and was the first to speak. "Ach, I see ya gots aroun' to planting those springy thingies into your metal box there, Oldsy! Is that'a why yer walking on yer toesies? The springies are back in your heel?"

"Yes, Bobby – it is hard to get much past you, isn't it? Besides being super light weight and maneuverable, we have been able to accommodate some additional toys into the suits to give the wearer a "leg up" on anyone they meet – including Dominion armor wearers."

James was still staring. "Master Oldive – just how fast can you run in that armor? I don't think a man of your …"

"Old age and flab?" Robby was ever so helpful.

"Ah, well, I was thinking more like experience and stature – anyway, could you have cleared those bales without the suit on?"

Oldive laughed heartily. "No, Warden. But I am not the best person to demonstrate the full abilities of the armor. I made this one for study and experimentation."

"So, have you made any more?" James had walked up closer to examine the suit in more detail.

"As a matter of fact, I have two others finished, and another that just needs some final work once I have final body measurements made. Now that I believe I have the bugs worked out, I have just begun ramping up the production of the various individual pieces in assorted average sizes – but you can get the most out of the suit with an individual fitting. Still, I have tried to make as many parts in a way that they will interchange between suits, and I think we could begin making about a dozen a week, maybe more if we can get any more metal production. That is the bottleneck right now."

"Ach, I think the bottleneck may be o'top yer shoulders, friend Oldsy! The way the helmet goes on is sort of like the cap of a bottle!"

"Very funny, Chief Engineer. But let me have my assistant give you a much better demonstration. As Robert stated so eloquently, I am getting a bit old for this … though I rather take exception to the flab!" Oldive waved his hand at an assistant, who disappeared into a small shack.

A few minutes later, a suited figure emerged from the far side of the shack and began a slow run, building speed with every spring assisted step. Shortly the armored assistant was bounding around a test track at an astonishing velocity, leaping larger and larger hurdles put in place by other helpers.

Oldive glanced over at Robby and saw him scowling and squinting, looking from one corner of an eye to another at the dashing figure. As the Chief Engineer turned toward him, Oldsy somewhat hurriedly turned away. "Oldsy, there is something … something peculiar about yonder assistant of yours. The armor … it looks somehow different. At this distance I canna quite make out what it is though."

Oldive gave a demur smile. "Oh, it is just a somewhat different style than mine."

The armor wearer was now running what must have been full out, going faster than any non-enhanced person would have been remotely capable of. A last hurdle was dragged out, this one with a bar that must have been over eight feet off the ground. The assistant gave a last burst of somehow even more speed and gave a particularly hard bounce onto the heels of the suit and sprang skyward. A loud gasp proceeded from the mouth of every onlooker as the figure cleared the bar … still standing vertically. The landing was far more graceful than Oldive's, with only a few steps forward after returning to the ground to stabilize.

The assistant proceeded to a small shack and with no weapons other than the armored suit itself began to smash the wooden structure to splinters. The figure then started walking towards the group as other assistants ran forward, swinging all manner of clubs and other blunt weaponry.

James was staring. "Master Oldive, you said that this other suit was of 'a different style'? I think I am noticing some of the … uh … styling. Am I seeing what I think I am seeing?"

Oldsy grinned. "Well, Master Warden, that largely depends on what you think you are seeing, now doesn't it?"

Robby was staring too. "But Oldsy … why woulda' ye design a suit o' armor with those big bumpy thingys out in the front? I mean, if I did not know better I'd … I … I-ya-yie! OLDSY! You've got a WOMAN out there?!"

The suited assistant was now standing only ten yards away while several other assistants came up alongside the group of onlookers. These assistants had bows. Turning their backs to the observers, they began to rapidly fire off a volley of arrows. Their target did not move, other than to flinch when the first arrows were let loose and began to hit. Several must have dented the suit, as the decidedly feminine formed figure moaned a couple of times and staggered back twice, but then stood firm.

"That concludes our demonstration, James, Robert, and gentlemen guests. I put before you the best suit of armor the world has ever seen, stronger, far lighter, agile, and which not only provides the wearer a very high level of personal protection, but which also imparts amazing capabilities due to the strong springs located in the soles. If what you see before you meets your approval and if you agree that this is what you would like for our army, I can get my assistants cracking at making as many as possible. Given the expected very short time we have, we can likely only produce a dozen or maybe two before the Dominion arrives."

James, with one eyebrow held very high, turned toward those under his command that he had brought. "I think we should outfit the Alpha Red Watcher team. If we can get enough suits, we can do the Blue team as well. I want the men to have some time to work with the suits before they have to see any real action – I think we can maybe come up with some rather nasty surprises for any Dominion soldiers who meet them! It is a real strategic benefit to us – we need to think about how to use it to the maximum advantage. I want all of you to consider that, and we will meet at 8 tomorrow morning to discuss ideas.

Meanwhile, Master Oldive, I will send our Alpha Red team here this afternoon so you can take whatever measurements you need. I suggest you show them a small demonstration like this first, and then I am very sure you will get not only their attention, but their full cooperation." James grinned and shook his head. "I can hardly wait to see what our top Special Forces commando team could do with that capability. I suspect they will come up with uses and tactics we can't even well imagine yet."

The other men reluctantly tore their eyes from the suit before them and turned to leave. The suited assistant began to walk toward Oldive and Robert, exaggeratedly swaying her hips suggestively. A low tinny female voice altered by the small holes in the helmet throatily spoke out "What about you, Chief Engineer? Does what you're staring at meet your approval?"

Robby's mouth dropped open and his eyes were indeed staring. "I ... er ... I mean ..." stammering, Robby turned a light shade of red.

"Cat got your tongue? Hmm, too bad." The figure now right before him tapped lightly on her helmet visor as Robby worked hard to gather his wits about him. Not only was he amazed and startled that Oldive had subjected a female assistant to such physical abuse as what had just been shown to them, but he was also rather taken aback by the rather exaggerated feminine form of the metal clad warrior, who stood eye-to-eye with the rather tall Chief Engineer.

A metal hand reached out to run a finger down Robby's arm. "Do you want what you see? The armor, of course!"

At this, Robby's red face started regaining more of its normal color as his eyes narrowed to slits. He did not even notice Oldive slowly replacing his own helmet back onto his head and take a few steps away. "Mr. Oldive, I do believe I may recognize a certain woman's voice, even if it is inside a tin can."

Laughter began to pour out of the suited figure before him, and Arianna slowly lifted and twisted off the helmet, shaking out her long locks of hair which cascaded down over the shoulders of the suit. "Were you impressed, my sweet engineer?" Arianna's eyes were sparkling with delight and humor.

"OLDSY – you allowed me precious wife to be nearly clubbed to death and let arrows be shot at her? Are ye out of yer blessed mind? I'm agonna

take that there suit 'o armor of yours and ram it down yer … HEY, COME BACK HERE!"

But it was too late. Even as the Chief Engineer took a long stride over toward where Master Oldive had been, his quarry was making a remarkably fast exit get-away, springing in incredibly long strides toward the other end of the testing grounds, at a speed that Robby could not have kept up with even if he had tried running flat-out. He began to mutter under his breath about what he might do if he ever caught up with that older engineer. Then a metal clad hand turned him forcibly around.

"Now look here, mister! I volunteered for this demonstration and you will not take out your misguided chivalry on your best friend Master Oldive. He would not have let me do it if he thought I would be in the least bit of real danger, and if you calm down enough to think straight you will know that is true."

"'E's not me best friend anymore."

"Now Robert, you had better not …"

"You are me best friend now, sweetpea."

"Robert, I said …" His words registered and her voice faltered.

"I donna' like the idea one little bit of you in that suit and people swinging clubs at you or shooting arrows … but I do like the idea of you being safe in a metal cocoon, out o' harm's way."

"I am not a Watcher or a warrior, you big lunk. But in a suit like this I think just about anyone could be quite a formidable foe."

"Formidable, I don't doubt that in the least. If they did not drop over from the initial heart attack I figure you could smother them with a frontal attack with those big …"

Robby next discovered just how painful a full swing of a metal gauntlet could be. He cried out in pained surprise and crashed to the ground, landing quite hard and not moving. Arriana ran over to him, as best she could in the bulky armor. Bending over was another skill that took awhile to master. "Oh … Bobby … I didn't mean to … I mean, I didn't even think that I had this metal on … oh Bobby, are you alright?"

Her husband shook the haze from his head. "Why is it that so many times I am around you, I end up getting knocked about?"

"Probably because you so often seem to think with your mouth rather than your head!"

"Aye, that be true, leastwise while I be around such a beautiful filly as you."

"Bobby, if you weren't such an awfully lovable lug I don't think you would have ever survived my choosing you."

"Now wait one minute there, lassie! What do you mean you choosing me? I seem to recall be'in the one doing the choosing now!"

Arianna smiled sweetly. "Ok, if that is what you want to think. I need to get out of this sweat bucket. Will you help?"

Robby began to sputter … she had ended that conversation none to his liking, not one tiny bit. But helping her out of the armor … now that had some possibilities …

Chapter 18

Re-acquaintances

Gaeten had spent all of the first day back debriefing in great detail what he had learned during his travels talking to very many people in the Dominion. One thing that had particularly stood out to him was the fear the average people had of the Dominion in general and of the Dark Magicians in particular, yet the helplessness they felt with no way to oppose them. The Dominion armies would first take over an area militarily and rule with an iron fist to crush any organized resistance, and then the Magicians would arrive with the Dominion administrators. It seemed the Magicians not only abolished any other religion but their own – which was primarily the worship of both demon demigods and of the Overlords, accompanied by occasional human sacrifice and of course hefty taxation payments – but they also brought with them their own secret police who constantly spied on the populace and reported back who might not be acting in full support of the new regime and religion. The Dark Magicians would then systematically and regularly make many "examples" of "traitors" and "heretics" by public torture or execution and confiscation of not only all of the worldly goods the person might have, but also that of their extended families. Thus within a short time not only did the spies rat out dissidents, but family members would begin to turn in their own kin they might suspect as a means of protecting their own assets – and for the chance to be rewarded.

Within a year of taking over a new area, the Dominion would also set up schools for the children which had mandatory attendance – at the point of death – and brought in their own teachers. The schools were run by the Magicians themselves and strongly indoctrinated the children with the ways of the Dominion, and to be on the constant vigilant look out for disloyalty toward the Dominion, even from their own parents. The best and brightest students were forcibly removed and sent off far away to special academies in the deep South, where more indoctrination and training was given. Many of those students went on to become Dominion administrators, and a select few were chosen to become Dark Magicians. Others were simply never heard from again. Within a generation of conquest, new territories of the Dominion were usually totally subjugated in body, mind and spirit.

However, there were exceptions everywhere, just not publically seen. Servants of the true God were seeded throughout the territories, and while they now had to operate unseen, the underground church was alive and growing in many areas despite horrific persecution. Gaeten had learned about some of these from the old prophet in Kardern.

Gaeten also had much to disseminate about the sailors and ships that he had heard about in Kardern. In all, he was able to give a very accurate assessment of the war preparations taking place in the few cities he visited. In conjunction with the documents obtained by Chu, the leaders of Freelandia had a very good picture of what the Dominion planned for their beloved country.

On his second day back however, he was done debriefing and had time to himself – and that meant he had time to go check up on Maria. Gaeten admitted to himself that he really had been concerned for her welfare, though it seemed that Vitario had taking a keen and personal interest in her. In fact, maybe she would hardly remember him, being so busy with all of her academy activities.

He stewed on that thought for awhile as he walked up toward the Music Academy campus. Gaeten was not one to get overly attached to people, but with Maria ... well, she was a special case. But how did she fare while he was gone? When he had left she seemed like a lonely, scared little girl, albeit one with incredible gifting from God. Surely she had changed, at least a little in the intervening weeks.

These thoughts coursed through his mind as he arrived to the Commons area on the campus of the Academy. Gaeten cocked his head to one side. Something seemed ... different. The music he could hear sounded somehow different, but he could not immediately put a finger on what it was. But even more than that, he could feel a difference just by walking onto the campus. That puzzled him awhile. It was not like he was overly used to the sounds and activities of the Music Academy anyway – it was a place he certainly did not frequent, seeing little value to what they did in general. But he had been awakened to the spiritual power of music through the gifting of Maria. Wait … that was what was different! There was a … a … spiritual freshness and intensity and … expectancy? … about the place that was not there before. It was not something he could specify very well, but it was real, and it was encouraging.

"Hello there Gaeten, old chap! How good to see you!" Sir Reginaldo's voice boomed out across the Commons. In a moment the big man had a hand clapped to Gaeten's back.

"Well, at least one of us seems overtly cheerful today," Gaeten grumbled, though in fact he was finding it rather difficult to remain grumpy or worried within the atmosphere that seemed to pervade the Academy grounds.

"And what is not to be cheerful about my friend? The sun is shining, the sky is clear, the birds are singing … God has given us so very much to enjoy today!"

Gaeten had to acknowledge that. He began to smile, a first for the day. "Well, it seems the world-famous singer has recovered from the latest sea voyage well. I admit to being surprised you came here to Freelandia though – especially since you were as aware as the rest of us that within a handful of days we are to expect the Dominion invasion fleet. Or are you planning on leaving with the Alterians later today?"

"Oh, so Prince Erkatan and his crew will depart today? I should bid him goodbye … it would be most impolite of me not to do that."

"Wait … did you know the Captain was the Crown Prince of Alteria all along?"

"Well … yes, actually. I had given a performance in Alteria a few years back for his father, a quite royal affair don't you know, and all of the princes and princesses were there. I was even properly introduced to him. Now I admit, when we first boarded I was not a hundred percent sure … that beard and outfit changed his appearance considerably from the smooth shaven face and royal finery when I last saw him. But after a few words I recognized his true identity and agreed to keep it a secret from you Free-landians – and any Dominion people we just might run into."

"Hmpf!" But the grump died out as soon as it got that far. "You kept the secret well, then."

"Why thank you. I do have a few of them I keep. Now to your other question. I came back here …" Reginaldo breathed a giant sigh. "I came back because I think this is where I truly belong. Dominion or not, this is where I first learned to sing properly, and this is where I think I need to come back to learn to truly … well, sing I guess. Here I learned how to use my voice. Now I want to learn how to sing with my heart and with my spirit." His voice grew faint and strained. "Gaeten, what is the point of singing if you are just performing for others? It is rather empty inside. I once thought that I sang for the money, for the prestige and glory and honor I would receive. I worked hard to become the very best … and yet I kept asking myself – what comes next? What is the encore going to be of my life? Then I met …"

"Maria?"

"Yes. Then I met Maria and things began to change. And then … then I met …"

"Maria's God?"

"Yes again, my good man. I had an emptiness that gnawed on my soul. Now it is beginning to be filled. I do not care if the Dominion comes or not, whether I survive the coming weeks or not. I have found where I belong. I now have a real reason to sing – and a most important "Audience of One", as that delightful young lady puts it.

But you are surely not here to listen to me ramble. If I am not mistaken, you are here to be reunited to your young former ward! She asked about you yesterday, and was rather disappointed your duties would keep you away for another day. I assured her you would come as soon as possible. You know, she thinks very highly of you, my friend."

A smile slipped out across Gaeten's lips, though he had tried to bottle it up. It was terribly difficult to not be overtly happy in this place!

Reginaldo watched the play of feelings run their course over Gaeten's normally so shielded face and began to chuckle. "Let's go find her. I believe she was supposed to be in the concert hall about now, directing a group of singers."

"Directing? My little Maria is directing a group of apprentices?"

"Ha, I could think she is almost running the place ... she certainly seems to have turned the old Academy upside down. It's like a new place, with a decidedly changed focus. And can you believe it – they are preparing for war ... here ... at the Music Academy! A few weeks ago I would have laughed at them. But now ... now I think I will join them. After all, these 'worship warriors' just get to give glory and honor to God with their musical skills ... now that is my kind of warfare!"

Gaeten was puzzled, but anything that could get Reginaldo to talk about worshiping God and warfare with the Dominion all in the same breath had to be good.

The two wandered their way in the direction Reginaldo had indicated. As they went, they could hear laughter and instruments and voices that all seemed to blend into a haphazard and yet somehow coherent background that joined with the wind and birds and all other sounds to be a musical tribute to God's creation. Both men stopped to listen and marvel.

"Beautiful, isn't it? It used to just sound like noise. Somehow it now sounds beautiful."

Gaeten had heard someone walk up to join them and recognized the tread. "Kory, I believe?"

Kory laughed. "Right you are, Grand Master Gaeten, sir. Maria said you would be coming by about now and that I should go out to greet you."

"But ... how would she have known when I was coming?"

"Oh, I stopped asking awhile ago. She just says God showed her. That sort of thing has been happening around here a whole lot recently. Come on, she was last in the practice auditorium ... though that is no guarantee of where she may be now."

Kory led them into the hall and to a sizeable side room. Several dozen apprentices stood grouped in the center with Maria standing in front. Everyone was just looking at the far-away expression on Maria's face.

Reginaldo spoke up. "Is she having another vision?"

One of the apprentices put a finger to her lip and nodded. Kory whispered, "That's her second one this week. It seems like with all this worshipping going on that God is speaking more ... or maybe we are just hearing more of what God has been saying and doing all along."

Reginaldo seemed skeptical. "But really ... isn't this a bit ... well ... emotional? I mean, does God really do such things?"

Kory looked up at the large man. "I don't think God forces Himself onto us, Sir Reginaldo. But I do think He loves us immensely and wants us to commune with Him as a standard, typical way of life. I picture Him in part like a close friend who is always standing next to me. This friend rarely shouts – usually just whispers and gives gentle tugs on my arm to get my attention – but always has valuable things to say and show me. My problem is that I get very busy with activities or my own thoughts, and so often ignore my friend." She sighed heavily. "I could wish that God was more insistent. When I am talking with my other friends I sometimes interrupt them to be heard. God almost never does that. He waits for us to quiet down and listen."

"So you think that maybe God is whispering to us … to me … right now, right here?" Reginaldo gave a furtive look around.

"Maybe He is. I don't mean to be rude, but would you know what to listen for? For me it seems to take a lot of practice, and I don't think I am very good at it yet. Some people seem to be better at listening – like they have a quiet place to go where they can hear Him better."

Maria seemed to give a start, and then she shook her head as though to clear it. The apprentices gathered closer excitedly. One of them spoke up. "What did God just show you, Maria?"

Maria smiled but there was a hint of sadness. "As we were all singing, I saw each of you transformed into something that looked like giant guitar strings stretching up to heaven. God's Spirit began to move among you. Some of the strings began to vibrate, creating beautiful music that reached up to God. The Spirit was not playing the strings – instead the strings would vibrate in resonance with the Spirit. Some seemed to be tuned into the same resonance and vibrated strongly, others only partly. Sadly, a few did not resonate at all, even though the Spirit was right there, moving right next to them."

The young men and woman began to look amongst themselves. Some giggled and excitedly smiled, nodding in agreement. A few look puzzled and unsure, and a few others gave a rather stony stare.

Maria turned her face toward them fully. "Don't you see? The more we are tuned in to God's Spirit – the more time we are thinking about Him and aware of Him, then the more we begin to do His things, His way and the more beautiful our lives become." Her voice took on a far-away quality.

"And the more of His power flows in our lives ... and the closer we can get to His glorious presence. Some of you may not have experienced this yet. Maybe something stands in the way, holding you back. Yet there is nothing comparable, nothing worth more than experiencing more and more of God Himself and His Spirit.

I think I noticed something else. Those who seemed to vibrate the strongest somehow seem prepared to do so ... like they were expecting and just waiting for the Spirit to move among them. Some of those that only vibrated a little seemed unprepared and taken by surprise. I have a question for all of you. When you come here, have you already done your warm-up exercises? If you come to play an instrument, have you already tuned it before class? "

Several of the young people nodded affirmation.

Maria paused and then continued. "Well, of course ... you come already prepared for the class. But what we are really doing here is practicing our worship of God and our joy of Jesus. So, have you prepared for that?"

Most of her class looked dumbfounded, while a few smiled knowingly. One piped up, "But how, Maria? How do we prepare – or practice – for worship?"

"You must prepare your hearts and minds. You cannot really worship if your mind is jumbled with worries, concerns, idle thoughts and busyness. Take care of those things before coming. Set your mind on God and His beauty. Spend some time in prayer, seeking His peace. Welcome the Holy Spirit inside you. Seek God's presence. If you walk in here like that, worship will come spontaneously – actually, you will already be worshiping and the class will just be an extension of that, where you learn how to make even better use of the talents and skills given you for His glory."

Though she could not see the many heads nodding and wondering eyes, everyone could feel the truth of what was said sink in deeply. Maria turned and began to make her way toward the newcomers. "I heard you come in. Thanks for bringing them, Kory." She had held her composure most of the way across the room, but once she had cleared the few chairs she knew to be present she broke and ran the last few steps to fling herself in the direction of the breathing she knew to be from the man who had protected her several times from beatings and worse in the little town of Westhaven only a few months ago when she had been an unknown, poor blind orphan.

Gaeten was responsible for 'discovering' her and bringing her here to the Keep. No, that was not right. Gaeten was the man God used to turn her former life upside down and introduce her to a new life she was so very sure she was created for.

Gaeten heard her coming but did not expect what came next. He barely had time to open his arms before she wrapped her own around the older gentleman, tears streaming down her face. "Oh Gaeten! It really is you! You really did come back safe! I was so very concerned for you."

The wizened Grand Master Gaeten, well known for his gruffness as much as for his mastery of the Watcher arts, wrapped his arms around the young blind girl and joined his tears with hers. The two just stood there holding each other for minutes as everyone in the room smiled.

After their initial arrival, Ethan had almost no time to talk to his parents for the first two days he was back, given all of their scheduled activities. He was very busy debriefing from his Dominion adventures, and several different people had asked him in multiple ways how much he may have disclosed to his captors or to Taleena, and how much that Dominion spy may have picked up herself. By the end of it, Ethan was feeling rather low and wrung out, wondering how many people who formerly thought of him as a hero now truly thought of him as a traitor to Freelandia.

So when he finally finished the last interview, he trudged back to his parents' house, wondering if he could really even call it "home" anymore. Though he felt forgiven by God, he was none too sure others were offering that forgiveness to him as easily or thoroughly.

It was late afternoon when he approached the door to the house, with the ever-present Watcher standing guard outside. Ethan was almost surprised when the man smiled at him and briskly opened the door. He entered and wandered back to the kitchen, where the aroma of whatever was being prepared for dinner was wafting pleasantly throughout the house.

His mother Lydia was there, testing the contents of one of the cooking pots. She looked up as Ethan entered the room and motioned him over, handing him a clean spoon. "Try this, Ethan."

He rather tentatively held up the spoon, giving a casual glance at the cooking staff. They were busily working and acted as though nothing out of the ordinary was occurring. He smiled, noticing how it seemed like his mother had grown shorter since he last saw her, and carefully tasted the stew. "It is wonderful, mother. I might add a pinch of salt though."

"Agreed, that is exactly what I was thinking too. Are you ready for a full home meal?"

Ethan had been through so very much, and now here he was, standing in the kitchen with his mother, and everyone was acting like everything was normal. He began to tremble, slowly at first but building, despite his attempts to stop it.

Lydia saw what was happening and knew its cause. She gathered her son in her arms and held him tightly. "Ethan, you are my son. You will always be my son. No matter what you have done or might do in the future, I will always love you. I do not love you for what you do, or on condition that you treat me any certain way or even that you love me back. I love you because you are the son God gave to me. My day to day expression of that love will likely waiver at times – I am all too fallible – but the foundational love will always be there."

Ethan had begun to cry softly. "But … but how can you? After what I have done? I am worse than the Prodigal Son in the Bible story."

Lydia pulled him in even closer. "In reality, I am just trying to reflect the love God has for us, as imperfectly as my ability allows. God in some mysterious and miraculous way chose you, Ethan, to be His child, adopted into His family. And you chose Him, chose to accept that position. God did this knowing full well you – all of us – would fail Him time and time again. If His love were conditioned on our behavior, on our total obedience, then none of us would be loved by Him very much since we all fall far short of His perfection. It is part of His love that continues to teach us, to take us along a pathway that bit by bit conforms us into His image. He knows we will stumble and fall. But He never condemns us for failure."

Lydia smiled and chuckled softly. "When you were little and learning to walk, you fell often. We did not think the worse of you for it, nor punish you for such mistakes. In God's eyes we are all like little children before Him. He is right there to help pick us up, dust us off, and set us back on our feet to continue the journey. I suspect God did just that for you at some point, when you turned back to Him. He was right there waiting for you, wasn't He?"

Tears still in his eyes, Ethan looked up. "Ye ... yes. I had given up, bound in the hold of that Dominion ship, drugged so I couldn't think straight, betrayed by someone I thought cared for me and held prisoner knowing I was to be used against everyone and everything that I held dear. I ... I was so helpless and hopeless, so angry at myself and alone. I knew I had betrayed you and everyone I loved, and God too. I figured there was no way out for me, that no one would ever accept or love me again, that even God had turned His face away from me. If I could of, I would have thrown myself overboard into the sea – but even that escape was denied to me by the ropes they kept me bound with."

Lydia shuddered at the image. "And then what happened, son?"

Ethan grimaced, remembering his captivity. "I called out to God. I stopped my self-pity and guilt, and I remembered what God had done for me, and who He really was. He showed me a part of Himself, there on that ship. And the funny thing was, He didn't condemn me. I deserved that, but instead He ..." Ethan's tears welled up again and his throat constricted. He swallowed hard and continued. "Instead as I neared Him my ugliness began to slough off. As I got closer to Him, in my vision I became pure white and stainless. It was as though this was how God actually saw me, on the inside. I felt so accepted, so loved. I think I understand His love a bit more now."

Lydia smiled, tears streaming down her own face. "Learning about God's love is a life-long process, Ethan. We all need to learn and practice accepting that love. We need to learn how to love others in reflection of the love God has toward us. The more of His love we accept into ourselves, the more of it is available to love others with – and to love God back with."

She released her tight hold of him and reached over to a pitcher of water and a cup. "We are like this cup – empty and rather useless all by itself. A cup is only useful as a holder of something else." She poured a few drops in. "When we only accept a little of God's love, it barely wets the bottom of the cup – there is barely enough there to even notice. Notice the pitcher still is full – it has not changed, it still has lots more to put into the cup." She poured more in. "Now the cup is half-full and is starting to fulfill its purpose, but it still is not full." She began to pour more. "God's love is endless and boundless – think of this pitcher as though it held an ocean full of pure water. Eventually we are filled with God's love for us." Lydia continued to pour, even though the cup was full to the brim. In a moment, the water began to cascade over the sides and over the counter top. "And if we continue to take in more of God's love, we cannot help but start to spill it out all around us, splashing God's love all over whomever we come into contact with."

Lydia began to laugh as the water flowed all over the counter and began to spill over onto the floor. Several of the kitchen staff were chuckling too and raced over with towels to contain the mess. "And yes, God's love can be wonderfully messy too – you never know where it might flow or land, but it does not matter. You can never run out if you are getting constantly refilled, and His love affects everything it touches for the good."

Ethan looked up into her eyes and saw … acceptance, and more – joy of being filled with God's love. "I want more of that, mother. I want to be filled with God's love like I see in you, filled to overflowing."

With a sly twinkle in her eye, she reached to hug him again, but just as she came near she upended the pitcher directly over Ethan's head. "There you go, filled to overflowing!"

His eyes popped out of his head at the cold blast and he began to laugh and cry and laugh some more. Lydia put the pitcher down and, heedless of his sopping wet attire, grabbed him into a mighty bear hug, laughing and crying with him. In a moment, the kitchen staff crowded in with their own hugs, not a dry eye among them.

Gaeten stood alone out in the woods, just outside of the Keep. He admittedly was quite concerned, and he blew for a third time on the extremely high pitched whistle. With both he and Ethan having been gone for such a long time, Sasha may have reverted back to the wild. Maria said she had called the gryph in several times and fed her sweet meats, but not in the last two weeks.

Finally, from a very long way off, Gaeten could just make out an answering cry carried on the evening breeze and coming closer. Life almost seemed like it was getting back to 'normal'.

Murdrock dismissed his senior Dominion assassins, and they seemed to dissolve into the overgrowth and woods around the small forester's hut. It was a slight risk to be this close to the Keep, with Warden patrols regularly traveling through the area. Yet it was so close that it was ironically safer – who would think anyone would ever try to stage this close to the Keep and the Watcher Compound? Now there were highly camouflaged tents pitched nearby – his main teams of Freelandian discontents – he called them Rats – who were poised to infiltrate key defensive positions to pave the way for the Dominion invasion – D-day he was telling the young men and older boys who made up his insurgent 'army': Dominion Day.

He knew this was his final and greatest assignment. The others had been bungled by incompetent subordinates, he kept telling himself. This time he had hand-picked men and he had gone over every tactic, every possible outcome, every back up plan. He had performed the incantations and spells himself. All was set. They were ready.

Tomorrow he would send out his top team, led by the Freelandian young man who had worked his way to become his right-hand man. They would position themselves and make ready for their most important mission, right on schedule for the invasion force. He had great confidence that Jarl could pull it off perfectly.

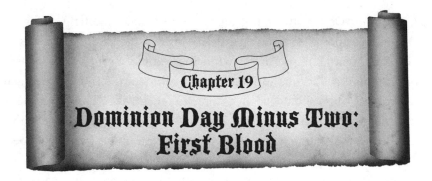

Chapter 19

Dominion Day Minus Two: First Blood

Commodore Moorhead was not used to his new rank or duties, though he did not mind being automatically given the best quarters on the fleet's flagship. As captain of the fleet that had first battled the Dominion and handily won, thanks to the new weapons from the engineers, he was comfortable in knowing what to do in nearly every circumstance. But now he had a much larger mission. He truly did believe it when he was told that several prophets and discerners had confirmed that this was the correct strategy. But that did not make him have to like it, did it? He was the commander of the main Freelandian naval task force, out on the high seas on the lookout for the Dominion attack fleet that was expected to show up any day now. He had seventy vessels under his command, a large majority of what Freelandia could put to sea, and he was itching for a fight. And he was sure to get one, but not the head on colossal collision that he dreamed of.

Instead his mission was to find the enemy and harass the daylights out of them. Moorhead knew this was probably a better strategy for his much smaller but faster and more maneuverable ships. He certainly did not relish the idea of going head-to-head with one of the newest Dominion Dreadnought battle ships, at many times his size and with catapults that had at least double the range of his own. Maybe not head-to-head ... but with some of the new weapons on over half of his ships, he dearly hoped and prayed to get close enough to one of those battleships to try them out. With conventional weapons, he knew his ships would not stand a chance against those sea monstrosities. He expected the Dominion commanders would think so too. Moorhead counted on it.

His ships were at full sail heading south to take the fight as far from Freelandian shores as possible. Battle groups of twenty-one ships had veered southeast and southwest, while his group of twenty-eight ships had split into four squadrons and were heading due south. If their intelligence was correct, they should begin to encounter advance Dominion patrols anytime now, though he did not expect them to want to engage with his fleet just yet. Bringing the battle to the enemy when they did not expect it was nearly always preferred when it was feasible.

The sky was noticeably darkening to the immediate south. Moorhead had heard many reports of similar storms that seemed to accompany – and somehow even assist – Dominion attacks. Commotion on the forward deck attracted his attention.

His first mate came running up. "Sir, signal flags from God Is Our Rock. Dominion scout ships were just spotted to the south-south west. They appeared to have immediately veered to the southeast upon seeing our ships."

"Very good. They will be running to inform their first attack fleet. If our information is accurate, the Dominion forces may have several hundred vessels coming our way, followed by a second wave of troop transport ships with additional warship escort. Our goal is to harass all of them, but to especially try to get at those troop ships – they are the main focus for us, and of course they will be the weakest but most protected asset of the Dominion."

"So … should I sound general quarters? How long until we should expect a repelling attack group coming our way?"

"I'd say within a few hours, and then they will be here with a large force. No, don't sound the alarm yet, though let the men know the time is short. Meanwhile, we let the enemy come to find us! Signal the other ships to begin Dispersal Plan A. Then make a fifteen degree swing to port with full sail. Keep in sight of our squadron mates. And keep close watch on the winds, especially with the storm coming. They will likely shift to be right in our teeth, so we need to make sure we are not meeting them head-on – there will be far too many Dominion ships for us to even think about a frontal attack. And by all means we need to do our best to be upwind of them for our own greatest range and maneuverability!"

"Aye Aye, Commodore." The mate hurried to carry out the commands.

"Gunnery Mate reporting as ordered, Commodore." The short, stocky man who stood before him had the reputation of being the best shot in the fleet … and the most trained and practiced with some of the new weaponry.

"Start preparing those aerial 'Thunderclap of God' devices. I expect we won't have many chances to get very close to the enemy, not once the Dominion Captains see what a Thunderclap can do. Let's hope they come at us with a few of those Dreadnaughts and that we can get close enough to Thunderclap one!"

"Aye, Commodore. Are you thinking they may come at us massed up close together … in a pack?"

"Well, I'm figuring they have several attack task forces sailing ahead and around their first wave of troop carriers. They will be expecting our navy to be stationed right off our coasts. So I figure they will have three main attack groups going north in a pincher array, designed to trap our fleet – to pin them up close to the coast with limited maneuverability. I am sure they plan on hitting us from three sides with overwhelming strength, hoping to crush our navy in one massive blow. If they can own the seas, it will make their invasion so much easier. And I am guessing they will be very sure of themselves that those Dreadnaughts are totally undefeatable.

So my best guess is that the Dominion will be coming directly at us with a sizable force, with one or possibly even two Dreadnaughts and a couple dozen supporting ships each. I expect they hope we will dash ourselves against those floating fortresses, and let their smaller ships mop up whatever remains. They don't know the size of our force, and may guess it is a scout patrol looking for them. They hope to surprise and scare us with the might of their Dreadnaughts. Let's see if we can give them a surprise of our own, shall we Gunny?"

"Aye Aye, Commodore. May I send up the Thunderclap signal flag to let the other ships in our fleet know to get ready?"

"Yes Gunny. If we see a Dreadnaught I will try to get us as close as I can dare – but I cannot risk getting into range of their big cats. Follow the protocol the engineers gave us, and we will pray that one or two of our aerial bombs will go off close enough to inflict severe damage."

"Aye to that, Commodore. But if God guides them straight we may even sink one."

"We can pray for that, Gunny. But I am not so sure even those new-fangled bombs will be powerful enough to take down a Dreadnaught. Yes, I heard of what happened before in the Bay, but that was a larger bomb than we can work with."

"Yes sir, but the engineers said they had improved on their designs."

"That may be, but they are untested, not in a real battle. The best laid plans are usually laid waste once the fighting truly starts. And even if we somehow did take out one of those mountains, there will be dozens of other ships to deal with. We are going to be outnumbered three or four to one. The best I can hope for is to even out the odds somewhat and pray for a miracle. Carry out your duties, Gunny. We will leave the results in God's hands."

"Double Aye Aye to that, Commodore! But begging your pardon sir, our God is in the miracle business!" The Gunny Mate trotted off to the rear of the ship, stopping part way to give instructions for a signal flag to be raised. Once reaching the stern, he took charge – when it came to battle preparations, the Gunny Mate was second only to the captain – or commodore in this case.

By the time the lead Freelandian squadron reached the storm front, they were ten miles to the east of where they had been an hour before, and the squadrons that had been to the east and west had tightened their formations with at least one ship of each within sight. The darkening sky would make signaling more difficult until it became truly dark and they could use lanterns instead of flags. All hands were on deck now, and extra men were up in the rigging to watch for the enemy ships they knew had to be close by.

A sense of unease was washing over the various crews, more than what could be naturally expected by the looming battle. All of the crews had been warned to expect this, and on every ship at a nod from their captains several sailors began to whistle one of the popular tunes recently coming out from the Music Academy. Several captains had scoffed at such an idea, but Commodore Moorhead had been at the worship concert. He had personally felt the power and believed it could well be a weapon against the spiritual forces of darkness arrayed against them. And even the doubters would rather adopt every possible advantage offered them against an enemy with such an advantage in ships. In the face of the dark storm approaching, with the wind beginning to whip against them and the threat of warfare imminent, the ship crews began to do something they had never, ever done before while on alert duty. They began to blend in worship with their work.

Commodore Moorhead had veered them easterly, and was now starting a shallow swing back westerly, which should position his squadrons with the wind to their backs ... though the storm winds could shift around quickly enough. Based on the winds, the current and where they saw the Dominion patrol ship, Moorhead predicted they should make contact with the enemy fleet at any moment now.

"Ships ahoy! Ships ahoy – to the southwest! I count two ... three ...six ...looks like a whole fleet!"

Moorhead shouted up. "Raise the Enemy Contact flag! Lookout - see any Dreadnaughts?"

"No, not yet ... wait ... I see something that looks like a small mountain on the surface of the water – could that be it?"

"That it would be, sailor. Give the coordinates to the helmsman and the distance to Gunny. Gentlemen, this is our hour, this is our duty. May God be with us!" As Commodore Moorhead turned back to watch the enemy ships growing ever closer, he turned his head northward in puzzlement. He thought he had just heard the faintest sound on the breeze coming from the north. The sound of ... music.

The Dominion Attack Force One commander Torgach looked contemptuously from his lofty deck far above the water. His flagship, the Dreadnaught *Terror*, was far, far larger than any of the Freelandian vessels he could see on the horizon. "Good", he said as much to himself as to any of the sailors near him. "Let them throw themselves at this mountain of terror and dash themselves to pieces. Then we will sail unopposed the rest of the way to that cursed Freelandia." He laughed ominously, hoping they would dare to try their magic fire against him … if it even existed outside of the imagination of the sailors who had reported it. He had top ranked Dark Magicians aboard, and the Overlord Rath Kordoch himself followed in the Dreadnaught assigned to escort the transport ships that would bring the Dominion invasion right into the heart of Freelandia.

Torgach was positive there was not a single thing on earth that could stop them, and that his magic would be far stronger than anything the Freelandians could hope to bring with them. After all, they were far from that northern country, and so the gods of that land could not possibly extend their reach this far. And he even had a secret weapon. He had personally seen to having several cubic yards of earth from the Deep South loaded aboard, which his Dark Magicians had assured him would guarantee that their gods would be along with them.

He gave out attack orders to his second in command. "Let them come in as close as they would like – let them fear as they see us tower over them and find their weapons ineffective. I want to see the terror in their eyes before we rain down our hellfire and consume their puny ships."

He lifted his voice. "Today will be a mighty victory for the Dominion! Today we will crush the Freelandian fleet and rule the seas!"

The storm was not as intense as Moorhead had thought it might be, though it looked much darker to the further south. The wind was gusty, but fairly steady. He hoped his Gunnery Mate could estimate the fuses correctly.

The Dominion fleet was spreading out, with the huge but lumbering Dreadnaught lagging behind the smaller faster vessels. With the speed difference, the more normal sized ships began to spread out and tack back and forth, creating a shallow "V" shape with the Dreadnaught at its vertex. It looked to Commodore Moorhead more like a large jaw ready to swallow his ships. It was his job to see that did not happen … but to get to the Dreadnaught itself several of his ships would have to sail directly into that gaping maw of Dominion ships.

"Helmsman – steer us directly upwind of that Dreadnaught. Gunny – I think it's time to get our little presents packaged up and ready to deliver."

"Aye Aye, sir!" The Gunny Mate turned to his crew. "Inflate the bubbles!"

Three sailors connected hoses to small pressure pots. As they turned valves, a loud hissing noise began and a large silk sack began to fill and lift off the deck. Once it was stretched full, they tied it off to seal in the gas and another was filled. Each pulled upward, but stayed a dozen feet off the stern, tied with a stout cord to one of the pressure pot bombs the engineers had created. After a fifth bubble had been inflated the bomb began to rock, nearly lifting away but for the heavy rope tether that held it firmly to the ship's deck.

The Gunny Mate carefully filled the last bubble, judging the wind and light rain that had started. When he was satisfied, he tied that off and added it to the others. A second bomb was moved into place and they repeated the process. In a few minutes they had three bombs, each with its own complement of inflated bubbles. An assistant attached a thin yet very strong cord to each bomb.

"We are ready, Commodore. With the wind we have, I put in fuses for twenty, thirty and forty seconds. We are going to have to be pretty close before we launch them."

"Understood, Gunny. Helmsman, First Mate – you heard the man – take us down their throat!" Moorhead looked at the other Dominion ships he was now passing, albeit at quite a distance. He could also see the other ships of his squadron likewise charging in, following their plan. His other squadrons should be nearing the perimeter of the Dominion ships, form-ing a wide line to the east. To reach the relative safety of their numbers, his squadron would have to pass right through the Dominion line.

"Gunny, I think this is going to be tight. Prepare the mine strings, wide spacing."

The Gunny Mate, whistling one of the new songs from the Academy of Music, began hooking up large wooden kegs with a hundred yards of line between them, with small kegs spaced evenly along the line to keep it afloat and hopefully aid visibility of where the kegs were to the Freelandians. The line had to be handled carefully, since it had sharp spurs and hooks along it which in testing had been shown quite effective in snagging ships that tried to pass over it. Each of the large kegs was festooned with knobby spikes, which the engineers promised would set the explosions off when and if they collided with a hard surface like a ship's hull. The Gunny Mate lit the fuses of the kegs, knowing they should stay burning for several days. He hoped they would be used up far sooner.

Torgach grinned evilly. "Arm the catapults with double loads of hell-fire." His crew chief looked up with surprise. "But that will cut our range in half, Commander!"

Torgach strode the three steps over to the chief and gave him a back-handed blow that knocked the sailor completely off his feet. "NEVER question me again! The next person who questions my orders will be loaded in WITH the hellfire!"

The crew jumped to do his bidding. Several sailors grabbed long-handled shovels and dug into a vat of burning tar and rocks. They lifted several heaping shovels over to a mixture of tar and large smooth round stones already loaded into the huge catapult on the fore deck. The contents began to smolder and then to burn brightly. Crews at the stern were doing the same, and amid ships others were finishing the loading of smaller cats with fire arrows.

"Helmsman – keep us pointed right at them. When I give the command, turn hard to starboard. We will shower them with the forward cat, and then with the stern. Crews, be ready with a quick reload – the other ships are not far off and they all are likely targeting us. I want to be ready with a second load even as the next ship comes up."

Torgach looked over to his First Mate. "I doubt they will even get an arrow on us. Look at how small those ships are compared to us! Our cats must have at least triple the range of their puny weapons." Then he looked puzzled. What were those … those sacks floating up off the stern of the Freelandian ships? "What magic is this?" He bellowed. "Dark Magicians – cast your spells to thwart whatever it is they are up to."

Several dark-hooded figures scuttled forward and began incantations. One bared his arms and drew a small knife, cutting himself as an offering to his evil god and letting the blood drip down onto a tray of dark Southern dirt. Satisfied, Torgach smiled. Even with their magic they would be no match for the Dreadnaught *Terror*. And he, Torgach, would have the honor of drawing the first blood in the final assault on Freelandia, preparing the way for the invasion forces to land in two days. This was going to be a great victory!

Commodore Moorhead knew what he was doing was crazy. He was steering headlong toward the biggest warship he had ever seen, in the middle of a Dominion attack group. To top that off, he had eighteen bubbles holding aloft three dark black metal canisters on five hundred foot cords. He would have to pull nearly into range of the enemy's huge catapults and then turn sharply at just the right instant. The fuses would then be pulled and the bubbles could float down wind to their intended target.

Maybe he was a bit crazy. He sure hoped and prayed it would work. Otherwise he had nothing with which to stop those mountains of the sea other than the floating mines, and he was unsure whether they would be powerful enough to punch through the metal clad hull of the Dreadnaughts … if the ship even hit one. The mines seemed like very useful tools, but haphazard ones that could not be counted on to take out a moving ship out on the open ocean. Now in a more fixed position like the mouth of the Bay of Freelandia … now that was another matter.

"Steady, men!" Moorhead eyed the rapidly closing distance and began a countdown out loud. "Ten … Nine … Eight …"

Torgach raised his right hand as he stood near the helmsmen at the stern, ready to signal the sharp turn and for the fore deck cat to launch. "Eight … Seven …Six …"

This was going to be so very close. "Three … Two … One … NOW!" The Freelandian ship surged to the port sharply even as the Gunney Mate yanked the fuse cords and other sailors released the wooden weights that were designed to skim along the water's surface, balancing the upward pull of the bubbles to keep the bomb swinging at the appropriate height. The bombs began their solo flight toward the behemoth Dominion Dreadnaught.

"Four … Three … WAIT!" bellowed Torgach. What was that Freelandian ship doing? He dropped his hand to shield his eyes from the light rain to try to see.

Communication on a ship the size of the *Terror* was more complicated than on smaller ships, since there was no possible way the crew on the foredeck could hear anyone from the stern. The crew chief on the big forward catapult saw the Commander's arm lower and believed it was the signal, at right about the expected time – even though the helmsman had not changed course yet. His catapult was turned sideways to have it positioned for a broad shot at the tiny Freelandian ship, and so now was aimed directly at … nothing. Yet the crew chief had no intention of disobeying a direct signal from the Commander himself. With a shrug he gave the signal to fire.

The big cat's long arm sprang forward, hurtling its fiery contents directly toward the path of the dodging Freelandians.

Something was not quite right with the third aerial bomb. It was losing altitude compared to the others, though still heading true toward the huge enemy ship. One or two of the bubbles must be leaking, thought the Gunny Mate.

Torgach was ready to have his fore deck cat crew dumped overboard, but then saw the long arc of the hellfire heading directly for the path of the Freelandian vessel. He was extremely puzzled by that ship's maneuver – but then he roared with laughter. "Look men, they are turning tail and running even before they could get off a shot at us!" He had completely forgotten about those strange floating bags. Anyway, his magicians were supposed to be taking care of that.

Moorhead saw the Dominion catapult heave its brightly sparking load of projectiles on a trajectory that was directly in the path of his own ship. He squinted and then sighed in relief as he could see that the load of large burning rocks would fall short. It was a fearsomely large load – easily enough to have sunk him had it hit – but perhaps those enemy cats were not quite as strong as he had heard. He figured he might have been just within range, but this shot was falling short.

With a few minutes to spare before needing to confront any other Dominion vessels, Moorhead saw two other ships in his squadron who had also released their Thunderclaps, hopefully with longer fuses since they were further out compared to the Dreadnaught. All seven ships had turned now and were heading directly for the nearest line of smaller Dominion vessels – though many were still larger than the Freelandian warships. His own crew was busily preparing their own catapults and spring launchers with the smaller versions of the Thunderclaps.

Moorhead turned and tried to pick out the light gray bubbles against a slightly darker gray sky, but he could not make out those launched from his ship or the two others that had loosed bombs from a further distance at the colossal Dreadnaught. Nearly twenty seconds had passed since they were launched …

Nine sets of bubbles carried their payloads toward the huge Dominion ship. One was sinking fast and went underwater before crossing half the distance. Several others were caught in updrafts that carried them far higher than desired, and others were drifting off course. In their practice sessions, the Freelandian captains had been shown that the only way to improve the probability of a direct hit was to launch a multitude of bombs. There was just too much variability with the wind and a ship's movements for a more surgical strike.

In the gray sky of the gathering storm, the fuse of the first of Moorhead's Thunderclaps burned through the cork stopper and ignited the explosive gas in the outer shell of the bomb. With a terrible boom the metal shell burst apart, spraying fuel soaked pellets and metal shrapnel outward. Moments later, the secondary fuses triggered and a gigantic ball of flame bloomed in the sky no more than fifty feet in front of the Dreadnaught. A thunderclap boomed out which deafened the enemy crew. The force of the explosion made a crater in the surface of the ocean, pulling the lumbering Dominion ship down toward its center. Then other bombs began going off in rapid succession.

The second Thunderclap from Moorhead's ship overshot and caused no damage. Another, hanging lower than the others, tangled its drag line in the uppermost rigging of the Dreadnaught just as the engineers had proposed and then ignited. The fuel did not have time to mix with air to create the true Thunderclap of God, but at such close proximity it did not really matter. The first explosion hurled the additional fuel directly down onto the decks of the enemy ship where the secondary fuses promptly ignited it.

With a horrific flash, the entire deck of the Terror became awash with fire, even as the metal casing of the bomb was shot with tremendous force down through its top decks. Meanwhile, the three high-flying Thunderclaps simultaneously exploded nearly a thousand feet above.

To the nearby Dominion ships it seemed like the sun had exploded directly overhead. There were three bright localized flashes, a pause, and then the dark became like noonday sun as three simultaneous humongous bright fireballs burst out and a awful gigantic rolling thunderclap sounded. Moorhead had never witnessed three of the devices going off all at the same time, or at that great height. It was awe-inspiring … at least if they were not directly over your own head. He was glad to be moving away. A verse came into his mind: "Our God is a consuming fire."

From that height a single Thunderclap may not have been as effective, but the effects of three at that altitude seemed to synergistically combine. The pressure wave slammed down and outward, snuffing out the burning decks of the Terror while it splintered the huge masts like kindling and cracked the top decks down the middle. Even so, the massive ship held. The sheer force of that massive pressure wave pushed down on both the huge ship and the water, dropping the Dreadnaught into a hole in the ocean deep enough that it could no longer be seen. Torgach looked up in terror as the ocean seemed to rise far above him on all sides and then came crashing inward. The Dreadnaught Terror was gone.

Commodore Moorhead's eyes were wide in astonishment and wonder, but he did not have any more time to gawk. He forced himself to look away and began to bark out further orders. They now had a gauntlet of more conventional enemy ships to deal with, and he wanted to extract every ounce of advantage the fireworks and destruction behind him might offer. The Dominion ships were not responding yet to the course change of the seven Freelandian vessels, and each of them closed in on their closest targets.

Four were too slow to come out of their shock, allowing the Freelandian war ships a close approach before they began maneuvering to bring their own catapults to bear. The smaller Thunderclaps that had already been launched sounded and three more enemy ships were destroyed under the great balls of fire. A fourth was badly damaged. The three other Freelandian ships were not able to get close enough as the Dominion captains, terrified by what seemed like explosive attacks from sky demons that they had just watched, steered well clear of this strange new menace that had somehow caused the unsinkable "mountain on the seas" Dominion Dreadnaught to be swallowed up by the very ocean itself and disappear with little more than flotsam left over under a fiery cloud of destruction. Murmurs raced among the enemy crews of sky and sea demons or gods that were reaching out to destroy them.

The intimidation was short-lived, however, and three Dominion vessels turned back to pursue the Freelandian ships. The closest to the Freelandian ship God is our Rock was tacking in from the west, while another vectored in from the east. Commodore Moorhead ordered the deployment of the sea mines on their long rope strings. This lightened his ship to allow for more speed. As the last rolled off the stern, he ordered a sharp turn to starboard. That caught the Dominion ships by surprise, and the closest even launched a volley of fire arrows, which just barely fell short of the fleeing Freelandian ship.

The range of the Freelandian spring guns was greater. Even as the Dominion arrows were falling into the ocean no more than thirty feet away, the heavy metallic twang of the largest spring gun sounded and a long iron-tipped bolt traced a flattened arc toward the Dominion ship in pursuit. It fell short of the deck and the Dominion crew cheered, figuring the target had been their main mast, even as the broadhead drove deep into the hull just above the water line with a loud 'thunk'. The force sent a shudder through the wooden ship and splintered the beams it hit. The Dominion ship began to take on water. More immediately though, the long pole considerably hindered steering of the ship, and it skewed sideways and slowed.

The second approaching Dominion ship plowed over the floating line of mines and several of the hooks lodged securely into the wood of its hull.

Moorhead had his ship swing around for another pass at the slowed vessel, which now could only sluggishly maneuver. The second Dominion ship, mine kegs now rapidly swinging through the water on the rope snagged by its hull, began to close with the Freelandian vessel. Timing was everything. As God is our Rock swung broadside to the stricken first Dominion ship, just out of the range of the Dominion catapults, the second ship crossed the bow of the first, several kegs trailing in the water behind it. As the two Dominion ships passed by one another closely, the keg mines struck and detonated. While not nearly as flashy as the Thunderclaps, they were just as effective on these smaller ships … especially when they were directly in contact with a wooden hull.

Geysers of water shot into the air, along with splinters from shattered hulls. In less than a minute both Dominion ships slipped below the ocean's surface. Up and down the Dominion line, other ships appeared to be suffering similar fates. One Freelandian ship appeared to have gotten too close and had small fires scattered over its deck, but even as he watched, Commodore Moorhead saw that they were put out. From his count, he figured eight or nine Dominion ships had been sunk plus the real prize, the Dreadnaught. Not a bad afternoon's work and a stupendous first encounter. Moorhead sank down on one knee and praised God for His mercy … and His continued blessings.

Further back in the fleet, the new Dominion Attack Force commander was uncomfortable in his very sudden promotion. The top naval strategists and leaders had been on the *Terror*, and with his own eyes he had watched in stunned awe as the heavens had opened up above the doomed Dreadnaught and the ocean opened up below, seemingly swallowing it whole. What terrible magic was this that those Freelandians had used? What other-worldly sun demon had been unleashed and had opened its gaping mouth to breathe fire down to consume the Dominion 'mountain on the sea'? At least after that morsel, the following sun-bites had been smaller, though not less damaging to the smaller ships to which it had been aimed. And what sea demon had bitten the other ships, created gaping fang holes that sank them just as effectively?

Whatever it was, he for one was not going to be over-confident like his late predecessors. Commands were issued and spread over his fleet: avoid engaging any Freelandian vessel without at least a four-to-one advantage. Even so, the word spread quickly throughout the entire Attack Force and no Dominion captain wanted to go head-to-head with the Freelandians, even with a large numerical superiority. A four to one advantage would not do you much good if you were the one selected to become the appetizer for the sun or water demon. Captains gave lip service to having no fear and that they were just waiting to take the battle to the enemy ships. Every one figured they would be best off being the third or fourth in line. Maybe the demons would get full by then.

Though the new enemy commander could not know it, similar skirmishes were happening with the other forward Dominion Attack Groups, and many other sub-commanders and captains were coming to the same conclusions.

But not Rath Kordoch. He was the Supreme Commander of the entire Dominion invasion force. He was a full day behind the forward Attack Force ships and therefore no word had reached him of the defeats that some might call catastrophic. No human word, that is. Within minutes of the various sea battles he felt it inside, in his spirit that had long grown accustomed to listening to those other spirits. He did not know the details, but he knew enough.

A dark shadow entered his luxurious cabin aboard the Dreadnaught *Dominance*. Not that this was altogether unusual, but this one was new and not supposed to be there. Rath motioned to an attendant, who hurriedly moved to a side room and returned with a ragged and obviously drugged slave. The attendant locked the chain attached to a harsh metal collar around the slave's throat to a ring set into the deck, forcing the slave to bend over awkwardly. The attendant looked up expectantly, and Rath nodded. The slave keeper picked up a short multi-ended whip and scourged the open back before him, drawing rivulets of blood that splattered over the dark red area on the floor below. Rath smiled in approval. It was not really necessary, but severe punishment and blood seemed to satisfy some deep part of him.

The new shadow coiled in a corner, waiting. Rath motioned it toward the slave, who in his drugged stupor had not done more than whimper at the pain. In a moment the slave contorted wildly, as though trying in vain to fight something off. Then all became still. A voice that did not entirely sound natural to the slave's body spoke. "Betrayed, Master! We have been betrayed by our own!"

"Nonsense."

"I saaww ... fire and brimstone! Death from above and death from below. It could not have come from the Freelandian ships – they cannot have anything like this! And they did not even fire on the *Terror*!"

"Tell me what happened."

"We were almost upon them, laughing at their puny ship – what could it possibly do against the *Terror*? Then ... flashes in the sky, a horrible boom high above us and the sky itself became fire that rained down upon us. The magician I was in was badly burned. Then ... I do not know what happened. The ocean was suddenly above us, mountains of water all around that came crashing down upon us. One second I was on the deck of the ship in a dying body, the next I was fifty feet under water. I do not like being under water – it is dark and so very, very cold!"

"Hmm. Fire from the sky, but not from any catapult? Could God Himself be entering this battle on the side of His blessed little Freelandia? It would be just like Him to cheat us! But no, that is not possible. It was only one ship, big as it is … or was. If God had sent true fire and brimstone it would surely have wiped out the entire Attack Group, maybe even the entire fleet. No, He should stay out of this conflict and let us do as we want. Our Master has said so. We will snuff out those Freelandians before God may even notice, if He cares to look, if He really even cares about them anyway. And why would He? They are so contemptuously weak and fail all the time. No, this must have been something else."

"One of us has betrayed the Master! It must be!"

"That is not possible … is it? No. It cannot be. None of us would ever side with the Freelandians. And certainly none would dare go against our Master."

"Then an angel?"

"One of our confused brothers? Perhaps. But God keeps them tightly leashed, they do not do anything without His command, like little sniveling spirit slaves. No, they would not have the presumption to do such a thing, especially against our Master. Unless … unless one is going renegade? Is that possible? I thought our Master gathered to himself all of those once, long ago. Could another have developed such independent thought? Surely not. But … possible? Or … no, our Master would not be setting one of us up against others? A house divided? No."

Rath paced the room for a few minutes. "No, it must be a rogue angel. Be on the watch for such a thing … it would only be a matter of time before such a one would come completely into our fold anyway, no matter how much he might be thinking he was doing God's own work. Ha, you cannot take God's matters into your own hands or into your own timetable. Foolish one … or rather, perhaps one of those squeaky clean ones has wised up and will shortly join us. Our Master will win in the end, even against God. He has told us that himself, many times."

"Where can I go, Lord Kordoch? I am much more useful to you than to remain in this … this slave host."

"Yes, you probably are. But you failed to protect one of the only six Dreadnaughts the Dominion has. And you do not even know what caused your destruction. You have been slothful."

"N …N…Noooo Lord! My magician was full of cuts from bloodletting and hoarse from incantations! None of us could have seen this coming!"

"Nonetheless, you failed."

"But Lord … that is not fair! Don't send me to the … the dry places! Not back to hell! Let me remain here, to continue to work out our Master's plan!"

"Fair? Fair! Do you think I care about fairness? You must be getting weak. What now to do with you? I don't know, your failure was colossal." Rath liked to watch the spirits squirm.

"Send me … send me into a fish … or a bird then. Maybe into one of our ravens?"

"Alright, into one of the birds then. But do not kill your body until after the invasion – your punishment is to be condemned to a raven until we have crushed the Freelandians."

"Oh, thank you Lord! I will go immediately!" The slave shook violently. With a sadistic grin, one final twist broke his neck and the body slumped to the floor dead.

"Dispose of that rubbish." Rath looked over at his attendant and then pondered the news. What might this mean to the invasion or the fleet?

Warden James watched as a swarm of engineers scurried and fussed over the Alpha-Red team to finalize the fit of their new armor. He wondered if this would be as helpful as promised. His team was used to stealth, speed and agility, and a suit of armor, even made of this new sillarium alloy, was certainly not stealthy. As his team began to practice with it, though, he had to admit it did allow for real speed – his men could run far faster, and for real agility – they could make prodigious leaps and amazing aerobatics. But he did not like the idea of relying on a thin metal suit to supposedly stop deadly blows. Avoiding them altogether or blocking blows with a weapon in your hand was far preferable. Yet as he watched he began to wonder ... perhaps the armor was a weapon too ... one you wore over your entire body and which was always in your hand ... or your hand was always in it.

He knew that the initial shock wave of Dominion Bashers would likely not have any other armor than crude shields, and likewise the poorly trained mass foot soldiers that often composed the next line of standard Dominion armies were designed for rapid advancement even at a relatively high cost in troop life. However, the second and third waves would be highly trained professional soldiers, probably the best the enemy could muster. They would have mounted heavy cavalry at the fore to lead the charges, and more lightly armored rear and flanking units. And while their leading foot soldiers would be lightly armored if at all, they would be immediately followed by heavier units to help push through any resistance.

In contrast, Freelandian Watchers were typically lightly armored at best but highly mobile and very highly skilled. What little real armor he had was put into defensive positions guarding entrances into the Keep, and to complement other fixed defenses. Freelandia had not had a standing army – or needed one – for several hundred years. Now they had defensive forces that ranged from being better fitted for Special Operations to being farmers and laborers with only basic training in military matters. James had few options. One he certainly did NOT have was to try to meet the enemy on an open battlefield. The Dominion had a vastly larger army with well trained soldiers. What he did have were tactics well fitted to the terrain and resources he had, some really superior weaponry, the inherent advantage of fighting from fortified defensive positions and most importantly ... God.

Even so, how was he supposed to repulse the enemy, still put men into harm's way, still expect death and destruction to reach their icy grip into the ranks of men who expected him to lead them to victory? How would his own faith stand up to this ultimate test? That question probably bothered him more than most others. Faith was easy when living was easy.

He feared his men might balk at putting up a very real defense when Freelandian blood began to flow around them, even when their own actions could affect the extent of the casualties. The Watchers would fight to their last breath, but what about the civilians? How could he bolster their courage and resolve?

For the umpteenth time he prayed. That, he felt, was a key thing he could do, and by extension, it was a key thing his army could do as well. James had asked Chaplain Mikael to appoint chaplains throughout the volunteer army ranks, and encourage them to lead the men in regular prayers. And James had heard what Mikael had done even more recently – he had assigned apprentice musicians and singers to each of the chaplains. They led the men in singing some of the new worship songs that were coming out of the Music Academy regularly now. James had raised an eyebrow at that, but he did not deny there was real spiritual power in that worship. But would that translate into physical power on the battlefield? It certainly was encouraging the soldiers though. And maybe it would reduce the normal fear and hesitancy of men waiting to face life-or-death conditions.

Yori, the leader of the Alpha Red team, was unsure about the new armor. He liked his team to be highly comfortable with every weapon and tool they might use, and preferred battle-tested and proven items over brand new. Yet he had to grudgingly respect the armored suits. His men were already devising new tactics to take advantage of the far greater speed and leaping capabilities, and they were already testing out the strength and damage resistance of their new tools. It was truly impressive. A few of his men seemed especially proficient already, like the suits were a second metallic skin. If they had time to practice with these and work out the tactical possibilities, the team would be the most effective Spec Ops team on the planet. Of course, they already were that before the advent of these armored suits.

Yori watched as the three men most adroit in using the suits, Prentice, Olaf and Dimitri, made coordinated leaps over a tall wall, landing right beside each other, having drawn weapons while airborne. Those three were already almost acting like a single fighting entity, one that was very rapidly acclimating to both the defensive and offensive enhancements the suits offered.

Yori surely hoped they would have the opportunity to give them a real try in battle. He figured he and his team would not have to wait very long to see.

The amphitheater of the Music Academy that stood on a tall hill facing the Bay was constantly in use now, with round-the-clock worship being offered as a fragrant sacrifice to God. Today an urgency seemed to be in the air, pulling them to join together to both worship their loving God and to combat a common enemy. Kory led Maria out to join those already engaged in this duality that was both strange in concept and yet felt so very right within their spirit. And while physically tiring, spiritually it was exhilarating, empowered and endowed as it was with God's Spirit and power.

Grand Master Vitario was already playing and motioned for the girls to join him. "Do you feel the Spirit's presence? It seems particularly intense today, similar to when our fleet first met the Dominion."

"Yes … yes I do." Maria smiled, though it was a bit forced. Worshiping with abandon for the sheer joy of being in God's presence was one thing, but knowingly going into spiritual battle threatened to add a heaviness that so easily seemed to burden her.

Chaplain Mikael walked over to where Vitario, Maria and Kory were huddled, and joined in their whispered conversation. "Is it always like this?"

"Like what?" Vitario looked at him with a perplexed expression.

"This … this wonderful unity. It is like you are all individually praying with your music, but all speaking variations of the same words at the same time in a unified whole. I have rarely experienced such marvelous corporate Christian unity."

Vitario mused over the words. "I had not thought of our worship music as prayer, but I suppose you are right. And the music does encourage unity – otherwise it would be so very discordant."

Maria was listening in, even as the music being played around them seemed to be inexorably pulling and tugging at her to join in. "But Chaplain Mikael … how could people praying to their Creator not be unified, at least in purpose? I mean, when you lead a prayer, doesn't everyone join in with you to speak to God from their hearts even as you speak out loud?"

Mikael shook his head gently and then hurriedly added, "No, Maria. Unfortunately not. Sometimes I pray with my eyes open, and when I look out I see many people who are obviously not participating. Sometimes I wonder if I am the only one truly praying."

"Oh, that cannot be! How could .. how could anyone not join it with you? I mean, God Himself is listening! I have heard you say that when two or more are gathered in Christ's name that He is with us! Since He is right there next to us … and even in us … how could anyone not pay attention and join in? And when I am praying, I often am listening too … it is a time when God helps me to be still enough to really hear Him more clearly."

Mikael reached over and held one of Maria's hands. "Dear child, may God grant that you never change! I would wish everyone else had such a relationship with their God as you do. Meanwhile, I am filled with wonder and hope seeing and hearing all of this unified worship."

The tugging on Maria's spirit was getting stronger and stronger. She gently pulled her hand away and lifted her violin, a far-away … or was it so very intimately close? … look coming over her face as she began to slip immediately away into her special place with God.

Vitario, watching, nodded to Chaplain Mikael. "If you think it was unified before, my friend, keep watching with both your physical and spiritual eyes and heart. I suggest you find a seat. This gets rather intense!"

For Maria, their hushed voices had already faded. The insistency of the call was not to be denied any longer. In her mind the worship sounds already formed a rainbow of color swirling in a coherent river of musical energy. Her Audience was of course already there. But as had been more common lately her stage where she saw herself standing was far larger than befitting a personal performance. Instead it was if she stood atop the cliffs overlooking the Bay, gazing southward at a roiling black thunderstorm of palpable menace and doom. Every day it grew closer, obscuring more of the sky. It now blotted out perhaps a third of the sky before her. But today it was not just a seamless wall of dark dread.

Maria shuddered even as she began to play. Today the front edge of the darkness was beginning to take a shape, black clouds coalescing slowly into the form of … She gasped as fear welled up, fear that threatened to turn

into full blown terror. She saw a huge gaping mouth form from billowing dark clouds and malevolent blood-red eyes begin to look piercingly directly at … her. It was her dream, her nightmare coming to life. It was the evil dragon intent on devouring and utterly consuming her very existence.

Her body quivering, a large part of Maria wanted to turn and run, or drop into a little fetal ball with her eyes squeezed shut. Yet the beast was still a long ways off, and the worship music was swelling ever stronger around her, buoying her spirit. Resolutely, Maria set her face, planted her feet, and began to play with real earnestness. At the same time she began to collect the musical streams and ribbons into a tighter and stronger weave, and to direct it toward the approaching storm. The spiritual energy swelled as their musical praise rolled out of the amphitheater, down across the Bay, and further … reaching out across the ocean water to combat the enemies of their God.

❧

Far out at sea, Rath Kordach grimaced as what had been a slowly building inconvenient headache suddenly grew in ferocity. He staggered a step in his cabin and he could feel demons about him howl in spiritual pain and anguish. Confound those Freelandians! This onslaught made it immensely more difficult to plan clearly, to even think clearly at all. IT HAD TO BE STOPPED! He would order all magicians and evil spirits to redouble their efforts. In this war with both physical and spiritual fronts, Rath was fully committed to winning both.

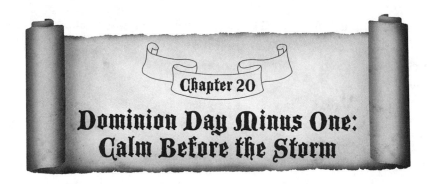

Chapter 20

Dominion Day Minus One: Calm Before the Storm

ommodore Moorhead and his crew were bone-tired; a sentiment the entire Freelandian navy could agree with, at least the large majority of them who were stationed out at sea. They had had little rest over the last twenty four hours as they flitted in and around the Dominion ships. So far, the *God is our Rock* had no more than a few arrows that had managed to land on her, while they gave three more enemy ships a watery grave. Moorhead ruefully figured the Dominion captains and crew likely were far more tired. Even during the night some of the ships had kept up the harassment, launching several of the bubble Thunderclaps set to go off high in the sky to be visible for many hundreds of square nautical miles. Those had no specific target and no one expected them to actually damage any Dominion ship. But the psychological effect would be devastating, keeping most hands on deck peering out into the stormy darkness trying to figure out if the thunderous booms were merely from the occasional lightning or from something more ominous.

The first Dominion fleet they had encountered was now well to the north, with only a few Freelandian ships continuing the harassment mission. The bulk of the Freelandian navy was now searching for the invasion force, with their lumbering troop carriers and likely heavy escort. The storm, however, severely hampered their ability to find anything. The wind was blowing strongly from the south now, propelling the enemy's ships northward at great speed and an accompanying fog was shrouding them from searching eyes. With the darkness, fog and rain, Moorhead knew the Dominion ships could be passing by only a few miles away, and he would be unable to detect them. And even if detected, it was doubtful he could have done much anyway. His small sloops were tossed about upon the waves and he expected that even his most skilled Gunny Mate would have been sorely tested to score a hit on any ship more than a few dozen yards away.

The Freelandian commodore also had no knowledge of how much cumulative damage all of his ships and crews may have exacted upon their enemies. He and his own crew could account for the vessels they sank and those observed sunk from others in the their immediate line of sight, but the weather made ship to ship communication highly limited. Yet in the midst of the actual fighting he had never seen his gunners shoot better. His helmsman seemed to anticipate his every command and begin to enact them even as he was just beginning to speak. And the Dominion vessels seemed to turn in just the most advantageous ways … advantageous to the Freelandians firing upon them that is. But now they would all have to continue with the prearranged plan. He did not have any control over the weather …but he knew who did, and went to Him in prayer.

The storm had reached the Freelandian coast, which was the final sign Jarl was waiting for to indicate it was time to get all of his men in place. Over the last several days his teams had painstakingly clamored their way up along the eastern coastal cliffs, under the very eyes of the Freelandian defenses. Now they were in position and readying themselves.

Jarl did not have enough men to cover both sides of the coastal cliffs, and had been told to focus all of his efforts on the side furthest from the Keep and the Watcher reinforcements. There was a small garrison half way up the cliffs, but between it and the main catapults there were several steep mountainous passes. Jarl's men had scaled high above the passes and were prepared to create landslides to bring down enough rock and boulders to prevent access for days – which was all that should really be needed anyway. Other men were positioned around the eastern cliff big cats, ready to overwhelm their crews. With the catapults on that side of the coast silenced, Dominion ships should be able to remain out of range of the catapults on the other side and have clear sailing across the Bay and to the Keep itself. Jarl licked his lips in anticipation. Finally, a big chance to prove himself, to prove his worth. His luck had been bad ever since ... ever since that certain little blind girl from Westhaven had ruined the good thing they had going there ... and caused the death of his two brothers and their Rat Pack leader. Some day, he thought ruefully. If that little mouse somehow survived the invasion itself, some day he would track her down and make her pay. He had learned that she had been whisked out of Westhaven and now was in the capital city. Maybe ... once the eastern coastal defenses were silenced ... maybe he could even sneak back to the Keep with a few of his men and take out one little target of his very own. One little target with the name of Maria.

Freelandia was no stranger to storms, but there was something decidedly strange and chilling about this one. The winds carried odd noises that seemed like subliminal screeches and faint, far-away screams. Few slept well, but time not sleeping was put to solid strategic use. The people prayed.

At the Music Academy, though, people also worshiped. Grand Master Vitario had instituted around-the-clock worship and now had increased the participation to help combat the feelings of dread and doom that seemed to accompany the storm darkness. He could tell it was having an effect as the Academy campus felt like a bastion of hope and purpose. Those not involved with the worship rotation were busily preparing both themselves and their instruments for the intensifying battle. It was certainly a fight unlike anything anyone had ever heard of. Reginaldo seemed to be hovering near Maria, rarely letting her out of his protective sight.

For her part, Maria acted strangely calm, though her friends noticed worried and even fearful looks that would pass over her face in unprotected moments. Kory knew it was at least partly an outward act. Maria was now regularly crying out in her dreams loudly enough to wake her roommate. Yet daily, Maria was also wandering among the other musicians and singers, listening and offering occasional suggestions, and she often stopped by one of the worship warfare sessions and joined in. Those seemed to energize and encourage both the others and Maria.

The whole mood of the entire Academy of Music was one of excited anticipation, mixed in with concern, and the intensity was growing by the hour. Some of the younger apprentices were afraid, and Master Ariel was talking with each one. The strongest antidotes for fear, they were all finding, were earnest prayers and focused worship.

As might be expected, the Watcher Compound was a beehive of activity as the various warriors further honed their skills and memorized the strategies and battle plans. There was no fear, only a sense of urgency to finalize all preparations. Late in the evening groups of Watchers departed to their various posts. Some would need to ride through most of the night. The greatest amount of work was going into final touches to the vast maze of narrow pathways created with a tremendous amount of moved earth and timbers by the large volunteer army. It lay between the main beach and the Keep itself. The beach was less than a mile from the city walls, but getting from there to the city was now much more complicated … and decidedly deadly.

The other main route to the city was from the shipyard docks. The docks themselves were being rigged so that any ship attempting to dock would be severely damaged from a variety of sources. The most clever were reed pipelines connected to large tanks of highly flammable lighter-than-water oils. On command, valves could be opened to dump large volumes of these oils onto the wharves and into the water under them. One flaming arrow would set the whole area ablaze. Tar and pitch containers were strategically located around the area too, so that any such fires would burn fiercely for several days. While the loss of their main docks would be painful to the Freelandians, they hoped the sacrifice would be much, much more painful to their enemies.

It would be possible for the Dominion army to try to land at the beach and then cross the Keep River to bypass the docks themselves and enter the Warehouse District. That area had very well constructed streets and blocks of large buildings interspersed with offices. The district filled a valley that sloped upward, ending in a large open field that narrowed at its furthest end to a very solid stone bridge that crossed the river. From there it was a short run to the Keep itself. The Warehouse District was a very busy place with considerable commerce, the busiest commercial district in the entire country. It could not readily be blocked. Instead, it had feverish activity now, but most of that had nothing to do with commerce.

Yori's suit chafed in unexpected places, and it was totally impossible to scratch any place that itched. Of course, that meant that itches were commonplace and everywhere. The Alpha Red team members were virtually living in their suits, as that was the best way to acclimate oneself to them as fast as humanly possible. And with prayer, they were not altogether limited to human possibilities. Everyone on the team was now quite at ease moving around in the suits … and in many cases moving much more rapidly than they ever could have before. Part of that were the springs, surely. But they had also learned that they no longer needed to slow for doors, or even most walls for that matter. They could run full force into all but the thickest planks or support timbers and often crash right through.

They had even worked up a tactic where one member would run at full speed at a wall, and at the last moment hurl himself forward shoulder first. Most of the time the wall crasher would smash through, creating a sizable hole and significantly weakening the entire area. Those following could then immediately push through the already created hole, or just run through the weakened remaining structure and so force a very unexpected entry. Just today, several team members had extra metal reinforcement added to their right shoulder area to enhance that capability. Several men had requested another improvement, which Master Oldive said he was working on anyway – additional springs were being added around the elbows and shoulders that greatly increased the arm strength in the suits. Only a few had those on a trial basis, but if they worked well they could become standard on additional suits.

If they only had more time … but with training there almost never seemed to be enough. Still, God was undoubtedly blessing their practice and the suits … well, there was no further skepticism or doubts within the Alpha teams. The suits were a colossal force multiplier, giving the wearer in some cases double or triple the capability he had before. And considering that the Alpha team operators had already been some of the most capable fighting men in the world, then with the suits they were unequaled, a group of men who could fight individually or in a highly coordinated team or sub-teams with capabilities the Dominion would not have even dreamed of in their worst nightmares. Or so they hoped.

Several dozen ships were out in the Bay of Freelandia, but by morning most would be upstream in the largest rivers, saved for later operations to repel invaders who bypassed the Keep. The crews set about installing heavy ropes and chains across most of the rivers, and dispersing many of the engineer's mines on ropes along the river mouths. When ready, fuses could be lit and horses used to pull the ropes across the rivers. Any ships attempting to pass would be in for a very rude surprise.

It chafed the captains to no end not to be allowed a head on fight with the enemy, but it was clear that the Freelandian navy would never succeed in defeating the Dominion armada, and to put ships in the Bay would certainly doom them. The captains knew that stationing them in the rivers was really not that much better, unless God showed up and showed off His power.

Besides, they all told themselves, the coastal cliff catapults and spring guns should decimate much of the incoming enemy fleet, and more would be likely taken by the various other launchers, mines and bubble Thunderclaps. If the weather cleared they might even be able to put aloft the huge bubbles that could carry the largest Thunderclaps along with a few human riders, though Chief Engineer Robert only grudgingly allowed their potential use if conditions were nearly perfect. He said he recalled all too clearly seeing his beloved Arianna falling from the sky in one of the baskets strung beneath those huge bubbles, and he had no desire to see anyone else attempt to fly without wings again.

But even with all of those preparations and defenses, everyone knew they were tremendously outnumbered. None of their history books save one recorded any other wars where such hopelessly out-matched defenders had not been utterly defeated. Of course, that one – the Bible – carried much more weight, being written under the direction of the Spirit of God.

Out in the Bay, only a single ship could be seen, edging close to the narrow waterway entrance that was the only connection to the ocean. A barge had already been located directly upstream from the inlet, anchors holding it fast in place against the steady current that always ran out to the sea beyond. The small but fast yacht reached the barge and carefully eased up and tied off just before the sun had fully set. The crew had a full night's work ahead of them, readying the load of sea mines already stacked on the barge and adding to it another dozen or so the engineers had just rushed to complete hours before they had set sail. They had a risky mission. They were to light the fuses on the mines and begin dropping them into the channel as soon as the first Dominion ship was spotted. The fuses would stay lit for up to three days, patiently waiting for some ship to come along and break off or push in one of the many spines sticking out at random angles all over the outer surface. The latest mines were larger than the others, a further improvement in destructive yield.

The crew's location, however, also made them the first Freelandian target those enemy ships would meet ... and therefore the recipients of the full brunt of the largest and most deadly naval armada the world had ever known. To a man, they considered theirs a suicidal mission. But if their actions would save others from a cruel Dominion fate, then they were all quite willing to lay down their lives ... for their country, their fellow citizens, and especially for their God.

Grand Master Vitario led the musicians at the amphitheater, and tonight he was praying and playing specifically against the dark storm that had lingered over the Keep for the last few days, along with the dreadful and strange noise that accompanied it. The Dominion and its forces liked the darkness and the eerie weather that often foreshadowed their attacks. Vitario had in mind to change that. Night was coming, but normal darkness held no fear. He and the others prayed and praised, petitioning God to clear the clouds.

The worshipers could feel the spiritual resistance. They pressed on and on. As the last evening light dimmed, the storm clouds did began to thin and disperse, and along with it the strange noises that seemed to come in with the wind. The spiritual oppression had lessened somewhat, but was still present and very threatening. But at least it looked like the morning would dawn clear. It was a calm just before the invasion storm.

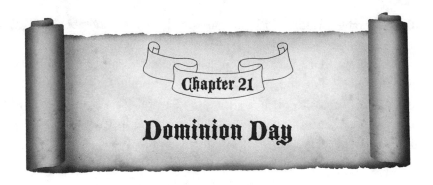

Chapter 21

Dominion Day

The day started for Jarl and what he called his 'mountain rats' midway between midnight and dawn. Teams used the scant unexpected moonlight that shone through the now scattering clouds to finish the preparations. Well before sunlight sizable rock falls blocked access to the Coastal Defenses on that side of the Bay. Even as the mountain rats carefully descended along well laid out routes, others scrambled across the rough terrain to reach the huge catapults and spring guns mounted in strategic sites. There were twenty such locations, and their crews had simple barracks nearby, often housing the complement of two or three of the launchers. Teams of Rats were assigned to each barrack, and others were to take out any sentries posted along the trails. They struck just before dawn.

The ominous dark cloud to the south had grown sizably, and deep red eyes seemed to glow within the blackness. Maria could see a horrific mouth of roiling clouds filled with dark fangs. Tendrils of evil were reaching toward her, getting ever closer. The terrible eyes were fixed upon her, drawing all hope and joy from her weak body to burn away to nothingness in those fiery pools of hatred, trying to suck the very life from her. She wanted to turn and run, but she was paralyzed with fear. The baleful eyes captured her attention even as the awful mouth opened in a full snarl of gaping cloud teeth. Maria watched in horror as hundreds of dark tentacles lurched out toward her, stretching to toss her immobilized frail form into the waiting jaws. She was helpless, hopeless, totally overwhelmed and totally vulnerable, waiting with terrible dread for the inevitable devouring. Maria screamed.

"Wake up! Maria!" Kory shook her friend again and finally Maria stopped wailing out and began to violently tremble. She began to sob, clinging to Kory with all her strength. Several girls from surrounding apartments came running in and all looked at the stricken girl as Kory sat on her bed and rocked her back and forth comfortingly.

"It … it was so awful! It was so much worse this time!"

"What was it?" Several girls blurted out at once.

"I don't know for sure … but it was huge and dark and had fangs and writhing tentacles and was totally evil, coming from the south. It was … it was coming to devour me!"

With the first light of day, the first wave of the Dominion fleet approached the outer cliffs that guarded the entrance into Freelandia Bay. Right at the entrance the coast was much too rough and inaccessible to mount defensive works. With the rising tide, the first warships were being made ready to make the daunting run through the narrow channel. The first Attack Group of warships had been ravaged by the Freelandian navy, losing over half of their vessels. Those remaining had first set up a cordon around the entrance to Freelandia, allowing the slower troop transport ships to catch up and finish the voyage. Most of the transports of Attack Group One had made it through the stormy night to arrive safely, and even as they waited in the early morning light the first ships of Attack Group Two began to show on the horizon.

Further out at sea but rapidly approaching, the remaining transport ships were also coming, ringed with outer warships to protect them. The bulk of the Dominion warships in this last wave were staging a rear-guard defense from marauding Freelandian vessels that still occasionally seemed to call on sky and sea demons to destroy unlucky ships. Those were getting rather sparse now, so the Dominion crews expected the demons were tiring, that they had worn them down or satiated their hunger for human flesh. Barring those, the Freelandian naval ships were very fast and had surprising range of their launched weapons, but the far superior numbers of the Dominion fleet made for much more than an even match. That allowed the transport ship captains to just concentrate on getting to Freelandian shores as quickly as possible. None wanted their passengers aboard any longer than absolutely necessary.

Rath Kordoch looked out over the largest invasion fleet the world had ever witnessed, high up on his perch on the Dreadnaught *Dominance*. In the distance he could see just one other Dreadnaught, and he scowled. Three of the massive ships had been sunk and one damaged enough that its captain had to turn back to make a run for a Dominion port specially prepared for very rapid repairs, accompanied by several other warships. There was much too much invested in these mountains to risk them limping back to a safe port alone. Rath still did not understand what power had been unleashed on the pride of his fleet, and he had not yet witnessed any of the Freelandian attacks himself. But it did not really matter. He had over a hundred warships remaining, and nearly that many transport vessels bringing his invasion force of nearly two hundred thousand soldiers, a thousand horses, and a dozen huge pachyderms. Freelandia did not stand a chance.

While Rath was the Supreme Invasion Force Commander, he did not pretend to be a military strategist. Fleet Admiral Nartusk stood nearby, surveying the many vessels under his command as they prepared for their run through the channel into Freelandia Bay. Ten of his biggest frigates would charge through first in rapid succession, splitting up immediately upon passage to engage with the expected enemy ships waiting for them. One goal was to bring the fighting up close to the Freelandian ships, which should silence coastal defenses from firing lest they strike their own ships. These would be followed by several dozen lighter, smaller, faster warships that would make rapid dashes closer to the shores to lure the coastal catapults into trying to hit the quickly moving targets, whose captains expected to continuously jinx this way and that to avoid being struck.

Next would come the first transports, built smaller and lighter than the others, which would dart in to drop off their contingent of specialty soldiers skilled in mountaineering. Their job was to take out all launch weapons endangering the fleet in this outer Bay area. In rapid sequence three quarters of the remaining fighting ships would enter the Bay to crush any and all remaining Freelandian naval vessels, with the remainder left ocean-side to ensure the entrance – and exit – of the Bay remained under complete Dominion control.

Fleet Admiral Nartusk smiled. All the planning, all the preparations were coming together now. This was his hour, his day, his moment. After their success, he may even be appointed Lord Admiral, the highest rank possible, only one step below that of an Overlord. *Ah*, he thought, *but first stay in the here and now. The only true reality is what I can see and hear.* He hoped all of the captains remembered to steer to the eastern side of the Bay … that is, if the coastal defenses there were not functioning as his intelligence reports had promised. He did not put too much stock into those promises, but if even some were out of commission it would make that side of the Bay less dangerous.

Not that they had come here to stay out of danger. He expected that while the smaller ships may indeed have to be very careful of shore-launched hazards, the *Dominance* did not. With the heavy metal clad hull and heavy timber construction, he doubted any but the heaviest of rocks could cause much damage to a Dreadnaught – and those heavy rocks could only be flung so far by even the largest catapults the Freelandians could have.

The original plan had two Dreadnaughts left out near the ocean entrance, but now that was down to one. All other mountains-of-the-sea were going to enter the Bay directly after the smallest transport ships had made safe passage, adding their immense size to draw fire from enemy ships and allow the troops rapid access to the nearby rocky shoreline. The Dreadnaught *Dominance* was the only such ship moving into the lineup position for early entrance and a signal flag was raised from its highest mast. The nearest ship, Southern *Menace*, seemed to leap forward, as if just barely held back by a leash, ready to tear into their enemy.

Rath Kordoch watched first one, then a second and third Dominion frigate turn confidently to make a run at the strait. He fully expected to lose a few warships – but really they were serving their duty … the war would be won on land, not on the sea. But to accomplish that, the majority of the transport ships needed safe passage.

Kordoch grinned evilly and turned toward the two dozen most senior Dark Magicians behind him with a nod. Each had a drugged slave before them, and at the nod each thrust his wavy edged ceremonial dagger forward and upward. Two dozen slave bodies fell to the ship's deck, blood pumping out over the already stained wooden beams. The magicians dipped their fingers into the fresh blood and began to paint first themselves and then the sailors around them and even the ship itself with strange rune symbols.

Let the Freelandians pray to their puny god, Rath Kordoch thought. *The weaklings will shortly feel the full wrath of the Dominion, and of our very real power. Their foolish god will not even know we are here until it is too late. And even if aroused, their god is no match for the demonic power overshadowing this awesome demonstration of might. In a few short days the world would see who is stronger … the peace-loving weakling Freelandians, or the proven conquerors of the world, the Dominion!*

The sky above seemed to darken with the arrival of thousands of black ravens. The birds wheeled through the sky as if in formation, then turned and shot forward, climbing high to clear the coastal cliffs. Though Rath could not see it, he knew the lead raven had deeply red bloodshot eyes.

Kory led a shaken Maria to the outside amphitheater by the Bay. As they neared, a booming voice welcomed them.

"Maria – you don't look well!" Sir Reginaldo strode forward to lift one of her hands.

"It … it has started I think. The *Dominion*. They are out there." Maria waved her other hand out toward the sounds of the waves. "They are coming for me."

Reginaldo looked perplexed first at Maria, and then at Kory. Kory shrugged. "She woke up screaming from what sounded like a very bad dream. She said something about a dark monster from the south that was coming to … to eat her."

Sir Archibald Reginaldo, the world's most famous and illustrious singer, sucked in a mighty breath and puffed out his immense chest. "Maria!" That was said with a loud commanding voice that demanded full attention.

Maria lifted her head toward the voice, a still-scared look on her face. Her body began to tremble again.

"Maria, whose battle is this? Is it yours? Would God EVER expect little you to fight His battles … alone, all by yourself?"

"Ah … no, I suppose not."

"Suppose nothing. KNOW the truth! Now tell me this … who would want you to feel afraid?"

Maria pondered that for just a second, and her trembling stopped. "The enemy!"

"Right you are, child. And let me ask you another question. Why do you think the enemy sent you that dream? What did they hope to accomplish?"

Maria stood straighter, and her voice sounded stronger. "To scare me?"

"Right again. Why?"

"Hmm … maybe because if I was scared I would not … would not …" Maria's face hardened in defiance. "Because then I would not be able to fight back!"

"And why pay you in particular this kind of special attention? Why would evil seem to be specifically targeting you?"

Now Maria looked angry but also a bit confused. "Why, Reginaldo?"

"Because they are afraid of you … and your gifting … and your God. They are afraid of what God can accomplish through you! Are you going to let them win?"

"NO!" With grim determination, Maria lifted her violin. Then she unexpectedly giggled. "I have my violin, and I'm not afraid to use it!"

Reginaldo grinned. "That's my Maria. Punch them with praise and whack them with worship! I think the enemy absolutely hates and fears our worship. Let them have it, my little worship warrior!"

Reginaldo was about to go on, but he could see a far-away look coming over Maria and knew that she was already fixing to do just that. He was so very glad he had had a long talk with Minister Polonos the night before. He far better understood what was really going on now. He rubbed his hands together. This could get interesting!

The captain of the *Southern Menace* had moved to the forward deck. He stared down at the flotsam exiting through the channel and laughed. Some poor merchant ship must have lost an entire load of barrels in the Bay, and it must have been awhile ago based on the odd barnacle growths. The barrels were spreading outward upon exiting the channel. He concluded they could not possibly pose any threat when the first bumped into his hull.

The blast shook the ship as if it was in an earthquake and a great geyser of water sprouted into the air. Many sailors were knocked to the deck, and the captain himself barely stayed upright by grabbing at a railing from only a few yards away from the impact. "What sea demon was that?" he shouted as the spray washed over the ship. "First Mate, check the forward hull below decks … see if our metalwork held!" He strode over to the still creaking side and leaned over the railing to examine what he could see firsthand. The blast had created a wide dent, but did not appear to have punctured the metal cladding.

"She's leaking slightly Captain, but no mor'n we'd expect in a moderate storm. It will take more than a Freelandian sea devil to stop our *Southern Menace!*"

"Very good! Let them throw whatever they have at us! The *Southern Menace* can take anythi …" A second barrel was hit and the proud captain this time was not gripping any railing. He and many others flew backwards and two crew men were even thrown overboard by the explosion. The captain stumbled to his feet, looking first down at his somehow still intact hull and then out at the many dozens of barrels passing through the strait that his ship was just entering. He had no idea if there was any connection between that flotsam and whatever sea devil lay beneath the water's surface, but he was not about to take any chances. "Helm, two degrees to port … now three to starboard! Steady … steady … now two more to starboard … now hard to port … back straight …"

The *Southern Menace* jinxed one way and then the other as the captain ordered the helmsman to steer around the barrels. Their passage through the channel was erratic, often coming quite close to the looming cliff walls, but they somehow made it through without further incident. That was not the case behind them.

Admiral Nartusk looked in astonishment as great sprouts of water leapt into the air around the first ship in his fleet to attempt passage through the straits. A moment later he heard the booming noise of the explosion. He turned wondering eyes toward Rath Kordoch, whose face looked as though by itself it could have sunk several of his ships had they been close enough. Nartusk looked away from that very unpleasant sight to another. His second ship in line was just entering the channel when first one, and then a second water spout shot upward, followed again by the dull roar. That ship began to list heavily to one side. They watched in horror as it dove bow-first beneath the waves.

"Whaaattt iissss tthhiiisss!" The Overlord whipped around toward his Dark Magicians, who were now cowering within their hooded robes. Several glanced up helplessly even as more explosions rang out. Rath Kordoch strongly desired to rip the heart out of someone, preferably bare-handed, but the noises distracted him, much to the magicians' short-lived relief. The Overlord turned just in time to see his third frigate shoot through the straits, triggering two separate geysers and booms, while the fourth turn aside as it began to sink lower into the water.

The *Dominance* was closer now, moving up toward the mouth of the strait. Nartusk could just make out several of the strange barrels as they spread outward. He watched curiously as one of the small and sleek Special Ops troop ships directly ahead of them in line casually bumped into one. Instantly, the trademark water geyser shot upward and Nartusk was close enough this time that there was no lag before the loud boom sounded. Horrified, he saw wood splinter from the bare hull and water pour into a gaping hole. The doomed ship drove forward under the momentum it had under half sail, forcing water in even faster. Within moments the ship had propelled itself completely under.

Rath Kordoch whipped back around, livid with fury. "Who is causing this? What is causing this? What sea monster is devouring our ships?" The Dark Magicians cowered in fear before the Overlord's wrath. "We need to know what spirit is lurking below us! You … and you!" He pointed to several from his personal guard. "Bind six of those cowering fools with the slave's chains!" The bodies of the slain slaves had long ago been pitched unceremoniously over the side. His bodyguards rushed forward, yanking up lengths of chain and cruelly wrapping six of the magicians with multiple lengths of the heavy metal bonds. The guards looked up at their master expectantly. "You six – since you are so useless up here, see what you might find … or appease … down below! Throw them overboard!"

The guards did not hesitate but immediately picked up the first bound magician and heaved him over the side. He hit with a tiny splash and instantly sank below the surface. The other five followed in rapid succession.

Meanwhile, Admiral Nartusk saw another ship run into a barrel which promptly exploded like the others. Geysers shot upward all around them now as the mines floated outward and struck the congregated Dominion vessels. Then his eyes opened wide as one struck the *Dominance* directly in front of him. The water erupted skyward and the huge ship shuddered, but it kept right on moving forward. Nartusk angled over the railing to look and could see no ill effect on the heavily armored hull. He made several snap decisions.

"Lookouts, helmsman – steer us directly into as many of those floating barrels as you can! Get in front of the smaller ships … NOW! Use the *Dominance* to stop as many barrels as possible. Gunners! Fire upon those barrels with every catapult you have and signal the other ships to follow our lead. Sink those barrels! They must be treats for the sea devils – see the fang holes in the smaller ships where the monsters have taken a bite! But they cannot chew through our metal hull! Gunners – fire at will!"

The Gunny Mates sprang to action and in less than thirty seconds the foredeck catapult let fly a load of fist-sized stones. Several struck nearby barrels. One sunk when its outer cask was ruptured without setting off the explosive swamp gas inside. The other promptly detonated with a loud boom, creating a crater in the surface of the ocean and spraying water high into the air.

It only took a few moments for the other captains who had been help-lessly watching as ship after ship struck barrels and sank to catch onto the idea. Dozens of other catapults launched loads of rocks and arrows at the floating bombs. Some barrels still made it through the barrage, but only a few were now hitting Dominion ships.

The *Dominance* plowed forward, past the smaller troop sloops and directly into the straits, triggering explosion after explosion as they cleared out the last of the floating barrels. When they had passed through the channel and emerged into the calm Bay of Freelandia, the barrel barrage had stopped.

Captain Nartusk steered easterly to clear the channel but stopped short of taking on what looked like a small pleasure yacht moored to a low-lying barge. He could see a crew of sailors scurrying around on the barge, but could not determine what they were up to. Regardless, they surely could not pose any threat to the *Dominance*, and so he disregarded them for the time being. To his great surprise, he could not see a single other Freelandian ship … anywhere.

He turned to survey the ships that had already made it in. With dismay, he could only see two of the large frigates, and only a small handful of the faster smaller ships that he had hoped would confuse the shore gunners, who for some unknown reason had not begun firing. 'Perhaps the Dominion spies had done a more thorough job than expected,' he thought. That would be a first.

Admiral Nartusk could hear continuing explosions, but they were few and far between now. He hoped few of the large soldier transport ships had been hit. Maybe the sea devils were satiated, finally. At least they did not seem to have to contend with the Freelandian navy here in the Bay.

Other ships now came pouring through the strait, one after another. Eight ships had entered the Bay when the first catapult on the western cliffs launched its payload of large rocks. They fell several hundred yards short and the Dominion captains noted the distance even as their crews cheered. Right nice of those Freelandians to show us their range, several thought.

Jarl's men caught their adversaries rather easily, as no one expected such a surprise attack. Within minutes every barrack was taken, with only a few offering serious resistance. The crews were bound and held under guard, while several groups of Rats ran to man some of the catapults themselves, in case any help might be needed by the Dominion. Per plan, black flags were raised to indicate the weapons had been successfully seized.

Dominion ships were now entering the Bay rapidly. Even though they should have spread out further, the captains felt greater safety in closer proximity, especially after what had happened outside of the Bay. Now they could only hear an explosion every ten minutes or so, but none in the Bay really knew how many ships had fallen prey to what they all thought of as sea devils. All dutifully kept outside of the range of the western catapults, with one brave Dominion captain having moved his ship to indicate the safe distance.

The *Southern Menace* had been in the bay the longest. With the large influx of new ships they were feeling confident once more in their far superior numbers … though perhaps somewhat less far superior than they had been a few hours ago. Emboldened, the captain had his helmsman steer directly toward the yacht and barge, only a few hundred yards away. As they turned toward the only Freelandian vessels in sight, the Dominion crew saw odd white floating … balls? …lift off from the barge and lazily drift upward in groups of eight to ten. As the third such group lifted skyward, the yacht dropped its moorings, all crew scrambled aboard and it began to pull away from the now empty barge.

The *Southern Menace* began to pick up speed. The yacht might be sleeker, but it had a fraction of the total sail cloth the frigate had, and they actually were rather even in top speed. The chase was on, and the Dominion sailors trained their catapults on the fleeing small ship, though they were well out of range at the present.

The bubbles were played out on long thin cords, now floating just south of the barge, catching a higher altitude breeze that pushed them toward the sea cliffs. Not yet noticed, other similar aerial balls were floating out from the Western coastal defense works further inland, where the higher level breeze would carry them nearly down the center of the Bay and toward the narrow channel to the sea.

Maria and a large assembly of fellow musicians were earnestly playing now, and many singers had joined in a series of rousing choruses of praise to God. Reginaldo joined in, as best he could without knowing all the words. He did not even mind when he stumbled over a few new phrases. He was happy. He was actually more than happy. He felt like he was accomplishing something, perhaps something more important than he had ever done before.

For her part, Maria stood before her Creator. While part of her was still a little scared inside, most of her was worshiping with abandon, giving all she had to the rising power of praise. It buoyed her spirit and she could sense the exuberance of the others around her. All of the spiritual power was being funneled as a mighty weapon out toward the dark evil present in her mind toward the south, now taking up well over half of her mental horizon. And the black cloud still had its menacing dragon head and evil red eyes. But it now did not seem quite as fearsome. But it was growing larger and larger … and getting closer. Clawed cloud tentacles reached toward her, growing bigger and coming nearer and nearer. The worship seemed to be slowing their progress, but they still slithered and writhed ever toward her diminutive form.

The Freelandian Western Coast Commander, could not understand why the eastern launchers were not starting their barrage. Most of the ships he could see appeared to be much closer to the eastern defense batteries and within range of the largest launchers. He understood why they were not letting out Thunderclaps … the prevailing breeze would not have allowed anything sent airborne on their side to be effective anyway. At least his were floating out nicely over the Bay. He hoped the fuses were estimated correctly – the range was much too far to trigger the Thunderclaps with attached cords, and so all were launched purely on fuses. He could also see the yacht out in the Bay, well north now of any of the bubbles, with their own armament drifting in the air along behind them and a Dominion frigate in hot pursuit. He was not sure if the frigate was too close to introduce to the Thunderclap, but there were plenty of other targets as several other Dominion ships neared the anchored barge. The shore launched bubbles were now well out into the Bay and being carried by the wind over the rather tightly clustered Dominion ships. The Freelandian coastal defenders prayed for the skills and wisdom needed to defeat their enemy. Any time now …

Admiral Nartusk smiled broadly as he watched so many Dominion ships streaming into the Bay. So far, it appeared the sea devils must be confined to the outer ocean, for no explosions, water geysers or gaping holes were showing up here. Perhaps the magicians sent into the deep by the Overlord had achieved something. Nartusk was still surprised by the near total lack of defensive actions from the Freelandians. Only one coastal launcher had sounded and shown that the Dominion ships were well out of their range, and there was only that one small yacht being pursued by one of his few remaining metal-cladded frigates, plus an old abandoned barge that one or another of the ships would soon either ram or sink with a catapult load. It was odd, very odd. The fleet had certainly been harried by Freelandian naval vessels several days out from the coast, where they had somehow conjured fire-breathing air demons to destroy many ships. Thankfully they had not seen any of those here … perhaps those sky demons only operated out on the open ocean. Sure, that must be it, he thought. A demon could only be in one given area at a given time. Even multiple demons could still only work in a limited locality.

But now … nothing. Well, the sea monsters were not 'nothing', but it was not the flesh-and-blood naval response he was expecting. No, this was too easy. The eastern shore defenses were supposed to be compromised by Dominion spies, and indeed his lookouts had reported seeing black flags raised on several obvious shore catapult batteries. But nothing was coming from the western coastal crags either. Those were too far away to see if any black flags may be flying there as well. Nartusk gave a command, and his signal flagmen sent out a quick message that the smaller, faster warships should dart closer toward that shore to draw fire. The Admiral certainly did not want to send his special mountaineering troops to land there until he had a better understanding of the full range and positions of the launchers that had to be ringing the rocky coasts.

At least the Overlord had calmed somewhat. Nartusk looked up at Rath Kordoch, who was pacing above on the highest stern deck. As he looked upward, the Dominion admiral could see strange white bubbles drifting overhead. Beneath each was a dark black round object. What trickery could this be? First there were strange floating barrels that apparently could only have been particularly tasty appetizers to attract sea devil monsters. Now strange floating contraptions were drifting over his fleet ... up in the sky, right above his ships.

Admiral Nartusk, commander of the largest and most powerful naval armada the world had ever witnessed, shook in sudden terror and his eyes bulged. If the barrels had been used to attract sea demons ... then what might these strange floating ... sacks attract?

Even as these thoughts filtered through his mind, the first Thunderclap of God went off, high above three warships. Nartusk winced and involuntarily ducked as the early morning sky lit up brighter than the noonday sun with a flare of fire. He was just straightening up when a gigantic fireball blossomed over the warships, accelerating burning metal projectiles and creating the characteristic pressure wave that slammed downward. In horror he saw the two ships furthest out hailed with high velocity burning shrapnel. Rigging and sails were destroyed and he Nartusk grimaced as he realized nearly everyone unlucky enough to be standing topside on the deck would have been killed. The hellfire tar containers on both vessels were hit and ignited just before the outer vestiges of the pressure wave struck. The minor fires already started were fanned into flaming infernos as the hellfire tar pots were knocked over. In dismay, Nartusk saw both ships fully ablaze.

The crew of the vessel directly beneath the secondary air explosion never had to worry about their ship being on fire. The immense blast of air pressure slapped down on them, splintering masts like matchsticks and pushing the entire ship down into a sizeable crater in the sea.

Nartusk watched in utter terror-filled amazement as that ship first sank into a ... a HOLE created in the water and then disappeared as water rushed back in to refill the void. In seconds, all that remained to be seen were bits and pieces of wood flotsam. "Fire-Breathing Sky Demons!" he bellowed. "Steer clear of those floating … ah … demon sky snacks!"

Within seconds another Thunderclap ignited, and then another. It became difficult to see clearly with all the flashes and the rolling thunder that became a deafening and constant bone shaking noise signifying death and destruction.

The entire crew of the *Southern Menace* heard the Thunderclap behind them and turned. In shock they saw three Dominion warships destroyed by some form of fire breathing sky demon. They had been closing the distance with the much smaller Freelandian yacht, but as the captain of the *Southern Menace* turned back to his immediate pursuit, he could see several sailors on the yatch ahead of him appear to cut some kind of cord that trailed upward into the very air. The little yacht now seemed to leap forward and rapidly began to pull away, as though some kind of sea anchor had been dragging behind but was now suddenly released. The captain did not have more than a few seconds to ponder what this might mean when a sky demon breathed its fire above and just behind him.

The Freelandian Coastal Defense commander noticed half a dozen smaller Dominion vessels cut through the water directly toward the western coast. They did not look like the troop carriers he was expecting, and so he allowed them to get rather close before ordering only his smallest catapults to fire. His crews were only all too eager to comply. He held back on firing the longest-range cats, and the even longer-range spring launchers. There was no reason to let the enemy know the full extent of Freelandian capabilities just yet.

Per strategy, catapult gunners ganged up on targets, with one aiming where the ship should be when the payload arrived if it stayed on its present course, and two others aiming where the ship might go if it suddenly shifted in direction. Gunnery crews touched their payloads and prayed a blessing on their aim. A dozen catapult arms slammed forward simultaneously.

Out in the middle of the bay, the captain of one of the remaining armor hulled frigates had already decided to at least sink something from Freelandia even before the Thunderclaps began to rain down like so many open handed slaps from the Hand of God. The *Despoiler* had raised full sail and was bearing down directly on the old barge. The Gunny Mate had requested using it for target practice, but the captain had declined, wanting to save ammunition for the supposed fleet of Freelandian vessels expected to attack them here in the Bay … or failing that for shoreline bombardment. Besides, he eagerly wanted to try out his metalized hull with the sharp-edged prow that could be lowered just for the purpose of ramming.

The *Despoiler* picked up speed and raced forward to collide solidly with the barge that appeared empty, other than for a large box with odd prongs covering its bottom and sides, which was hanging from a pole in the center. The metal prow easily crumpled and splintered the sides of the barge and it immediately began to list severely in the direction of where water poured in and where the *Despoiler* now worked to extricate itself.

Upon collision, the box broke free of its loose knot on the rope and dropped. The burning swamp mud under its prongs stabbed into other combustible fuel inside. The box slid and tumbled on the pitched deck directly toward the *Despoiler*. It exploded, propelling large tar and pitch soaked bundles primarily in the direction the box had been moving. Several landed in the Dominion sails, dripping burning pitch as they tumbled. Others bounced over the decks, leaving a trail of sticky burning goo. Sailors scrambled to dump sand on the deck fires, but the sails and rigging were swiftly consumed. The *Despoiler*, now free from the sinking barge, drifted helplessly in the current back toward the channel leading to the ocean.

Thunderclaps sounded all over the area now, and ships frantically tried to escape by sailing further into the Bay. The *Dominance* was no exception, as Nartusk commanded the helmsman to get them away from the angry sky demons that were devouring ship after ship. He watched in dismay as heavily loaded troop carriers shot safely through the straits from the open ocean, only to sail into chaos and fire-breathing destruction. Even now he saw a frigate, desperate to escape, inadvertently ram into a slow-moving transport vessel. The troop carrier's hull must have cracked, as it began to list and sink low while the frigate desperately tried to disengage and pull away. It could not, having seriously damaged its own bare wooden hull when hitting the much heavier carrier, and in despair the Admiral watched both ships sink under the water's surface. The whole region was awash with debris and flotsam, along with hapless Dominion soldiers and sailors both alive and dead.

Rath Kordoch was not in despair. He was in barely contained fury. The remaining Dark Magicians on board had tried to sneak below decks, but the Overlord had them all rounded up and leashed together amidships. He now stomped in blazing anger up to the cowering crowd. "WHAT IS HAPPENING?" He glared malevolently around the sniveling group, none of whom answered. With a massive hand he reached to the nearest and lifted the man up from the neck with his right hand. "None of you have answers to this? What magic is Freelandia using? Why can you not defeat it? Why are you not even now calling on our gods and demons to assist us?"

The man in his grasp writhed in the choking fist and then went limp. Disgustedly, the Overlord reached to grab the body with his left hand and violently cast it over the railing into the sea. The rope leash bound around the former Magician's waist went taut and the next Magician in line was jerked from his feet to slam against the ship's railing. He mistakenly stood, while desperately trying to hold back from the terrible pressure threatening to cut his body in two. He tried valiantly to brace his feet against the deck, but in two steps Kordoch was next to him and pushed. The magician screamed as the rope cut into his waist and pulled him over the rail and into the sea.

The rope connecting him to the next in line snapped instantly taut and with a terrified yell the next magician was jerked so forcefully to the railing that his flailing arms could not grab hold. He too was dragged overboard. Realizing their fate, the rest grabbed onto the mast and each other, holding the fourth member from sharing the fate of the first three. This man's face grew bright red as the rope tore into his flesh from the dragging weight and pinched off internal organs. Blood began to spill out of his mouth and he went white, then his body sagged limp. Still the others held on against the mighty strain.

After watching them for a cold minute, Kordoch nodded to a sailor holding an ax and the rope was severed. The dead body was cut away from the others and pitched unceremoniously over the side. The remaining magicians looked at each other, relieved that now perhaps the blood lust of the Overlord may be filled. They were wrong. "Bind up the first six you can lay hands onto!" His guards rushed to comply. "The sea devils were mostly satisfied when we offered them magicians to feast on earlier. Let's see if the sky demons will likewise find our offering to their tastes! Load them into our biggest catapult, and since the demons appear to like fire, load in some hellfire with them."

The six doomed magicians began to wail and beg for mercy, but it fell on deaf ears. They were bound securely and thrown into the large metal cup normally reserved for rocks and hellfire tar. Large shovelfuls of the molten tar were thrown over the squirming and panicked magicians. At a nod, a torch was lowered to touch off the flammable hellfire and the catapult triggered to launch. The blazing payload went upward and outward in a high arc, but there was no responding fire in the sky and the still-burning bodies plummeted into the ocean several hundred yards away.

Rath grunted in dismissal. No further Thunderclaps sounded and he looked over the fiasco in the outer Bay. As if to echo his foul mood, one final explosion sounded directly over the straits, catching two transport ships sailing through. One was sunk immediately, while the other was blown violently off course and struck the solid stone walls that made up the cleft in the cliffs. It held for a moment, then broke apart and sank with all its passengers. Kordoch trembled in white hot fury over the catastrophic loss of men and animals. The finest and most potent armed forces of the biggest and most aggressive country in the world had been cut nearly in half within hours, without a single Freelandian warship in sight.

Admiral Nartusk constrained his anger in check so that it would not cloud his strategic thinking. He watched as a dozen ships fell to the impossibly long ranged Freelandian coastal defenses. It would take several more minutes and quite a few more ships before all would be safely out of range, and now one out of every two or three new ships entering the Bay got pounded. That had to stop, and as quickly as possible. "Give the signal for the rest of the decoy ships to make their close runs, and get those mountaineering troops to the western shore!" His flagman scrambled up the rigging to his perch and frantically began signaling the rest of the ships in the down-sized fleet. The message was repeated by every ship that saw it. Within twenty minutes, two groups of smaller Dominion ships broke away from the rest. Then Nartusk turned to Rath Kordoch. "Its time for our ravens."

Rath nodded, impressed by the level-headedness of the Admiral. He would have to watch that one … it would not do for an underling to appear better than his master. Then the Overlord turned to the eight remaining Dark Magicians. "Call in the birds." They nervously looked around at each other, and then within the confines of their rope tethers they began to invoke a complicated spell which involved ritualistic dancing and bloodletting. Within a minute, a large swarm of ravens appeared from somewhere nearby and began to make their way toward the western coast with raucous caws.

The speedy warships set full sail in what their crews suspected to be suicide missions. Once within known range of the Freelandians, their captains began to jinx them about, all the while sailing closer and closer to shore. The specialized troop carriers spread themselves out widely and made a mad dash toward the coast.

The Freelandian commander watched the group of ships break away and head slightly northwest. It was obvious some were transport ships. Their target was just as obvious – his coastal launchers. When they were still half a mile offshore he gave the command, relayed down to the north-ernmost launchers.

He could not hear the shrill metal-on-metal sound that the huge springs made inside their launch tubes from his distant perch, but even at this distance he could just make out the round projectiles. About half way through their downward arc, cloth chutes opened out above the bombs, slowing their decent and ensuring all were pointed straight down.

Rath Kordoch watched approvingly as the first invasion force headed toward the western shore. It would be a proud moment when the first Dominion forces actually set foot on Freelandian soil. His smile froze in place as he saw projectiles arc impossibly far out over the water, much further than anything he had ever heard about being launched from the largest catapults. As they neared his ships though, they miraculously seemed to stop in their arc and float lazily downward.

"What Freelandian magic is this?" he demanded of no one in particular. "What could these be? They travel too slowly to hurt anything!" Rath turned toward the Admiral with a questioning look.

Nartusk shrugged, but then his sharp eyes noted that the specks of dark floating down on what looked like small white clouds were actually quite similar to what had been floating overhead … under the white bubbles … which predicated the fire-breathing sky demon attack. His knuckles whitened from his intense grip on the railing in front of him. No … it cannot be … they had made the sacrifice of the magicians …

The smaller tube-launched versions of the Thunderclaps could not create the percussion pressure waves of air like the larger versions which had already decimated so many Dominion ships in the Bay. But on the smaller ships rushing toward shore they were just as effective and could score much higher hit rates since they could be aimed and fused more precisely. Still, with rapidly moving ships at quite a distance the gunners targeted two or three launchers at each of the lead ships. Several detonated too early, and while terrifying to the Dominion soldiers, they caused no real damage. Meanwhile, the other improved catapults and spring launchers out of range of the transport ships had nothing to do … except target practice on the dodging Dominion decoy warships. Burning arrows and stones showered first up, then down in long arcs.

Two transport ships survived the deadly Thunderclaps and raced shoreward. One caught half a load of burning arrows from a nearby catapult and nearly capsized as its rudder spun out of control after the helmsman was killed. As it wallowed unsteadily, two volleys of rock broke through its hull and it went down. The other ran straight for the shore. It had a very shallow keel in front and the captain obviously was expecting a one-way voyage. The ship ran aground on a sandbar several hundred yards from shore, and within seconds skiffs were lowered and the soldiers began to scurry over the sides on rope ladders. A launcher sent out its last Thunderclap at the ship, but it was too late. The explosion peppered the vessel with burning debris and it caught fire, but the soldiers were already gone.

Minutes later, the first but greatly reduced contingent of Dominion soldiers disembarked on the Freelandian shore.

The biggest launchers sent out their last payloads of grooved smooth stones toward the Dominion ships that were still entering the Bay and had not yet reached safety to the east. The crew commander could not understand why not a single eastern coast weapon had been fired, and he feared for the worst – that somehow Dominion forces were already in control of those coastal defenses. He did not have much time to wonder about that as the sky became thick with the raucous calls of the most numerous swarm of ravens the Freelandians had ever witnessed. The large black birds weaved through the air directly above them and some even began to dive at the launcher crews. Several men cried out in pain as talons or beaks scored upon unprotected flesh. Crews began to wave sticks in the air as they valiantly loaded and fired again. Their aim was off on this volley, and only a few shots scored on the distant ships.

A team of Watchers saw the landing of about eighty Dominion soldiers. Most moved off to their prepared positions, while several blended into the rocky terrain to observe and keep track of where the enemy troops went. Other teams up and down the coast shifted their resources in response to the reduced threat, but remained ready if reinforcements were sent from the still-massive armada out in the Bay that was now slowly grouping into formations and beginning to head northward.

Rath Kordoch walked over to a sailor who stood in gape-mouthed shock at the destruction he had just witnessed. In cold rage Rath ran him through with his own sword. That bloodletting seemed to settle the Overlord, though he was still seething at the loss of ships and more importantly of soldiers. Yet he knew both his remaining navy and army still should greatly outnumber the Freelandian defenses. He would surely make these wretched northerners pay dearly. Rath could feel the evil spiritual forces swelling in strength and fury even as his attack and invasion forces continued to grow as more and more ships streamed into the Bay. It was time. "Raise the signal flags! Charge forward! Get out of this confining and confounded area and take the fight to the Capital of Freelandia!" Sailors rushed to comply. Within minutes the flotilla began to sail toward the Keep.

Moorhead had one thing to his advantage. Actually, he had several, but now he had an enemy with a known location, guarding the entrance to the Bay of Freelandia. Every ship at his disposal headed straight for those waters, where he could now hope to have some small advantage in ship numbers. He gave thanks to God for their victories and prayed for further deliverance.

He expected there could be a Dreadnaught or two left, but he had reserved a few Thunderclaps just for that potential. First, though, were the outer sentry vessels. No longer was he relegated to hit-and-run attrition warfare. His attack groups formed up, smaller than before but still quite sizable. Moorhead figured they had destroyed in total something in the neighborhood of eighty Dominion ships … so far, at a loss of no more than thirty of his own. A three to one win ratio was superb, but not good enough to stay floating by the end of the hostilities. And if Freelandia were left without a navy, they were doomed. He was not sure how, but he knew he had to try to increase that number substantially. The current tactical situation had been expected, with battle plans to use the Freelandian ship's speed and agility to the best possible advantage to the Dominion ship's size and greater firepower. With greater confidence than he had at any time before, he looked for Dominion ships now with eagerness. If Freelandia were to be defeated, he surely wanted the world to know it had bravely stood against an overwhelmingly larger foe and never turned back. But they had not been defeated yet. He had not been defeated yet. God was not done yet.

As the Dominion ships began to pull away, the launcher crews tried to reload their weapons and fire at the fleeing ships, but it was nearly all they could do to keep from being viciously clawed by the wheeling black birds. There was scant shelter on the cliffs other than their barracks, but with soldiers heading their way and Dominion ships that were still straggling in, they knew their place was at their stations. The Commander only knew of one place help could come from. He sank to one knee and prayed, holding one arm over his head for protection.

Even before the final words left his mouth he heard a high pitched avian screech high above the cliffs. Dodging between the attacking ravens, he caught a glimpse of a truly wondrous sight. A formation of what must have been several dozen mountain Gryphs were coming in from the north in a steep dive, straight toward them. The Commander worried that this might be another wave of attackers and ordered his men to draw swords – ravens were one annoying thing but Gryphs were quite another and far more dangerous. But as the great birds dived it was not his crew that was their target. The large birds of prey tore into the unsuspecting ravens, breaking their attack of the men. The air became thick in a frenzy of bird-upon-bird aerial combat. The raucous screeches deafened the ears of the defenders as they bent low to the ground. With broken bodied black birds raining down, the ravens suddenly scattered off down the coast and the Gryphs gave chase.

In a moment, they were out of sight and the Freelandian crew manned their launchers once more, except for the few who ran down the trails to their assigned observation posts. There were still a few Dominion transport ships flitting through the straits, and none of the newcomers knew of the full range of the largest spring launchers. The Freelandians were determined to introduce that to them.

The Dominion captain split his men into four groups. Each took a slightly different path up the steep terrain from the beach. They knew there had to be trails above that reached the catapults, and once they could reach them they would have a clear path to the coastal defenses. The captain figured the Freelandians would consider the cliffs insurmountable and therefore likely have only a light guard for them at best. Even with less than a quarter of the men he had expected to land on the shores – cursed be those air and sea demons! – he really did not expect more than a token resistance from the enemy his leaders had always described as flabby, weak, and more likely to run and hide or fall to their knees to beg their God for mercy than to stand and fight. He was in for a rude surprise.

It took no longer than a few minutes to come. The team to his left was making the best progress up the steep mountain side. The lead man reached a flat outcropping of rock that formed a sizable ledge. He began to help his fellow climbers up to the ideally situated resting stop. Too ideal. A well-camouflaged Watcher fifty feet higher up the hill waited a moment longer, and then tugged on a black string that traced down through hollow bamboo pipes down to the ledge below and to a peculiar metal pot buried under loose rock at its base, right along a horizontal crack that ran the length of the large rock outcropping. Less than five seconds later the bomb exploded, sending rock shrapnel out in a wide arc. Those that were not killed outright by the high speed projectiles did not escape death as the slab itself upon which they were standing cut loose from the cliff wall and tumbled with the men back down the steep mountainside, taking out several climbers on its way.

The captain realized too late that they were in a trap. A dozen Watcher archers opened up on them from places of concealment and clear angles of fire. The Dominion soldiers scrambled up the cliff face as fast as they could propel themselves forward, but before they made the relative safety of the top, over half of those left had been thinned from their ranks. The remaining thirty men grouped together on the mountainside path, which made for particularly ideal targeting for the three teams of Watchers.

The Dominion soldiers regrouped and started up the path at a slow run. They had not gone more than a hundred feet when all three spring launchers were triggered by the waiting Watchers. A small glowing ember at the mouth of each tube was sufficient to ignite the powder, which produced scorching gouts of flame that shot out over fifty feet. The stones went much further – at least those that did not encounter Dominion soldiers first.

Those left alive turned and ran, as best they could with singed skin and smoking clothing. In their disorganized rout from the fire-breathing land dragons that their leaders had somehow failed to mention, they were very quickly caught and subdued.

The first land battle of the invasion had not gone well at all for the Dominion.

Chapter 22

Landfall

aria slumped in exhaustion, though spiritually she felt the lingering joy that filled her when she was singing or playing before her Audience of One. That joy was tempered, though, with the realization that the dark evil Dominion dragon she could see in her 'special place' had grown substantially in size and power. When she had finally stopped worshiping at the amphitheater to give her fingers and voice a much needed rest, the blackness in her mind had swelled to engulf three quarters of the space she could see. It now eclipsed most of her spiritual vision, pressing down around her, threatening to drown her within its darkness. The tendrils emanating from the black cloudy dragon-form had nearly reached her, and a small little-girl part of Maria was terrified of what would happen when they reached her.

She wondered if God would stop them. So far there had been no direct indication of that though. Maria was trying to trust, trying to stay faithful in the face of her fear. But it was becoming increasingly difficult. The terror of the dreams she had been having for the last several months was mounting and it was all Maria could do to not feel her doom was inevitable. A part of her had already accepted the thought that she would not survive this battle, this war. That part wanted to just give up. Yet she was also angry, knowing that feeling was not from God, but from the enemy. Maria was determined that even if the worst happened, she fully planned on going down fighting. She would be a worship warrior to the very end. But now she had to rest, and even try to sleep – if the dragon dream would let her.

As the light was beginning to fade in the west, the first Dominion warships arrived a mile out from the Keep docks and began to patrol in wide sweeps. Every captain was surprised … there was still no sign of the Freelandian navy, not even protecting their most important port and seat of their government. The transports began to arrive, and they arrayed themselves so that the first wave of shock troops were out front, ready to launch their landing skiffs as soon as it became dark enough to afford them some level of protection from the inevitable shore catapults.

The shore defenses were silent, biding their time and hoping ships would come within range. Aerial floating Thunderclaps were made ready, but the prevailing wind was at an angle that prevented their use. It was unnerving, seeing a horizon full of enemy warships just outside the door, and having little to do about it. Well, there were some things that were being done. A flotilla of barrel mines had already been dropped off by small private boats, and the current was slowly carrying them further out to sea.

Nartusk eyed the Keep dockyards and beach. He would have rather met a defending navy, where his superior numbers and ship size should have guaranteed a quick victory. But the absence of any obvious defensive actions at all was somewhat unnerving – almost as much as the Overlord's constant pacing back and forth over the raised stern deck, muttering curses and dire threats under his breath.

The *Dominance* was the only Dreadnaught present, and as such was not only by far the largest vessel here, but also the most protected by its thick metal-clad hull and massive timber construction. "Take us in closer," Nartusk quietly commanded the helmsman. The big ship slowly turned northward and left the relative safety of the amassed warships to plow through the water closer to the shoreline. Still nothing. Nartusk was about to turn back when several lookouts, peering out into the waning light, shouted warnings. Hundreds of floating barrels were slowly spreading outward on the current. Without even waiting for any command, the catapult gunny mates let loose with loads of fist-sized stones.

The cats made a racket of noise as they whipped out a rain of rocks. The floating barrels were easy, slow-moving targets, and the current was actually congregating them into a relatively tight formation that moved towards the *Dominance*. The first volley struck half a dozen barrels, sinking four and triggering two to detonate with bright flashes against the darkening sky. With the barrels fairly close together, the results were truly spectacular. The first two exploding mines triggered several others, and then a chain reaction of deafening detonations spewed water and unexploded barrels high into the air.

Even Rath Kordoch stopped his pacing and looked in awe and terror as the better of sixty mines blew holes in the water harmlessly in a swath that started a hundred yards ahead and stretched forward for over a mile. Many barrel mines soared through the air from the force of nearby explosions, and when these landed they detonated from the impact, creating yet more secondary detonations. Several barrels landed near the *Dominance*, and water geysers drenched portions of the ship's deck.

Finally, the numbing explosions stopped and every sailor looked at one another in dumbfounded shock. Nartusk was trembling and had to hold onto a rail to steady himself. The mad feasting orgy of the sea devils was like nothing his long naval experience had ever prepared him for, and he vehemently hoped to never see such a spectacle ever … ever … again. He turned and noticed the few remaining Dark Magicians, who were reduced to blubbering pools of absolute terror both over what they had just witnessed, and at what they expected the Overlord might do to them, given his seeming penchant to sacrifice them to soothe the monsters that the Freelandians somehow seemed capable of unleashing upon the Dominion fleet. But Rath Kordoch appeared to be too much in shock to do anything … at the moment.

Within a few more minutes, darkness descended over the water with an eerie quietness, with only the water lapping at the prows of the moving boats sounding out over the still water. The moon rose dark red, as it had been the night before, making the wavelets seem to reflect blood. The highly superstitious Dominion sailors and soldiers hoped it foreshadowed the spilling of Freelandian blood. So far today, it had only been Dominion blood spilled out by the tens of thousands of men.

Several small groups of four or five warships and several troop carriers broke off from the main armada out in the harbor and began to slowly make their way further northward in the Bay by the moonlight. They would station themselves at the mouths of several larger rivers and along the coastlines looking for additional landing sites. While the main and likely conclusive battle would be for the capital city, there would likely be other smaller skirmishes elsewhere, and the Dominion planners had prepared for that.

Master Warden James squinted as he strained to see the vast Dominion fleet now setting anchors more than half a mile out over the Keep's harbor. The massive mountain-of-the-sea Dreadnaught was still easily discerned by its huge outline. From what his commanders had told him, that ship appeared to have been responsible for the destruction of the barrel mine field that they had sincerely hoped would be able to take out a large portion of the enemy fleet in a last ditch effort to prevent enemy soldiers from setting foot on Freelandian soil here at the Keep. It had even been reported that one mine had detonated right against that behemoth's hull but had no effect whatsoever. Unless its captain unwisely came close enough to the shore to be within range of his spring launchers, that vessel would pose a tremendous threat to any Freelandian ship that might dare to come into the entire Bay. James also guessed its mere presence bolstered the enemies resolve and morale, a bold symbol of the might and power of the Dominion. And unless something could be done against it, he feared his other defenses would prove inadequate. Even if against all odds and expectations his rather sparse army could somehow repel the invaders on the land, Freelandia would still fall if the Dominion ruled the sea.

James still had the engineer's Thunderclaps to work with, but the breeze had died down to nearly nothing at dusk, and he doubted if any of the air-floating bubbles would reach that far out into the Bay before drifting away. And besides, they were too small. The Dreadnaught dwarfed any ship he had ever seen. The black outline looked like a floating mountain. Surely nothing could stand in its way. Surely … James shook his head to clear it. By God's grace and mercy, they would find a way. They had to find a way.

The small Thunderclaps would be saved for the landing boats that would surely be preparing to swarm the beach anytime now. The exceedingly gentle breeze might just work for that. James judged the breeze direction and strength and re-examined the harbor in the faint twilight. He shrugged. They would have to work. He had only a few other options.

But something had to be done about that Dreadnaught. By morning, it would be too late to try to send out any remaining Thunderclaps – the beach and coastal defensive works would surely be overrun by then. If they were going to do anything, it would have to be tonight, even as the landing boats ferried the invasion troops to shore. James sighed. He would have rather Thunderclapped that mountainous ship. He would have really enjoyed seeing three or four big Thunderclaps going off right above that monstrosity, as though God's hands were making like a percussion drummer right over their heads. But that was not to be. He had prepared for this potential outcome. James was nothing if he was not thorough.

Alpha Red Team Leader Yori got the message from the Master Warden's command post. He grinned. This was what his team was trained for … and truly lived for. They even had practiced such maneuvers on ships in dry dock, and twice on Freelandian naval sloops out in the Bay. His team was ready. Yori strode into the makeshift barracks. The look on his face was enough. Every man leapt to his feet, grabbing gear and weapons. With a silent nod, Yori led them out and toward the docks, several of their marching feet punctuated with a peculiar metal clang.

The Dominion ground troop commanders had scanned the beach before the darkness of dusk became too great to make out any details. They had observed pretty much what was expected: large pikes planted into the sand, pointed outward to make landing a small craft difficult, but those would be easily defeated by throwing ladders and even heavy mats over them, and once on the other side they could be pulled out or chopped down. What lay just beyond the beach was the most puzzling. The harbor ended to the east with the main commercial wharves. Those would certainly be pleasant to land at, but they would be heavily sabotaged and only a fool would try landing a ship there. Away from the docks themselves was a fairly large sandy beach in an open crescent shape surrounded by high banks. The beach ended with a gentle slope upward where time and erosion had flattened the high shoreline that led directly to the Keep itself. From his briefing, the commander knew the city itself started about half a mile further inland.

The strategists of the Dominion had prepared rough maps for the invasion, and the harbor and docks looked to be quite accurately portrayed. The beach area, however, looked considerably different. Tall earthen embankments protruded outward toward the shore, each over 20 feet high, creating multiple narrow channels of sandy pathways leading up toward the city. This did not particularly concern them, however. The first troops to be sent ashore would be the Southern Bashers. These barely civilized giants were hard enough to contain within the transport ships – indeed, there had been reports of near mutiny aboard many when those cursed fire devils had descended on the ships near the Bay entrance and fearful talk of Freelandian demons had swept over the Southern ships. Only extra rations of Fireweed had calmed the savages.

No, the troop commanders were sure that regardless of what defenses the Freelandians may have dreamt up, the Bashers would surely overwhelm them by shear strength and numbers … though there were fewer now than planned as whole ship-loads had been sunk … many whole ship-loads. Nearly half of the Dominion's contingent of Bashers had drowned out in the Bay.

And now several ship captains were looking uneasily in the moonlight toward the Freelandian docks as their ships were taking on more water than the sailors could bail. Unless they were unloaded of their heavy load of troops shortly, they would have little choice but to either try the docks or run their ship at the beach and hope for minimal loss of life from crashing into reefs or sandbars.

But the order would surely be given shortly to begin sending troops ashore – for the land invasion to truly begin. The Bashers would be sent out first, but they would not be alone. Along with them were their Hellhounds, huge dog-like beasts even more savage than their masters and barely controllable with the Fireweed added to their feed. And the pachyderms – one could never forget the wild and nearly mythical pachyderms that were so difficult to transport but which caused so much fear among their enemies!

The Freelandians would barely know what hit them before they were massively overrun like every other country they had ever gone up against.

Throughout the day groups of musicians and singers had wandered around the Keep, stopping every few minutes with a song of praise and worship. It was like slow moving patches of sunlight, sweet smells, and calm that dispelled the fear that seemed to hang in the air. There was no room for despair when minds and hearts were turned toward and tuned into God and His might, power and mercy.

As night approached different groups replaced those needing rest and non-stop worship continued to pour out. It was not expected that any serious fighting would occur during the night aside from perhaps the beaches and docks … the Bashers supposedly were rather afraid of the dark anyway.

Maria fell into a fitful light sleep. Kory had asked Master Ariel and a few others to come over to help pray over their friend. Even as they did, they noticed her slumbering form twitch this way and that as she dreamed.

The black roiling dragon head was now so very close. Maria could smell fetid and noxious odors emanating from its fanged mouth. The red eyes seemed to pierce right through her to see every failing, every worry and fear, every weakness she had ever experienced. She felt so very, very unworthy. Unworthy to think she could somehow find favor with God. Unworthy to lift her head up and think she could stand before the Dominion onslaught. Unworthy to have a single friend, a single scrap of goodness within her. The weight of guilt and shame was pummeling down on her in wave after wave, all under the watchful, baleful glare of the dark dragon.

She was now closed off from everyone else, closed in with nowhere to hide and nowhere to run. The gaping jaws of the dragon were now directly over her, closing in.

Maria could not even scream. She was rooted to the spot, helpless and all … alone …

That thought went too far. A back part of her mind rebelled. She KNEW she was never ever alone. She had never been totally alone. She knew that she knew that she knew she always had an Audience. Even in her dream state, she turned from the horror that was before her and all around her and instead turned inward to where her only true hope dwelt.

Maria melted into that spiritual presence, willingly ignoring the ominous doom that seemed to encompass her outwardly. Here she was safe.

Her sleeping body had finally stopped trembling and whimpering. Those praying over Maria slumped back in their chairs. This small battle of the war appeared to be over. Wearily, they found their own beds. The next battle would likely not be very far behind.

In fact, a great peace seemed to settle over most of Freelandia, like a great warm comforter on a cold night – even though the enemy and war was right on their doorstep. Prayers continued unabated, as did the worship warriors.

Jarl was not at peace. He shook his head to clear out the thoughts of sleep. His main job was done, and Murdrock had not given him additional plans. All of the Dominion ships that were coming into the Bay of Freelandia were surely in now – leastwise those that were still floating –so what use was there for his Rats to stay? By mid-day next, surely the Dominion would have taken the Keep, and with it control of Freelandia. It would be far better for most of the Rats to join in with the fighting – and such initiative on his part would surely look good. Besides, his Rats were becoming very antsy just standing around here, and some might take it upon themselves to slip out and join the fighting … or at least the looting afterwards.

That prospect made him lick his lips in anticipation. But there was an even greater prize than loot that drove him. Revenge gnawed at his soul. There was a particular someone in the Keep that he felt needed payback, and he would not be settled at all until he could personally see to it that this person … that she … got what was coming to her.

With an evil grin Jarl ordered his Rats down the pathways in what was now becoming blood red moonlight, reaching the ropes that they had used to climb down the cliffs after causing the rockslides earlier. They had plenty of time to scale the sheer rock faces and find the narrow trail they had used to reach those heights, and the thin moonlight was just enough for them to use to slowly work their way safely along the path. With any luck, by morning they could be down the mountainside and reach the outskirts of the Keep.

In the twilight, dozens of very light, very low to the water canoes quietly launched from the rocky coasts out past the wharves and beach. Each was silently rowed by two of the Irregulars who frequently fished these waters and knew every nook and cranny and could tell exactly where they were – even in the moonlight that was giving a silvery red sheen to the water's surface. They could do nothing against the Dominion ships, which would surely have lookouts posted along every rail while so close to enemy shores. They really could not carry out any kind of direct attack at all. But they were ideal for the mission at hand.

As these small canoes began to quietly make their way out into the Bay, three slightly larger outrigger canoes gently pushed off from the dockyard wharves. They were painted pitch black and were paddled with cloth muffled paddles. Several bubble sacks had been cleverly fitted underneath and then inflated, causing the boats to lift much higher in the water so that they could skim over its surface with considerable speed … especially when rowed by men whose arm muscle girth rivaled most men's thighs. This would be the first amphibious operation the Alpha Red team had ever executed outside of training. Each face painted member was anxious to put their extensive training to deadly use.

Prentice, Olaf and Dimitri were the only three team members who were not totally comfortable with the mission, and it was not because of the armored suits they were wearing. Commander Yori had insisted that each have a swamp gas pressure pot strapped to their backs with several large empty bubble sacks folded up just above with tubes attached to the pot. It made for a bulky and awkward backpack, but Yori had absolutely insisted. If for any reason one of them went into the water, the forty pounds of armor weight would cause them to rapidly sink … and the armor could not be quickly removed. None of the three relished the idea of going for a downward swim tonight. Master Arianna had said the folded sacks would very quickly inflate by a sharp pull on a special cord that snaked back to a special valve on the pressure pot.

Though they had very nicely requested that she personally demonstrate the buoyancy the sacks supposedly would provide, their requests were summarily squashed by the arrival of the lady's over-protective husband, whom they recalled also had a suit with who-knows-what kind of engineering 'extras' built in.

So they took her word that the sacks would work, but none appreciated the extra weight or diminished agility from the backpacks. Each warrior fully expected to remove the hindrance once they had boarded the Dominion Dreadnaught … at least until they had planted the hull bursting bombs they had stowed in the canoes and were ready to make their get-away.

Rath Kordoch felt the spiritual peace settling in over the countryside before him and it infuriated and exasperated him. The Dominion always struck fear and terror into their enemies, and they used that to demoralize defenses so that they much more easily succumbed to the ferocity of the Basher onslaught. He could sense the dark demonic forces building around him, but being repelled back from the shore. Darkness swirled around him as his anger grew, and he knew that anger could be a magnet for evil forces. The dark power around him felt invincible. "Light the signal fires! Start getting our troops ashore!" His minions scurried to do his bidding. Large torches began to light up, and in minutes every ship had responded with their own flares. It was the signal to begin the invasion.

To the shore launcher batteries, the lights also made great targets. Not that they could reach those far-away ships, but it just made it all the easier to fine tune the alignment of the guns to where the skiffs would be carrying the enemy troops. On cue, great bonfires were lit on the shore as if to welcome the invaders. The furthest light of each marked the furthest range of a given catapult or spring launcher, and these launchers were the very latest design from the Engineers, with the largest payloads and greatest range. The invasion force was going to get a very 'warm' welcome both on their way to and once they arrived at the beach that was now relatively well-lit by the flickering bonfires.

Jo-Nakar was the chieftan of his Basher tribe, most of whom were present on the transport ship *Najiri*. As leader, it was his responsibility to be the first off the ship and onto the landing craft, assuring it was safe for the others. His red-glowing eyes surveyed the distant shoreline and down to the rather flimsy skiff bobbing up and down on the water below. The torches from the ship's deck cast an eerie glow down to the waterline and only partially lessened his nervousness and intense dislike for being out on the open water.

He felt the light breeze blowing shoreward and caught a glimpse of light further out on the Bay, which seemed to be slowly floating shoreward with the light breeze. *That was nice*, he thought. *The outer patrol ships must have launched other small boats with torches to help us see better.* With a smile he swung over the side and climbed down the rope netting to reach the landing craft. After assuring himself that it was not leaking … much … he motioned for the others to follow. The floating lights he could see moving up and down on the short waves would be nearly along side when they had fully loaded this skiff and were ready to push off and man the oars to take them ashore.

It took nearly an hour to prepare for the massive first wave of landing craft to be loaded and readied. One by one the transport ships lit a green flame torch to signify their readiness, and once the majority had done so, the signal was given by Rath Kordoch to launch the skiffs. Over four hundred boats began moving shoreward, rowed by the very strong backs and arms of the Basher shock troops.

No one knew where the floating torches had come from, nor how such small little rafts could give off that much fire light when all anyone could see was a jet of flame shooting up out of some metal pot. The Freelandian Irregulars quietly paddled their canoes, taking pathways back through the many Dominion ships anchored at regular intervals that kept them out of sight.

Jo-Nakar sat in the prow of the skiff, urging his Bashers to row harder. His eyes widened in red unbelief as magically a jet of flame several feet long appeared in the sky a few hundred yards away, slowly floating in his direction. He turned in panic and yelled at his men to row faster, before the fire-breathing flying creature would be upon them. The Bashers turned to look and began to curse in fear. All redoubled their efforts to see if the landing craft itself could fly ashore.

The Freelandian shore catapult crews saw the first skiff pass one of the floating torches, which marked the approximate range of the shore batteries. Several of the floating bubble torches lit up, casting a flickering pale light onto three other skiffs in close proximity to each other. "That was rather kind of them, wasn't it?" The launcher captain who had spoken grinned over at his crew. His chief answered, "Aye, sir. Shall we send them our greetings?"

"Please extend to our guests the right hand of the Thunderclap of God."

"Right-O Captain!" The chief made a minor correction of aim and triggered the release of the giant spring. With a metallic rasping 'sproing', the spring extended in the tube, propelling the metal canister upward and outward.

"We cordially welcome you to Freelandia," muttered the captain.

Jo-Nakar did not see or hear the launch. He was still wildly eying the tongues of downward-directed fire when a small explosion and flash occurred far above and behind him. The Basher chieftain immediately turned to look. A split second later, the secondary fuel ignited, creating an intensely bright flash of fire that seemed to cover a quarter of the sky in his vision. The surprise nearly caused Jo-Nakar to topple overboard. He was just regaining his shaken balance when the sonic boom rattled them all to the bone. Everyone fell to the deck of the skiff crying out in terror. A moment later they felt a surge of water propel their craft forward with great speed. Knowing that they were nearly to the apparent safety of the beach, he screamed at his tribesmen to take back up their oars and row with all their might.

The Bashers in the skiffs were now too afraid to notice anything but the nicely lit shore only a couple of hundred yards away. Few noticed the strong smell and oily sheen on the water's surface. Three shore battery catapults went off, sending a shower of burning pitch-soaked rocks out over the water in seemingly ineffective shots. When the flames hit the floating oily liquid pumped out onto the water's surface through long reed pipes from reservoirs positioned high up the coastal hills, the surface of the water erupted in flames ten feet high. The waves and breeze prevented the oily slick to extend very far out from the beach, but for the hundreds of incoming skiffs it appeared that the only direction they could go was straight into the mouth of hell.

The effect terrorized the Bashers, though did little actual damage since the flames could not set the skiffs on fire. The first few skiffs scraped on the beach bottom. Jo-Nakar leapt out and raced the ten yards to the shore, figuring his fellow Bashers had better follow, because he surely was not going to wait to help them, fire or no fire burning in patches around him. Solid ground never felt so welcome and he worked to control the trembling in his arms before any of his men could see it. When all had landed he ordered the youngest to row the skiff back out to the ships for another load of soldiers. The Basher, no more than fifteen years old, had eyes wide with fright and began to blubber in protest. Jo-Nakar withdrew his foot long knife and traced a bright crimson line across the young man's chest. Blood began to drip down from the very shallow cut and the Basher's eyes were riveted to the point of the blade, now held only inches from his face. "I have given you your first war wound. Wear it with honor. If you do not return this skiff you will have shamed me, shamed your tribe, and shamed the honor of the scar you would like to proudly display. Decide now. Shame or honor. Death or life."

The young warrior gulped hard and sat still with a determined look on his face. "Good, come back quickly and join your tribe. Great honor awaits us as we destroy the Freelandians and their accursed fire gods!" He and a few others turned the skiff about and pushed it off. Jo-Nakar hoped the lad could make it back to the ship, and even more that reinforcements would pour in to cover the beach.

He turned, noticing that most of his men had gathered by the nearest bonfire, drying and warming themselves with its heat. As he and the six others who had launched the skiff began to walk over, Jo-Nakur heard a whistling sound in the air that could only come from one source. He and the other seasoned warriors dove to the sand as hundreds of smooth stones tore through the air, and then through the flesh of his comrades around the fire.

Rath Kordoch could not be contained. Every soldier around him tried to become invisible and outside the wide reach of the huge sword arcing through the air with every step. "WHAT MAGIC IS THIS!" he bellowed, but none could answer. His current chief Dark Magician was cursing the night air between shrieked incantations. The man jerked his body this way and that around the deck in a frenzied dance, his own small knife busily bloodletting his life essence from dozens of wounds. Rath strode over. "Let me help with that!" With a powerful swing, the man's upper torso fell away from its lower mate. Usually such violence calmed the Overlord, and this did subside some of his blinding rage.

He looked out over the continuing scene of destruction, noticing the pattern of strikes. "Douse all torches and fires, immediately! Shoot out those wretched floating torches too! They are using the light to target our troops!"

By candlelight his catapult crews at once took aim and began sinking the floating pressure pot lights with scattershot of heavy rocks even as the ship's crew hurriedly threw torches overboard to extinguish them. Within seconds, the captains of the other ships took notice and followed suit, and within ten minutes the fleet and most of the harbor waters were blacked out. Even the burning oil slick out on the water's surface was already dying out and washing ashore.

On the beach, Jo-Nakar saw the mighty Dominion warships blink out into the night darkness. While no Basher seemed particularly bright, and especially not with a double dose of fireweed, Jo-Nakar somehow put the events together. "The fires! They are targeting the fires! Put them out!" He ran to the nearest and grabbed a burning log, fireweed making him oblivious to the pain, and threw it into the harbor where it went out with a loud hiss. All over the beach, the Bashers began to imitate him, though few really understood why. In minutes the beach and harbor were both only illuminated by the thin light of the partial blood red moon.

The catapults and launchers continued to pound the beach, but now they were firing blindly and only occasionally scoring significant hits. The enemy had also scattered over the beach, and were congregating on the eastern side of the beach, closer to the river and dockyards which were the furthest from any of the defensive batteries and thus largely out of range of the death raining down from the dark sky. But the desired damage was largely done. Several hundred skiffs had been hit, with the Thunderclaps having done by far the greatest destruction, each destroying everything under them in a roughly circular area over a hundred feet across. Some of the skiffs had merely been overturned, and both men and animals swam to shore as best they could. But the remaining skiffs were now having to row through a harbor filled with floating bodies, and landing on the beach shore now involved pushing aside dead comrades and beasts before any could reach the sandy shore. The Freelandian welcome had wiped out over a quarter of the landing troops either before they even reached the shoreline, or within minutes thereafter.

The cats and launchers were all mounted high up the slopes of the hills surrounding the harbor, with reinforced rock walls and pikes defending them from all but the most dedicated foe. They might last the night, but almost surely not long at all in the morning. The crews had scant ammunition left anyway, and so they abandoned their posts per plan and climbed ladders placed up the hill sides to join their companions closer to the gates of the Keep. The ladders were pulled up after them, leaving the now empty and useless heavy weapons behind.

The three squads of the Alpha Red team nearly noiselessly threaded their way between Dominion ships, now blacked out as they had expected them to eventually become. So far, all was going according to plan. Two slowly coasted up to the massive hull of the Dreadnaught, just darker patches on the dark water's surface far below the rear deck, while the third stopped further out, where the stern sea anchor chain disappeared under the water. Three shadowy figures began to spider crawl up the chain in silence while their outrigger moved near the hull.

As the first figure reached the highest point possible where the chain exited a hole in the thick timbers, the Special Forces operator hung for a moment by the short rope he had slung over the chain. He uncoiled a thin but very strong black cord with a treble hook on one end and waited. It took perhaps five terribly long minutes before odd screeching sounded far off on the other side of the Dreadnaught as an Irregular shot several arrows skyward that had specially fluted heads that created the unique sound. At once the warrior swung the grappling hook upward and over the top railing. A strong pull indicated the hooks had caught tight. The climber threaded the loose end of the cord through the anchor chain for his comrades to reach and then adroitly climbed hand over hand up the last few feet. He paused at the top once his eyes could see over the railing, seeing several sailors thirty feet away peering off into the dark night in the direction of the sounds. He silently swung his feet over the railing and crouched, ready to spring into action. In moments his comrades joined him on the darkened deck that only had a few dim torches set in irregular intervals, leaving long black shadows such as the one they were now in.

The second man up affixed strong hooks onto the railing and then lowered over the side of the ship a narrow rope ladder that he had carried in a small backpack. As the other team members began to clamber up, the first three spread out to better secure the deck area that they now claimed. The Dominion sailors remained on the other side of the ship, nervously murmuring about the odd noise.

Commander Yori was the first man up the ladder, lugging one of the five explosive pressure pots they had brought. They were directly behind and below the upper decks of the stern, where no one else on the ship could likely see them unless a sailor came purposely walking this direction. The two sailors who presumably were assigned to guard this area were standing to the far side, looking away. There was no one else in sight.

Yori breathed a prayer of thankfulness and gave a nod in the dim moonlight. Two of the team stole behind the sailors. After a quick check that they remained out of sight of the rest of the deck, thin black cords were looped over the sailor's heads and pulled tight. In sixty seconds the bodies were carried further to the back and propped into slouching shapes against the inner wall, looking to any passersby that they were napping. It would take a fairly bright torch light to see the thin red marks on their throats that told a different story.

The men split into teams, with two staying near their ladder leading to the canoes and the others evenly divided to the left and the right. Yori did not know how many sailors to expect on the deck of the Dreadnaught. It could easily be seventy or more, especially as they were so near an enemy's shore. He could not risk an all-out battle … the entire ship's compliment of sailors and soldiers could be many hundred. The sixteen members of the Alpha Red team were incredibly skilled, but stealth would serve them far better.

Which brought him to his only armored team members. Prentice, Olaf and Dimitri were by far the best in their suits, and they were trying to be as quiet in their movements as possible … but there was only so much you could do even with metal joints even when they were well oiled. Even with cloth coverings, the suits made much more noise than any of the men were used to. At least they were not bumping into anything, having removed their bulky inflatable packs.

Before the teams eased out from the stern shadows, one from each group scrambled up the rigging, a short bow strung over their backs. Sniping in the dark on a wave-rolling ship was none too easy, but considerable practice did give his archers considerable skill. He hoped it would not be needed.

The Freelandian commandos began to infiltrate the main deck of the Dreadnaught, looking for ways to access the lower decks by other means than the main stairways. The cargo hold hatches were amidships, and so the teams moved toward that direction.

Meanwhile, the two left to guard their exit lit the fuse on one pressure pot and carefully lowered it on a rope over the stern to hang just above the rudder. They fastened the rope securely and tied the thin triggering cord to a rail. Once that cord was jerked, they had less than three minutes to be well away from the explosion that should render the warship without steering. This was not their primary desire … sinking the ship was the goal. In case that did not work, disabling it was the next best outcome they hoped for.

Several additional deck sailors were dispatched silently before the port side team came to the mid-deck catapult. The machine was huge, the largest by far anyone had ever even heard of on a ship. A small crane made with a block and tackle set up was located directly over a hatch perhaps three feet square, apparently to lift stone projectiles out from the hold below. Right beside the cat was a large pot set atop an iron stove filled with glowing coals. Inside was a gooey black bubbling tar, which when lit was what the Dominion called 'hellfire'. Three sailors were stationed near the catapult and the tar to keep careful watch – uncontrolled fire is one of the things sailors fear most while out at sea.

Dark shadows crept forward, low to the deck. The sailors stationed at the catapult talked amongst themselves and mainly looked over the water to the beach, where a hundred small campfires were now lit indicating concentrations of Dominion troops who felt they were out of range of any Freelandian reach. Other sailors were only twenty-five feet away, so great finesse was going to be needed.

The lead Alpha Red warrior who was closest to the catapult sailors pulled something out of a pocket. He purposely made a slight scraping noise as he hunkered down amidst a line of barrels filled with sand … one of the best fire-fighting materials aboard the ship, since water would not quickly quench burning hellfire tar.

One of the sailors heard the noise and glanced over. A couple of glass marbles rolled out over the deck, moving across from the sailors. It caught their attention and without thinking all three scrambled over to catch the slowly rolling balls before they could reach the other end of the deck and fall off the ship. With their attention focused away, three Freelandian warriors leapt out of the darkness. It was tempting to just assist the forward momentum of the sailors and pitch them right off the deck, but the noise of the splash would very likely draw attention. Instead, each was dispatched with a blow to the head or neck. Three more Dominion bodies were propped into sitting poses as if they were asleep.

Yori knew they did not have much more time. Surely some form of walking patrol would have been set up, and therefore within a few short minutes the supposedly sleeping sailors would be discovered. They had to get the hull bursting bombs positioned very quickly.

The hatch by the catapult was opened quietly and half of the team slithered down ropes into the upper hold with four of the remaining five pressure pot bombs. One was left topside with the remaining team, which included the three armored warriors.

The hold below the catapult contained a large quantity of arrow bundles, which could be dipped in hellfire tar and lit before shooting. Another hatch revealed the lower hold, where a large stockpile of stone ammunition was kept, along with two additional heavy iron pots filled with thick cold tar. Yori grinned. The Dominion was making it easy on them. Two commandos placed swamp gas bombs under and on the top of each tar pot and their fuses lit. The commandos then climbed their ropes back upwards to the upper deck, trailing thin black cords that would trigger the three minute fuse burns. They wanted to be well away when the lower hold of the Dreadnaught filled with burning hellfire.

Dimitri watched carefully as two Dominion sailors with cutlass scabbards hanging from their belts came walking along the starboard outer deck rail. Across on the port side he could see two more beginning their ritual walk around the deck circumference. While Commander Yori and the others had only been below decks for no more than two or three minutes, it did not appear they were going to be able to remain stealthy for too much longer. Even as those thoughts flashed across his mind, one of the guards stopped and pointed. The pale red moonlight and few small torches aboard the ship did not proffer much lighting, but as Dimitri glanced in the direction of the sailor's hand he could see one of the 'sleeping' sailors they had leaned up against a barrel must have sprawled over. The two guards strode in that direction purposely. It was nearly show time.

Dimitri took a step forward. In the dim light, the green, yellow and red paint on his armor looked convincingly like a fairy tale monster that Minister Polonos had described as being commonly told to young Dominion children to scare them into obedience. One sailor bolted away while the other stood in transfixed horror at the apparition that had suddenly appeared before him. Dimitri swung his arm in a tight arc. Double blades that were attached to the arms of the suit looked remarkably like claws, and these claws found their mark upon the hapless sailor.

The dying man's scream alerted the deck crew. Prentice and Olaf stood and spread out, blocking the catapult hatchway from view. The first dozen deck crewmen ran up with daggers and swords drawn, only to stop short and turn away in fear at the mythical monsters that stood a foot taller than anyone else present. One particularly brave fellow ran forward with a hatchet and threw it right at the nearest monster.

Olaf cringed inside his suit, but the short-handled ax bounced harmlessly off the armor with a loud metallic clang. Staying in character, he gave an animal roar in response and took a step forward. The sailors, eyes wide in fear, stumbled over each other as they tried to retreat.

Commander Yori heard the commotion as he started to climb up from the upper hold, still clutching the thin cords that would trigger the pressure pot fuses below. As his blackened head popped above the deck timbers he saw a dozen sailors rush at the three armored Freelandians. He nimbly pulled himself up to the deck surface, crouching low. He looked as shouts began to sound above on the stern decks above his head. Several Alpha Red team members rushed over to the main door leading down to the sailor sleeping quarters. They placed a metal bar over the door. With massive blows with the hilts of their daggers they drove in metal spikes that would secure the bar and prevent the door from opening, at least for a few more minutes. There was no easy way to secure the open stairway leading to the upper decks.

Prentice stepped forward, figuring the best defense is often a surprise offense. He had climbed up onto several barrels and as a rush of sailors came forward he made a tinny growl and leapt forward, making sure to land squarely on his heels with bent knees. The springs located there compacted and then propelled him forward, and extending his legs he sprang toward them in an impossibly high arc, actually landing behind the surging attackers, spinning to land facing back at them. Without even pausing he charged at them from behind. Olaf, meanwhile, was charging forward and the two suited warriors met in the middle, swords and bare metal arms swinging wildly. Against the unarmored sailors, it really was not much of a fight. Bare-fleshed bodies went sailing in all directions, some whole, and some in unnatural pieces.

Footsteps racing down stairs heralded the arrival of Dominion reinforcements, but the first half dozen found no footing on the last five steps as their feet shot out from under them due to the extremely slippery oil a Freelandian had poured onto them. They landed in a jumbled pile where shadowy movements ensured none rose to join the fight. The sound of bow strings vibrating indicated those higher up on the stairs were also being restrained ... some permanently.

Rath Kordoch had already packed his personal items and had commandeered a skiff to be lowered from the bow. He and the remaining Dark Magicians were going shoreward, regardless of whether Admiral Nartusk thought it safe or prudent yet. The Overlord was not about to miss his place to rally and send off the ground troops.

Yori assisted the last of his team up through the open catapult hatch. They raced to the stern as another wave of attackers pressed in on the armored monsters only a few feet away. Yori whistled loudly and the two archers in the rigging scrambled down to join the retreat. As the last of the unarmored Alpha Red team members ran past him, Yori tugged on the bomb ignition cords. He whistled the loud signal to retreat and turned to race himself to the rope ladder in the stern, which was now packed with team members scrambling down as fast as they dared to the waiting canoes. Unfortunately, between the noise of the battle and the limited hearing inside the suits, none of the three armored Freelandians heard him.

Dimitri finished off two Dominion sailors with a sword swing. He turned to see Commander Yori's back disappearing around the bend of the stern. He tapped on Olaf's arm and jerked a thumb backward. Prentice, however, was busily hacking into a half-dozen sailors, whose own blows were bouncing and skidding harmlessly off his now dented armor. All three Freelandians could see what looked like a horde of Dominion soldiers and sailors pouring out of the forward deck hatches. Olaf pointed behind him and Dimitri nodded. They ran the several steps over to the boiling tar pot, wrenching off the claw-swords on their arms. Dimitri grabbed an iron shovel off the deck and shoved it under the pot. He put the shovel handle to his shoulder and began to heave upwards. Olaf meanwhile grabbed the lip of the pot with his gauntleted hands and pulled. Together, the pot began to tip over.

Prentice was bruised from the many blows, but slashed forward with his sword-claws to send the remaining attacking sailors to meet their Maker. His eyes inside his suit widened as he saw a mob of over forty soldiers make their way toward him, several with large battle axes that just might be powerful enough to cause real damage. He glanced backwards just in time to leap aside as a wave of molten tar splashed out of a big pot toward the front of the ship.

Dimitri reached down and grabbed a handful of burning embers in his metal hands and flung them over the spreading tar. It instantly burst into four foot high flames. The added heat caused the tar to spread even faster, blocking access to the Freelandians, who turned and raced backward.

The three remaining Freelandians loped in unnaturally long leaps to the rear of the ship. Olaf immediately swung over the railing and began to descend the rope ladder. Prentice realized his comrade had forgotten his swamp gas life preserver and picked up both his and Olaf's. Dimitri grabbed his arm and shook his head, pointing down. Prentice dropped the heavy backpacks and scrambled over the side. Dimitri shrugged one of the packs onto his own back and was slinging his arms through the straps of the two others when a crowd of racing soldiers rounded the far side of stern and immediately attacked with swords and axes swinging.

Dimitri really had no choice. If any of the soldiers or sailors cut through the rope ladder, his two armored team mates would most certainly plunge into the sea and sink to the bottom of the Bay. Worse, one might land in a canoe and break right through it. Instead he turned and swung both of his arms together, the backpacks knocking aside the weapons of the foremost. A loud hissing noise commenced, and Dimitri realized one of the rip cords must have been yanked. The backpack on his left arm burst open with a very rapidly expanding white bubble sack.

He staggered backwards as the large sack filled the narrow space between the ship's railing and the vertical walls comprising the construction of the upper stern deckway. The Dominion attackers backed up in sudden fear, unsure of what this new phenomena might be. Dimitri afforded a quick look over the railing and saw that his comrades were all down and safely into their canoes. Two vessels had pushed off, leaving Yori holding the end of the rope ladder in the final remaining canoe. For some reason, Yori seemed to be shouting something, but Dimitri could not make out what his commander seemed to be saying. He grabbed the top of the rope ladder with one hand as he tried to shrug off the fully inflated bubble sack that was pulling his arm over his head as it stretched out and tried to rise up into the night sky. As it lifted, the sailors saw their chance and lunged forward.

A moment later it did not matter what Yori was yelling or that the gas sack felt like it was pulling his arm off, or that the Dominion sailors and soldiers were charging at him with drawn weapons. The pressure pots in the ship's hold exploded.

Dimitri saw the hatches on both the lower and upper holds burst outward off their hinges and the decking crack, but the integrity of the ship held. Flames began to shoot out of the deck cracks. Dimitri felt the mighty Dreadnaught shake and tremble violently, and roll in the water.

Though unseen deep down in the hold, both tar pots rolled about in the blast, and one tipped over to cover one of the remaining swamp gas bombs. The other cauldron rolled to a stop against the other pressure pot bomb.

Dimitri was shoved hard by the rocking ship. He clutched his arms instinctively to try to regain balance. The rope ladder in his right hand was yanked completely free of the deck railing to which it had been tied. Dimitri's flailing hand tried to find something solid to grab onto, and only succeeded in tangling in the ropes helplessly. The same flailing arm held the other life preserver backpack, which was not designed for such antics. It promptly blew its valve and its bubble sack shot upward.

The rocking of the deck began to subside. Dimitri looked up at the Dominion soldiers and sailors who where only a few steps away, staring with wide eyes at what looked like some misshapen butterfly whose wings were giant white sacks and whose body was green, yellow, red and bright metallic. Dimitri groaned. He was quite in a pickle. "Lord God … save me!" he cried out as the crew took tentative steps forward, weapons extended.

The pressure bomb hanging directly over the rudder erupted, blowing half of the rudder right off the ship, cracking the upper deck work and shearing the connection to the helm wheel. The pressure wave also sent the now barely-heavier-than-air Dimitri slamming upward into the upper stern deck works. That abuse was sufficient to trigger the third and final life preserver in the pack on his back.

The exploding pressure bomb at the rudder rocked the canoes and creating a deep depression in the water directly behind them. Yori fell to the floor of the canoe onto his back. Looking upward, he figured he must have hit his head much harder in the fall than he had thought. He knew he must be hallucinating. Dimitri was swinging over the railing, clearing it by several feet, suspended beneath three large white bubble sacks. Looking nothing less than a gigantic moth, Dimitri floated out over the railing, tethered to the canoe by the rope ladder.

If not for the strength of the armored suit, Dimitri felt his arms might be pulled cleanly away from his body. As it was, the sacks seemed to be valiantly trying to lift the canoe up out of the water even as they were caught in the breeze and pushed strongly away from the stricken ship.

Rath Kordoch commanded the skiff's crew to cease their rowing as red hot embers shot skyward from both the hold hatches and the burning hellfire on the deck. He was staring when the last two swamp gas bombs exploded deep down in the lower hold.

One tar cauldron careened sideways down the length of the hold, smashing through watertight walls through the length of the ship. It finally banged up against the front bow hull and rolled to a stop. Then the last swamp gas bomb, buried under the overturned tar cauldron, exploded. The pot launched directly upwards.

Rath's mouth hung open in utter astonishment as a heavy iron hellfire cauldron burst through the decks and rose skyward nearly to the height of the tallest mast. It flipped over and began its descent. The heavy pot crashed through some of the same holes it had made during its ascent and struck the bottom hull. The massive timbers were designed to withstand any storm, but the ship's designers had certainly never planned for such abuse. The cauldron punched a four-foot hole directly through the hull as it sank to the bottom of Freelandia Bay.

The Overlord could not believe his eyes as he watched the mightiest ship that had ever sailed sink lower and lower into the water as men scrambled to launch lifeboats and as other nearby ships drew closer to assist in rescuing survivors. He just could not believe the *Dominance* was … sunk … and next doubted his sanity as he saw a huge white moth appear to be pulling an outrigger canoe rapidly across the dark red water toward the shoreline well to the east of where his invasion troops were bivouacked.

Chapter 23

Morning Light

Vitario noticed that his hands were trembling with nervous energy. This was easily the most faith-stretching and crazy thing he had ever done ... maybe those two normally went hand in hand. He would have to think about that some other day ... if he lived through this one. Before dawn, a large contingent of musicians and singers were gathered in the Academy Commons, finding their place in the growing assembly. As Vitario inspected the troop he nodded at Maria, Kory, Ariel and even Reginaldo who were at the front of the line. For the umpteenth time he looked at Maria and asked, "Are you really sure about this? Is this really what God requires of us?"

Maria smiled up at him sweetly, though her lips trembled. "Yes, Master Vitario, and you are supposed to lead us, the Worship Warriors of Freelandia!" She said that in a brave tone, but as hard as she had tried, her voice still quavered.

Vitario smiled even if Maria could not see it. "Then let's do it. Let everyone know the power of praise and the might of our Maker!" He lifted an old trumpet, one his father had passed down to him from his grandfather. He hesitated just for a moment, thinking about how God had been preparing them for this very hour. Then he pressed the mouthpiece to his lips and let out the sound for battle.

The troop began to slowly march forward to circle first the inner Keep and then the outer city walls.

✦

At the beach, Rath Kordoch had slept very little. He thought about running through every Dark Magician they had brought along, and although it brought a wicked smile to his face, it was not something he would actually do ... at least not yet.

Now with the morning dawn the troops were getting better organized, what was left of them. Rath rubbed his bloodshot eyes. Well, they were red now anyway. He removed a small silver tumbler and removed a pinch of finely ground fireweed from the best stock known in the Dominion. He held it up to his nose and snuffed it in. A moment later his eyes took on a darker red cast and the headache and tiredness were barely noticeable. It was time to send the Bashers in to rout the enemy behind their quaint little barricades that blocked the pathways up from the beach. It should truly be a glorious day, finally.

The sky was just beginning to lighten, though dark shadows swirled around the Overlord as always. He could sense the dark evil spirits about him and it lifted his mood. Rath turned toward his newly appointed chief Dark Magician. "Our little friends will feast on the flesh of men today. Bid them in."

The Magician nodded gravely and began the incantation to summon the ravens. Their numbers had been reduced but there was plenty enough to darken the sky and pester the defenders to distraction. Minutes later a huge flock of ravens appeared out of the twilight, cawing raucously. They swirled around and around the beach and then flung themselves inland.

"Come, my Magicians, let us drink the blood of Freelandia and ..." He frowned. Something had just stirred out over Freelandia, something he had only ever encountered a hint of before and never, ever just before a battle. Something in the spiritual realm was happening. Normally when the Dominion came against an enemy he could feel the despair and gloom coming from them, and in a large way he actually fed on it, growing even stronger and more powerful. Fear and doubt and agony were like aphrodisiacs to the dark evil about him. But this ... this was nothing like that ... it was more like the opposite! In his spiritual mind's eye he saw a bright light emanating from some specific spot within the Keep, and it was growing far stronger, pushing away the evil shadows congregated around the city for a feast. And … it was coming his way.

The Dark Magicians who stood by were looking at the Overlord uncertainly, not knowing what the play of emotions that coursed over his face meant, though they too felt a distant unease that was growing substantially by the minute. Rath shook his head. Curse, curse, curse these Freelandians! They must be stopped, they must be utterly wiped out – they were utter anathema to the Dominion and the power that stood behind it.

Maria was in her special place, playing before her Audience. But it was not the easy-going praise of other days. The dark clouded dragon dominated her spiritual sky, looming dreadfully above her. Only her tiny little stage area was lit with bright white and color. A portion of Maria's mind balked in terror. Her playing faltered and the colored ribbons of sound she could see and manipulate had a ragged appearance that lacked coherence and its full vibrancy. Nonetheless, it still pushed out against the blackness, now acting more like a defensive shield than an offensive power to oppose evil.

Maria could sense she was battling for Freelandia, but today it also seemed like she was also in a personal battle, for the dark dragon image in her mind seemed to be coming specifically for her. That thought threatened to overwhelm what bravery she had. The dragon's tendrils were now starting to wrap around her ankles and their fiercely cold touch spawned all the more doubts and fear that she desperately tried to beat back. It seemed like she could just not continue onward.

In her special place Maria turned away from the darkness in terror. She wanted to run, but turning around brought her spiritual gaze to look at her Audience. God's power and majesty had not changed at all, and within that gaze she felt His love melting away her fears. And now, most unusually, God spoke directly to her in a voice at once gentle and yet with undertones of tremendous power.

"I am always here, my child. I will NEVER leave you or forsake you. In your greatest fear, turn to look at Me. When you think you will falter, look to Me. Your enemy's strength is but a shadow. Do not fear the shadows.

My light will dispel any gloom. Now be filled with my Spirit and fight against the evil – but do so by first concentrating on Me."

Maria felt warmth infuse her small body and the bright glory around her audience seemed to swell in beauty and immense energy. Basking in His presence, she wondered why she had been afraid and doubted. She thought about it a moment and realized she had again tried to take responsibility onto her diminutive shoulders when it did not belong there. The burden had been much too heavy for her to bear. But it was truly not her burden. As though it were a physical weight, Maria put her worries, fears and doubts down before her Maker. Laid out before her, in the light of her Audience, they seemed tiny and insignificant. Maria smiled and lifted her eyes. She knew where her help came from, that her Deliverer stood right behind her. Resolutely she turned around. She was not alone. Her Father stood right behind her. And her Father could whip the shadow dragon any day.

Maria began to sing to the worship song being played. The ribbons of sound in her special place began to glow with renewed energy and purpose. In a moment, Maria was dancing among them, weaving the worship into a mighty weapon which she flung with gusto at the engulfing darkness beating down around her.

The darkness seemed to tremble and shudder at the onslaught and it seemed to Maria that the small area of light around her grew in size just a little. She grinned.

Rath Kordoch trembled as he felt the surge of spiritual opposition. No! This should not be happening! He must find the source and destroy it! He looked out over his assembling troops who were nervously pacing about. He shook his head, trying to clear it but was only partially successful. His rage grew and he concentrated on his anger, feeding it with attention to make it stronger. Rage and hatred sustained him. Normally fear would make the spiritual forces behind the Dominion stronger, but anger and hate would do.

Rath felt renewed power surge around him. The dark demonic forces of the Dominion would prevail … he would see to it himself!

Murdrock and a dozen assassins were already in the Keep, keeping a very low profile since the majority of able-bodied men were manning the city walls and streets as volunteer soldiers. They were in a small room overlooking the town square, and Murdrock could not help but recall the failed attempt made earlier at this spot. But this time that dratted Ethan would not be present. The Chancellor had called for a prayer meeting out in the square, and in a few minutes most of the top Freelandian leaders would gather together and bend their knees or prostrate themselves before their pitiful weak god and beg for mercy. *They would be begging the Dominion for mercy before the day was through*, he thought. But all those leaders, face down would make for some fine targets.

Several of his men strung their bows and set quivers of arrows down by a curtained window. The others went downstairs to a private room Murdrock had rented and waited, swords ready, for the order to storm out and once and for all chop the head off the mighty Freelandia.

Murdrock gloated. He would be a hero for this … this coup-de-grace of the invasion. He limped out of the building, the only one among the Dominion men that did not appear fully able-bodied. His bad ankle, still not healed from the first assassination attempt, was hurting again and he felt it made him look weak in front of his men. So instead he was acting as point man, coming to a small outdoor table to sit with a cup of tea with a few older patrons at the café.

Officials from the government offices were beginning to wander out into the square. It would not be long now.

Robby sighed with exasperation while rolling his eyes. "I'm'a tellin' ye that ye canna go out to the front lines, armor or not!"

Arianna stood defiantly in Master Oldive's workshop with both of her hands on her hips "But Robby, what's the point of having armor if you don't use it when your country needs it the most?"

"We are engineers, lassie, not Watcher warriors. We'd be just in the way. Besides, I think our prayers are needed more than our metal … as nice looking as yours is, mind you."

"Bobby … watch yourself!"

"Oh my, but I'm sur'in to be watching you, my deary!"

Master Oldive clanked up. "I think the prayer time is about to start. Let's stop the bickering and get to praying!"

Four pachyderms each dragged several large wooden skiffs across the sandy beach and over to the edge of the river. Two others had already crossed the eight foot deep torrent, barely getting the feet of their Basher riders wet, pulling across heavy cables. The Bashers attached the cables to stout posts they had pounded deep into the sandy soil. On the other side the cable ends were being threaded through eyeholes in the bows and sterns of the skiffs. One by one, the skiffs were attached to the cables and pushed out into the rapidly moving water. When they had enough to completely cover the river's surface, the cables were pulled taut and attached to more posts. Boards were next laid down over the skiffs and attached, finishing their work on the floating bridge. It would not take the weight of a pachyderm – but those could ford the river themselves. It would do nicely for the Dominion cavalry and foot soldiers, though.

The bulk of the Bashers formed into loose tribal groups. Jo-Nakar only had a few men left, so he brought them over to a half-tribe who appeared to be struggling to replace a leader. The time was short, so the combined tribe group allowed Jo-Nakar to lead them forward to the easy honor and glory they had all been promised and come to expect. So many Bashers had been killed out in the Bay that it was difficult to form cohesive fighting units. The Dominion generals had to be content with three battalions of nearly seven thousand Bashers and animals each. Heavy doses of fireweed were freely meted out to each of the huge warriors.

At least the shore defenses were silent. During the wee hours of the morning the hills had been scaled and the Freelandian positions overrun – only to find them all empty of crews and the equipment solidly fixed to secure mounts in the rocky hillside.

A trumpet sounded from the Dominion camp. A rippling stir ran through the waiting warriors on the beach as the leading ranks surged forward. Chains were attached to several large pachyderms and hooked to the large metal gates that barred entrance to the narrow pathways up the hill from the beach. With seemingly little effort the beasts ripped the gates from their posts. With wild war cries, thousands of Bashers charged forward. The pathways were much too narrow for the pachyderms, but the excitement caused several to lift their large trunks and add their nasal trumpeting to the Basher yelling.

The wave of Basher warriors surged up the trails. Those first in line got no more than ten strides before the floor before them gave way and they plunged down onto sharp metal spikes. Those not killed outright were severely wounded. High on fireweed, more Bashers raced forward, and the charge barely slowed as the following horde trampled over their fallen comrades.

Jo-Nakar's face was a mask of fury at the dishonor that his new tribe was one of the last to leave the beach. He urged his Bashers to run even faster, ignoring the dead and wounded. As they moved up the pathway, surviving Bashers who were still mobile joined them, often with clothing tied over cut feet and legs to staunch bleeding. As they moved forward, Jo-Nakar's tribe swelled in size.

The Bashers came up the hill considerably faster than expected. Dozens of Freelandian farmers with fine netting over their heads brought large covered baskets forward to the edge of the pathway embankments. As the Bashers came into view, the farmers dumped their loads of beehives in front of the enemy. Further up the trail, pressure pots with long metal tubes pointed down into the pathways. Each had a burning cloth attached to the end of the pipes and a Freelandian hand clutching the handle of a valve. As the first Bashers came into sight, wildly swatting at the remaining stinging bees, the valves were opened wide and great gouts of fire shot outward to form a solid wall of flame.

Not all of the Bashers were running up the deadly beach pathways. Several thousand Bashers had grudgingly crossed the floating bridge, along with over fifty hellhounds and the entire compliment of a dozen pachyderms that had survived the sea voyage. They raced over to the wharves and docks ahead of them, but found no enemy. The frustrated Bashers turned from there to surge through the streets of the dockyard toward the warehouse district. It was unnatural to them not to face an immediate enemy, as was racing through empty streets that turned this way and that. Many were blocked off with tall gates set into the ground. The pachyderms could remove them later as needed.

Dominion soldier engineers marched over to the secured dockyards and quickly dismantled the fairly crude booby-traps they found. Once finished, they signaled to their ships in the Bay. Several were barely afloat, and a good many of the cavalry horses were still berthed, along with more pachyderms. It would be much easier to unload those at the docks. Two dozen ships lifted anchor and began to converge on the wharves. Two hundred cavalry troops had made it safely to shore the previous night. They now galloped to meet their comrades. The Dominion cavalry were renowned for crushing any troops opposing them.

Rath Kordoch watched as the horses charged across the bridge. It was an inspiring sight, and it seemed that finally something was going right. He motioned for his huge bay charger to be brought over, gilded in gold and purple finery … but with very functional armor plate protecting much of its head and chest. His contingent of elite personal bodyguards and Dark Magicians also mounted. Together they rode toward the bridge and the pathway already trampled out towards the dockyard. The cloud of ravens that had been circling overhead swirled outward and seemingly broke ranks, released to find their own targets of opportunity.

Several miles south of the entrance to Freelandia Bay, Commodore Moorhead had his hands full. The outer ring of Dominion patrol ships was putting up a considerable resistance, even without the Dreadnaughts.

He had lost several ships already, but the enemy was taking the far worst of it. His squadron was battling several larger Dominion warships when his lookout high up on their mast reported seeing huge sails approaching from the south. In minutes, the unmistakable outline of a 'mountain of the sea' Dreadnaught could be seen racing in their direction. Moorhead scowled. If the Dominion had more Dreadnaughts in reserve that they were sending in, this might not be very pleasant. He ordered his helmsman to tack hard to port, narrowly missing a catapult launch of flaming arrows from the nearest Dominion ship even as his own crew scored a hit, breaking their enemy's main mast half way up with a spring launched stone.

The spring launchers could fling a rifled rock with amazing distance and accuracy. With them, his small ships were more than equal to any Dominion ship he had come across … except for the Dreadnaughts. He figured there may be at least one of those to deal with just outside of Free-landia Bay, and perhaps another one or two inside. And now it appeared yet another one or even more may be coming up in reserve. Moorhead had no more swamp gas mines, and had used up all of his Thunderclaps of God. There was not much left in his arsenal to go against those behemoths. But there was one supreme weapon left. He prayed.

A dozen Dominion ships sailed into the dockyards as fast as they dared. Most had holds filled with horses and their riders, but several ships leaked water badly and would need repair work at the dry docks. None of the Dominion engineers had given more than a cursory look at the reed pipes directly under the docks, figuring them to be some sort of drainage system. Which, in fact, they were – just not for excess rain water.

As the first eight ships came within fifty feet of the docks, spring launch-ers were triggered by a dozen well hidden Irregulars in tiny camouflaged kayaks low to the water and muck where the wharves meet land. Large metal-tipped poles sprang outward, nearly level with the water. When they struck the ships they were just beginning to break the water's sur-face. The weight of the poles coupled with tremendous velocity punched right through Dominion hulls. Ships shuddered as water gushed into their holds.

Horses whinnied as the ships stalled their forward movement and began sinking. Only one actually made it to the dock, but it had already taken on so much water than its deck was below the dock level. Ship crews and rider-less cavalry men leapt into the water as the ships with their steeds sank below the waves. The men thrashed about, wondering about the strange smelling oily scum on the water's surface. A few wondered if it could possibly be from the liquid spewing out of the pipes directly under the dock planks. Several of the hidden Freelandians lit oil soaked rags wrapped around long arrows and shot their burning projectiles into the oily slick. With a horrific flash the slick burst into a conflagration.

Another set of ships tried to turn away, but six more were hit with the flying poles that punctured their hulls as well, drowning more men and horses.

With no further ships daring to approach, the Irregulars shoved their narrow kayaks through a channel dug out in the shoreline mud to scoot out from the docks much further to the east. Ten minutes of hard paddling brought them around a narrow promontory and away from any Dominion eyes. Two ships in the Bay tried to give chase, but the Freelandians scooted their craft into a narrow stream a hundred yards further down the coast and were out of sight and out of catapult range before any ship could get close enough to even try to fire upon them.

The Musician's March was halfway through the city, heading for the eastern gate. From there it was a short walk down to a massive stone bridge that crossed the river, and then to the road that led to the warehouse district and the docks. It was a slow and purposeful march, and Maria walked along, but her mind was elsewhere. The true reality was what was happening in her 'special place'. There, standing before her Audience of One, she had never felt so alive and full of energy. God seemed to fill the area behind her with His presence, majesty and wonder. Yet evil dark clouds billowed before her, absorbing all hope. The darkness was growing in size and menace. The light and power where she stood seemed like a tiny pinprick of hope and truth against a torrent of despair that kept pressing down all around her. With every step the doom grew closer and more oppressive. Several of the other musicians had already grown faint as fear and doubt drained away faith and courage. Maria was not sure how long they – or she – could hold out.

Yet she knew she must fight on, regardless of the outcome. She would remain true to her purpose. At least she would try to as hard as she could.

The strands of colored musical ribbons danced all about her, mixed with a myriad of wafting sparkles that she somehow recognized as prayers of God's people. And in the middle of it all, dancing with impossible gymnastics and grace, Maria flew amongst the colors and movements, pulling the many strands and ribbons together. As she touched each one, it pulsed with additional power from God's Spirit. As she walked, she also shaped the music into an immense cable of pulsing, vibrating spiritual energy that coursed around and overhead of the marchers like a bright spiritual cloud of fire that was somehow also a shield. The darkness beat down upon it constantly and Maria shuddered with the strain.

Kory was by her side and let out a whimper. The heavy weight of despair seemed to be barely kept at bay and part of her wanted to turn and run away as fast as she could. Yet she knew with certainty that her place was exactly here, and in her own special place before God she purposed to keep her eyes and heart on her Audience and play on.

The intensity of the spiritual attack on the musicians increased even more, and many stumbled as the marching came to a stop. Fear beat upon them and even Vitario's trumpet playing faltered as a pained expression crossed his face and one hand clutched at his chest.

In her special place Maria could see the ribbons of musical energy begin to fade and several shriveled up to fall lifeless to the ground. The darkness seemed to sense their weakening resolve and pressed down even harder. The black fangs of the cloud dragon were nearly closing down on her and Maria could not go any further. Yet she did not back away or curl up into a little ball. She shivered in palpable fear and the light seemed to be shrinking around her. The enemy was winning.

In her mind, the dragon spoke. "You are mine now, puny little girl. Did you truly think you would ever amount to anything? Did you truly think you could stand before my might and power? You are nothing. You are less than nothing, not even worthy of my contempt. What have you done to think you could resist me? Who do you think you are? Some noble

warrior? Some great scholar of your pitiful sacred writings? Some learned theologian? A minister or missionary perhaps? What have you ever done for your God? How many times have you failed him in your short little life? Ha! How many times have you failed him this month? This week? Today? How can you call yourself his follower when you resist his ways time and time again? How could he possible still want you? How have you earned the right to resist me, or to even stand here?"

Maria hung her head. It was true. She had no education, did not come from some great family of priests or leaders, and what did she have to show for herself in her short life? Memories of past sins flooded over her and her head hung in shame. She was unworthy. Totally unworthy. She did not deserve to be here, to even stand before her God. She had failed so very often. Her resolve crumpled and in her mind she dropped to her knees, cringing. The blackness and despair were all before her, closing in all around …

But not everywhere. She looked up in terror at the horror before her. In a quavering voice she defiantly whispered, "I … am … NOT … YOURS!" Maria turned in her special place. Though a large part of her wanted to run in shame away from the holy Presence, she instead prostrated herself before the Audience of One who had always been there for her, had always accepted her and loved her.

God's voice spoke again to her, "No, my child, YOU ARE MINE! No one can take you from Me!"

"But I am so unworthy! I have failed you so often! How could you possible love me?" Maria sobbed.

"You cannot possibly earn my love, Maria. But you ARE worthy. Not because of what you have done or who you are. Not because of anything the world may see you as. It is because I CHOSE YOU. I adopted you into MY family. You are worthy because of who I AM!"

These last two words reverberated with power that seemed to shake all of Maria's spiritual surroundings. The dark dragon snarled behind her but the radiance of her Audience grew stronger and stronger, washing over her anew. The fear was not totally gone, but it had no real power over her anymore.

"And I have chosen you to lead this battle. Not with your own strength, but with MINE!"

Maria was lifted to her feet by the spiritual power. Around her the faded ribbons of music began to brighten. She turned to face her enemy and saw that indeed it was just a dark cloud with no real substance. How could she have been afraid of that … mist, of that shadow? And she knew the way to dissipate shadows was to turn up the light.

Maria began to sing a song of worship. She gathered together the renewed strands of music in her mind, building it stronger until she could barely contain it in her grasp. Then, with all of her might, Maria directed the bright light of energy directly toward the dragon, an immensely powerful weapon of worship.

Chapter 24

Hellhounds

Something was wrong. Gaeten could feel it inside, like a heaviness that constricted his breathing. He did not know what was wrong, but there was a particular sense of evil coming from the dockyard area. It was more than just the Dominion forces. Someone – or something – else was down there too, and it had immense evil spiritual strength.

Miguel looked at the deep wrinkles developing on Gaeten's forehead even as he too felt unusually uneasy about what might be coming their way. He knew of the fortifications and preparations in place to meet the Dominion army. But as the strength of the uneasiness grew, so did his concern. Miguel looked around him. He and Gaeten were stationed close to the end of the warehouse district, just before the large open field leading to a stone bridge that was the last step before reaching the walls of the Keep. Gaeten and he were positioned to mount a counterattack that should allow retreating Freelandians time to regroup at the bridge and mount a final stand before the enemy reached the Keep.

Miguel looked back at Gaeten even as a wave of nauseating dread washed over him. He nearly gagged and heard several other defenders less successful in quelling the bodily reaction.

Gaeten flinched but stood straight. He then slammed the butt of his staff down onto the cobbled flagstones at his feet. "Come Miguel. We need to tell the sub-commander of this area that a greater need has arisen for us. We have to try to stop whomever or whatever is the source of the evil presence behind the Dominion army."

❧

Miguel had to nearly jog to keep up with the pace that Gaeten set as he strode forward with a stern expression of determination. They hurried down empty streets, with each turn taking them closer to the approaching Dominion forces. Seeing their general direction, Miguel steered Gaeten through several buildings and backstreets, emerging into a small courtyard over half way to the dockyard. As they exited a building, Gaeten jerked to a stop. "What is that noise?" He pointed upward.

Miguel shaded his eyes from the rising sun. "I don't see anything ... wait ... it looks like ... like a huge flock of large black birds – and they are coming this way!"

Even as he finished saying this the first ravens cried out overhead and Gaeten could feel an evil presence with them. One dived right at him, cawing raucously. Gaeten's staff swished through the air in a tight arc, knocking it aside. But behind it he could hear many more, and overhead it sounded like hundreds or thousands. An idea flashed through his mind and he grabbed the thin metal whistle on its strand around his neck, put it to his lips and blew. Miguel looked at him oddly, not having heard anything. Then he had no time for his curiosity. Ravens were diving at both men with great speed, seemingly with murderous intent. Miguel sliced his two long swords through the air, littering the ground before him with bird halves. Gaeten's staff was a blur of motion itself, clearing a path before them in air now thick with flitting black shapes.

Miguel glanced forward. "This way, Gaeten – we can duck into one of the warehouses to escape!"

Gaeten did not have time for another blow on the whistle as he shuffled towards the sound of Miguel's voice while still sweeping ravens from the air before him. The cawing and screeching from nearly every direction was disorienting, even to one with Grand Master Watcher skills. Miguel was half of a block ahead when the flock broke off their attack and wheeled upward momentarily. Gaeten snatched at the whistle again but just before he could use it he heard a guttural low growl from down the street. He turned toward the new threat and the lone growl turned into a chorus of howls only a few dozen yards away.

Miguel had raced ahead and found an unlocked warehouse window. He threw it open even as the growl sounded behind him. He turned to see half a dozen Bashers entering the courtyard, each barely holding back a huge hellhound. His eyes went wide as he saw they were between him and Gaeten.

If that were not enough, another mass of ravens from the circling flock above broke away and with a loud chorus dived back toward the two Watchers.

Gaeten heard the hellhounds and Bashers pause at the sound of the birds, and used that few seconds to blow again upon his special whistle. A wry grin lifted the corners of his mouth as he heard a familiar high pitched screech from far above, suddenly joined by dozens and dozens of similar avian voices. Gaeten had no idea where the other gryphs had come from, but their battle screech never sounded so pleasant to his ears.

The other part of his mind that was tracking the Bashers and their beasts now came to the forefront. The hellhounds were still growling, but now it sounded to be more in pain. Gaeten could not see the hounds shaking their massive heads back and forth, sending red spittle flying in all directions and pawing at their ears.

Miguel had an inspiration. He yelled out "Gaeten ... blow that thing again!"

Though he was not sure why, Gaeten complied. He pursed his lips and blew with all his might.

Sasha distractedly pulled out of her dive, having already rendered several ravens into shreds. The gryph looked down and saw her long-time benefactor in an open area between buildings opposed by strange and dangerous-looking animals. Those were more the gryphs size, and Sasha instinctively realized that both the canines and the Bashers were enemies. The great bird wheeled off from the melee and flapped her mighty wings to gain altitude. She would need more speed to go against these new foes.

Hellhounds could produce very loud and menacing growls. It seemed they could also produce howls of pain that were unequaled. Every one of them within a long earshot let loose a racket and began to roll on the ground while pawing at their ears. It was not a particularly safe way to lie on the ground with gryphs hunting above. Sasha had been joined by many of the other gryphs and now one after another dove at the hellhounds, still rolling belly up on the ground. Only a few of the Southern attack dogs survived. The Bashers holding the chain leashes of those remaining jerked hard to get the hellhounds back to their feet. Between the pains in their heads, the fireweed burning in their veins and the Bashers jerking on them, those remaining went berserk.

The beasts turned on their masters and on anything else in sight. Gaeten heard running feet and a chain dragging on the ground coming directly toward him. He leaned forward on the balls of his feet and carefully timed the swing of his staff. It connected with the hellhound solidly, but the drugged animal felt no pain and the staff barely deflected its charge. A leap sideways just kept the savage jaws from his skin. The hellhound did not pause but leapt again.

Gaeten drew a knife from his belt and stabbed in an upward arc even as he let himself fall backwards. The blade plunged into the thick fur of the animal's belly, but the thrust angle was not quite right and only gave a superficial cut. Gaeten curled as he fell backwards, shoving his legs up and outward to send the hound hurling beyond him. The long chain leash however dragged directly over Gaeten, and he felt his knife yanked away as it was caught in the links. He twisted sharply to leap back to his feet, hearing the hellhound slam into the ground, rear up and come charging back.

Gaeten's sharp hearing picked up the sound of a Basher charging in his direction, and of several more hounds bounding around the courtyard, wildly snarling. He thought he heard swordplay a ways off, in the direction Miguel had been, but he had no time to help his fellow Watcher. The open area of the courtyard was not to Gaeten's advantage, and he was finding these hellhounds considerably harder to dispatch than expected. It was time to turn his environment into his advantage. Gaeten did something he very rarely resorted to. He turned and ran.

Miguel watched helplessly as several enemy combatants raced after Gaeten, but there was nothing he could do. His own swords were a blur of motion as he countered the attack of two Bashers. Their brute force was extremely difficult to block directly, so Miguel had to work at deflecting the blows while trying to rapidly attack back. Step by step, he was being backed away from the courtyard that he had leapt into, trying to reach the side of his friend and mentor. Miguel sensed his back was only a few feet from the wall of a building, and still the Bashers pressed in, their long arms and swinging weapons not providing Miguel any opportunity to strike.

Miguel drew in a deep breath and gave an incomprehensible roar as he charged forward. The Bashers took a few startled steps backward, blocking the Freelandian's sword strikes. Miguel spun around and raced full out directly at the blank wall of the building. Both Bashers paused only a moment and then surged forward after the seemingly crazy Watcher. Miguel leapt directly at the wall, planting his left foot at chest height and then gave a mighty shove even as he twisted his body into a back flip.

It was a desperate maneuver, but one that was executed perfectly. Miguel soared backward, rolling his body even as he slashed downward with his long swords. At the last instant he straightened his body and landed solidly on his feet behind the Basher warriors. Both swords dove forward to finish the fight. Miguel smiled, inwardly congratulating himself on his acrobatics. He turned back toward the courtyard and noticed Sasha wheeling above, dispatching one of the few remaining ravens. A deep-throated growl to his side announced the lunge of a remaining hellhound and Miguel's attention was suddenly taken elsewhere.

Sasha craned her head to find another enemy. Her extremely keen eyes could only see one ... a lone raven fluttering toward the dock yard with a damaged wing, surrounded by what looked like a thin but dark roiling cloud and having strange bright red eyes. With a great flapping of her immense wings, she gave pursuit.

Rath Kordoch sped his horse up from the shoreline and towards the wharf district roads. Dominion soldiers were amassed and at his signal they stormed forward. What was left of the cavalry charged ahead of the foot soldiers, figuring the first wave of Bashers had most likely cleared away any sizable enemy resistance directly ahead.

Rath was gloating at the power of his troops as they moved forward. He sneered and spoke to the retinue of guards and Dark Magicians around him. "No power on earth had ever stood against the might of the Dominion! We will crush these weaklings as we have crushed all other peoples, nations and gods!" He urged his mount forward but had gone no more than a few steps when the spiritual world around him exploded. Dark shadows gathered about him shuddered and contracted. The blinding light seemed to singe his consciousness and he recoiled from it forcefully. Many of the Dark Magicians at his side tumbled off their mounts to the ground, clutching their heads in agony and the Overlord had to work to remain seated himself. As he overrode the pain he recognized the devastating assault as resembling what he had felt once before. The source was somewhere close to the north, perhaps in the city ahead of him.

Rath shook his head from side to side to try to clear his thinking. He did not know exactly where the spiritual attack was coming from, but he certainly recognized its nature. It was full of hope and joy wrapped up in a musical praise to the Freelandian god. Anger boiled within him, quickly turning to hatred, and he fed on that, regaining some of his strength. His eyes narrowed to slits. "With me!" he shouted at whatever Magicians remained horsed. Rath urged his mount forward, death in his glare. He had to stop this powerful force that could potentially defeat even his great army. It must be destroyed! His mind tunneled down to those simple thoughts and his rage and hatred muddled all other considerations. Carefully laid out battle plans became irrelevant as the supreme commander of the Dominion army charged blindly ahead, pushing aside and even in a few cases trampling down his own foot soldiers whose ranks broke as they raced forward to try to keep up.

Chapter 25

Bashers

The front running Bashers headed through the wharf district at a frenetic pace, leaping along in gigantic strides but not even seeing the Freelandians who lay hidden, allowing them to pass. The lead Bashers kept looking around, expecting to find some form of enemy to attack as had always been the case in past invasions. The confused look on their faces might have been almost comical, were it not for the murderous weapons in their hands. The fireweed induced haze compounded their bewilderment and the lead warriors slowed as they came to a major intersection of streets with still no enemy in sight.

Directly ahead of the Bashers, one street curved left. Garish paintings adorned the building walls they could see, depicting mythical monsters devouring what looked like fellow Bashers. Master Chu stood near one such wall, perfectly blending into the building upon which he leaned. He stood directly in sight of the Bashers, though none could discern his presence. Chu observed the Bashers swiveling their heads back and forth at the option in pathways forward. The left street itself had been painted a particular shade of slime green that Minister Polonos has reported looked very much like a poisonous fungus that grew throughout the far south Dominion territories.

The other main street curved right, going slightly downhill and lingering smells of fresh bread wafted up from the outdoor market and several bakeries that until two days ago had been in business down the street in that direction.

The Bashers were not generally known for their higher thinking skills, and with the double doses of fireweed they had been given their cognitive abilities were even further reduced. The lead Bashers were clearly not in favor of heading up the left street, yet Chu could see indecision among them as a few took tentative steps right but then wheeled around to rejoin the growing crowd of nervously fidgeting warriors. A small group detached itself from the milling throng and began heading left. Chu frowned. That would not do.

The group of Bashers were about halfway across the intersection when they saw what appeared to be part of a building wall detach itself and begin running toward the main thoroughfare to the right. Dumbfounded, they stopped and stared for a moment. Then one noticed that the running wall had legs and pumping arms. With a bloodcurdling holler he leapt forward to give chase. He was not entirely certain what he was charging toward, but it was on enemy soil and was running away from them. That meant it just about had to be an enemy.

The battle holler catalyzed the entire mass of Bashers. As one they launched after the running figure, who was now racing down the rightmost street and dodging around a corner. The first Bashers to turn the corner did not notice the odd bumpy section of wall along a nearby building and their long strides quickly took them racing down the next street. A barricade had been erected at the next intersection, allowing further travel in only one direction. A furtive movement far down the street prompted renewed war cries from several Bashers and away they flew down that street. The following horde followed suit until Chu was left alone, hunkered against the rough building stonework. He smiled. These Bashers were in for a wild goose chase through the warehouse district, and would likely only enter the real fighting to the rear of the professional foot soldiers. There they should cause considerable commotion and confusion. Confusing his enemies is something Master Chu did best.

He stood straight, seeming to disengage from being part of the very stone wall upon which he had been leaning. He figured he and his fellow camouflaged Watchers had no more than twenty or thirty minutes before the front wave of Dominion foot soldiers would arrive and the real fun would begin. He wanted to make a final check on his team, if he could find them … though all should be in sight. They would let the first soldiers pass right by them, and then begin to decimate them from behind.

Gaeten raced back along the path he and Miguel had taken. His hand reached for the doorknob he knew was right … there! … from when he had closed it only minutes before. A hellhound was literally nipping at his heels as he turned the knob and leapt inward. Even as his foot touched the floor inside, Gaeten twisted sideways while sliding his staff backwards at a low angle. The hound was very close. The moment it took to open the door had allowed the hellhound to close the distance between them and even as the hellhound's legs tangled with the staff, its fangs scoured over Gaeten's left leg in deep furrows.

There was no time to do more than grimace and ask a quick prayer for grace. Two Bashers were charging toward the doorway right behind the hound and Gaeten crashed his shoulder back into the door to slam in shut with great force. The foremost Basher was just entering when the solid wooden door smacked him right off his feet and toppled him backwards into the second rushing Southern warrior. Meanwhile the hound inside had regained its footing after tripping over the staff and was just turning toward its adversary when that same staff smacked down right between its eyes, bloodying its nose and sending shooting stars into its vision. It howled ferociously and sprang forward, shaking its head in attempt to see more clearly. Gaeten had caught the door, swinging back and nearly off its hinges from its abrupt meeting with the Basher's face, and now he pulled it wide open while tucking himself between it and the wall. The Bashers were disentangling themselves on the ground, the topmost with a heavily bleeding and broken nose, when the hellhound caught both sight and smell of what its fireweed dulled mind told it must be the source of its sudden pain. With a bared-teeth snarl it bounded out the door directly at the Bashers. Gaeten nearly caught its tail as he slammed the door shut again, and his questing fingers found the latch to lock it. The door would never hold back the Bashers, but from the sounds coming from its other side Gaeten did not think it likely that would ever be tested.

Gaeten could feel warm liquid running down his leg where the hellhound's teeth had torn his flesh. He retrieved a knife from the several he had hidden within his clothing and cut a strip from his outer garment to tie snuggly over the wound. He had no time for pain, and he willed it into a corner of his mind. It would catch up with him later without doubt, and he gave a silent prayer for strength, and that it would not be infected with some canine malady. Gaeten tentatively put weight on his leg, ignoring the increased pain and found it to be steady … for now. It would have to do. He could feel the evil presence close by, and coming closer. He moved through the building and out a back door on what he prayed was a correct intercept course.

It was terribly difficult for the hidden Irregulars furthest toward the docks to let the Dominion cavalry charge by, and then the thousands of running foot soldiers. Many fingers twitched on the strong cords strung through thin reed pipes buried a short distance underground. When the last lines of soldiers were in sight, one jerked his cord and several pressure pot land mine "Fists of God" detonated sixty feet away. At the horrendous noise the others pulled their cords and all hunkered lower in their single person buried bunkers. The Dominion troops above had no such solid protection as it seemed like the ground gods of Freelandia had risen up to take their turn at drinking foreign blood. Many of those not killed outright in the blasts were perforated with high velocity shrapnel.

The troops in the rear paused at the awful roar of erupting earth behind them, and other hidden Irregulars triggered additional huge Fists of God swamp gas bombs hidden in the first row of buildings. Walls had been weakened, allowing thousands of small fragments to blast outward as a deadly hail. Secondary bombs were housed in thick iron cauldrons loaded with small stones and chains, which were triggered immediately after the first to fire their projectiles outward without the impediment of intervening walls. Several nearby buildings crashed to the ground, blocking streets further and adding yet more to the maelstrom the rear Dominion troops were finding themselves in.

The explosions continued, one after another in succession, following the pathways the foot soldiers had taken, moving forward far faster than any could escape. The disorganized main mass of the Dominion army had only gotten several blocks into the warehouse district. Over half never had a chance to leave.

Soldiers ahead began to panic, scattering in any and all directions but backwards, some even dropping their weapons in sheer terror. First Freelandian sea monsters, then sky demons, and now ground gods bent on devouring them! What might come next? The wounded and shell shocked troops were just thinking that when the very walls came alive with swords and other weapons to set upon them.

Master Chu and his fellow Watchers took no prisoners.

Jo-Nakar's eyes were wide and he knew he was afraid. It was a very strange feeling for a Basher warrior. Thousands of fellow Southerns had run ahead of his trailing tribe, but the Freelandian magic must have been dropping them like … like … he absently swatted at a fly and stopped cold. Somehow an image had come unbidden to his mind of a strange white haired blind man back in Kardern who had warned about men dropping like … flies. His blood ran ice cold as a hail of arrows showered down upon his tribe from a high cliff. Without thinking he sprang ahead and finally cleared the deadly twisting pathways and emerged into the bright sunlight in a clearing. He saw many hundreds of other Bashers, milling about, obviously without a leader and unsure of which way to go next.

Drugged Bashers rarely could keep a goal in mind very long, being much more used to simply fighting onward until there was no more resistance. Leaders had to only point them towards the next obstacle, but with no obvious enemy directly in front of them they were confused. Jo-Nakar had a thought. Those did not come all that often during battle, but this one came into his dull mind like a comet. I could be their leader, he thought. I SHOULD be their leader. I WILL be their leader.

He charged forward, calling on the others to join him and promising they would finally find an enemy to fight and blood to spill. Bashers all over the clearing looked up and saw a tribal leader striding forward with grim purpose, and the throng quickly fell in behind. The thousand or so that could keep up started a slow jog forward. Jo-Nakar did not know for sure which road led to the Freelandian city that was their main target, but his sharp eyes could just make out what appeared to be wooden structures across the clearing and through a line of trees. He ran in that direction at a pace that would allow his sizeable army of Bashers to easily keep together.

Minister Polonos and Chaplain Mikael stood at the forefront of the heavily armed defenders atop large earthen barricades, watching through small breaks in the trees as the Bashers regrouped and began coming their way. Polonos strode a few steps forward to the outer edge of the steep man-made hill the enemy would have to climb. He doubted the defenders around him could withstand the onslaught. For a fleeting moment he wondered if he should excuse himself from this prominent position and retreat. He knew how to live off the land. He could escape into the forest and hide from the Dominion. Sure he could, and he could even set up a resistance movement, maybe start a ministry among the refugees …. Polonos frowned at those unbidden thoughts and shook his head hard to one side. "Get behind me, old deceiver! You will not trick me so easily," he muttered.

Polonos held his old and weather beaten head high and his eyes shown bright. He lifted both hands heavenward. "God who is our Defender, You see our plight and You hear our cries. Blind the enemy even as they come upon us. Cover us with Your protection. Defend Your people and Your Name." He held his hands high even as the Bashers surged across the clearing and the leading element broke through the trees right before him.

The worship warriors were winding their way down the last hill before leaving the city gate above the bridge. Each played like they had never played before, caught up in the praise they were giving to their Creator. Though each knew they should be scared to death at what lay before them, somehow, incredibly, they were filled with joy as they focused wholeheartedly on their Lord and God. And from that joy flowed a strength that drove them on.

Master Vitario, leading the procession with his trumpet, was not playing as loud as he had been. He lifted one hand up to rub his right shoulder, which had begun to ache for some unknown reason. Behind the musicians marched an army of several thousand volunteer defenders. These were the last of the Freelandian army at the Keep, swords following singers and marching musicians. Vitario smiled. God's ways were certainly not man's.

Commodore Moorhead maneuvered his ships to put the smaller Dominion vessels between the Freelandian ships and the colossal Dreadnaught that was now nearly upon them. He could see Dominion sailors on the warships cheering at the arrival and he sincerely hoped his crew could find even one Thunderclap left, somewhere. So far none had. If the other ships under his command were similarly scarce he could do nothing more than attempt hit and run tactics to keep his ships outside of the long firing range of the Dreadnaught's huge catapults. Maybe a massed run could allow some of his ships to score hits on that monster while the others were dodging the catapult launches. That was at least worth a try. Moorhead turned to his second in command to give the order when he stopped, a perplexed look washing over his face.

The Dreadnaught was coming right between two other Dominion warships as though to take the lead against the Freelandians. His ships were still much too far away for even the mighty catapults on that huge ship to reach them, yet he clearly saw the cat's arms fly forward from the deck that stood impossibly high above the water's surface.

Loads of burning rock and tar rained down on the Dominion ships to the right and left of the Dreadnaught. The huge ship turned to port as if to give a broadside volley toward the Freelandian ships – though they were still a few hundred yards too far away – and instead ran in front of the third Dominion warship in the triad that Moorhead had been maneuvering to attack. As the Dreadnaught passed in front, the Dominion warship was hidden from view, but moments later Moorhead could see it again, now with its deck aflame and listing severely to one side.

The Dreadnaught turned again and did not bother to launch another round. Instead it rammed right into the middle Dominion ship, splitting it in half as though it had been a toy. The other two attempted to steer away, but with shredded sails and burning decks they had little ability to run or maneuver.

Not to miss any God given opportunity, Moorhead commanded his ships to attack the third hapless Dominion warship, even as the Dreadnaught bore down on the first ship. Within just a few minutes the only Dominion ship before them remaining afloat was the Dreadnaught.

As Moorhead's ship cautiously approached the Dominion flag was lowered and an Alterian flag was raised high. Prince Erkatan looked down at the approaching Freelandian ship. "Oh, hello Captain ... or is it Commodore by now ... Moorhead I think? May I present to you the Alterian ship, the *Dreadful*. Not a very original name if you ask me, and one we shall surely change shortly ... but not just yet I think. How may we be of assistance?"

Moorhead looked bewildered, but also very relieved. "It is Commodore, sir. But how ... I mean, surely this was not built by Alteria?"

Erkatan laughed. "No, Commodore – this is certainly not our style of ship. Much too slow and unwieldy. Really only good for one thing. No, this one was being restocked at one of the Dominion's island ports, not really much of a place after the Dominion took it over, though it had been quite a nice tropical resort rather strategically located just off the south western corner of Alteria. I'd been there the year before ... beautiful sandy beaches, crystal clear water ... it should actually make a quite nice royal vacation spot, after the appropriate renovations are finished. It seems this vessel was still docked when that little island officially became a territorial possession of Alteria. Of course, that made it ours, regardless of what that stubborn Dominion captain said or threatened. We really did not give him much choice. He and his crew should even now be setting about those renovations. It was so kind of them to 'volunteer' for such duties since they were liberated from Dominion control. Since they had so kindly restocked the ship's stores I thought we'd sail on over and show you our new toy."

Moorhead had to laugh. "Your ... your new toy?" he chortled.

"Yes, and I must say I am not overly fond of it. It sails like a fat drunken sow. Would you like it instead? As a gift from the King of Alteria? I'd have to keep my crew aboard – over the last week they have become quite adept at handling it and even with operating its weaponry. I'm afraid they would be rather unhappy with me if I made them leave, at least just yet. But you are more than welcome to come aboard and assume ownership. I'd even be pleased to serve as your First Mate, if you'd have me, at least for a few more days."

Moorhead did not know whether the Prince was being serious or jesting, but at the comical low bow being given in his direction, albeit from thirty feet higher in the air, the Commodore bent in half roaring with laughter and his crew joined in.

"Well, sir! I must say you Freelandians have a rather strange custom of saying 'thank you'! Regardless, you are very welcome." Erkatan smiled warmly. "So here we are, sailing northward to say hello and I see what appears to be the entire Alterian fleet, out on maneuvers. And we get here, and it appears those nasty Dominion folks are out bothering our dear Freelandian allies. Did I mention my men had been practicing their gunnery skills with these monstrous catapults? My Gunny Mate claimed his men had a distinct need to practice, preferably on moving targets. You can never get too much practice in, that's what my father often says. Anyway, those Dominion chaps seemed to oblige us."

Moorhead had regained control, barely, and these last remarks nearly sent him into a renewed paroxysm of laughter. With difficulty he straightened up and, though still smirking, he settled into a more professional composure and looked quizzically at his unknown benefactor. "Sir, you appear to know who I am, but I'm at a loss to know who you are, or by what authority you seem to speak for the king of Alteria." Moorhead was getting a sneaking suspicion about what the answer might be, and in a moment he was not disappointed.

Chapter 26

Assassins And Armor

hancellor Duncan and Lydia finally exited the administration building and walked, hand in hand, down to the assembled people who worked under them to keep Freelandia running smoothly. All looked up, many trembling visibly knowing a bloodthirsty enemy was at the doorsteps to the city and wondering if this was the last day they might live. "Good people," Duncan began in somber tones, "God has never forsaken His children. Let us not fear. Let us join the fight. Let us pray." He dropped to his knees in the dust and bowed his head. Robert, Arianna and Oldive, standing close by, tried to copy that as best they could in their stiff armored suits, and all of the other administrators did likewise. Only a few Watcher guards, led by Suevey, continued to peer around the town square. And even she closed her eyes momentarily to join in.

It was what he had been waiting for. Murdrock raised his hand and brought it down in a chopping motion.

"Oldsy, ye dinna leave room in the knee thingys to properly kneel!" whispered the Chief Engineer.

"Well Robby, I didn't really expect anyone wearing the armor to be down in that position much! I rather figured on praying standing up."

Robby just couldn't master the technique and gave up trying to get into the awkward position that his amour just would not cooperate with. He rose to his feet.

Two arrows careened off the shoulders of his suit, intended for the Chancellor who was kneeling down just to Robby's side. Robby turned toward his fellow engineer. "Hey Oldsy, you donna have to cuff me for criticizing your design!"

Oldive looked at him quizzically, standing himself and taking a step closer to his friend. "But Robby, I didn't cuff you."

Robby turned, trying to look at Arianna behind him, but needed to take a sideways step first. As he was accomplishing this two more arrows shattered into splinters as they intersected with his back. He finished the turn and spouted, "Arianna – what was that fer? Why'd ye go and smack me a second time?"

Arianna had figured a way to drop to one knee rather gracefully, but now she stood. "You lout, if I was to smack you it would be for a very good reason ... I can usually think of several at any given time ... but I didn't touch you ... yet."

Robby began exaggerated gestures with his arms. "Then what ..."

A couple of administrators nearby had started, and now were pulling wooden splinters from various parts of their bodies. One of them spoke up. "Hey, what's the deal with the splinters?"

This time three arrows struck various parts of his armored body as he continued to wave his arms and shift his weight. His antics had already caught the attention of Suevey, who was chuckling when this next volley of arrows struck.

"ATTACK!" She screamed out that one word even as she leapt over prostrate bodies to position herself between the Chancellor and Lydia and the source of the arrows which her mind calculated to be ... "THERE!" Her arm pointed up at the window from which the would-be assassins were launching their arrows. Her own weapon was out and twirling rapidly through the air in tight arcs. More arrows began to be fired rapidly, but every one that came within three or four feet of Suevey was deflected out of its intended path.

Oldive grasped what was truly happening. He took two steps and bent his body over Duncan and Lydia, shielding them from any further danger from that direction with a wall of metal. The other Watchers had weapons out, and as the archers tried to select alternative targets, every arrow was being deflected or shattered outright by the highly skilled protective services. But that left no one able to go after their source. No one, that is, except two rather annoyed engineers.

Robby leapt toward the doorway at the base of the building from which the archers were firing. He took three clunky steps forward only to see his beloved Arianna flying past him with heel-spring power. He was a full step behind her when Arianna landed on the heels of both feet several yards in front of the building. The thick springs propelled her skyward and she soared upward and crashed right through the archer's window.

Robert was not nearly as coordinated as his wife, nor had he anywhere close to as much practice time in the armor. He tried to land as she had, but instead tripped as one toe caught on the ground and instead of sailing skyward he launched almost horizontally off from one heel and ended up cartwheeling through the doorway, just as the six waiting Dominion swordsmen tried running out.

Robby's flailing feet and hands sought to stabilize his crazy flight, but mainly ended up knocking three of the assassins senseless while he landed very heavily on a fourth. His visor had dropped and Robert had no idea of who or what he had just careened into. "Oh … sorry about that … so sorry!" He began to rise just as the fifth swordsman swung down on him with all his might. The sword shattered on Robby's helmet from the left side, and he swung himself roughly in that direction. With the heavy dose of adrenalin coursing through his bloodstream, the awkward armored suit followed his rapid jerk and his outstretched arm, with no real direction from the engineer, smashed into the swordsman's head. He dropped like a rock to the floor.

"Ach, sorry 'bout that!" Robert finally stabilized himself enough to peer out through his visor, just in time to see the sixth Dominion assassin, sword held ready, figure his fortunes were better upstairs with the archers. The man whirled around and raced to the nearby stairs.

"Oh no you don't – not so fast, you!" Robby was slowly catching on to what was happening. He stomped down on his heels and was propelled after the swordsman, landing rather flat footed. The springs pushed him forward and upward. He reached out and just caught the heel of the fleeing assailant and both crashed onto the stair steps. The assassin tried to twist his foot away but Robby was holding on with an iron grip. The man pulled as hard as he could while lying on his back and turned to look up when he heard a heavy clunking noise above him. All he could really see was a strangely shaped metal foot right above his face. His last conscious thought was wondering why the heel looked so very odd …

"Arianna love, are ye alright?"

She flexed her metal sheathed arms. "I kinda like this outfit. It could use a few frills, and it would be far better in pink or purple. Even so, it makes it rather easy to avoid the advances of unwanted men. Maybe every girl should have one."

Robby rolled his eyes, though no one could see that under his visor.

Murdrock wondered if this was all a bad dream, but the sharp pain from where that bumbling clown in armor had stepped on his foot reminded him that he was all too awake. He stood wincing, steadying himself on the small table where he had been sitting before taking a few tentative and quite painful steps away … any direction, just away. He figured this might be a good time to vacate the Keep. Maybe he could still get in on some of the action out in the countryside. At least out there he could hope to team up with his Rats. Staying in the Keep while the Dominion army attacked had never been in the plan anyway. With the assassination foiled – again! – he would just make his exit sooner than planned.

Jarl and his band of Rats had worked their way to a main road and were now nearing the eastern side of the Keep. From the top of a hill Jarl could see the old stone bridge and the large contingent of Watchers guarding it. He grinned. This would be a good vantage point to watch the slaughter.

He was just settling in when he heard something on the morning breeze. Music? MUSIC? He watched in amazement as the troupe from the Music Academy began to wind their way down the road toward the bridge with a large troop of soldiers marching behind them. Jarl squinted and could just make out the little girl second in line – it must be his nemesis, Maria! If she was going to be down there near the battle, then he would be too – there was no way he was going to let some random Dominion soldier claim his prize. He turned to his own 'soldiers'. "Come on Rats … the killing's this way!"

Chapter 27

An Appointment With An Overlord

aeten raced through alleyways and the occasional building that was along the path in his mind that would intersect with the focal source of Dominion evil. A mental image formed, with a brightness centered near the Keep and a dark fog edging closer. And he was right at the juxtaposition between them. Gaeten could not hear it, but he knew the musicians were playing, and that this powerful praise was pushing back at the approaching evil. But the evil was still growing and coming closer.

He had to hurry – he sensed whoever was coming would be intent on stopping that source of strength. And Maria … his Maria … would be at the center of the enemy's focus.

He was very close now. Gaeten ran up to a building wall and began feeling his way, searching for a door. The presence he was seeking was no more than a hundred yards away, maybe just on the other side of this building and closing fast.

Rath Kordoch sensed someone was near, some bright point of Freelandian light that stood out in the spiritual realm against the backdrop of the comforting darkness. His brow furrowed in concentration. There was something familiar with this, something he had sensed before, back in the Dominion. What was it? He shook his head in annoyance as the remembrance eluded him. No matter.

Rath pressed his horse to move faster. He and a handful of Dark Magicians and two dozen of his personal bodyguards had caught up with the tail end of the heavy cavalry as they clamored through the deserted streets. Ahead, the lead armored knights did not pay any attention to the metal pots hanging high above the streets from cables, and no one cared that each had a brightly burning cloth on top. No one paid attention, that is, until the first Fist of God detonated. Metal marbles and spikes hurled downward with terrific velocity. Horses whinnied and men shouted in fear, but no one could discern where the attack was coming from. The burning fuses of a dozen more Fists reached the propellant charge and few could see or hear anything other than the screams of horses and men alike. Walls blew outward directly across from the riders and several streets themselves erupted in gigantic explosions. Before the dust settled, volleys of arrows streamed out of windows, doorways and from building roofs.

From behind, Rath looked wildly around, looking for both an enemy and equally for an escape route. The explosions sounded similar to the sea and air demons they had met near the entrance to Freelandia Bay. Rath shuddered as he realized he had ignorantly thought they had left behind the northern monsters when they had disembarked. These deserted city streets now seemed like a death trap. He quickly glanced around and saw what looked like a large warehouse to the northwest. Rath kicked his horse into motion and reached the warehouse loading door, with several of his brawny bodyguards close behind. One was armed with a large battle ax, and within a few blows the door shattered. Several kicks cleared the remaining wood and offered a wide enough entrance for horses.

Rath kicked his horse through the opening and the Dark Magicians and bodyguards hurriedly followed. The interior darkness and rows of stacked materials slowed them to a walking pace, but at least there did not seem to be any earth-demons or enemy archers raining destruction upon them in here. After a moment of getting acclimated to the semi-darkness, Rath pointed roughly northward and his retinue began making its way through the warehouse, with several bodyguards urging their steeds ahead.

He had only gone a few paces when he pulled back on his reins, his forehead knotted in concentration. He felt a presence that he had only felt once before, back in Kardern. Rath's eyes went wide. It was the Freelandian spy who stole the boy from his very grasp!

Gaeten was just entering the large warehouse when he heard wood splintering far down at the other end of the building and the distinctive sound of moving horses. The evil he had been tracking seemed to roll forward like a thick cloying fog. Doubts and fears rose unbidden into his mind and the wound on his leg began to throb with sudden intensity. Gaeten was tired. Tired of fighting, tired of trying, tired of even standing. *Surely he could find some soft place in this warehouse to just sit for awhile. The others could get along without him. They probably didn't even miss him. They never really appreciated his true abilities anyway. He could just find someplace to sit and ... NO!* Gaeten shook his head forcibly. That was not truth! He mentally pushed aside the negative thoughts and turned inward into his own "special place" where he met with God. The purity of that Presence drove out the evil darkness. Gaeten's ears started to pick up a wisp of musical notes floating through the air, light and airy. He smiled and whispered, "Thank you, God. You have always been here for me. Fill me with Your strength and guide my hands and feet."

His smile turned into a calculating thin line of determination and he launched himself forward, weaving through the rows and racks that filled the warehouse, the faint echoes of his light tread creating a mental map of his surroundings.

Several bodyguards had trotted ahead along adjoining rows. There was no other noise besides that of their steeds, but those rhythmic clacks of hoof on wooden floorboards effectively hid the swooshing sound of a staff slicing through the air. The second bodyguard heard a thud of something falling and he frowned, lifting his ax into a more ready position. He tried to peer over toward his leading companion, but the only thing he saw with clarity was the end of a staff moving with great velocity into his face. His eyes crossed following its movement and a moment later a second thud sounded.

Rath Kordoch had not heard the thuds, but he did see the second bodyguard up ahead tumble from his horse to fall motionless on the floor. His eyes went wide and his face contorted into a mask of rage as he spit out, "It's the Freelandian spy from Kardern! Find him! Kill him!"

Gaeten had never met the Overlord, but he certainly had felt his presence. And without doubt this was the source of evilness he was seeking to stop. He leapt atop a pile of what felt like grain sacks and threw one of his knives in the exact direction the words had come from. Unfortunately, one of the Dark Magicians had just kicked his horse to surge ahead and the first projectile buried itself in the wrong person. The Magician wondered what magic had caused an odd wooden handle to just appear in his side before the pain burned through the fireweed in his veins. He shrieked and reflexively kicked his horse, which bolted ahead of the group. One of the bodyguards spotted Gaeten and charged forward with a yell. Gaeten did not know for sure who he had hit, but did not think it was the Overlord. Then he had no time left to wonder about that.

Even as the bodyguard and his mount closed the distance, Gaeten was lifting one of the bags of grain at his feet and swung it and his entire body in a full circle before releasing the bag. The guard was only a dozen feet away when the heavy sack smacked into his chest. He was lifted right out of his saddle and flung backwards, but the other guards and Dark Magicians saw the movement and converged on the spot where the grain bag had originated in its flight.

Gaeten had already leapt off the pile of grain sacks and was circling around other stacked items, working his way to close in on the Dominion Overlord. His wounded leg was aching and he was concerned about how it would impair his fighting ability. The noises of the horses and moving men bounced around inside the warehouse, making a confusing mash of echoed sounds.

Gaeten rounded a bale of something that smelled like slightly musty cloth and someone spotted him. Two men came rushing, weapons ready. Gaeten thrust his staff at one in a blocking maneuver and nearly simultaneously kicked at the other with satisfying results. The first parried with what sounded like a sword, but Gaeten's staff was faster. One end blocked the sword thrust and the other end spun forward to strike the Dominion attacker squarely on his forehead.

But even as that man fell, two more rushed in and Gaeten could hear others coming from both sides. Worse, he heard horse hooves clicking away – the Overlord apparently was continuing northward through the warehouse, leaving his underlings for Gaeten to fend off. Gaeten could not let him get away. He twirled to his right and sprinted directly into the Dominion fighters coming from that direction. He dodged one and clubbed another, continuing his pursuit. Yet he could hear the Overlord's horse moving faster and nearing the far exit. Gaeten picked out a sound he was searching for, leapt upon a stack of earthy-smelling crates and launched himself through the air.

The rider-less horse whinnied in surprise as Gaeten landed awkwardly upon its back. There was no way he could have done better without knowing exactly where and how the horse was situated, but the landing was good enough for Gaeten to grab a handful of mane and he quickly pulled himself into a more proper position. The horse had begun moving forward on its own from shock, and it took little additional prodding for it to gallop toward the other horse it could see ahead. Even as he squeezed inward with his legs, he felt renewed wetness trickle down his injured leg.

Many of the Dominion bodyguards and Dark Magicians saw their adversary's escape and scrambled back to their own horses to give chase, with all of the others close behind.

The Dominion foot soldiers were in barely recognizable regiments as they surged forward, trying to follow the path the cavalry and their Supreme Commander had taken. Their sergeants and captains were cursing the horse soldiers who had sped ahead and would likely get the honor of breaking through the enemy lines first, and thankful the ground gods of this cursed Freelandian soil had stopped their awful fury after having eaten up well over a third of the rear troops. As the front line foot soldiers came within range, roof mounted catapults opened up, hurling thousands of smooth stones which pounded down upon the unsuspecting attackers. Hurriedly the soldiers raised their small shields, while the cat and spring gun launchers turned to heavier projectiles.

A Dominion ground commander recognized the threat and yelled out, "To the buildings!" Rough ranks dissolved as the Dominion soldiers scrambled off the streets of death. Even as they barged into buildings and raced upwards, Freelandian crews hurriedly abandoned their mounted weapons and escaped over planks placed across adjoining rooftops, which were dropped to the streets below after use.

The Freelandian defenses were formed in rings, and as one layer collapsed the next opened fire on the advancing troops. But the sheer volume of Dominion forces was rapidly overwhelming the defenders, who were now falling back faster and faster. The Freelandians finally seemed to be in the process of being routed.

Miguel knew he had little chance of reuniting with Gaeten, though he had scoured the immediate area where he had last observed the Grand Master to be. Instead, he began to engage and dispatch the groups of two or three Bashers that were roaming his area of the warehouse district. But he felt a constant nagging in his mind that he was needed elsewhere … somewhere northward. Miguel jogged up a street and turned into a long narrow alleyway heading north. He had traversed most of its length when a contingent of several dozen Dominion infantry men marched past the alley opening ahead. Miguel sprang sideways in an attempt to avoid being spotted, but to no avail.

Their leader shouted out, "Finally, a flesh-and-blood Freelandian! Get 'im, men!" The squad sprinted into the alleyway. Miguel spun and raced away from them, but had only made it a short distance when a hellhound rounded the corner at the other end of the alley, nose to the ground. It obviously had been tracking him. The chain trailing behind the hound ended in the grasp of a huge Basher, with two equally large companions.

Miguel stopped. He took a deep breath and smiled thinly. "I am and have always been Your servant, my Savior. If this is to be my end, so be it. But I know I am immortal until the moment you are done with me!" He stood sideways, one sword in each hand raised toward opposing foes.

The hellhound's chain was loosed and it lunged forward in a gallop. It was faster, but the leading foot soldiers were closer and already running. Miguel turned to face the more immediate human attackers. His swords flicked outward far faster than the closing fighters expected, and the first two tumbled to the ground, not to rise again. The low growls from the hellhound behind him were very near, and Miguel was wondering how he would deal with it and the rest of the arriving soldiers. He stole a glance backward while fending off the first sword strokes. His eyebrows shot heavenward when what looked like part of the wall just behind him erupted outward and a long black sword cut short the hellhound's rushing attack. He had no time to consider that further, but gave his full attention to the pressing attacks from the Dominion soldiers who were now filling the alleyway in front of him.

The alley was narrow enough that only two or three assailants could confront Miguel at any one time. And he was thankful that none had bows. While the Watcher's skill was considerably greater than anyone he faced, a new soldier automatically filled in any fresh vacancy. After dropping the eighth or ninth soldier, Miguel's arms were tiring from the constant blocks, parries, thrusts and slashes. His slower movements took their toll and he inadvertently cried out when an unexpected spear thrust penetrated his defenses and nicked his right arm. His rhythm faltered momentarily and an attacking solider pressed in aggressively, his sword slipping past Miguel's parry. For the second time Miguel's eyebrows rose in surprise as a long dark blade appeared from behind him to block the blow and deal its perpetrator a fatal reprisal.

"You seem to be slipping, my friend. Perhaps you would like to sit this one out and allow me to finish these off?"

"Chu! I wondered if you were the animated brickwork that stopped that hellhound! But why were you in this alley?" Miguel did not stop his swordplay while speaking, and if anything he acted almost casual as he finished off one solider before him while engaging yet another. Yet Chu could see his friend slightly favoring his right arm.

Chu's blade flicked out and another soldier fell. "I was heading this way myself and saw you duck into this alley. I was right behind you and slipped in just before the Bashers and that hellhound sniffed you out. You know, my friend …" Chu was momentarily interrupted as he dispatched yet another attacker. "… I think I could track your scent nearly as easily as that hound. Did you really have to put on that cologne before joining the defense against the Dominion? It is not like this is Rhoditian, after all."

Miguel's face turned red, but his sword did not pause in its lethal dance. "Just because I choose to face death like a gentleman and not like a … a …" His sword flicked out and finished the last of the soldiers. A sly grin stole over his face. "… like a flaming wall-spider, doesn't make my sword any less lethal than, say, certain drumsticks I once encountered!"

Miguel had slid a step sideways as he spoke, and even so just barely missed a flying forearm snapped in his direction.

"You smelly ingratiate! I should have let that hound see if you tasted as well as you stink!" Chu was scowling as he stared with squinted eyes at his fellow Watcher.

"Oh, so you like this cologne? I picked it up for next to nothing in the Keep just yesterday. Seems like the few stores that were open had heavily discounted supplies, for some odd reason." Miguel had sheathed one of his swords and was now smiling innocently while twirling his mustache with his free hand.

"Miguel, you are incorrigible! Now let me pass. I have a strong sense that I am to be elsewhere. I feel I am supposed to be heading …"

Miguel stopped his antics and stared at Chu. Both finished the sentence simultaneously. "… northward!"

Chapter 28

A Race To The Finish

than and Quentin were on the rooftop of the tallest office building in the area, located nearly at the end of the warehouse district just before the open field that led up to the bridge. Hundreds of other archers ringed the buildings nearby, many having nearly exhausted their arrow supply while decimating the Dominion cavalry. From their vantage point, Ethan and Quentin could see a swarm of Dominion foot soldiers advancing through the streets in their direction. Ethan could just make out other Dominion cavalry and what were likely Bashers off in the distance in different directions. It seemed to him like they were moving in confusing patterns, but all seemed to be converging toward the field to the north.

But there was now no more time to think about that as the enemy soldiers charged forward and into his considerable bow range. As Ethan nocked his first arrow though, the enemy soldiers suddenly seemed to slow, at least in his eyes. A few moments later, they seemed as though slogging through thick syrup. He began to fire, sending arrows along the blue ribbons that glowed brightly in his mind.

Quentin did not mind being assigned as an assistant to Ethan, knowing his fellow Watcher's awesome ability with a bow. Even so, he figured his own preparations may have been overly zealous. He had better than a thousand arrows up on the roof top, packed in bundles of twenty-five to a quiver. Quentin was looking out at the advancing Dominion troops when he heard the bow string start to thrum with a nearly constant buzz. He turned with a second quiver in his hands and had to avert his gaze before his eyes crossed from the strain of trying to actually see what his comrade was doing. Wisely, he just held up the quiver. In less than a minute he felt it getting lighter, though he could barely see the arrows actually being removed and fired. With his other hand he reached for another quiver, barely in time to keep the streak of motion next to him fed with deadly projectiles. Quentin swallowed hard, wondering if his supply of a thousand arrows was now perhaps shortsighted.

In her 'special place' Maria could see that the darkness had been pushed back somewhat, but now a sprawling cloud of especially thick blackness was pushing back against the headway they had made and was inexorably advancing upon her. She was growing very tired, but began one of the latest worship songs that spoke of God's goodness and love. It filled her with renewed hope and Maria pushed back at the darkness that threatened to engulf her, not even noticing two particularly black tendrils that were curling out from the sides to nearly touch her. But the dark dragon was again moving closer and it seemed as though its entire focus was solely on her.

"I will destroy you, little girl. I will devour you and then each of your companions and then everyone you have ever held dear. You cannot stop me. No one can stop me."

Maria winced as the evil words seemed themselves to bite into her. But she knew there was One who could stop the evil.

Rath Kordoch lifted a foot from his stirrup and kicked at the door he somehow knew would be an exit from the warehouse. Evil power flowed through his body and the door broke free from its hinges. He urged his horse out into the street and began a slow trot. His face was contorted into a fearsome sneer as shadows seemed to thicken and concentrate around him. Rath could nearly see the dark power around him, and also the focal point of the Freelandian resistance – a near pinpoint of light that lay not far to the north. It was close. It was time to snuff it out once and for all. Without a thought to those he was leaving behind, the Overlord dug in his heels and charged forward. The street before him split into two paths. He choose the wider, better paved option, figuring that would be the most likely path leading toward the Keep itself and what he knew would be his ultimate destiny. The smile on his face became even crueler. *Rath the Destroyer*, he thought. *That would be a fitting epitaph …no, engraving on the golden statue in my honor*, he corrected himself.

He travelled no more than a block when he ran into the remnants of a cavalry unit, who immediately formed up around him. His progress was slowed, but it was no matter. The horsemen would be his new honor guard.

Gaeten was less than a minute behind, and ducked just in time to avoid being unseated by the doorway designed for human rather than equine travel. Once out on the street he urged his horse after the sounds of the hoofs ahead of him. The horse cantered forward and with no visible prompting veered up the narrow path. Gaeten had not been able to find the reins, and so pulled on the horse's mane, trying to alter its course as he heard the sounds of the Overlord's horse veer off in a different direction. It was to no avail. His horse stubbornly refused to turn. Gaeten considered leaping off, but something seemed to keep him in place and ease his concerns. "Alright, Lord … have it Your way. Send me where You want!"

The Overlord's bodyguards and accompanying Dark Magicians thundered down the street. They did not know in which direction Rath had gone, but they could clearly see their Freelandia adversary, and they were gaining on him rapidly.

Jarl and his team made their way slowly, avoiding notice as they eased their way into an intersection where the path they had taken from the eastern coastal road merged with the main thoroughfare that ran from the warehouse district across the stone bridge and up to the Keep. They were just out of sight through the trees from the city and the thousands of defenders who would be stationed at its entrance. Jarl motioned for his men to wait alongside the empty section of road, the better to attack the Freelandians when they fled the bridge and the inevitable slaughter. It was a perfect spot for an ambush. He would catch the fleeing Freelandians between the swords of the Dominion invasion force and the pack of his Rats here. Jarl smiled. Surely this would earn him great praise. Surely his initiative would be well rewarded.

He could hear the music coming from the direction of the bridge most clearly, and it filled his mind with hatred and anger. With his men well positioned, Jarl left them with his second-in-command and took a different course of action. He jauntily strode down the road acting like one of the other volunteers arming the Keep. The bridge was almost in sight, and that must be where the musical instruments were being played. That was where Maria must be. Jarl blended into the defenders, working ever closer toward the ludicrous band playing while a war was raging.

Ethan had nearly run out of arrows, firing them at impossible speeds. Quentin merely held first one full quiver and then three at a time. When only one remained he tugged on Ethan's sleeve. His comrade's eyes had a far-away look, but at the insistent tug they refocused. Ethan turned to look at Quentin and in a moment he nodded in understanding and lowered his bow. Time returned to normal speed as Ethan could see Dominion soldiers climbing over the strewn piles of bodies decorated with feathered shafts.

The two young men ran to the far side of the roof and clipped strong ropes attached to shoulder harnesses they wore to a taut line running from a post on top of the building to a point several hundred yards away on the ground. Giving each other a shrug – they had never tested this before – each jumped off the building.

The hooks attached to the line held as both Quentin and Ethan slide down the steep rope, gaining speed as they went. Seconds later they reached the ground and came to a running stop on the street, now quite a distance away. They removed their harnesses and had just started to jog across the open field when they were met by Miguel and Chu.

The foursome neared the bridge but turned at the sound of hooves. All turned to see Gaeten on what appeared to be a Dominion horse heading their way at a full gallop, reins dangling from the horse's bridle. Bearing down on him only a few yards behind were over a dozen enemy riders. Even as they were taking this in, Dominion forces began pouring out of the warehouse district from every possible angle. And all were charging directly at the Freelandians making their last stand at the bridge.

The Watchers turned back and hurried forward to make a united stand with the Freelandian forces. As they arrived Miguel turned to look back and was startled to find Chu missing. *'Just like him to disappear when the fun is about to start',* he thought.

Chapter 29

Focal Point

C ommodore Moorhead shook his head in amazement at God's grace. He and the Alterian crew had sailed the Dominion Dreadnaught right past the outer guard of Dominion vessels and up to the sole enemy ship attending the very entrance to Freelandia Bay. That ship, however, had been another Dreadnaught, the *Darkness*. But it had shown no suspicions as they approached, knowing that no other navy could boast of the awesome and indomitable size of these mountains-of-the-sea. The Alterian crew had pretended to be Dominion sailors, replete with the correct clothing and lightened skin to match. They had come to within a hundred feet of the unsuspecting enemy vessel, and then had turned the loaded catapults directly at them. With a good many of his crew on deck to see the unexpected arrival of a second Dreadnaught, the Dominion captain had little choice but to surrender. Prince Erkatan had led a mixed crew of Alterians and Freelandians to immediately board and commandeer the vessel, putting the former crew into locked and guarded holds.

Moorhead had only a short time to reflect on the blessing. The rest of his fleet arrived an hour later and a pitched battle began with the remaining Dominion ships. Both he and Erkatan hoisted makeshift Freelandian flags from the two Dreadnaughts and entered the fray. As Dominion captains saw this turn of events they panicked and scattered, trying to escape the jaws that closed in on them from before and behind. The naval war was effectively over, but no one knew what might be happening within the Bay or shores of Freelandia. For all of the mercy shown to them thus far, Moorhead knew he very well could be the Commodore of a navy that had no country left to come home to. Before the entire crew he knelt and prayed a prayer of thanksgiving, and of deliverance. On the other Dread-naught, Prince Erkatan was already doing the same.

The re-flagged *Darkness* was left with a large support fleet of Free-landian and Alterian vessels while the *Dreadful* and sixty other ships of the combined ally forces shot through the straights. Commodore Moorhead, knowing the abilities of the coastal gunners, made sure every ship was fly-ing large and highly visible Freelandian flags.

Jo-Nakar was terribly confused and becoming frightened. The head-ache caused by using too much fireweed did not help at all. His large group of Bashers had moved as fast as they could muster toward what looked like the city, but as they approached, it did not seem like their intended target. All they could see was a blinding white light up the road before them, so bright they could not look in that direction for more than a second before turning away or shielding their eyes. Worse yet, he could just make out huge white beings holding what appeared to be flaming swords standing in obvious guard to the north. No, that was certainly NOT the way he was going. Those white beings terrified him down to his very core. Nothing in this world could make him go that direction.

This must not be the way. The thought came into his mind clearly through the fireweed haze. He heard the sounds of running feet to his right, down a road that seemed to curve away and downward. That MUST be the way, he figured. Jo-Nakar turned and began to jog down the road and his Bashers followed, glad to get away from the terrifying visage. Be-sides, running downhill was far easier. This day was not at all turning out like they had expected. Every Basher was just itching to finally fight something they could see and hear and touch. It was driving them crazy. Their pent up fireweed rage had been stoked and bottled up far too long, and now they were ready to attack the first people they saw that gave them the least bit of resistance.

Rath Kordoch had finally worked his way to the front of the cavalry unit when he turned a corner and faced an open field. *Finally*! he said more to himself than to the horsemen behind him. Then he winced in pain as the power of the worship music blasted against his evil bulwark of strength. Movement to his left caught his attention, and he scowled in fury as he first felt the presence and then saw the Freelandian spy, who he thought had been finally finished back in the warehouse, galloping across the open ground. His own retinue appeared to be hot on his heels. Everything seemed to be focused on the stone bridge he could just make out across the field. Rath also sensed the dark presence of the Bashers who now were running toward the same goal from behind. *How nice of them to congregate in one place where we can finish them off once and for all*, he thought as he spurred his horse to charge forward. It was all coming together now. Now he would crush this cursed enemy. Now he would fulfill his destiny. Now he would be known forever as "Rath the Destroyer." Now the Dominion would rule the world.

The blasted source of the spiritual strength seemed to lie just ahead also, and Rath's keen eyes could see a man at the front of a troupe of musicians holding a trumpet. The loathsome brightness was emanating from right in that vicinity. As he rode forward the dark tendrils of evil concentrated around him. He pointed his arm forward. "Get him!"

Master Vitario was very winded – actually too winded. He was no longer playing his trumpet and he stopped walking just short of the bridge, leaning on a nearby Watcher for support. The pain in his shoulder had gotten stronger, and seemed to be spreading both down his arm and back toward his chest. If he could only catch his breath … He choked as an icy presence seemed to wrap itself around him, squeezing. Vitario's eyes bulged as his chest constricted inward. A gust of cold fear swept over the Freelandians, paralyzing them in place. It seemed as though all color drained away and everything took on a death-like pallor. Sound seemed to deaden so that even the music seemed to lack life.

Maria was utterly exhausted as she danced and wove the strands of music, even though the dark shadows were blotting out large portions of her vision and obscuring even the living sounds in which she was moving.

A black wisp of cloud coiled out and grabbed one of the strands with which Maria was working, choking it off. Its bright blue color faded to a dull translucent gray, and she winced as a shooting pain seemed to lance back at her. Maria cried out and faltered, and the dark cloud pushed in further as though it sensed weakness. Fear washed over her again. Even in her special place, color seemed to drain away and a bone numbing cold washed over her and totally immobilized her.

All sounds of life around her were drowned out. Maria felt all alone as the gaping jaws of the dragon again opened directly in front of her. Death seemed to be all about her. She shivered in the stillness.

Yet Maria knew she was not alone. Even if she could not turn, she knew in her heart that her Audience was always present. The fearsome evil edged yet closer and Maria seemed to feel its chilling breath wash over her. *This must be the end*, she thought with resignation.

The heavy spiritual oppression had caused nearly all other movement of the defenders at the bridge to stop, frozen in place. Even the music had faded away as each musician battled internally with the fearful dread and lifelessness that drained away all vitality and chilled them to their bones.

Rath sneered. The foolish Freelandians ahead were standing at the bridge with gaping mouths – finally the demonic forces had battled through and were overwhelming all resistance. Rath almost laughed. And they thought they could stand before the Dominion! They thought they could stand before the all-powerful evil lords who empowered the Dominion forces! They must be terrified down to their souls at the fearful apparition about to run them down – as well they should. *They should pray to their puny weak god that they will die today*, he thought to himself. For anyone remaining will surely pay a heavy price for the blow they had made to the Dominion war machine. Freelandia would be punished most severely for the trouble they had caused.

Rath saw two young men at the forefront of the Freelandian forces at the bridge ahead of him and recognized one as the son of the Chancellor, that mongrel who had somehow escaped his clutches back in Kardern. *How nice of him to join the others, just before they all die*, he thought smugly. He drew his huge long sword. It was time to begin to satiate his thirst for Freelandian blood. And he was so very much going to enjoy beginning that feast first with the boy and then with those musicians who stood such a short distance across the bridge. And maybe that dratted spy too, if his bodyguards did not finish him off first. Rath did laugh this time, more like a feral snarl. They thought to repel his horde with a song, did they? In time they would learn the music of the Dominion, music calculated to tear down resistance to baser thoughts and behaviors, to lead away from the light and inexorably draw men's souls into darkness.

Even as the dragon jaws were closing over her, a memory flitted into Maria's thoughts. She saw herself sitting by still water in the darkness, light rain pattering over her and creating its own cadence at the water's surface. All creation seemed to be palpably present, waiting in anticipation. In growing wonder Maria saw her current situation superimposed over that memory. One was so very, very peaceful and full of pent up joy, just waiting to be expressed. The other was so terrifyingly dreadful … but in both she could sense an immense waiting … waiting for the dawn.

Maria closed her eyes to the imminent doom moments from consuming her. She mentally turned from her consuming fear and searched out to feel the presence of her God. It was there, right behind her, unchanged. Her heightened spiritual senses spread out to take in her surroundings. All was frozen in fear, but there was more. She began to sense God's presence not just behind her, but all around her, infusing all of His creation. And everything seemed to be holding back somehow, waiting. Waiting not for its destruction … but for its release. Maria could sense an immensity waiting, like a gigantic flood of spiritual energy barely held in place. She knew what to do now. It was time for the joy of the Dawn Chorus of creation to be released.

In that moment of time, Maria saw the pent up prayers of saints, also waiting for release. It was rather like a gigantic mountain of water, restrained until now, ready and waiting to be released. She had not seen this before, but realized it had always been here, held back by the hand of God until His appropriate time. Why had she feared? Their Deliverer was prepared and standing by.

Maria lifted the Diamond Violin. She cocked her head to one side, listening to the low resonance of creation itself as it continually praised its Maker. It was not one of her songs she would play. It was one of His.

As she became even more attuned to this primal spiritual energy she even began to feel her own body respond ... it too was part of creation like everything else. A portion of this energy poured into Maria such as she had never known before, not even when she had battled the dark forces during the first battle the Freelandian navy had had with the Dominion fleet. Her face began to glow with supernatural radiance to the point that it obscured her features. She could not tell – both because of her blindness but also because she was totally caught up with God's presence in her special place. Maria began to play and as once before it was as though all of creation began to join in ... or perhaps better, she was joining it. There were no words, just a primal joyous tune that thundered like a thousand mighty waterfalls singing praise to the Creator. Maria joined in, adding the praise and prayers of the people. She felt her body begin to tremble and shake as though the very cells of her body were taking part.

Rath was only a short distance behind the contingent of Dark Magicians and his own bodyguards, having a shorter distance to the bridge from where he had exited the warehouse area. He almost hoped the lead elements would stumble so that he ... Rath the Destroyer ... would be at the apex of the Dominion's final, decisive blow. A moment later it appeared that his wishes were coming true. Directly before him, the lead horses of his bodyguards suddenly stopped and reared skyward, whinnying in fright. Bodyguards and Dark Magicians began sprouting feathered shafts and toppling from their mounts. The horses and men right in front of him shied left and right and at a flash of black steel one mount became rider-less.

Directly before him was some apparition, some Freelandian earth monster who was dealing death to all who came near. Rath's eyes bulged and he instinctively goaded his horse to the right, swinging his own sword at the dirt and grass covered figure. But the ground fiend had already moved to the left after one of his hapless bodyguards.

Rath saw no Dominion forces between him and the focus of his rage ahead. He would let the others deal with this latest monster. It seemed rather limited after all, not like the sky and water demons they had prevailed against earlier. He kicked his horse forward.

A Dark Magician tried to follow his leader, but as he turned his fidgeting horse he found himself heading directly into … The lead Magician's eyes widened in fear as the earthen monster swung a long black sword. It was the last thing he was afraid of … at least in his earthly life, which ended a fraction of a second later.

Chu swiveled and swung again, taking down another Dominion enemy. Additional enemy cavalry was charging forward. Chu's sword rose and sliced in a steady, frightful rhythm of death.

Jo-Nakar and his band of Bashers thundered down the path. To the right and to the left blinding white light shone. His fireweed clogged mind only saw one way forward, straight down the road they were on. A short ways up from the bridge there was a turn in the road that led down to the stonework itself, and there he saw dozens of young men with weapons drawn. Finally! An enemy to attack! Even as his mind focused – as best it could – on the armed men before him, his feet felt the ground below begin to quake and the air around him somehow tremble in unison. If he had been afraid before, now he felt a terror welling up that overwhelms all rational thought. In this mindless rage he charged at what must be an enemy force directly in front of him.

The band of Rats were watching the curve of the pathway towards the bridge, expecting at any moment to hear running steps as terrified Freelandians tried to race for the temporary safety of the Keep. They heard pounding feet and for a moment thought their time had come. Each raised their weapons but then realized the sound was coming from behind them. The Rats spun, weapons high and ready.

Jo-Nakar saw the enemy turn his way, weapons up … but they were no match for the pent up ferocity and strength of the Southern Bashers. The Rats were cut down where they stood. Their blood lust barely whetted, the Bashers raced down toward the corner of the pathway, looking for more enemy.

"Gaeten, over here!" shouted Miguel. He helped his fellow Watcher down, noticing the large red patch on the horse's coat. "You're hurt, my friend! Let me bind that better." Miguel's knife was whipped out of its sheath and he cut off the end of his own sleeve. He expertly tied it over Gaeten's wound.

"Thanks, but a sword, Miguel! Get me a sword!" Gaeten knew he had no time for niceties. Without hesitating Miguel pressed one of his own matched pair into the Grand Master's outstretched hand. Ethan came alongside his elderly friend, having exhausted the arrows from the last quiver Quentin had brought along. Gaeten smiled, recognizing the presence of his young sparring partner. They turned to face the threat bearing down on them with thundering hooves.

The other musicians could only sense a tiny part of the creation chorus stirring around them, but they could hear Maria's violin. With greater skill than most had known they possessed, they rapidly picked up the tune with newly found energy and enthusiasm. None but Maria had ever played anything like it before, but each somehow tuned into what the Spirit of God was doing, getting on board a massive musical and spiritual juggernaut that thundered outward, breaking the strength of evil. The power swelled, and Maria danced among it in her special place, feeling more alive than ever before. The ribbons of sound crackled with energy and she joyously wove the strands into even tighter coherence and sent it blasting directly into the cloud dragon right on top of her. It recoiled in surprise, giving

Maria more room to dance and weave the worship. Yet she did not even notice. She was no longer fighting or fearing. She was just worshiping before her Audience and in some incredible glorious way joining in with creation in praise.

Maria noticed a complimentary tune spring up in her mind. Somehow the words to Reginaldo's Masterpiece seemed so very fitting, sung to this … this anthem of God. She began to sing.

Reginaldo was right beside her and was starting to take a step forward to help Vitario when he felt an awesome power welling up, one that could not be ignored and that made the hairs on his arms stand up and his massive body begin to quiver in resonance. The air around him began to sparkle and snap with energy, and as he turned he could not even look upon Maria's face other than to see it was upturned toward heaven. He both heard and felt the ancient song of creation swelling around and somehow in him and he marveled. Then in a few moments, Reginaldo heard the words to his … no, Maria's Masterpiece begin. Without a moment's hesitation he stopped everything else he was doing or even thinking and joined in.

The two singers had taken a few steps forward and now were just standing on the bridge itself, and the spiritual force seemed to funnel out clearing a pathway before them. In a moment, the only others on the bridge were the four Watchers out front, defiantly holding their position.

Miguel finally noticed the earthen figure a stone's throw out into the field. He leapt forward and sprinted toward his friend, his single sword swinging.

Rath saw the Freelandian warrior sprint past him and let him go. The massive Dominion army behind him would chew the lone soldier up and spit him out as an appetizer before a great slaughter. Rath kicked his steed forward, only to see the Chancellor's boy swing a long bow over his head and launch it directly toward him. The bow flipped end over end and somehow struck the head of the Overlord's horse squarely. Rath Kordoch awkwardly leapt off as his mount faltered and then crumpled to the ground. He was only a few yards away and closed that gap at a staggering run. Rath noticed the music had changed, and now it seemed like the very air around him was closing in and the ground below seemed to be clutching as his passing feet. He shrugged it off. He knew the evil power filling him would prevail, as it always had.

The Overlord's huge sword swung at the empty handed Ethan. In Ethan's perspective, the sword moved in slow motion. The sword sliced through the air missing him, but now was headed straight for Gaeten. Miraculously, Quentin somehow managed to get his long curved sword in its path, deflecting the blow even as Gaeten was swinging his own sword to counter it. Gaeten's sword struck Quentin's and spun it out of the youth's hands.

Ethan saw the slowly spinning sword swerving through the air to come directly his way and followed the path of action outlined by the blue line in his mind. His hand closed around the sword's hilt as he rolled and bounced back up to stand ready. Quentin prudently scurried backwards and both Ethan and Gaeten stepped in close together to block the Overlord's path. Ethan recognized Rath Kordoch, and a small grim smile grew onto his face.

Gaeten also recognized the evil presence and spoke first, loud enough to just be heard over the swelling music from behind him. "I missed meeting you in Kardern. How thoughtful of you to come for a visit. Pity it will be so short."

Rath was in a wild rage, with shrunken black tendrils curling over his arms and around his body. He was personified evil. Gaeten's words frothed him to a fever. "You!" The accusation had just left his mouth when he swung a mighty blow not at the older man, but at what he hoped was an unsuspecting Ethan.

The blade inched along its path and quivered as though the Overlord was fighting to keep its aim straight. Ethan saw how to deflect it and grasped the long tang two-handed and swung in the prescribed blue arc he saw in his mind. Then as fast as he could move his leaden-seeming muscles he countered with a devastatingly fast swing of his own at the Overlord's legs.

Somehow the large man jumped upward in time and the blade passed just under him. At the same time, Rath drew a long knife with his left hand and deflected Gaeten's fast sword strike. The three became a whirl of action so fast-paced that the onlookers could not really tell what was happening. Thrust. Swing. Parry. Jump. Crouch. Lunge.

Ethan and Gaeten had sparred for years, and so knew each other's likely actions quite well. But both were hard pressed to find an opening or weakness as Rath Kordoch fought with inhuman strength and speed even as his weapons appeared to balk within his grasp. His eyes were glowing red as he pressed forward a step, and then another. They were now on the bridge proper, and slowly the Freelandians were being pushed backward by a foe whose visage was becoming blacker and darker as thoughts of doom and despair and doubt flooded outward from him to wash over both his combatants and everyone around them.

Chapter 30

Finale

aria and Reginaldo could not even see what was happening around them. They were totally immersed in the song … the Masterpiece of Creation. As their voices merged into a perfectly harmonious duet, Maria blended in the ribbons from the instruments in her special place. She saw an immense number of bright prayer sparkles and began to blend those in as well. The ribbon worship swelled with each addition, growing more vibrant and pulsing with power. She flung it at the dark tentacles of evil and the cloud dragon that were right before her. The blackness writhed and while it backed up, it seemed to hold. Malevolent blood red eyes shone with hatred and fury.

Maria could feel all of creation around her join fully into the battle, all tuned to the same spiritual frequency that resounded with their joy and praise to their Creator. And it all seemed to be channeling around and through Maria. Yet for her, it was all just a marvelous awesome dance of praise. If she lived, she did not care. If she died, she did not care. Her entire being was here and now before her Audience of One, before her Creator, before her God.

Rath Kordoch swung again at Gaeten. Ethan could see that the blow would not connect, but then realized it was not really intended to. At once he could see several likely moves in advance. In anticipation of the next moves of both Gaeten and the Overlord Ethan lunged, dropped to one knee and stabbed forward and upward with all his strength and blinding speed, saying a frantic prayer.

The thick coiled clouds of spiritual darkness held for a moment longer and then shattered. The evil dragon roared in impotent fury as the wispy curls of dark shadows dissolved into the bright glory that now banished all else.

Gaeten swiveled backwards and to one side, swinging his sword at the exposed head of the Overlord. Rath Kordoch's heavy sword arced past where Gaeten had just been and sliced through the air where Ethan's body was standing a fraction of a second earlier, even as he tried to jerk his head out of Gaeten's reach and parry with his knife. Too late, he realized Ethan's move and twisted his torso toward that threat. It perfectly coincided with the upward thrust, allowing the blade to miss the ribcage and stab directly into the Overlord's heart.

The song of creation continued, now seemingly amplified and lifting high above the battlefield. Ethan and Gaeten took several steps backward and parted, leaving the body of Rath Kordoch alone in the center of the bridge as a massive earthquake began to shake and roll outward from where they had been standing. Chu and Miguel walked in from the edge of the field, as their confused enemy had pulled back, seemingly to regroup.

Jo-Nakar and the remnant of the once strong Basher battalion rounded the last bend in the road at full run. Their first real taste of bloodletting had mixed with the copious amount of fireweed coursing through their veins and turned them into mindless berserkers. The bright white light would not let them turn or stop, and so they raced blindly forward, past the Freelandian army lining the way and then onto the bridge, past the rest of the Freelandians and out into the open field, where what remained of the finest and strongest army the Dominion had ever fielded or that the world had ever witnessed were charging forward to meet them. The ground was heaving around the Dominion troops, and they were blinded by dazzling bright light and deafened with noise like immense rushing wind. Into that chaos came the loud war-whoop of Bashers in sight of their mortal enemy. The soldiers panicked. Each thought the Freelandians were upon them and they all attacked the nearest figure they could make out.

James had come down to the bridge, having tried to keep up with the Bashers when they had been redirected away from the Keep. At his command, the Watchers formed a protective ring in front of the bridge – more to keep the Freelandians from entering the battlefield before them than from any apparent need to keep the enemy away. And there was apparently no particular need yet to use the large spring launchers set up next to the bridge. The Dominion forces were annihilating one another, and as more poured out from the warehouse district they seemed to immediately join the fray. In time, even a few of the wounded pachyderms charged into the incredible brawl, scattering soldiers like toothpicks wherever they ran. One even charged forward toward the bridge, but even as the Watchers prepared to try to stop it the huge animal halted in its tracks as though it had run into some kind of invisible wall. It reared back in confusion, turned, and plunged back into what was becoming a total slaughter.

Maria and Reginaldo sang through the Masterpiece several times, and then both fell silent, knowing their work was done for now. As their voices quieted, the musicians around them slowly wound down as well, until the only major noises seemed to be coming from the self-destruction occurring out in the field. Reginaldo shook his head like he was coming out of a trance and knelt down next to Master Vitario, who was being tended to by a healer. Kory and Ariel were at Maria's side, supporting her as the energy drained away and she might have fallen if they had not been there to catch her. The brightness of her face was still difficult to look directly into, but was slowly fading.

Jarl had worked his way quite close and had his dagger out and by his side. He could not comprehend what he had just witnessed, and was even still seeing and hearing out in the field beyond the bridge. It was her fault … it had to be! Somehow Jarl just knew this utter disaster had to somehow be tied to that little snot of a girl, now being supported by two others who likely were just as bad. But never mind them. His only focus now in life was to sink his knife into that helpless weak form before him.

Jarl lurched forward, raising his dagger. A huge hulking figure was bent over an older man next to Maria, leaving her drooped against another girl of about her same age that Jarl did not recognize. No matter. If needed, he could easily dispatch both of them.

The rather rotund man turned just as Jarl raised his knife to its full extent. With surprising speed, the man launched himself upward. Jarl was totally focused on the point of his blade, oblivious now to all else. He stabbed downward with all his might.

The brightness in her special place had overtaken even the ribbons of sounds, and Maria stood silent and still. The vision in her mind began to fade, and into this transition she heard an odd noise behind her. Maria turned and looked up. Through a haze of light she saw a deadly blade descending, and then a blur of motion intersected her vision. Maria screamed, not knowing what was happening or if she was somehow still in her special place or not.

Reginaldo felt a sharp prick and then a deep burning pain. He ignored it as best he could as his meaty right fist connected with Jarl's evilly grinning face. The blow would have done a prized boxer justice. Jarl was lifted completely off his feet and the force sent him flying backward to land in a crumpled heap, never to rise again. Reginaldo grunted at the effort, and then sat down heavily. The pain was now becoming intolerable and Reginaldo's focus was narrowing as he slumped yet lower to the ground.

Someone held his hand and he looked up into Maria's face staring down at him.

"Maria ..." His voice was weakening. "Maria ... did we ... did God ... is Freelandia safe?"

"I think so, Reginaldo." Maria stared down at her benefactor and friend, reaching a hand out to touch his face, marveling at the double sensory impact. "God has given us a great victory. And He used you to bring it about. You are a hero, Reginaldo."

"Maria – I am no hero. I have been a fat conceited pompous oaf who ignored God most of his life. You on the other hand are a true heroine, who loves God above all and follows His ways." Reginaldo blinked hard and squinted up at Maria, with the bright glow fading now from her. He struggled now to speak, barely getting out a faint gasp. "Maria ... your ... your eyes!"

Maria stared down at him with a pained expression, noticing his dark brown eyes for the first ... and last time. Reginaldo's eyelids fluttered and closed with finality.

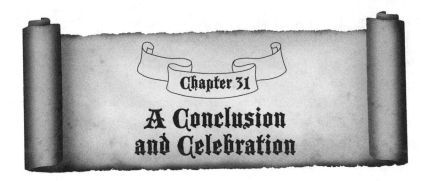

Chapter 31
A Conclusion and Celebration

The next day, Watchers carefully went through the warehouse district and the beach areas looking for any surviving Dominion soldiers. The citizen volunteers began the monumental task of collecting the dead, and Arianna had most of the remaining swamp gas on hand brought out to the field to create a colossal crematorium. There just wasn't any other way to dispose of them all in a timely manner.

A few Dominion ships that had headed toward other ports in the Bay of Freelandia and up some of the larger rivers had been turned back by stalwart shore defenses and had turned to join their comrades out in the Bay before the Keep, but every Dominion captain and sailor had looked with astonishment as a huge fleet of not only Freelandian but, against all expectations, of Alterian navy vessels completely cut off any hopes of escape out to sea. And with sinking hearts they trembled as they saw one of their own mighty Dreadnaughts leading the armada, clearly flying a Freelandian flag atop its highest mast.

In the last two days the remaining Dominion sailors had witnessed their invasion fleet reduced to less than a quarter of what it had been by hosts of sky demons and sea monsters and by impossibly long ranged and accurate shore fire. Even their flagship Dreadnaught the *Dominance* had been scuttled by some unknown terrible forces, whom the few surviving sailors had described as metal scaled fish monsters, impervious to any of their weapons. They even seem to have been attacked by a giant white moth, the likes none had ever heard of. And now they were surrounded by an enemy fleet twice their size and led by a ship so mountainously huge they knew their own puny ships were helpless against it. There was only one thing they could do. Ship after ship raised white flags of surrender.

The Dominion Invasion was over.

Murdrock could see the signs too, even as he holed up in a rundown tavern in ... what was the name of this forsaken place ... Westville ... Weaslewood ... no, it was Westhaven. It had taken most of a day to hobble out of the Keep, keeping a very low profile. And then another day was spent in the back of a farmer's wagon heading any direction as long as it was away. And it would likely take weeks or months before he could walk halfway well again, with a broken foot and a bum knee. Maybe he could take up farming somewhere ... or maybe open a restaurant ... one that specialized in spicy Southern cooking. *Hey* he thought, *that might not be so bad. I've lived on my own these many years; I'm a half way decent cook. I can handle pretty much anything in a skillet or pot, though for the life of me I've never been able to get the hang of baking. It would not be for long term of course ... just until I heal and things quieted down. I could work in a kitchen as a chef, but it would be best to not be out front serving customers. I'd have to see what kind of eatery might exist in this forsaken little town. And preferably one that already had a decent baker ...*

It took a few more days to assess the damages and losses, and to round up the last of the surrendered Dominion forces. Minister Polonos was put in charge of the prisoners, and while technically they were indeed conquered prisoners they were treated with great dignity and kindness. After all, Polonos had argued, they were not the ones responsible for the war and many had been forcibly pressed into military service. Once the fireweed was out of their systems, even the Bashers had calmed and seemed to accept they had been defeated. All were medically examined and given the same level of attention and treatment that Freelandia's own wounded received. And all were told about the one true God that had shown His strength and might against the Dominion.

Duncan was busily going through reports when Chaplain Mikael knocked politely on his door. At the proffered smile and nod, he entered the Chancellor's office.

"Sorry to interrupt you, but I have a pressing matter that needs your personal attention." Mikael sounded serious, but there was a twinkle in his eyes and a warm smile on his face.

Duncan welcomed the break. "Lydia mentioned you would be stopping by, and that I should agree with what you suggested."

Mikael laughed. "God's Spirit certainly has gone before me then, preparing my way! Do you want the details?"

"I would not want to miss them, though I expect it to coincide with what is burning on my heart as well."

"God coordinates His leadings well, doesn't He? Chancellor, we have witnessed the greatest outpouring of mercy and grace since the founding of Freelandia. We had also experienced a tremendous and unprecedented revival of faith and outpouring of the Holy Spirit. And against all human odds and expectations, God has delivered us from the greatest threat we have ever faced." Mikael's tones had risen as he spoke, ending in a fervor that would have been right at home from his pulpit.

Duncan chuckled and played along. He narrowed his eyes and responded, " And so …?"

Mikael's smile was quite contagious. "And so … we need a celebration! A celebration the likes of which we have never had before! And …," his face turned more serious. "a Day of Remembrance. A holy day our children and children's children and all those after will observe. And when they ask why we celebrate that holy-day, what means this Day of Remembrance, we will tell them of how we humbled ourselves before our Creator, worshiped Him in the face of peril, and were delivered by His mighty hand. And, I might add, of the truth of God's Word and of the prophecy given concerning these last days."

Duncan's face had frozen as the Chaplain's words painted a vivid picture in his mind that harmonized completely with what God had already been fomenting in his own mind. A single tear trickled down his face and he could do nothing less than sink to his knees in thankful prayer. In a fraction of a second, Mikael joined him.

A gentle breeze tousled Maria's hair as she slowly made her way down the same path where just two weeks before she had led marching musicians toward a meeting with the Dominion army and the evil spiritual power behind it. She had retraced these steps several times, and always with a disquieting mix of emotions.

Maria could now see the way, but she was unsure if that made it any better. Before she had to walk more fully in faith, but now her sight gave her greater independence, almost as if she did not need God's leading and help as much. But that was not what troubled her most or drew her to the old stone bridge which her feet had now reached.

A few more steps brought her to the very spot, and as each time before, Maria knelt down to touch the dark brown that was etched into her memory as permanently as it seemed stained into the rock. Here is where it had happened. Here is where it ended.

A tear trickled down her face and Maria attempted to intercept it's fall with a jerk of her hand, but failed. The droplet intruded itself onto the stain, seeming in her mind to deface it. She angrily snapped her head back.

"I could not move fast enough either." The voice came from behind her, on the other side of the bridge. Maria spun to see who was intruding on her sorrow.

"I had just finished with two Dominion soldiers, bodyguard of the Overlord I think. I saw a young man on the far side of the bridge, and even at this distance I could see murder in his eyes as he moved toward you." Miguel absently twirled his mustache with one hand. "I tried to yell, but it was much too noisy for anyone to hear me. My feet would not move fast enough. I was no more than half-way across the bridge when the dagger flashed." The Watcher's shoulders slumped and he sighed heavily. "Maybe if I had started off sooner, not even tried to yell a warning. Maybe if I had thrown one of my swords. Maybe …" His words trailed off into silence.

Maria, angry at first at the interruption, saw tears streaming down the face of this man she could not recall having seen before. Her voice broke as she stammered out "You were here?"

"Yes. Or actually just over there." Miguel pointed absently. "I saw Sir Reginaldo move. I had never seen him move that fast! And I saw the knife moving. I knew what was going to happen. But I could not stop it."

"It was not your fault, sir." Maria looked back to the dark stains. "It was mine. Jarl hated me, not Reginaldo. That blade was meant for me. If I had only been stronger, then others may have seen Jarl coming. If I had only done something different back in Westhaven, so Jarl would not have hated me so much. If only God would have …" Maria's words stopped in mid-air, as she finally voiced what was truly troubling her.

Miguel had not noticed. "No, young ma'am. It was my fault. It was my plan that brought Reginaldo back to Freelandia. We could have found another way. The war with the Dominion was no place for a great singer such as Sir Reginaldo. This was a Watcher matter. A Freelandian matter. Bringing a non-combatant into a war zone is inexcusable. The blame is mine."

Maria's eyes were now dry and wide. "You … you brought Reginaldo here? With Gaeten and Ethan and the Alterian prince?"

"Yes, little lady. I see you agree. I am sorry. I brought him here, and it now seems I brought him here to die."

"But sir, you could not have known that! I heard that you and the other Watchers rescued the Chancellor's son, and convinced the Alterians to join us against the Dominion. You are a hero!"

"A hero? Hardly. A servant of God, at best. Grand Master Gaeten did most of the work. And it certainly is God who deserves all the credit." Miguel looked critically at the young woman before him. "And you must be Maria! Reginaldo spoke of you on our journey. He was very fond of you. And from what I saw that day, he voluntarily gave his life to save yours."

Maria looked down, tears again welling up. "Ye …yes. It was voluntary, wasn't it?" She looked back up, searching the Watcher's eyes.

"Yes, Miss Maria. He gave up his life for a friend." Miguel tilted his head in thought. "Perhaps, little lady, it is neither of our faults. Reginaldo made a choice. He chose to value someone else's life higher than his own. He sacrificed himself to save you."

"But …" Maria could accept that Reginaldo's death was not really her doing, not really her fault. But that did not quiet the source of what distressed her the most. "But then why did God choose to save me instead of him? Why did God let him die?" Maria slumped. She had finally said it, finally put words to the jumble of thoughts and doubts and questions that had been plaguing her. She began to cry softly.

Kneeling beside her, Miguel wrapped his long arms around the diminutive girl. "Maria, I truly believe Reginaldo gave his heart to Jesus. We will see him again, you and I. He is now in a far better place. He has been promoted from this life into the next, to now be with God forever. He just gets to start there earlier than us."

Maria leaned into the supporting embrace. "But why did God let that happen? Why would God have wanted Reginaldo to die?"

It was a question that Watchers dealt with perhaps more than most. Miguel pondered his response for a moment before answering. "I don't think anyone can answer that for you, Maria. It is a question only God Himself can truly answer. But know this: His Word says that all things work together for good for those that love Him. I do not know the answers, but I do know that this too is part of "all". God has provided for us magnificently. I have come to trust Him even in such loss." The Watcher sighed. "Perhaps even especially in such circumstances. Faith is easy when life seems good. My faith grows most when it is stretched."

That struck a responsive chord within Maria. She thought back in her own life, recalling how she had learned to trust in God through the many difficulties she had faced.

The sobs quieted and Miguel let the silence hang, allowing time for reflection. After a few minutes, he continued. "I believe both Reginaldo and God would want us both to move on, to continue on in God's service. God may show us His reasons, but even if He does not, yet will I serve Him with all my heart, soul, strength and mind.

I will miss Reginaldo, but I am also happy for him. And I will honor his memory by telling others of his great service to Freelandia and of his final sacrifice. But mostly I will tell of God's great grace and mercy, and of His love for His people. And I will continue to try to do my best at what God directs me to do. For me, that is being a Freelandian Watcher."

Miguel loosened his hug and with a gentle finger lifted Maria's chin to look into her eyes. The tears had stopped and he thought he could detect a hint of resolve forming in his new young friend. "But what, my little lady, is God planning for you?"

A small smile crept onto Maria's face. "So far I think all I know how to do is worship."

Chuckling, Miguel stepped back and gave an exaggerated low bow before her. "That, milady, is a very worthy calling indeed. And if I'm not mistaken, one surely to be put into great use tomorrow at the Day of Remembrance celebration!"

Maria slowly rose. "Thank you, sir Watcher! You have given me many things to think about." She looked down at the brown marks that now somehow looked more like simple discolorations that joined with others on the stone bridge. She looked back up. "I do not even know your name! But I have heard of the rescue mission and of the arrival of the Alterian ship with Ethan, Reginaldo, Gaeten and two other Watchers."

Drawing himself to his full stature, Miguel began another bow.

Maria continued. "By the way you snuck up on me, you must be Master Chu!"

Miguel moaned and rolled his eyes heavenward.

Maria looked over the musical score spread out on the table before her. She, Kory and Master Ariel had spent much of the last two weeks visiting the various classrooms within the Music Academy, listening to ideas the apprentices and Master's alike offered. Then they had condensed it all down into a new song, blended with the Freelandian Anthem ... and even with inspiration from Sir Reginaldo's Masterpiece. The entire Academy would present it: every apprentice and every Master, from the least to the most experienced and talented.

It was ready, as ready as it would ever be. But Maria did not feel she was. The words of the Watcher – with a pained voice he had corrected her that his name was Miguel – still echoed in her mind. And to be honest with herself, her worship had been diluted lately by the feelings of guilt and loss they had discussed on the bridge. She felt that conversation was the start of a healing process, but the questions still lingered.

With all the excitement within the Academy and the last minute preparations, there was no place here she could find the quietness she needed to finally bring her questions to the only source of answers. Maria looked about the room and noticed a flute slung in a protective cloth sleeve hung up on a wall. A memory flitted across her mind, bringing a smile to her face. It was late, so she slowly walked to her and Kory's apartment. She wanted to get as much sleep as she could before her planned very early morning departure.

The darkness of the pre-dawn posed no problems for Maria as she picked her way along a familiar trail. She wondered if she would lose some of her confidence in the dark, now that she could see. She figured it would be a well-worthwhile trade.

The quietness of still water soon overcame the nocturnal noises. Maria made her way to the same spot she had been those weeks before when she had sought to escape from the doubts and insecurities that had threatened to overwhelm her. She sat, letting the stillness quiet her current worries one by one until the peacefulness of the location was all that was left.

Inside, she pictured herself standing in her special place, before her Audience of One. His comforting presence spread over her. Maria was about to begin a song of worship when the familiar voice came clearly to her.

"You are troubled, my child. Be still and rest in the knowledge that I am your God. I made you. I work all things together for good, even the things you do not understand. You have learned to trust me in the past. Trust me now! I taught you to trust me in little things so that you will be able to trust me in bigger things. You are weak … I made you that way! In your weakness I am shown strong. But do not let your confusion or fear or doubts stop you from doing what is good and right. Did I not use you – in your weakness – as my chosen weapon against the Dominion evil? Did I not infuse you with my power when you needed it? I choose the foolish, the weak and the base things so that no one can claim glory in my presence. I delight in using these, and I delight in my children … and I delight in you!"

Maria could not stand or speak, and tears streamed down her face. She felt a wave of … of delight … wash over her as though God were sharing a tiny portion of His view of her. It overwhelmed her senses, ushering in an immense feeling of contentment, completeness and of wholly belonging right where she was. She had never felt so … so entirely loved. Not for what she could accomplish, not for who she might become or even for what love she could give back. She was fully loved for just who she was, just for who she was created to be. It was somehow peaceful and energizing all at once. And the love was not passive. It was intense, active, right now. It reached down to her innermost being and engulfed her.

Maria could not tell for how long this lasted. She could only be totally held captive by it, unable to think about anything else. Slowly the feeling toned down enough that she could think clearly, and Maria was dumbfounded that the God of the universe could possibly accept her so fully; He who knew her innermost weaknesses, fears and doubts. Her eyes opened very wide as she marveled at the immensity and love God had toward her.

"Reginaldo fully served my purpose. I set the time to bring forth life and to take it. My timing is always perfect, for I see the past, present and future, the beginning and the end. No one dies on the earth prematurely or before their proper time. I created time. Trust me with both life and death, for death on earth is but a passing into the rest of your everlasting life. I gather my own to me, to live in my presence forever.

I left you on the earth for a purpose. Never lose your awe and wonder as you hear my voice and see my glory in all of my creation. It shouts of me, if only people would recognize it. That is part of my mission for you – to remind my children of me through my gift of music and song. That is its purpose. Now my child, again experience my song, the song of my creation."

At once Maria heard everything around her. She seemed to hear every insect, every amphibian, and every bird in her surroundings. She heard each individual source and yet somehow could comprehend them all at once. And the sounds, though muted, were joined together in praising their Creator who gave them life and breath. The sounds filled her mind, and yet somehow, beneath that, she seemed to hear yet more: the rocks, the water, the trees – even the air around her. All were in hushed undertones, praising God while waiting with palpable anticipation. All of the sounds were distinct and yet joined in a low orchestra. In her mind, the various sounds formed intricate ribbons of muted colors slowly flowing around her. Maria could somehow feel the sounds as well as hear and see them, but she made no effort to manipulate or change them in anyway. It was not her place. They were already perfect.

In amazement Maria detected a specific sound and saw its ribbon, coming somehow from herself and weaving into the rest of creation that she was a part of. It fit right in with the rest and there was a waiting.

Maria turned toward the glow on the eastern horizon. The anticipation seemed nearly unbearable, as though creation was waiting with her, like some unthinkably immense volume of water held back by a thin barrier, waiting for its proper time of release.

Then, in the twinkling of an eye, the first rays of sunlight burst over the horizon. Joy filled her being and it was as though the dam burst. The muted sounds and colors flashed into loudness and brightness, and in Maria's mind the ribbons of sound now flew through the air all about her. The outpouring of joyful worship of God caught Maria up, and she could not be still any longer as the intensity had to have an outlet. In her mind she leapt with amazing acrobatics, dancing before her God amidst the now gyrating vibrant colored ribbons of sound. She did not know if she was singing or not. There were no words to express the worship and time had no meaning. On and on she danced as all creation joined with her in passionate worship before their Audience of One who had formed them and gave them their being.

The song had a beginning, but seemed to have no end. Yet after awhile the intensity diminished as the sun rose fully in the east. The song remained, but it gradually faded into Maria's background, becoming softer and softer until she felt she could not really hear it anymore, though she knew it was still going on.

Maria became aware of her earthly surroundings, but a remnant of the glory-joy remained deep within her. It was euphoric and empowering. She sighed, not wanting it to end. She looked up. "Thank you, Father God. Thank you for letting me experience your creation-song. And thank you for letting some small part of it remain within me!"

Peacefulness blanketed the pond. Maria lingered for a few more minutes, soaking it all in while knowing deep within her the song went on, never ending. Eventually she stood, knowing she should leave but wishing she could stay here forever. But there were other responsibilities. It was time to go back.

The soft light of mid-morning guided her footsteps as Maria strode toward the Keep in the morning light. This was a day of remembrance. A day of thanksgiving. A day of worship.

Something was missing. Maria cast about the preparation rooms at the Academy of Music, but saw nothing amiss. Yet the nagging feeling remained, and it was only half a day away from the celebration. She spun to go into another room, hoping something would quell the disquiet, but then stopped in her tracks. Maria rolled her eyes and laughed at herself. Taking a deep breath, she instead closed her eyes and turned inward to pray.

"God, I don't understand. Something seems wrong or incomplete. Will you please show me what it is?"

Almost immediately an image came into her mind of her conversation with Miguel on the bridge. Maria's face screwed up in thought, replaying the conversation. It was not as much what he had said, as it was the combination of Watcher and worshiper that held her attention. God had won the victory right there on the bridge, and He had blended together the musicians and the Watchers to make the final battle stand.

Her eyes popped open. Maria nearly gasped. They were planning a wonderful, joyous celebration of God's victory, with every musician, singer, dancer and everyone else in the Academy involved. But at the final battle, both Watchers and worshipers joined together as God's warriors.

Their current plans would not do. They were missing a crucial element.

There was not much time. Maria scurried over to the Watcher Compound. Suevey was exiting the main entrance and they nearly collided. "Maria! It is such a pleasure to see you again! But why the so serious expression? And what brings you here of all places?"

A smile formed immediately on Maria's face. "Suevey! I did not expect to run across you … or to be nearly run over by you! Do you know where Gaeten is?"

"I believe he is in his apartment. You will not believe though what he had delivered this morning!" Suevey wore a conspiratorial look and her voice lowered.

"Oh, what would Gaeten possibly have delivered?"

"Well, I just so happened to find a lad looking lost in the Compound and helped him locate a certain Grand Master's apartment. He was carrying a rather large box. I told him I really should inspect the contents, for securities sake of course." Suevey giggled. "It was … a suit!"

Maria somehow gasped and giggled all at the same time. "A suit? Delivered to Gaeten? Was it a mistake?"

"No," Suevey confided. "The lad gave a passing description of Gaeten and said he had been in for a fitting a few days prior."

Maria's face screwed up into a quizzical expression. "Now just what would Gaeten of all people be doing with a suit? It can't be to stuff and use for target practice!"

"I sincerely doubt that!" Suevey laughed. "It is a mystery – but one I am sure you can wheedle out of him far better than anyone else I know. Just make sure you tell me!" With that the older woman snickered and turned to walk away, tossing a "Bye, Maria." over her shoulder as she went.

Maria shrugged. Gaeten was still mysterious, though not nearly as much so as when she had first met him. Now she knew he had a soft inside that he studiously sought to hide from everyone … well, everyone but her.

She was halfway to Gaeten's apartment when Maria's sensitive ears detected an extremely shrill whistle, at a pitch so high she knew very few people could even hear it. Maria headed for the source, which not unexpectedly was very near Gaeten's apartment. She had not gone more than a dozen steps before an avian screech sounded overhead. Maria quickened her pace and in a minute turned a corner to see Gaeten sitting at a bench with Sasha perched next to him.

While still twenty paces away Gaeten spoke. "Ah, Maria! What an unexpected surprise. And to think I was coming to find you within the hour myself! The Lord surely works in mysterious ways!"

"Hello, Gaeten! Maria walked directly up to the wizened Watcher and without asking reached in and gave him a big hug. She felt the old man flinch slightly – nobody but his Maria had the audacity to give him a hug … and lived to tell about it. She noticed and laughed. "You needed a hug, Gaeten … I could tell!"

With a guttural clearing of his throat, Gaeten was about to grouse when he thought better of it and joined her chuckle. "Oh, Maria! Only you can get away with that you know. And it is a good thing the only one who saw it was Sasha … and I can count on her keeping quiet about it."

Maria turned to the great bird and loosed a litany of clucks and coos. Sasha first bent her head sideways to listen, and when Maria had stopped the Gryph began to cluck and bob her head reprovingly towards Gaeten. Maria smirked while Gaeten looked slightly annoyed – but she could see the start of a smile hiding in the corners of his mouth. Gaeten clucked back at the bird in response and then added, "That is totally unfair, you both ganging up on me like that."

Maria smirked. "Oh, the poor old Grand Master Watcher being ganged up on by a little girl and a semi-tame Mountain Gryph. I would enjoy seeing some of the faces when I told them that line!"

"You had better not!" growled Gaeten menacingly. But he could not hold that posture against Maria for more than a few seconds. He laughed good naturedly. "Now what brings you here to see me, Maria?"

"Well … I have a question to ask you, Gaeten. At the celebration tonight I was wondering …" Maria felt tongue-tied and her sentence drifted off to silence.

Gaeten stepped into the awkward quietness. "Sorry to interrupt, Maria, but I need to ask a favor of you concerning the evening events. I expect Grand Master Vitario is planning a worship celebration to commemorate God's great victory over the Dominion. I think it would be most appropriate that a senior Watcher join you, acknowledging that our salvation came from God's hand, not by our own might or power. I brought it up with Warden James and he fully agreed, and while I thought it should come from him, James strongly recommended it come from me – so that I could recount the rescue of Ethan and all of God's miraculous grace in returning him to Freelandia and of the final defeat of the Dominion Overlord.

The people need to hear of how much God cared for us, how His hand protected us and guided us, and how it was altogether His victory, not ours.

We need to show we were all working together as one, the Watchers and the Worshipers. And that really, truly, we are all Worship Warriors, side by side.

So, Maria, I was wondering if I ..." Now it was Gaeten's turn to lose his words. "I was wondering if I could join you tonight, to be at your side. I even ... I even bought a suit for the occasion!"

Maria marveled again at God's ways. "Gaeten, I would be so very pleased to have you next to me tonight. And this time I will try extra hard not to fall over and bang my head on a wall!"

Gaeten smiled, though obviously uncomfortable at both the thought of being on stage and perhaps also of the memory. "But Maria, you said you had a question for me?"

Maria had to put a hand over her mouth to control the giggles that threatened to spill out. "Ah, I was wondering ... I have never heard you sing ... can you carry a tune?"

A New Beginning
(a few weeks later)

Duncan called a meeting of his main staff and invited Minister Polonos and Chaplain Mikael, and also Prince Erkatan. "Gentlemen, the Dominion army and navy have been shattered. Between the navies of Alteria and Freelandia, we collectively own the seas. With so much of their army destroyed, it is doubtful that the Dominion will be able to militarily hold many of the lands they have recently conquered – the natives will undoubtedly rise up in revolt and many or most will likely succeed in their bid for independence. We can lick our wounds here and let the rest of the world fend for themselves, or we can help them, both militarily and with supplies and advice. But most importantly, there will be a spiritual vacuum. The Dominion ruthlessly tried to wipe out any local religion in the regions it conquered, and forced all to worship their demon gods, or at least give lip service along those lines. Our God won a great victory, and we have a duty and privilege to tell everyone, everywhere about Him …that the world may know Him as we do.

I have asked Minister Polonos to draft ideas of how we might organize and accomplish this, and Chaplain Mikael on how we can recruit and train missionaries to carry it out. I'd like you all to hear what they have to say. Then we need to pray and ask God's guidance – we do not want to do anything outside of His direction and blessing."

Master Vitario looked up from his bed at the Ministry of Healing as Maria, Kory and Ariel entered. "How's my favorite trio of musicians?"

"We are doing pretty well, sir. But we were wondering how you are doing?"

"Well, the healer says I had a heart attack, and that I need a lot of bed rest and quiet activities. Mesha does not think I am fit to be the head of the Academy of Music anymore."

"No! Surely you will get better!" Maria looked imploringly into Vitario's eyes.

"I agree with him." Vitario sighed. "I have led the Academy for many years now, and I think it is time for fresh blood to take over and bring it to even greater heights – to tune it into what God is doing on a continual basis and not get stuck into doing the routine or only what we are comfortable with.

I have given this a lot of thought and even more of prayer. I was particularly pleased by how you all worked on the Day of Remembrance celebration. By any account it was a huge success in terms of organization, delivery and especially by impact. I have heard so many reports of how people connected to God and saw how He brought about such a miraculous deliverance that I have lost count. And everyone seemed to comment on how well it showed that all the glory went to God as both Watchers and worshipers led the activities.

That leads me to naming my successor. I am thinking that person might be you, Ariel."

The girl gasped and her face went white in shock. "No way! I am much too young and inexperienced! I could never ..."

"Both are true, but with wise counsel I think you could do well – and I think fresh ideas and direction may well be needed to complement the major change in focus we have wrought within the Academy over the last few months. And you three have been at the crux of changing how we view music – as a blessing from and a response back to God, not as an end in and of itself. We were so very concentrated on perfecting what I now view as just a tool ... a wonderful, complicated and rich tool, but still a tool. A tool for God's purposes: for worship and praise, to remind and instruct people, to bring us and everyone who hears to a closer relationship with their Creator. And, a tool to combat our real enemy.

No, with this new movement of God's Spirit in the Academy, I can sense a very humbling message from God to me: get out of the way. I think that may be in part why He sent along the heart attack, it rather forces part of the issue – it takes me out of any direct leadership role. I am content with that.

Nothing is final yet; we still need to have a board meeting to discuss it. But I think God's message is pretty clear. If we ask you, Ariel, will you accept?"

She stood up straighter and squared her shoulders. "If it is what God wants me to do, I am His humble servant."

"Good – that is exactly what I had hoped you would say."

There was a polite knock on the door. "Now there is another matter to discuss. Ariel and Kory – can you please excuse us for a few minutes. Maria – you stay."

The two young ladies looked curiously at each other and at Maria and then opened the door. "Oh, hello Mr. and Mrs. Duncan ... ah, Chancellor and Chancelloress ... uh ..."

Lydia beamed at them and pulled both into a warm embrace. "It is just Lydia for my close friends like you." They blushed and backed away, grinning ear to ear and talking to each other in hushed excited tones. Lydia smiled and glided into the room with her usual entrance flair, with Duncan close in her wake.

Lydia spoke first. "Hello Maria, Grand Master Vitario, and Mesha!" She nodded at each one while her husband smiled in turn and gave a short bow toward each.

Duncan picked up the conversation as he straightened. "How are our wounded doing, Mesha?"

"They are being tended to. I put Nurse Abigail in charge of the lot of them, and she has sternly warned them of the consequences of long recoveries. I think she will scare them well in no time at all – unless they see through her no-nonsense exterior. Then they may ask to be adopted."

Vitario began to chuckle. "Interesting segue way there. Before getting to that, Mesha – what is your prognosis for Maria's sight?"

The Master Healer looked thoughtful. "I have never personally known someone with her condition to ever regain sight. There is no medical explanation, which of course God never particularly seems to care about. Sometimes it seems He delights in confounding me! But this is not confusing at all. It is simple. God has totally healed her. As best as I can tell, she has perfect vision."

Maria gave a small girlish giggle. "I can even see you haven't shaved in a few days, Master Vitario!"

The Grand Master musician laughed with her. "Guilty as charged, milady." He looked over at Duncan and Lydia, who both nodded approvingly. "Maria, there are several things we need to discuss."

Maria's face took on a puzzled and apprehensive look. "Uh …. Like what? Am I in trouble?"

"No, no, my child." Vitario was gently laughing and beckoned the not-so-little-anymore girl over to his bedside. "Please, sit." She did so and he continued. "No, in fact quite the opposite. With Reginaldo's death I believe I am free to tell you something … something I think he would want you to know now."

While Maria was no longer feeling guilty of Reginaldo's death, the loss still hurt. A tear was forming in Maria's eye.

"We will all miss him, Maria. He was a great man … who became far greater still when he gave his life over to God's will instead of his own and started loving Jesus more than himself. Before the war, when he last left Freelandia, he made me responsible for several things. One was to see to it that you lacked nothing. He put a sizeable deposit in your name at several of our banks, and said he would also do that in other banks in Alteria and elsewhere, just in case our troubles with the Dominion turned out differently."

Maria gasped and her eyes went wide, and even Duncan and Lydia looked surprised. Vitario continued. "And he also left a revised legal form with me, with copies to be placed with the bank accounts mentioned – and with the many others he had around the world. I have my copy here with me now." Vitario pulled out a very official looking parchment. "I have had a lawyer read it and translate it to a form of wording I can understand. It boils down to this. Maria, Sir Reginaldo has left all his earthly goods to you. All you need to do is show yourself to any of the banks and they will grant you access to his considerable wealth. To prove to them that you are indeed the right person, he said you could sing his Masterpiece to them …" Vitario grinned, "… or show them this, his own special signet ring." Vitario held up a beautiful gold ring with small jewels forming a bright multicolored "R." "I was entrusted to watch over his accounts here, and use them to ensure you had whatever you might need. Because of my heart condition, I think it wise to entrust that responsibility to someone else – and for you to know what is now rightfully yours to claim."

Maria was totally speechless, her eyes filled with wonder and her mouth gaping open. Then she began to softly cry. "I … I don't deserve anything like this! I am … nobody. I am an orphan with no parents or relatives. Why would … he … do this for me?"

"I don't think that is the correct question, Maria. Gifts are truly from God, who surely influenced Reginaldo to do this. We do not and cannot really 'earn' or deserve them. And why would God show such favor upon you? Well, first it could be because of how sincere your faith is toward Him. And another is that you have shown faithfulness with what He has already given you. You have taught me about using my own musical gifts for His glory and His purposes. Perhaps He has plans for you to use this new gift likewise."

Maria's eyes rose slightly, but this was all still overwhelming. She had gone so very long with next to nothing, and still God has supplied everything she had needed. And she had learned to lean on God everyday for so much. Ever since meeting Gaeten she had no longer wondered about how she would eat or be clothed. Maria's face scrunched up in thought. Had she lessened her dependence on God with the security of those basic necessities? No, she decided, she had not. With the threat of the Dominion she had turned to God even more. But with that now gone, would she find she needed God less? And if what Vitario was saying was true – not that she doubted his words – now she was rich, rich beyond her imagination. Would she now ignore her Audience of One?

The play of emotions running across her face must have been fairly obvious to the onlookers. Duncan observed and commented. "Maria, God gives us blessings because He loves us, and to test our commitment to Him. He often gives us a little at first, and as our faith grows He gives us more. You have lived with little, but as far as I can tell you have been very faithful to use what you have for His kingdom. God gave you more when He orchestrated your coming here to the Keep. And again, you have been faithful with His added blessings. You now have an even bigger test – to be faithful with riches. That indeed is a big challenge that few seem to conquer. But God never, ever, allows us to be tempted beyond what we are able to bear, but with the temptation He gives us choices with which we can overcome.

You have a lot of friends, Maria. With riches will come many more people who will want to be your friend. Some will be legitimate, while many others will only want access to the wealth. If I may make a suggestion ..."

Maria nodded emphatically, and so Duncan continued.

"I recommend Maria that you seek help with these funds. Pick several trusted advisors and entrust the money into their care. Put some distance between you and the riches, and always seek God's direction on significant spending decisions. God has given you a great responsibility in this. Use it for His glory, and He will ensure you are never in want."

Maria nodded solemnly, but still looked very confused about the turn of events.

Vitario politely coughed. "I realize this is a huge change for you Maria. And it is not one that you have had a say about. There is another big change for you to consider also ..." Vitario looked over at Duncan and Lydia. Duncan nodded toward his wife and Lydia picked up the conversation.

"Maria, Duncan and I have discussed and prayed over a decision since well before the Dominion invasion. We don't want you to be an orphan anymore. We would like you to be part of our family – to be fully and officially adopted as our very own daughter. We had no idea what Sir Reginaldo had done, and it does not matter in the least to me." Lydia took on a most uncharacteristic hesitant look and lowered her head. In a very soft, vulnerable voice she asked, "Maria ... would you accept our offer? Would you ... accept us as adoptive parents?"

If she had felt overwhelmed before, Maria was now flabbergasted. Her eyes unfocused as she retreated into the one place she had always felt – and always been – safe. Her Audience of One was right there, as His Presence always was. She felt His peace and acceptance ... and love so overwhelming that it pushed aside all of her fears and hesitations. Maria looked questioningly at her Audience. She felt so very small and insignificant, yet at the same time so accepted and thoroughly loved. Part of her mind stayed there, while the other was back in the small room with Vitario, Duncan and Lydia.

"But … but I am nobody! I don't understand. Why would you … why would you want me? I don't deserve this!" Tears were flowing freely, and not just down Maria's face.

Duncan answered. "That is not the right question, Maria. Why would God choose us? We cannot possibly ever deserve it – none of us. He chooses us because He wants to, and we just have to accept that on faith. We have been grieved by your situation ever since we met you. Gaeten has taken excellent care of you, and so has Master Vitario. But that is not the same as a parent, even an adoptive one. We have discussed this frequently and taken it to God in prayer even more often. We are certain it is what God wants us to do. And, I should add … we have discussed this with Gaeten and Vitario and they are also in complete agreement and acceptance."

Maria felt like her world had just spun in fast revolutions, and she was disoriented and dizzy. "Well, Chancelloress … I mean Lydia … or whatever I should call you now! You are a Discerner – what should I do?"

Lydia swept over to Maria, embracing her into a tight hug. "No, no Maria. I cannot answer that for you. It is a decision you must take up with God."

Maria nodded, only partly comprehending. The part of her that stood before her Creator inside her mind looked imploringly at the glorious Presence before her. She did not hear any words, but images began to flash before her of the various interactions she had had with Duncan and Lydia in her short time here at the Keep. No one short of Gaeten had shown so much love to her, and even at her first meeting Maria had felt totally at ease sharing her heart with Lydia. The images ceased and Maria knew how she should answer. Even as she realized that, a wave of peace flowed over her.

"I know that maybe I should think about this longer, but I don't need to. I know what my Audience feels about it. I don't understand it, this is all so overwhelming, but yes – yes I would like that very, very much!"

Duncan rushed over to where Lydia had Maria in a bear-hug and joined them, tears starting to mingle with theirs. Vitario felt his own tears well up. He wiped his rolling eyes and mutter under his breath. "Oh bother!"

Gaeten and Ethan were sparring again in one of the more private lower level training rooms within the Watcher Compound, with Quentin trying to follow the incredibly fast movements – and giving up amidst the rapidly whirling and flying arms and legs. Gaeten was the main initiator so far, with Ethan working hard to block every move the older Master made.

Gaeten began a series of furious punches and Ethan watched closely as the fists slowly fired out. Blue ribbons showed the required movements needed to block every advance, and his body slowly responded to his rapid mental commands to twist aside and swing out counters with his hands and forearms. All the while, he was most carefully watching his blind and incredibly talented opponent. There. The slightest different tension of muscles was just beginning to show. It was a "tell" – an indication of what the Grand Master would do next. Time slowed further. Ethan rapidly compared it to his many other bouts with Gaeten and figured the probable action ... and best counter reaction ... and best way to return with an aggressive counter-strike. He had never put this all together before but had no time for excitement as he forced muscles that seemed embedded in molasses to bend to his will ... well, not a whole lot of time anyway. Time, after all, was rather relative to Ethan in the midst of a fight.

Gaeten shot out one more punch and then without any warning – any that he was aware of showing – lashed out a right foot at high speed toward Ethan's head. The young man ... who now seemed nearly full grown ... did not even try to counter the punch but instead began a massive twist of his body that seemed excruciatingly slow to him but was almost too fast to see for the watching Quentin. The punch passed into thin air even as Gaeten's kick was winding up. Too late, the old Master sensed the totally unexpected movement before him, but his muscles were already committed.

Ethan's torso bent forward and moved through the air, seeming to almost pivot around the fist that never was able to quite connect with his flesh. His own left foot sliced through the air and the left side of Gaeten's head was the only obstacle in its path. Already off balance from his own kick, and with his mind screaming that it was not going to like at all what was about to happen, the impact sent the older man tumbling sideways to land heavily on the matted floor.

Gaeten groaned from where he lay, and Quentin raced over to his prone figure. Ethan followed right behind as he regained his balance and time returned to normal with his worry over his good friend and mentor. As both bent over the groaning old man, Gaeten's hands shot out, grabbed each of their ankles and jerked hard, flipping them over onto the mat beside him. All three bounded to their feet laughing good naturedly. Gaeten turned his head toward Ethan and nodded. "You jump fast, little grasshopper! And if I am not mistaken, that is the first time you have ever bested me – though of course my leg has not fully healed yet." He said the last with great sternness in voice and a frown upon his face.

Ethan looked nervous for a moment, and then saw a corner of the old Master's lips twitch and curl, and with a smile gave a short bow – but never taking his eyes off the tricky Watcher. "I just anticipated what you would do next." He conveniently left off the part about the muscle "tell" … that might come in quite handy in future sparring.

Gaeten smiled and returned the short bow that he could hear and sense his young protégé had given. "I am going to recommend you be advanced to Apprentice Level Five. You still need more experience before I think you will be ready for Level Six, though with quick learning that level may not be more than a year or two off. As it is, you will be the youngest Level Five Watcher we have ever had. You have mastered many areas of combat, but there is much more to being a Master Watcher. I am going to assign you to work with Master Chu for the next year – his principle agreed on an extended leave of absence - your speed will not give you much advantage when the goals are stealth and disguise."

Ethan looked both excited and disappointed all at the same time. Sensing his emotions, Gaeten continued. "I of course cannot help you as much in that department. All of you are always camouflaged to me! However, I am expecting you here once a week – I want to make sure you do not start going soft on your hand-to-hand combat skills! And we need to figure out a way for you to begin instructing younger Watcher apprentices – that too is a very important skill and essential if you are to ever make Master level someday."

Ethan's smile just was not enough. He stepped in and hugged the wizened Master, very much to Quentin's astonishment. Even as he hugged back, Gaeten turned his face toward Quentin with a stern frown. "Not a word of this Quentin … not a word!"

"Oh, Grand Master Gaeten – I would never ever even think of such a thing!"

"Ach, not again! I've been quite the model o' patience, but really now, is this thingy necessary?"

"Oh, quit your complaining. Is the poor little Chief of Engineering having trouble with his bow tie?" Arianna grinned mischievously. "Perhaps I should help pull it tight."

"Oh no ye don't, lassie, keep those conniving hands away from my poor abused neckline now! There … are ye finally satisfied?"

Arianna looked over the tie critically. "Only one wee thingy missing …" she said in her most exaggerated faux accent. She reached up, grabbed his face between her hands and planted a big wet kiss on his lips. As she pulled back her eyes sparkled like the diamonds on the necklace leant to her by Lydia.

"Robert Macgregor, what have ye gotten yerself into?" He gave an exaggerated sigh.

"Are you finished with your fussing? Or do I need to work on you some more?"

"Well now, lassie … that depends on what kind o' work you have in mind!" He pulled his wife in close and she at first acquiesced, then at the last moment pulled away and punched his shoulder … hard.

"Will you keep your mind on the task at hand? We have to be at our formal wedding ceremony you promised me in just a couple of minutes!"

"Oh, I doubt they'd go and a'start without us now, see'in as we are the main attraction … or leastwise you are. I'm just a'tagging along for the ride."

"Speaking of that … are you going to tell me yet what you and Oldsy have concocted for our honeymoon? I saw you two hashing out some kind of arrangement, but you have not told me what it is!"

"An' the suspense is just killin' ya, right?" He showed her that she was not the only one who could grin from ear to ear mischievously.

"Men! Now get a'move on, you lout! I will NOT be late for my own wedding! Get yourself going or else I'll …" She found it next to impossible to get her final words out from under the big kiss Robby planted on her mouth. Well, not more than fashionably late anyway, she thought.

Turlock looked out over the dew-filled grass from the window of a house on the outskirts of Kardern as he finished his breakfast. He had felt the immense spiritual ripples that marked the end of the battle up north, punctuated with what felt like an earth tremor under his feet. He wondered just what indeed had happened. Maybe one day he would hear the real story. Meanwhile, it was a new day for the territories of the Dominion. Former territories, he corrected himself. It would not be many days before the news of the war came back. Already several damaged ships had limped back to Kardern with wild tales of destruction under the hands of angry Freelandian gods, seemingly bent on their demise.

Turlock had to address that. There was only one God, and He was not angry with the sailors, just with the evil they had represented. God was just – and that meant a price had to be paid for one's evil ways. But God was ultimately merciful along with that justice. "If they only knew …" he mused outloud.

"Knew what?" Nimblefoot looked up from his own simple breakfast. For the first time since he had taken on the prophet's mantle he could not see an evil spirit within sight.

"If the people here only knew God the way we do … if they only knew of His love for them."

"They will – when you tell them." Nimby smiled at his much older friend.

"Yes, you are right. As God reveals Himself through His servants and His creation and especially through His Spirit, they will come to know Him. I can't wait to get started! But what about you?"

Nimby shrugged. "Does that matter? God has appointed you to be a witness here in Kardern, to start what will become the largest church of the true God in these parts. As for me … well, there are many other cities that need to hear about Jesus and have leaders appointed to start churches. But the Creator's Truth will become known again in the Southern lands."

"Can I take off this blindfold yet?"

"Oh no, me love … me married wifey! Not quite yet!" Robby held Arianna's hands as the carriage rolled down toward the re-opened docks. Someone had attached broken Dominion swords to short strings and tied those onto the back of the carriage such that they made a quite noisy procession as they went along the streets.

"Tell me something then, husband. I noticed you fawning over that new instrument that Maria played at our wedding ceremony. Its notes were quite distinctive … I don't think I have ever heard anything quite like it. There was almost a …a metallic twang to it. It was incredibly beautiful."

"Ach, that little thingy? Oh, it be just some wee little thing I had experimented on in me spare time since finally getting out o' that metal can. Ye know how we finally got some time to spare, what with not needing ta be workin heaven-bent on war mongering ideas and equipment."

"Robby, are you telling me you invented a new musical instrument?"

"Well now, me love, there may just be a wee bit more of me than ye realize. There be a goodly brain betwixt me thick skull and ravishing handsome like good looks."

Arianna doubled over in laughter. "Oh, I already know there is more to you, husband of mine!"

"Now, now deary, this be not the time nor place for such wise-foolery, even with it being betwixt hubby and wifey. You will just have ta try and control yerself a wee bit longer, as direly difficult as such a task most certainly must be."

"Oh Robby … you are too much!"

A crowd had gathered near the mountainous royal Alterian sailing yacht, and Prince Erkatan stood next to a very large and strong wicker basket. He waved them forward as Robby carefully guided his blindfolded bride. "It is a pleasure to meet you, Chief Engineer. And this stunning lady must be your quite lovely bride?"

"Right'o you are, sir, though she's a wee bit quieter now, with the blinders on and all. Maybe I'll figure a way to keep those handy – just for when I need to get a word in edgewise like."

"Robert Macgregor! You let me take this thing off this instant!"

"Hmm, methinks I may needs to make a few corrections to the auditory adjustments."